Tatius wrapped his arm around my waist, and he turned me, tucking me against his hip so we were standing side by side. "You be on *my* arm tonight, Kita. Hermit, are you coming? We have an appointment with the Collector."

I'd seen Nathanial in a rage once before, and it had been a terrifying thing to behold. It was no less frightening to see now.

"Get a hold of yourself," Tatius chided. "We will present a unified front, with all of my council backing the fact my companion had nothing to do with the albino's demise."

"Your companion?" Nathanial's words were hardly more than a broken scratching sound issuing from his throat. He looked at Tatius. The rage had thinned in his face, a sharp edge of fear taking its place. I'd seen similar expressions on animals before. The question in their eyes wasn't an indication they were beaten—it was the panic of being backed into a corner. A cornered animal was deadly.

Tatius stroked my hair. "Yes, *my* companion."

A statement. No question. No room to argue.

I tried to push free. "No."

The master vampire cocked a dyed eyebrow. "No? My dear, you get no say in this matter. You are a novelty, a child, a commodity. And now, you are mine."

❧ • ❧

DATE DUE

Other Novels in the Haven Series, by Kalayna Price

Once Bitten

•

Twice Dead

Kalayna Price

Bell Bridge Books

This is a work of fiction. Names, characters, places and incidents are either the products of the author's imagination or are used fictitiously. Any resemblance to actual persons (living or dead,) events or locations is entirely coincidental.

Bell Bridge Books
PO BOX 30921
Memphis, TN 38130
ISBN: 978-0-9843256-7-2

Bell Bridge Books is an Imprint of BelleBooks, Inc.

Copyright © 2010 by Kalayna Price

Printed and bound in the United States of America.

We at BelleBooks enjoy hearing from readers. You can contact us at the address above or at BelleBooks@BelleBooks.com

Visit our websites – www.BelleBooks.com and www.BellBridgeBooks.com.

10 9 8 7 6 5 4 3 2

Cover design: Deb Dixon
Interior design: Hank Smith
Photo credits: Harlequin wall background
© Cinnamon | Dreamstime.com
Woman - © Bruno Passigatti | Dreamstime.com
:Lk:01:

Dedication

To Dad, who always accused me of printing books on his printer. You were right. Thanks for letting me do it anyway.

æ • ❧

Chapter One

I propped my elbows on the balcony rail that hung over the Death's Angel dance floor. Below me, industrial music pounded against scantily-clad bodies contorting to the beat. A man in a wolf mask and tight pleather pants ground against a girl wearing a tattered red cloak and strategically placed electrical tape. A zombie in more chains than clothes shambled past the couple, headed for a coven of dominatrix witches. Fictional characters and sexualized movie monsters milled everywhere. What most of the clubbers didn't realize was that among the costumed masses were real monsters—and I was one of them.

I glanced at the man beside me. Well, not a *man* exactly, more like vampire. Nathanial leaned against the wooden balcony rail, his back to the club and dancers. A white opera mask covered half his face, but unlike the famous mask of the fictional phantom, the thin porcelain didn't cover deformity or ugliness—far from it. Nathanial's features were as sharp and perfect as if they'd been carved by an artist. They were also currently set in an expression of annoyed arrogance that was as fake as the mask. He'd held that exact expression since we arrived at the club an hour ago.

"We showed up. We've been seen. Can we go now?" I asked, swirling the contents of my untouched Bloody Mary.

"Kita."

My name. Just my name, without any inflection. I took his meaning as 'No' or maybe that I already knew the answer. And I did. Tatius, the big bad vampire king of Haven, had summoned us to his little party for a visiting master vamp. So here we were. I balanced the acidic smelling drink on the rail. *And here we'll stay until we're dismissed.*

So far, my introduction into eternity as a vampire sucked—and not just blood. Sighing, I shoved the untouched alcohol aside. The bartender, dressed as, shock of all shocks, a vampire—complete with genuine fangs—retrieved the precariously balanced glass before moving on to a customer whose drinking habits required a lower iron content.

Without the glass, I had nothing to fidget with, and my attention returned to the writhing bodies on the dance floor. So many people. So many hearts racing and crashing below thin skin. So many heartbeats drowning out the blaring music. Pressure built in the roof of my mouth, turning to pain as my fangs descended.

A warm hand landed on my shoulder, and I tore my gaze from the dancers. Nathanial watched me, his fingers sliding from my shoulder, down my arm, to my hand. My knuckles were white where I gripped the balcony rail.

I pried my fingers from the wood. Nathanial's crystal gray gaze flicked to the movement, then back to my mouth.

"It's nothing," I whispered, trying to keep my lips pressed over my fangs as I spoke.

Not that it mattered.

"Perhaps we should mingle." His expression didn't change. Not a feature twitched, despite the fact I knew he had no interest in talking to anyone in the balcony crowd.

The balcony was VIP only. Or really, VIV—Very Important Vampire. Some humans were present, as snacks. Thankfully, I hadn't noticed any public bloodletting. *Yet.* But, as vamps didn't trigger my prey instinct, mingling with them was less likely to result in my accidentally eating someone. On the other hand, it also meant I had to talk to the other vamps—which was way more dangerous, in my opinion.

It wasn't an option I was eager to embrace. "I just need some air."

The edge of Nathanial's lips tugged downward. A small motion, barely noticeable. It was his first slip all night—and it wasn't approval. We disagreed on my eating habits, or more accurately, the fact I was subsisting on only animal blood. He was of the opinion that I needed human blood. I was of the opinion that it was his fault I was on a liquid diet in the first place, and he better put up with my sustenance of choice. I sighed, blowing a lock of my tri-colored hair out of my face and intentionally misinterpreting his look.

"I know, I know. Vampire. I don't *need* to breathe," I whispered in an exaggerated huff. "But I can't change twenty-four years of expressions just because I recently woke up slightly less than alive."

Nathanial shook his head, but a smile touched the edge of his mouth. "Walk with me."

His fingers slid through mine and tugged me from the balcony rail. Reluctantly, I followed him into the crowd of vampires.

The costumes on this level were more diverse than those on the dance floor below. True masquerade outfits, elegant dresses, velvet top coats, and jewel-encrusted masks made the balcony crowd colorful. But for every Victorian dress or harlequin was a vampire wearing only leather straps across strategic body parts. I couldn't recognize the native Haven vamps by sight, but considering my previous experience with the local vamps, and the fact Death's Angel was operated by them, I suspected the visitors weren't the ones in bondage gear.

Nathanial conformed to neither group. His porcelain mask was plain, unadorned, and his black hair hung in a long ponytail trailing down the center of his back, blending with the lush fabric of his opera coat. His costume defined elegance in simple stark black and white.

In contrast, my costume was garishly bright. Black and orange tiger stripes decorated my skin-tight unitard. Faux fur rimmed my white gloves and fuzzy white boots. A striped mask completed the outfit. My mess of calico locks—my hair's natural color and a reminder of what I had been until a couple weeks ago—almost matched the costume. Almost. Nathanial had asked me if I could be anything, what I would be.

I glared at the stripes. Tiger stripes. Like my father's. *Me and my big mouth.*

"Hermit, it has been a long time," a male voice said.

I cringed. Only vamps called Nathanial 'Hermit.'

Nathanial turned toward the voice, moving me with him, and I looked up, and then up some more. The speaker towered over us, and while I was on the short side, Nathanial wasn't. The man wore a fitted crushed velvet maroon frock coat I could have used as a dress. Falls of lace escaped from his cuffs and collar, and a gold mask set with rubies obscured wide features. He was so massive, it took me a moment to notice the small woman at his side. She was his exact opposite. Where he was all blunt edges she was sharp, petite. She was my height, but beside him she looked like a fragile doll in her frilled dress and silver mask.

"Three hundred years, I believe, Traveler," Nathanial said, his voice polite but disinterested.

"At least." The giant's gaze moved from Nathanial to me and then back. "A lot has changed in that time."

I groaned silently—or perhaps not all that silently, as all eyes moved to me. *Oops.* Still, I didn't want to listen as they hashed out three hundred years of vampire history as small talk. I glanced around.

There was an empty spot on a couch in the far corner of the balcony.

"I think I'll just . . . " I pointed at the couch.

Nathanial's eyes frowned at me. Not his mouth, or his expression, I'd just come to know those eyes, to know *him*, well enough over the last few weeks to see the fact he didn't think it was a good idea.

"It's just right there," I said, backing away as I spoke.

He didn't stop me, so I turned tail, all but running for the sanctuary of the couch.

Most of the seating on the balcony was filled—vamps tended to sprawl, but the couch I claimed had only one other person sitting rigidly at the other end. She wore a simple, black–and–white, harlequin jumper with an elaborate, full-faced mask, a large feathered hat, and brown curls that looked so synthetic they had to be a wig.

She didn't move as I collapsed onto the far cushion, and I let out a relieved breath. *At least I won't be expected to socialize.* I refilled my lungs—the habits of the living die hard—and that was a mistake.

The cloying scent of blood rolled over my tongue, caught in the back of my throat, filled my senses. The scent was cold, bitter, not all that appetizing, but it was very close and thus, tempting. Oh, so close. My fangs burst free in a flash of hunger, and I slid across the cushion without consciously deciding to move.

The woman didn't react or look up as I sidled up next to her. There was something *off* about the scent of her blood. But that didn't matter. Not right now. All that mattered was the smell of it.

My fingers brushed her shoulder.

The mask tumbled forward.

The hat and wig followed, the wig's synthetic curls flying.

I jumped to my feet. Above the frill of her collar was a stubby, raw neck. No head.

A fake mannequin head *plunked* against the floor. Rolled. It stopped finally, settling three feet from the couch. I backed away, aware of the heavy silence suddenly coalescing on the balcony. Industrial music still pounded below me, but the vampires had gone deadly still.

A large hand closed around my arm. The grip tight. Painful.

"What did you do?" A rough voice whispered the question behind my ear.

"I, uh . . . " I gulped and made a wild, floundering motion from the head to the body. "Her head just fell off?"

A woman in a gold-trimmed gown stepped forward and knelt to

study the fake head. Un-seeing glass eyes stared out of it. As if all tied to one string, every vampire in the room shifted their gaze from the head, to me, and then to the body, which was still perched primly on the couch. Her hands were in her lap, one gripping a glass balanced on her thigh, but she was definitely *not* a mannequin. The smell of blood aside, I could see the white of her exposed spine among the pinker flesh of her throat.

"What is the meaning of this?" demanded the woman in the gold trimmed gown. "Where is her head?"

I thought, at first, that the woman was asking *me*. As if I had any idea. Then I realized her glare went over my shoulder, to the man still gripping my arm. I glanced back, but didn't recognize the vamp holding me. Based on the leather pants loaded with silver studded straps, and the electric blue hair that fell to his chin in jagged tapered tips, I guessed he was one of the local vamps. Then I noticed his eyes: green and old, with a gaze that landed like a physical weight on my skin.

Tatius.

I swallowed hard. Oh crap, a decapitated body *and* the attention of the king of Haven. Did I know how to break up a party or *what?*

Chapter Two

"What happened?" Tatius demanded, his glare boring into me.

I looked around. Nathanial was several feet away, standing at the edge of the semi-circle that had opened around me. His posture was aloof, uninterested, but he watched me without blinking. He tapped two long fingers on his full bottom lip, as if idly contemplating an obscure thought, but again, his gaze didn't waver. *Something about my mouth?* I pressed my lips together.

Crap. My fangs were still out.

I willed the damn things to retract, and Tatius's grip on my arm tightened. He shook me.

"I said, what happened?"

"I touched her shoulder, that was all."

"Should we guess why?" A chime-like voice spoke from somewhere in the mass of vampires.

I gritted my teeth and resisted the urge to press my hand over my mouth. My fangs weren't visible anymore, I knew that, but it was no great mystery to anyone on the balcony what had been motivating me. "She smelled like blood," I muttered under my breath.

I should have known better. Vampire hearing was exquisite.

The woman in the gold-trimmed dress lifted an arched eyebrow dotted with rhinestones. "In this crowd, I should think more than a reckless *child* "—she dismissed me with the insult—"would have noticed blood. Unless there was some trick involved." She stared at the posed figure again. There was no blood on the collar of the outfit— there wasn't even blood around the cleanly severed stub of neck. The woman turned back to Tatius. "What have you to say of this, Puppet Master?"

"My apologies, Collector. I assure you, I intend to get to the bottom of it." Tatius's gruff voice crackled down my back.

Collector? Great. The Collector was the big bad star of this party. The guest of honor. I *so* needed to get out of here. In my old life I'd learned better than to pull an alpha cat's tail—though knowing better didn't mean it didn't happen anyway, sometimes. But I totally hadn't meant to land in the center of this attention.

"Nuri," Tatius said, turning toward the crowd. The mass of vampires who—now that the initial shock of the body's discovery had worn off—were murmuring among themselves, parted to allow a preteen girl through.

As the girl, Nuri, approached, Tatius released my arm. *Thank the moon.* I moved to step aside, but his hand slid around the back of my neck. The touch wasn't restraining, but it was overly personal, his fingers coming to a rest in the hollow between my collarbone and throat. *Oh hell no.* The last time I met Tatius, he'd considered killing me. Then he'd forced his blood in me. I did *not* want anything else to do with the vamp.

I tried to shrug him away, but his fingers flexed in response, his nails biting against my skin. Okay, so apparently I was going to have to make a scene—another scene—or stay put. I erred on the side of caution, for once.

Nuri, dressed as an ancient Egyptian queen with a large snake peeking out beneath her dark dreadlocks, knelt beside the harlequin. As I watched her lift the dead woman's hand, I realized where I'd seen Nuri before. She'd sat at the council table the first time I was brought before the vampires, which meant she must be a lot older than she looked.

After a moment of poking at the body, she stood and turned to Tatius. "Rigor mortis has only begun to set, so I'd guess she's been dead no more than four hours. There is no tearing of the flesh, so she was decapitated by a sharp instrument. The lack of blood suggests she was drained before death. I'll report more when I find it." The words were too old, too serious for her thin, girlish voice. Not that anyone else appeared to notice. She stepped aside and nodded to two pleather-clad vampires, who rushed forward to lift the body and carry it toward a private elevator in the corner. The fake head still lay on the floor, ignored.

The Collector stepped forward, over the forgotten head, until the train of her dress engulfed it. "You have your Truthseeker looking into things, and while I'm sure she will be very thorough"—the way she said it made it clear she was *not* certain of any such thing—"I offer the assistance of one of my vampires." Without waiting for an answer, she lifted her hand. "Elizabeth, attend us."

Tatius's fingers flexed against my skin. *Agitation? Anger?* But he didn't say anything as the small, doll-like woman I'd seen earlier in the night on the giant's arm stepped forward.

"I will be happy to assist," the woman said, curtsying to the Collector. Then she turned and her icy eyes caught on mine. "At least we know the harlequin wasn't this fledgling's *snack*."

Tatius's fingers flexed again, harder this time. "Hermit, find her someone to eat." He shoved me toward Nathanial, and I gladly retreated from the center of attention.

Nathanial's arm slipped around my waist as I reached him, and he wove us through the crowd, away from the couches. We passed the two vampires waiting for the elevator with the body, and I breathed deeply, rolling the decapitated woman's scent through my senses. The sweet tang of blood reached for me, made the roof of my mouth burn, but I focused on committing her scent to memory.

Nathanial didn't fail to notice my signs of hunger. "I am taking you home."

Home. It was a nice thought. I'd had enough with vampires. Enough of their double-tongued political games. And enough headless bodies. But . . .

I glanced back at the vamps loading the corpse into the elevator, but it wasn't her harlequin costume I saw. My mind replaced her with the image of another body, one bloated from several days of death. A human body that had been, in part, my fault, because I'd accidentally created the shifter who'd killed her. I'd tracked the murderer, stopped him, but the weight of his victims wore on me.

Nathanial studied me with eyes that saw too much. Eyes that stripped away my secrets. He shook his head, a small smile tipping the edge of his lips. It wasn't a happy smile. I looked away, and he drew me closer to the side of his body without breaking stride toward the stairs.

"I will take you to the hospital," he said. "You can visit them."

Two weeks ago, I would have avoided hospitals at all costs. But then, two weeks ago, I'd still had to breathe to live, I'd spent most of my time as a six-pound calico kitten, and I hadn't yet known I'd created a rogue who'd gone on a killing spree. A rogue whose victim count totaled fourteen women.

The only two survivors were currently in medically-induced comas at Saint Mary's Hospital. Two weeks ago it would have been easier to walk away from a headless body. To trust that someone *else* would deal with it. A lot can change in two weeks.

I glanced back at the gathered vampires. All the vampires in

Haven were on this balcony. The harlequin had been drained of blood. If the killer was a vampire, he was here. *It has nothing to do with me. This murder isn't my responsibility. It isn't.*

I let Nathanial lead me out of the club. But damn, guilt was a bitch.

⌘ • ⌘

Two hours later, I walked into Nathanial's kitchen. Without Nathanial. After all, we hadn't been formally dismissed by Tatius, so he had to return to Death's Angel after our visit to the hospital. I was still flushed from the flight home as I followed the sounds of the television into the front den. Even after dozens of airborne trips with Nathanial, I still couldn't get enough of the wind in my face and watching the world slip by below us. I could only hope the ability to fly would be a vampire trick I'd learn one day.

I pushed open the den door. "You up for a hunt?"

Bobby, a shifter from my home world of Firth, and once the big love of my life, was currently a couch-crasher in Nathanial's cabin and would continue to be until the gate to Firth reopened and he could return to his pregnant mate. He looked up as I entered. Our relationship was complicated, and awkward, but we were working it out. Mostly. When he wasn't threatening to drag me back to Firth with him, that is.

He hit a button on the remote, muting the brightly animated cartoon on the screen. Then he lifted his feet from the arm of the couch. I slid into the free spot.

"So, hunting?"

"Still hungry? We caught dinner before you left." He frowned, his brow creasing, and he rolled to a sitting position. "Did something happen at that vamp club?"

"It, no, well . . . " I grabbed one of the hunter green throw pillows and dragged it into my lap. "I'm just hungry."

Bobby slid closer, moving into my personal space. "You're starting to smell like a frightened rabbit."

Okay, this was what I meant by awkward.

I jumped to my feet. "I'll just go by myself."

"Kitten . . . "

"Forget I asked." I headed for the door. Bobby was right. We'd already hunted tonight. Even with the heightened metabolism of a shapeshifter, Bobby was only one person and his other form was a bobcat—he didn't need two rabbits in one night. Hell, in Firth, he wouldn't have eaten more than three or four rabbits a week. It was wasteful to kill more tonight.

He caught up with me at the front door and pulled his sweater off despite the blanket of snow spreading out around the cabin. He had to shift if he intended to hunt.

I took the front steps two at a time. "I said to forget it."

He jutted his chin and continued to disrobe. "We'll freeze the extra meat." His fingers moved to the button of his jeans. "You hunting like that?"

I glanced down. I was still wearing the ridiculous tiger suit, but unlike Bobby, my clothes didn't matter. He'd lose a lot of mass once he shifted, and a thirty-pound bobcat couldn't exactly wear a two-hundred-pound man's jeans and sweater. Technically, whenever I shifted, my clothing disappeared. That was my gift. Or it had been, before I became a vampire. Now I was stuck in one form. My claws had extended, once, when I'd been in a fight for my life against the rogues. But since then, my cat had remained locked in the cold coil inside me. Dead.

I kicked off my party boots. "Let's hunt."

☙ • ❧

Snow crunched under my bare toes, and my prey lifted its head, its long ears twitching. I went still, not even daring to breathe. Beside me, Bobby hesitated, his compact bobcat form disappearing behind a frozen shrub.

The snow hare's ears twitched again, his whiskers trembling as his nose worked. Muscles bunched as he prepared to leap, and I sprang into motion.

Brittle, ice-encased twigs shattered as I broke through the frozen brush. My dash was noisy, but that didn't matter now. Not at the speed I was moving. I pounced, snatching the hare in mid-bound.

It screamed, a piercing distress call. I grabbed at its pumping back legs, but one slipped away. Pain flared across my collarbone as the hare's back claws ripped through the thin material of my costume, tearing into the skin below. Not that the pain stopped me. I caught the leg with one hand, gripping the hare's scruff with the other, and effectively immobilized it. Fur brushed my lips, then my fangs sank into the back of its neck. Liquid warmth filled my mouth, slid down my throat. Heat, life, filled my torso, spreading contentment toward my limbs.

Then the hare's mind opened to me.

Panic raked across my senses, stabbing deep. *Run,* the hare's instincts urged me. Every cell in my body knew I'd die if I couldn't run. My heart jumped to my throat, making swallowing difficult.

A vampire bite caused euphoria in humans, but animals recognized death when it caught them. Still, even as the depths of the hare's fear enfolded me, I had other instincts—darker, more demanding needs which kept my mouth working, my throat convulsing.

The small hare drew one last breath. Then the connection between our minds snapped. The sudden absence of its terrified presence left a gaping hole in my mind—an emptiness which didn't fill as I regained awareness of myself and of the limp body in my fingers.

My hands trembled as I set the small corpse in front of Bobby. I swallowed hard. My tongue tasted like I'd been sucking on an old piece of copper, and I shivered despite the new warmth rushing through my limbs. *This is natural. The way it should be.* I'd been born a predator. A cat. I'd hunted with my clan all my life. This hare was prey, serving its function in the circle of life.

Bobby butted my knee with his tawny, bobcat head, his imploring, almond-shaped eyes watching me. My gaze refocused, and I realized I was still crouched over the dead hare, my thumb sliding along its cooling paw. I pulled my hand away and lunged to my feet.

Bobby stared at me a heartbeat or two longer. Then his paw lashed out, fast and precise, disemboweling the hare. *The animal version of field dressing*—or an appetizer. A scream sounded in my head again, starting as the dead rabbit's voice, then bleeding into a woman's sobbing cry. I turned away, but it was too late.

Finding the beheaded body earlier tonight had been too much of a reminder of the rogues' actions. Now, in my mind's eye, I saw claws rip through flesh. The flesh was furless, pale, human, and very much alive. The woman's scream redoubled in pain, and giddy amusement bubbled in me as I reached out to rip away more tender skin.

No, I won't see this—won't feel it. Not again.

I squeezed my eyes shut, but I couldn't block out images playing *behind* my eyelids. Bobby's feline call of concern grew distant; the first clue that I was running. My stride carried me effortlessly through the frozen forest, but I couldn't distance myself from the memories haunting me.

And memories they were. They just weren't mine.

I'd absorbed the memories when I'd tried to drain the rogue

during our fight. My mind had touched his, had seen through his eyes, had felt the high that rushed through him when he killed. Now I had flashbacks that put me in a front-row seat to the sense-surround biography of a sociopath. And those tainted thoughts I'd never be able to outrun.

Chapter Three

Running did little to clear my head, and I eventually forced myself to slow. Sticky blood seeped down the front of my costume from the hare's deep scratch on my shoulder. *I probably ruined the costume. At least I'll never have to wear it again.* Circling back to the cabin, I brushed the snow clinging to my bare feet on the welcome mat before stepping inside.

"Bobby? Nathanial? Anyone here?" I called as I pushed the front door closed behind me.

No one answered, but footfalls thudded in the hall—footfalls far too heavy to belong to a bobcat. I cringed as the double doors swung open and Nathanial's Newfoundland trudged into the kitchen.

"Sit, Regan."

The massive dog just cocked his head. He rounded the large table that monopolized the room, his black nose working as he approached. I pressed my back flat against the wall, my hand groping for the door knob.

"Regan, stay." I peeled my free hand off the wall and tried to mimic the gesture Nathanial used to control the beast.

Regan didn't pay attention.

He took another step forward. Phantom pain laced through my torso, tracing the path of old scars from an attack I'd barely survived as a child. The attack had been by a rogue wolf, not a dog, but dogs were still Canids, and close enough to wolves to make me uneasy.

The dog sniffed the air, his large muzzle lifting, and I shuffled sideways. Okay, maybe more than just "uneasy."

Regan stopped, his floppy ears pricking like he heard something. Then his head swung to the door and his ears dropped, his hackles rising.

"Niiice doggy," I whispered.

Regan's lip rolled back in a silent growl, but he wasn't looking at me. His gaze was fixed on the door. A loud *ding dong* sliced through the air.

I jumped. *The doorbell?* I hadn't even known Nathanial *had* a doorbell. And who would visit out here in the middle of nowhere?

The bell dinged again.

"Let us in, little one," a deep female voice called, the words heavily accented by a throat clearly more accustomed to pronouncing a harsher Germanic language.

Oh, this evening kept getting better and better. I knew that voice. It belonged to the vampire council's enforcer, Anaya. And I was willing to bet, even though I couldn't hear him, that her companion Clive was with her. I'd only met the pair of enforcers once before, but they'd gleefully delivered me to what they had believed would be my final death. I didn't foresee us becoming friends.

"You'll have to come back later. Nathanial isn't here."

"Open the door." This time the voice was clipped and masculine. Definitely Clive.

Regan apparently didn't appreciate the vampire's tone either, because his silent growl became increasingly less silent.

My fists clenched at the growl, my fangs descending. *He's not growling at you*, I reminded myself, repeating it like a mantra in my mind. The mantra didn't help. A great, growling dog was between me and the door. He could have it.

I scuttled further away, sliding along the kitchen wall. Regan fell silent, and if I hadn't been listening so hard, I wouldn't have heard the creak of the wooden stairs outside.

Anaya and Clive were leaving? Just like that?

Regan looked at me, his mouth falling open and his pink tongue lolling out one side. It was a happy expression, I *knew* it was, but I still shivered at the sight of all his big, white teeth.

"Uh, why don't you stay here in the kitchen, and I'll go somewhere else?" I asked the big dog.

He regarded me with shiny black eyes, and then plopped down on the tile.

I'll take that as yes.

Pushing off the wall, I crept across the room, angling for the swinging doors in the opposite corner. Regan watched every halting step. I was a yard beyond him when a loud bang crashed against the door.

I leapt backward, slamming into the huge table. Regan also jumped to his feet, his hackles lifting, his long fur fluffing out like an excited porcupine.

"I think you lost something," Anaya called through the door. She punctuated the statement with the sound of something hard hitting something meaty.

A pained grunt drifted through the door. I'd lost something that could be hurt?

Oh no.

Bobby.

Forgetting about the growling dog, I darted across the room and flung open the door. Anaya stood directly in front of the door, still dressed in the costume she must have been wearing at the party earlier—unless she normally dressed as an eighteenth century bar wench with a skirt far too short for the time period. Behind her, Clive was dressed as Napoleon—appropriate, given his height—but instead of hiding his right hand in his uniform, he gripped Bobby's once again human wrists. Clive's other hand curled in Bobby's shoulder-length tawny hair, controlling Bobby's head, pulling it back to expose his naked throat.

My knuckles turned white where I gripped the doorframe. "Let go of him."

"Let us in," Anaya said. I stepped aside, waving my hand to include the open entrance. She shook her head. "You are forgetting. The words, child."

Right, vampires had to be invited inside the first time they visited a residence. *Which means Nathanial has never let them enter before.* My hesitation was miniscule, only long enough to consider that if I allowed them to enter Nathanial's home, the invitation couldn't be rescinded. Then Clive tilted Bobby's head at a sharper angle. The short vampire bent forward, his fangs aimed at Bobby's throat.

"Come in, damn it," I said. "Come in."

A happy-crocodile smile crawled over Anaya's face. As she crossed the threshold, she held out her hand for her companion's, who released Bobby. I slipped outside as the two enforcers surveyed the kitchen.

"You okay?" I whispered, reaching out to help Bobby to his feet.

He took my offered hand, but only as a gesture, putting no weight on me as he rose stiffly. He wore only his blue jeans, and those were not even fully zipped. No sign of his shirt or shoes.

He rotated his arms, stretching his shoulders, but he didn't meet my eyes. "Sorry," he finally said, rolling his neck. "They jumped me while I was redressing. I didn't hear them coming. They're more powerful than they look."

"Wasn't your fault." I glanced inside. Regan had backed up all the way to the swinging doors, but that was as far as he seemed willing to retreat. "Well, the vampires are inside the house. I say we stay out here."

I was joking—mostly—but Bobby frowned. Gooseflesh puckered along his wide shoulders and chest. *Damn, I keep forgetting about the temperature.* Bobby must have been freezing, standing shirtless in the snow. Only a couple weeks as a vampire and I was already taking for granted the fact that blood, not ambient temperatures, affected my comfort level. But Bobby was a shifter, not a vampire, and shifters didn't do well in human form in the cold.

Well, I have to face the enforcers some time. I stepped inside, but I didn't go far. Regan was still growling.

Anaya turned to me. "Call off your dog."

"Uh, Regan, stop?"

The dog didn't so much as pause.

Bobby snapped his fingers, pointing at the dog. "Down."

Regan looked at him, then whining, lowered first his front half then his back half to the floor.

Oh, that was totally unfair.

With the dog no longer a threat, Anaya swept through the double doors leading to the rest of the house. Clive hung back. He leaned against the counter, crossing his arms over his chest and keeping an eye on Bobby and me.

"Rather quaint, isn't it?" He indicated the kitchen and its large birch table, bay window, and row of simple cabinets with a jut of his chin. His tone wasn't complementary.

I didn't bother answering, but rocked on my heels. My feet itched to move. I didn't like being in close quarters with the enforcers, especially not without Nathanial present. But I wasn't about to run for it and leave Bobby to them. That just wasn't an option.

Anaya swept back through the door, her dark gaze driving into me. "Where is your Master?"

"Not here. I told you that."

A muscle twitched over her temple, jerking the edge of her thick brow. "Where is the Hermit?" she asked, but with her accent, it sounded like she asked where 'de Ermite' was.

How many times did I have to repeat myself? "Not here. He went back to Death's Angel."

Her crimson nails slashed through the air, dismissing my

statement. "We just came from there."

I looked down and licked the corner of my mouth. Nathanial was missing? Not good. Spreading my stance, I crossed my arms over my chest and met Anaya's gaze again. I didn't care if I looked defensive. Hell, I *was* on the defensive.

"Nathanial dropped me off before heading back to Death's Angel. If you didn't see him, you must have crossed paths."

Anaya and Clive exchanged a glance, mirrored expressions of annoyance making their lips hard. Clive pushed off the counter and swaggered up to the kitchen table. He dragged a chair over the tile, and held it for Anaya to sink into. Then he sat, propping his boots on Nathanial's burnished table top.

"De Council—the Hermit not included, seeing as he was absent— demands your presence, little one." A cruel smile crawled over Anaya's face as she spoke. Nothing that made her smile like that would be healthy for me. I shivered, but she wasn't finished yet. "They have questions. I suggest you supply answers."

The pressure in the room changed, and another shiver tingled along my arms. Not a visceral response from Anaya's threats, but . . . *Crap. Magic.*

Not now.

Now was definitely a bad time. An almost inaudible *pop* whispered inside my ear, and Gil appeared behind the two enforcers.

I don't know what the mage had been doing before she arrived, but she'd clearly miscalculated something because she appeared three feet from the ground. She hung in midair for less than a heartbeat. Then she hit the tile with a yelp.

The enforcers jumped at the sound, springing from their chairs with smooth malice. They circled Gil as she pushed off the ground, her cheeks flushed.

Clive grabbed her wrist. "Where did *you* come from?"

Gil's eyes grew wider than the shiny brass buttons on her pink coat. "You're . . . vampires?" She threw a desperate look at me.

What the hell was I supposed to do? I cleared my throat. "Gil, please go back to the living room."

Gil nodded, her black curls dancing vigorously around her head. She stumbled back, but Clive still held her wrist. He glanced at Anaya. Her shoulders were rolled back, her fists clenched as if anticipating an ambush, but she nodded. Clive released Gil's wrist, and Gil darted from the room. *Thank the moon,* If they hadn't let her go, I had no idea what I'd have done. What I *could* do.

Anaya returned to the table, but her eyes were sharp as her dark gaze landed on me once more. Clive remained against the back counter, where I knew from experience he could see the entire room and both doors. Not that he could have possibly known Gil had honestly appeared out of nowhere. I was more than happy to let him think she'd simply snuck up on them.

Anaya's teeth clicked, and I smiled despite the fear clawing my stomach. They were on my turf—well, Nathanial's, at the very least, and he was a council member. He surely outranked a couple enforcers. Gil's appearance had unbalanced them. Maybe I could work that to my advantage. I dropped into the chair across from Anaya and placed my elbows on the table-top.

Anaya lifted an eyebrow, as if to say she couldn't believe my gall, but she leaned back against her chair. "We also came to deliver a message to the Hermit. Since he is not here . . . "

I laced my fingers together and propped my chin on my hands without lowering my gaze. "I can pass it along."

"No. I think we will report to the rest of the council. Clive." She stood, extending her hand. Clive, shorter than Anaya by at least a foot, scrambled over, taking his mistress's hand. She turned and studied me as if I were a bug she hadn't thought would make such a mess when squashed. "When the Hermit returns, he will take you to the council. I would suggest you not delay. We go now."

Clive flashed his fangs at me, then wrapped his arms around Anaya's waist. "See you soon," he said, but the menace in his tone made it clear I wouldn't enjoy myself when I returned to Death's Angel.

Then they vanished.

Chapter Four

A surprised sound escaped from deep in Bobby's throat. He pushed away from the wall, his eyes cutting across the room, searching for the vampires who'd disappeared.

I motioned him to keep quiet. I'd learned from my last encounter with the enforcers that they weren't bound by conventional travel, but I'd been under the impression they flew, physically *flew* through the air, like Nathanial. But the kitchen wasn't exactly a launch-pad, what with the roof overhead. The door was closed, so it was possible they were still in the room. Invisible. Watching.

Tipping my head back, I searched for scents betraying hidden vampires. Everyone who had walked into the kitchen tonight had tainted the room, and my olfactory glands simply weren't strong enough now that I was a vampire to detect if the scents were wafting off unseen bodies.

Before I could ask Bobby for help, Regan stood and trudged to the space where the vampires had last been seen. He sniffed hard. Then he snorted, turned, and trotted out of the room.

Well, okay, Regan had clearly dismissed Anaya and Clive. But did I really trust the instincts of a dog? Yeah. This time. He *had* realized they were on the porch before I did, and he had shown the good taste to dislike them.

Good enough for me.

Now to figure out what Gil wanted. I wasn't scheduled for lab-rat duty with the mage tonight.

"Gil." I pushed through the swinging doors and headed for the den.

It was empty. Had she left already?

"Gil?"

No answer. *Maybe she's in the window-less part of the house?* Nathanial kept an impressive library there, and I could just imagine Gil, a scholar, drooling over it.

"Gildamina!"

I pushed open the thick door separating the 'show' section of the house from the part catering to vampires. The light-tight seals slurped as the suction broke.

"What was that?" Bobby asked, a step behind me.

"What was what?"

"You screamed something," he said as the door swung closed behind us.

"What, 'Gildamina?'"

A frown dug into Bobby's forehead. "What's that? Some sort of human slang?"

I pushed open the study door. She wasn't there. "Gildamina. It's Gil's full name."

Magic surged over my skin, lifting goosebumps.

"*There* you are," I said, turning toward the twinge of magic.

Gil stood in the hall behind me. A bright flush ignited her cheeks, burning into her eyes. Her fingers flared wide at her sides, as if she'd just forced her fists to unclench.

"Where did you learn my name?" The words were a whisper, as if she were forcing them out around a solid knot of anger in her throat.

"Uh." Okay, this wasn't a response I expected. Gil tended toward mousey. She was a know-it-all, sure, but this barely contained temper was more like, well, me. Her voice wasn't even squeaky at the moment. I blinked at her. "The judge called you Gildamina."

"Don't use my name!" A nerve twitched under her eye. Then she took a deep breath, released it, and tugged on her coat in a stiff movement. "I've read that shifters have no *true* names, so you wouldn't understand." She frowned at me, her eyebrows cinching together. "You shouldn't have been able to hear my true name." Her scroll appeared in her hand. She jotted something down.

"Why not?"

She didn't bother looking up from her notes, but asked, "Bobby, what's my full name?"

Bobby, who'd been hanging back against the wall, shrugged. "Gil."

Huh? Hadn't he heard me say . . .

"See, Kita? A *mage's* name is protected. Only I can choose to share it." Gil tapped the feather of her quill against her thought-pursed lips. "So how did *you* hear it?" She cocked her head to the side and her eyes popped wide. "The Judge's mark. It must be." She scribbled something in her scroll, mumbling to herself. "The bond his mark created must have formed a link, a magical transference that allows you to access information the judge has mystical clearance for. I wonder if there are any similar cases." She looked up. "This could make a fascinating paper."

Right. Something else *interesting* about me for her study. I guess that was, technically, a good thing. After all, as long as I was useful as research material, she'd help me keep my protected, 'Rare Species,' status.

Gil vanished her scroll and looked around, probably for the first time since she'd popped back into the human world. "Well, I can look into names later. I need your assistance with something." She ran a hand through her dark curls and glanced over my bare feet and skin-tight tiger outfit. "You might want to change."

Let me think. Stay here and wait for Nathanial so he could take me to see the vamp council, or go with Gil? What a choice. It wasn't like the enforcers had given me an appointment time.

"I'll grab my coat," I said and ducked into the bedroom. I stripped out of the costume as I dug through the drawer Nathanial had cleared for me in his dresser. The wound over my collarbone had stopped bleeding, so I pulled a sweater on and slipped into a sensible pair of jeans before stepping back into the hall. "Where are we going, anyway? And for that matter, how are we getting there?" The cabin wasn't exactly close to anything but acres of woods.

"Like this." Gil's hand shot out. Magic charged through the air as her fingers landed on me.

Then the hall disappeared.

A darkness surrounded me, a darkness so complete it burned away memories of light. The inky nothingness had no sound, no scent, as if I'd been swallowed by a black hole. I could see my feet but nothing below them.

"Gil!" The air was too thick. I couldn't draw breath. "Bobby?"

I swallowed the nearly solid air, gagging. What had Gil done? And more importantly, was this what she'd meant to do? *Or did I get sucked into the backlash of a botched spell?*

I needed to scream, to move.

I couldn't.

Blood roared through my ears—the only sound in the darkness. I hung suspended in nothing. Crushed by emptiness.

Then light burst through the dark, burned my eyes. My hands flew up, blocking out the light. No resistance met my movements. Crickets chirped. Tires crunched over pavement. Wind tickled across my skin.

Slowly, I lowered my hands and risked peeking through my eyelashes. A dozen pinpricks of light met my limited gaze, none bright enough to be blinding. I opened my eyes the rest of the way, staring at the star-filled sky. I blinked. I could feel the ground and soft grass—not snow—beneath my back. My heart gave up its mutinous attempt to desert my torso, and I drank in a deep breath that tasted of spring and green life. *Where am I?*

And better yet, where had I been?

My elbows wobbled as I pushed off the ground, my palms sinking into the thick grass. I looked around. Small cement buildings surrounded me on all sides. No, not buildings. Sarcophaguses. Mausoleums.

I'm in a graveyard?

"Toto, I don't think we're in Kansas anymore," I whispered.

"You weren't in Kansas to start with," Gil said from somewhere behind me. "But we're not in Haven either."

I jumped. My vision spun with the sudden movement, and I squeezed my eyes shut. *Can a vampire hurl?* I sure felt like I might.

"Are you hurt?" Gil asked, her rain boots thudding as she moved closer. The lightest touch of magic tinged the air, and I cringed, my eyes flying open.

Gil knelt a couple feet from me, but she wasn't reaching out to help me stand. No, instead she jotted something in her damned scroll. Most likely something about *me*.

"Can you describe how you feel?" she asked, looking up from the tightly penned lines.

I forced my lips to curl into something akin to a smile. "Like I'd commit *mageicide* if I could only stand up."

Gil dropped her quill, her gulp audible.

She'd only recently started to trust me, and I needed to stay on her good side if I wanted to avoid the judge and his execution warrant. I was still on the magical equivalent of parole. I took a deep breath and let it out again, resisting the urge to yell as I asked, "So, should my first question be 'How did I get here,' or 'Where *here* is?'"

Gil licked her bottom lip. "Well, as far as *where*, this is King James Cemetery. The *how* is a little . . . uh, complicated?"

Understatement. Definitely an understatement. I waited, my teeth gritted. Gil fidgeted.

"I might have tucked you outside of time and space while I traveled here. But it appears not to have had any adverse effects." She fished her quill out of the grass and tapped it on her scroll. "I hypothesized that a short detour into the void between worlds would have no ill effects on a vampire. I wouldn't chunk anything fully alive in there, of course."

"You hypothesized? As in you guessed and then you threw me in a . . . a *void*?" I shoved to my feet. My face was hot, and the pinch against my lips told me my fangs were showing. I couldn't help it. I was well and truly pissed.

Gil stumbled back and her scroll vanished. "I did consider the possible outcomes thoroughly before trying it," she said, wringing her hands together.

When I only raised an eyebrow, she took another step back and her gaze darted away, skittering over stone monuments without finding a place to land. She tugged at an imagined wrinkle in her coat. "Well, that aside, my research points to this cemetery as the resting place of . . . someone I think can help us determine if you tagged any other rogues. I've narrowed it down to one sarcophagus, but I need help."

"Help with what?"

"A little research." She turned, her eyes still not meeting mine. "The lid is heavy. I can't lift it."

Great. I was here as muscle and we were what? Grave robbing? I pressed the palms of my hands against my eyes. A headless body, the rogue's haunting memories, the void, and now grave-robbing? Could this night get worse?

Wait, I forgot. When I returned to Nathanial's, I still had to appear before the vamp council. I sighed and dropped my hands.

Might as well get this over with.

"Which one?" I swept out a hand to indicate the rows of monuments that stretched around us for as far as the eye could see.

Gil indicated a small mausoleum with what appeared to be a sphinx watching over the rusty gate covered opening. The gate squealed as it swung on ancient hinges, and flecks of red rust stuck to my fingers. Inside, Gil pointed to the second sarcophagus. I gave the lid a shove, but the large cement slab barely budged.

Moving to a better angle, I braced my knees and shoved harder. If a human had been watching, they probably would have laughed at the idea of me moving the slab. After all, I was only a few inches taller than five foot and my five years of living as a stray on the streets had made me skinnier than a predator should be, but as a shifter I'd been stronger than a human, and as a vampire I was even stronger still. Not like toss-a-bus strong, but much stronger than I looked.

The stone scraped along the base, and a nail-bitingly annoying grinding noise filled the mausoleum. Beside me, Gil bounced on her toes, anxiously attempting to peek into the hole as it opened. I gave one last shove, and stopped, looking down at what I'd revealed.

Inside the sarcophagus, an ancient skeleton grinned up at me, its thin arms crossed over gray cloth hanging to its ribcage.

"This is it?" I asked, stepping aside.

Gil hung over the triangular opening. Her hands clung to the ancient cement, her dark curls quivering as she shook her head. "He's not here."

Oh, there was definitely someone in this sarcophagus, though since the name carved on the front read 'Mary Elizabeth Stanhope,' I was fairly certain *he*, whomever *he* was, had never been in the tomb.

Gil pushed away and dragged her feet to the mausoleum doorway. "I must have miscalculated something. Maybe if . . . " She pulled a scroll out of thin air again, glancing around the cemetery. "I could have sworn. But . . . " She frowned, vanishing her scroll. "I'll take you home."

Magic crawled over my skin.

"Wait." I stumbled back. No way was I going into the void again. I'd call Nathanial. I didn't know the number, but I'd seen the telephone on his counter. I could find his phone number and he could come pick me up. Okay, my reasoning might be flawed, but I'd just wait. The council be damned.

Gil ignored my protest. Her hand touched my arm. Then the mausoleum faded to black.

ॐ • ॐ

I lay on my side and blinked into the darkness. Not the nothingness of the void—the wood-paneled walls and ceiling were clear to my vampire eyes, so this darkness was simply the lack of light in Nathanial's hallway.

No more adventures with Gil.

Ever.

My stomach couldn't take it.

I fought the urge to hurl everything I hadn't eaten. Then I pushed away from the thick pile carpet. My knees didn't cooperate the first time I tried to stand, but the second time I managed to get my feet under me. I leaned against the wall before stumbling toward the main part of the house.

The swinging doors to the kitchen had gotten stuck half open, and I paused outside, staring in at Nathanial. He sat in one of the unpadded chairs, several books scattered across the top of the table and a laptop directly in front of him. He'd removed the opera mask. It lay face down, forgotten, on the edge of the table. He didn't look up from the book he leaned over, didn't realize I was there, so I had a moment to stare and let my eyes soak up the width of his shoulders, which tapered down to lean hips.

He wasn't large and bulky like Bobby, but had a quieter, more lithe strength. I was supposed to hate him. After all, he'd made me this blood-sucking aberration. But as I watched him, all I could hate was the fact my fingers itched to trail through the dark hair streaming over his shoulders. I could only hope he never realized it, never saw me staring when he wasn't looking, but sometimes I was afraid he knew me better than I knew myself. It wasn't a comforting feeling.

The book in Nathanial's lap snapped shut. He tossed it on the table and leaned back in his chair. He reached up, rubbing the bridge of his nose with his thumb and forefinger. If he'd been human enough to sigh, I think he would have at that moment, but he only wasted energy on breathing to speak and for show. As if a silent alarm went off in his head, his hand dropped, and he turned, peering into the darkness where I stood.

Caught.

I stepped through the doorway, and Nathanial flowed to his feet.

He glided across the kitchen. Awareness of his presence filled the space around me before the doors had time to swing shut. His grace wasn't feline like the shifters I'd grown up around, but it was definitely predatory. And it was all male. He ran a finger down the side of my cheek then pressed his lips, feather-light, across my forehead.

My heart lurched like it could propel me to step closer to him, to move into his embrace. Instead I scooted away.

"When did you get back?" I asked, hoping he hadn't been home long enough to note my absence. I doubted I was that lucky. Very little got past Nathanial. Besides, the pile of books on the table was impressive.

He frowned, and I squirmed under his measured gaze until I finally looked down to escape it. My palms were gray with dust from the sarcophagus, and flakes of red rust clung to my fingers like spots of dried blood. I brushed my hands on my thighs. It didn't help, and I scrubbed harder. Nathanial stepped forward. His hands slid around mine, stilling me.

"Where were you, Kita?"

I shrugged without looking up. "With Gil."

It wasn't an answer. Not really. But, after a beat, he stepped back as if he'd accepted more than I said. "The council wants to speak to you."

He'd changed the subject? Seriously? He never let me get away with half-answers this easily. Of course, it wasn't every day I discovered a body and got summoned by Haven's vampiric council.

I nodded and tugged my hands free. Without a word, he ushered me out the door and onto the porch, but when he turned, the frown melted off his face, leaving in its place a look of nonchalant arrogance. His expression, as empty of true emotion as if he'd put the opera mask back on, spoke volumes about the emotions he *wasn't* sharing.

At least, it did to me.

It was his public face, the one he hid behind. The fact he was wearing it while it was just the two of us made my anxiety level skyrocket. "What?" I asked, crossing my arms over my chest. "You're starting to creep me out, Nathanial."

He blinked, as if startled. Did he think I wouldn't notice he'd shut down and was being all secretive?

"I am going to say something you will not appreciate," he said, his tone as guarded as his face.

Like I hadn't figured that out. I tapped my fingers against the gray elbows of my coat, waiting.

"Tatius will not approve of your current condition. He instructed you to feed. You need blood before we go."

My hands clenched, my fingers digging into my arms until the pain became small red points I could focus on. I wanted to stomp my feet, to yell. I'd hunted not once, but *twice* tonight. *Can't he be satisfied with*—I cut that thought off.

Sucking in air, I filled my lungs with the scent of night, of the nearby woods, of the spicy scent of Nathanial's skin. I kept drawing in air until my lungs pressed against my ribs and expanded in my diaphragm. Then I let all the air rush out of me, emptying my body of every drop, every scent, every breath. If I yelled, Nathanial would wait me out. If I ran, he would come after me. If I hit something, it would break. So I stood there, perfectly still, perfectly empty.

The mask slipped from Nathanial's expression as his eyes warmed. One edge of his lips quirked like I'd amused him. What, had he expected me to have an outburst? *Probably.*

But I wasn't going to. Not this time.

"I've hunted. I'm fine."

Nathanial stepped closer and moved into my space, filled it. He wasn't a big man, but his presence, maybe even his power, closed around me. His fingers traced the edge of my face as he studied me, and my pulse quickened. It was like his touch pulled a girlish giddiness from deep inside to the surface, made me want to smile against my will. *Focus, Kita.*

"I'm fine. I'm not even cold." Not much, at least, but I didn't add that.

"You look drawn, tired."

Gee, isn't that what every girl wants to hear? I backed away from him, though it felt like losing a part of myself to pull away from his touch. "Let's just go."

"You need blood. Blood that is not from an animal. Take from me." He lifted his wrist, but I grabbed it before he could open a vein.

"No." Taking blood was too weird, too intimate. And he was already too . . . everything. Just the idea made heat lift to my cheeks. I shook my head. "No."

"I have been patient these last two weeks. I have let you try to survive on animals. I have never forced you—"

"So don't start now."

We were standing close enough that I had to tip my head back to meet his eyes, but I didn't dare look away as he studied me. The silence built between us, growing sharp. Then he shook his head, a low chuckle rumbling from his chest.

"If attitude alone determined power . . . " He brushed a strand of hair behind my ear and smiled. "Or denial."

"I'm not in denial," I huffed under my breath, which only made the edge of Nathanial's lips twitch higher.

"Of course." He wrapped his arms around my waist and drew me closer to him, engulfing me in his scent. "Tatius will want you to recount the events of the night. Please, mind your tongue," he whispered the last into my hair, the amusement fading from his voice.

Then we were in the air, the little cabin disappearing below us as we hurtled toward the council.

Chapter Five

I dragged my feet through the underground rooms of Death's Angel. I most certainly wasn't anxious to reach the council's chambers. Of course, I could only walk so slowly, especially with Nathanial steering me ever onward as Anaya sauntered down the dark hallway in front of us. She and Clive had been waiting for us when we arrived at the club, gleefully anticipating delivering us to Tatius.

Anaya stopped at a pair of double doors. I expected her to knock. She didn't. Instead she threw the doors open, the knobs slamming into the inside walls with a resounding boom.

Every undead eye turned toward the doorway. I cringed, inching behind Nathanial.

"The favored child and his companion have arrived," Anaya announced into the stunned silence enveloping the room. Then she turned and sauntered back into the hall.

Her name was so going on my shit list.

Tatius shook his head from the center of the room where he sat atop the council table. His gaze raked across me, bearing down as he hesitated. Then his eyes moved on and the weight lifted from my skin, but not the feeling that I'd been worn down just by the brush of his attention.

"Everyone out." Tatius's voice was smooth, not even lifted, but the non-council vampires in the room jumped. Then as one, they turned and headed for the door.

"Hermit, thank you for gracing the rest of the council with your presence. You'll understand that we moved on without you, so show yourself and your companion to the sitting room. I'll be there when I have time to deal with you," Tatius said, his attention returning to the vampires around the table.

Nathanial nodded and led me past the large council table before lifting a cloth panel and revealing the doorway to a small, dark room. Plush carpet muffled the sound of my steps as I followed him to a dark leather couch in the center of the room. Paintings instead of fabric lined the finished walls. The only thing missing was electric light.

Instead, unlit candelabras were scattered around the room. Anywhere else, the room would have been unremarkable, but its very normalcy made it remarkable compared to what I'd seen of the underground parts of Death's Angel thus far.

Nathanial sank onto the couch. He crossed an ankle over his knee, and I frowned as he pulled a small book from the inner pocket of his tux jacket. *How can he read at a time like this?*

"You should take a seat," he said, glancing up from the book. "We made Tatius wait. He will return the favor."

I didn't take his advice. I was too jittery to sit. Instead I paced a circle around the room and fidgeted with a marble from my coat pocket, rolling it through my fingers.

It was hard to mark time in an underground room, but it felt like we'd been waiting for over an hour when Nathanial leaned back, his gray eyes fixing on me. "Kita, sit."

"Sorry. I'm a cat. Not a dog. I don't do tricks."

The edge of his lips twitched in an almost smile, and the small change lit his face, breaking the mask of indifference I was growing accustomed to seeing tonight. The change was small, subtle, but even the air in the room responded, seeming less thick, less dangerous.

Okay, so we were waiting on the head of the vampire council, and yeah, Tatius had considered killing me once, but I hadn't done anything wrong this time. I'd found a body. Hell, he'd been in the same room when I'd discovered it. He couldn't have that many questions. I'd tell him what I knew and we'd leave. Simple as that.

I sank onto the couch beside Nathanial, and his hand slipped around mine, entwining my fingers with his. The warmth of his palm pressed into mine, spiraling up my arm to gather in a burn across my cheeks. Or, at least, I hoped it was just his warmth that made my cheeks hot.

"Uh . . . how much longer?" I asked, freeing my fingers and clamping my hands in my lap. "At this rate, it'll be dawn before we're dismissed."

The door banged open, and flames flickered to life on the wicks of the many candles scattered around the room. I jumped, squinting in the sudden glow of light.

"You have rooms here," Tatius said as he strolled through the door. "Dawn is not a concern."

He lowered himself onto the chair across from us in one smooth movement, then threw one leather-clad leg over the chair arm. Nuri followed. She sat perfectly straight in her chair, not leaning against the plush cushion.

Silence, aside from the slight hiss of the candles, filled the room. I held my breath, willing my racing heart to slow, to not disturb the stillness or draw attention to itself. Nathanial leaned back. His arm stretched along the back of the couch, his elbow bent so his fingers rested lightly on my shoulder. He looked relaxed, but the blank mask consumed his features.

"You summoned us?" he asked, the words as casual as if he'd mentioned a recent sport's score or offhand current event.

Tatius cocked his head to the side, making the pointed tips of his blue hair sway around his face. "I summoned her, Hermit. Just her. You're here as a courtesy because you are her sire."

I flinched. I couldn't help it. Tatius scared the crap out of me. I'd grown up in a society of predators, and no matter how often I was told I'd be *Torin*, clan leader, one day, it had been pounded into my small kitten body that the biggest predator made the decisions. Tatius was, by far, the supreme predator in the room.

"You found a body," he said, his tone deceptively cheerful.

I nodded. He knew I did. He was there. *Everyone* was there.

"Words, Kita. Unless a cat's got your tongue." He laughed at his own joke, and I gritted my teeth. "Why did you touch the body?"

"I smelled the blood," I said, and Nuri nodded.

The pre-teen council member stared at me. She wasn't just watching and listening, but studying me like she could read secrets under my skin. I readjusted my weight on the couch, uncrossing my legs and recrossing them.

"So before you smelled the blood, did you notice anything unusual about her? Did you see anyone else near the body?"

I shook my head.

Tatius frowned at me. "I need your words. Speak."

Okay . . . because that isn't weird or anything. I glanced from him to Nuri. She was still watching me with that same intensity as she perched perfectly straight at the edge of her seat.

I cleared my throat. "I didn't notice anything remarkable except that the couch was mostly free. I don't remember anyone else close to her."

Tatius looked at Nuri and she nodded. "All truths," she said.

I frowned at her, but she continued to stare at me, her over-expanded pupils absorbing the entirety of her irises. I swallowed, hard.

Vamp powers—it had to be. I looked away.

"Why were you at the couch alone? Why weren't you with your master?" Tatius asked.

"I needed . . . air," I said, and Nuri frowned at me.

"Truth," she said, but puzzlement made her voice turn the single word into a question.

Tatius huffed under his breath and swung his leg around to the front of the chair. "Air." He shook his head, and, propping both elbows on his knees, he leaned forward. "You sought out a hiding spot because you were hungry. You followed the scent of blood because you were hungry. And now you sit in front of me, still hungry."

Nathanial's fingers tightened on my shoulder. A warning? I couldn't deny anything Tatius had said, so I didn't answer. After a moment, Tatius's gaze left me to bore into Nathanial.

"I ordered you to feed your companion. Could you not find her an adequate meal?"

Nathanial's arm behind my head turned to unmalleable wood, like he'd frozen and dared not move.

I frowned. "He didn't need to feed me. I hunted."

Nuri cocked her head to the side. "Truth?"

The word was definitely a question that time.

"I did."

Tatius rolled to his feet in one liquid movement. He crossed the short distance between his chair and the couch and gripped my face between his thumb and fingers. He tilted my chin back, and I let my gaze follow sluggishly. I wasn't looking forward to meeting his intense eyes, but as I finally dragged up my gaze, I found him studying my face, not staring me down.

"You haven't hunted. I'd wager you haven't fed well in a week."

"I hunted," I repeated.

"She believes that she has," Nuri said, but I couldn't see her beyond Tatius's mesh-covered chest.

"She hunted," Nathanial confirmed. His hand still gripped my shoulder, tethering me like a lifeline amid Tatius's attention. He cleared his throat and added, "She hunted and she caught something."

Tatius's gaze swiveled toward Nathanial. "You mean someone."

When Nathanial didn't agree, Tatius's fingers tightened on my face. Just a quick flex, which he might not have been aware of. "Some*one*," he restated.

From the corner of my eye, I saw Nathanial's head move. "She has been hunting wild game on my property."

Tatius's fingers squeezed hard enough to make fire lance through my jaw. "Animal blood?" The question was quiet. The kind of whispered statement a person makes when they know that if they speak louder, they will yell. His hand flexed again then fell away.

I opened and closed my mouth, pain rushing in along with the blood filling my cheeks. I wanted to touch the tingling skin, but I didn't want to show that much weakness. Instead I sat as still as possible as Tatius rounded on Nathanial. He grabbed two fistfuls of Nathanial's tux and hauled him off the couch.

"Animal blood?"

Oh yeah, now he was screaming.

"What were you thinking, Hermit? She can't survive on animal blood. If she goes mad and loses control, whose head do you think I will have to come after, huh? Whose?" He shook Nathanial, who said nothing. "You turned her. *You* are responsible for her actions." Tatius released Nathanial's jacket and shoved him away.

Nathanial's back slammed into the couch, but his body melded to the seat. The fluid motion looked intentional as he propped an ankle over his knee. Undisturbed. Relaxed. His emotionless mask was still firmly in place. Tatius's words might have well bounced off it for all the effect they appeared to have.

Tatius's lips twisted. "Nuri, you can leave," he said without looking away from Nathanial.

She slid off the chair and glided across the room. At the door she paused. "Shall I inform the Collector you will meet with her shortly?"

"No. Just send Samantha to find Kita someone to eat."

I sprang from the couch. "No. I can't—"

I didn't make it fully upright before Tatius caught me, one large hand locking around my jaw again, his thumb and fingers digging into my cheeks. He lifted his hand until I was forced to balance on my toes. Then he leaned in, his intense eyes inches from mine.

"You can. You will. I have to make a show of strength. A half-starved vampire under my protection isn't good for my image. Now be silent. I have things to discuss with your master."

Without releasing me, Tatius turned, his attention moving to Nathanial. "As you missed most of the council's investigation, in brief, it has been uncovered that the body belonged to one of the Collector's . . . oddities. An albino," he said, ignoring my struggle to free my face. "We don't know when the body arrived on the couch, how it got there, or why no one but your companion noticed it. The location and theatrical treatment of the body indicates a message, but Nuri has not been able to find anyone who has knowledge of the crime. The Collector is incensed. She wishes to examine Kita's memories. I have granted her that right."

My memories? Oh hell no. I was not letting some vampire sink their teeth in me. Wrapping my hands around Tatius's wrist, I attempted to pry his hand off while pushing backward with my toes. My efforts earned only a tightening of his fingers.

"Let go."

He ignored me. "You will not interfere in the examination, Hermit."

I sagged, hoping my full body weight would pull me free, but Tatius held on. Pain radiated from my jaw into my throat, and I got my feet under me once again.

Nathanial cleared his throat. "Tatius, perhaps if you released—"

"No." His fingers flexed tighter and I couldn't hold back my yelp.

I could only see him in profile, but I didn't miss the smile that twisted his lip at the sound. *Prick.* Balling my hand into a fist, I slammed it into his elbow joint.

He rounded on me, drawing me higher until the toes of my sneakers trailed along the carpet.

"That's twice you've struck me," he said bringing our faces close enough I could have bitten his nose—if I could have moved my head. "Ever strike me again, and I will hit back. I promise, I hit harder."

He opened his hand, letting my jaw slip between his fingers. The release came so unexpectedly, I dropped, landing in a clumsy crouch. My hands flew to my face, and I didn't bother not rubbing my aching jaw this time. The sweet copper taste of blood touched my tongue from where my teeth had sliced through the insides of my cheeks. My fangs descended. *At least he let go.*

"Stand up," Tatius commanded.

I seriously debated not standing, to remain crouched beside the couch. Hell, curled in a ball sounded even better. But I wasn't a complete idiot. I pushed off the floor, keeping my head down as I straightened. Nathanial stood. His arm slipped around my waist, offering warmth and a measure of security, but I didn't dare lean into him. I'd shown enough weakness already.

"Shall we discuss how you are to act when I present you to the Collector?" Tatius asked, and I could guess the question was addressed at me based on the patronizing tone.

"Is this where I swear to tell the truth, the whole truth, and nothing but the truth?" I asked, not bothering to keep the sarcasm out of my voice.

"No. This is where you assure me you will not speak or draw any attention to yourself. And when I present you, you will concentrate your damnedest on what happened on that couch and not think about all that other fascinating stuff in your head."

"No one's biting me."

His hand flashed into movement, but I knew that was coming. I jumped aside, out of reach. Dropping into a crouch, I dared a glance at his face. "If you're so worried about my blood level, maybe you should stop grabbing me so I don't waste blood healing."

Nathanial sucked in a breath—probably at my words. I *had* promised him I'd watch my tongue. But Tatius pushed my buttons. What could I say? I'd always had issues with authority.

Tatius stepped forward, and I scuttled back until my butt hit the couch. *Crap.* I flowed to my feet.

"Don't move," Tatius said, but the words were a whisper.

I glanced at Nathanial. His mask had cracked, his eyes creased at the edges and his mouth slightly open as his gaze raked over my face. I faltered, only a single heartbeat, but it gave Tatius time to close the space between us. He bent low as his hand moved to my face, but he didn't grab me. Instead, he used one finger under my chin to tilt my head back.

"You bruised."

I gaped at him. "What the hell did you expect? You held me up by my face."

He shook his head, but it was Nathanial who spoke, his voice further away than his body. "Vampires do not bruise. Our blood heals us. Bruising is a sign of severe starvation."

"This is your fault, Hermit," Tatius growled. His angry gaze moved to Nathanial. "You haven't been feeding her."

"Didn't we just establish that I've been hunting?" I muttered at the ceiling, where Tatius's finger still pointed my face.

Tatius's finger traced my chin down to the center of my throat, and I fought the urge to swallow. He studied my face, examining the bruises he'd made but was blaming on Nathanial. As his eyes swept over me, they lost most of their more frightening—and homicidal—gleam. His mouth didn't so much soften as change from a pissed line to a determined one. His hand slid around my throat. My heart, which had been lodged there, trying to choke me, abandoned that plan. Instead it zoomed downward, intending to take my stomach out as it clawed free of my body. I braced for pain, but Tatius's hand slid along my skin until his warm palm cupped the back of my neck.

The gentleness of the gesture was so unexpected, my breath rushed out of me. A breath I'd apparently been holding long enough that it tasted of stale fear.

Tatius didn't notice. He was looking at Nathanial again. "When was the last time you opened a vein for her?"

Nathanial's gaze crawled to me, and then skittered away. His mask was truly broken now, panic clearly chiseled on his features. "She has had some difficulties adjusting and—"

Tatius cut him off. "When."

"Five nights ago."

Tatius's fingers twitched. "Are you trying to kill her?" His voice was quiet again, that low, calm before the storm quiet. He looked down at me, and I could almost feel the scales in his gaze—the weight of the decision in his eyes made me want to back up, but I couldn't. His hand on my neck, however gentle, held me in place. "I let you keep her," he whispered. "You flaunt my laws, Hermit, yet I still granted you your companion. Then you let her starve."

His hand loosened and his fingers drew circles on the back of my neck. A shiver I couldn't suppress ran down my spine, and Tatius smiled. Leaning down, he grazed his teeth across my throat. His fangs weren't out, so flat human teeth lightly nipped at my flesh. I stumbled back as a shiver that was only mostly fear shook me.

"You smell like blood." He pulled me forward two steps for the one I'd taken away, then he turned to glare at Nathanial again. "Did you bring her to me hurt as well as starving?"

"No." Nathanial's eyes were wide as they swung to me. "Kita?"

Oh, crap. "It's nothing. A scratch." I closed my coat tighter around me, but Tatius swept it open again, pushing the faded gray material off my shoulders.

He hooked his fingers under the collar of my sweater and pulled it aside. Both men stared as he revealed the rabbit's jagged claw marks crossing my collar bone. I could see just the base of the cuts. They weren't bad. They'd heal by morning. I'd certainly had worse.

Tatius frowned.

Nathanial stepped between my back and the couch. His hands

landed on my shoulders, but his touch was tentative, like an alighting bird ready to take flight. "I will rectify both situations. Please. Let me fix her."

I swallowed. The scratch wasn't anything, really, but I didn't like the way he said *fix*—like maybe Tatius thought I was broken. I glanced down and caught sight of the long dagger Tatius kept strapped to his thigh. I wasn't unfixable. I leaned into Nathanial, and his hands became surer weights on my shoulders, his fingers wrapping around my upper arms. If I had known earlier that all this would occur, I would have just taken his blood on the porch. Really, I would have at least considered it. Dammit.

I opened my mouth to apologize, then snapped it closed again. Now wasn't the time. Instead I said to Tatius, "I thought you were just going on about how I needed human blood."

His frown deepened. "You could gorge yourself on all the humans you could possibly swallow and it wouldn't do you any good because you couldn't convert the blood to energy. You need a base of master vampire blood in your body to do that, and a baby body like yours doesn't produce it. You have to be fed by a master to survive."

"I will fix her," Nathanial said again, pulling me tighter against him.

Tatius watched us, but finally he shook his head. "No."

No. Two little letters. One earth-shattering word.

Behind me, Nathanial's body went rigid, his fingers digging in hard enough to raise bruises on my arms. "Tatius . . . "

"I said no. You had your chance. Leave."

Chapter Six

"Leave, Hermit," Tatius commanded again.

One by one the fingers on my arms lifted. Nathanial stepped back. The withdrawal of his body in the space behind me created a chilled abyss. In his absence, panic curled into the newly opened chasm.

He's not really leaving. Is he?

My pulse rushed in my ears. I wanted to turn, to find Nathanial, but Tatius's hand on my neck kept me still. I twisted in Tatius's grip, my fists clenching at my sides. My eyes slid to the dagger at his thigh again. He'd said if I hit him again he'd hit back, but if he was planning to kill me anyway . . .

I cocked my arm back. Prepared my punch.

Fingers slid over my fist and Nathanial stepped into my range of sight.

"Be calm, Kitten." The whispered words were gentle, but his grip was tight and the set of his shoulders defensive.

Tatius cocked a blue eyebrow at Nathanial. "I told you to leave."

He didn't. Nathanial brushed his lips over my still clenched fist. Then he sank onto the couch, not leaving.

"So be it," Tatius said and then he lifted his wrist and bit deep. He held out the wrist for me. "Drink."

I didn't want to. I was sure I didn't want to. But when Tatius tugged me forward, closer to his body and his bleeding wrist, I found my mouth closing over those small punctures.

"Do not bite me," Tatius whispered into my hair.

He told me that last time he forced blood on me too.

I drank hungrily. When the pulse of his blood slowed, I pulled back. The sweet, coppery taste tainted my senses, filled my body with new warmth. My tongue darted between my lips, searching for lost drops, and Tatius's fingers flexed on my neck.

"Drink more," he commanded again, lifting his wrist.

My gaze fell to the mostly healed wounds. He cursed and ripped his skin open, wider this time. It looked like it hurt, but he simply shoved the once again bleeding wrist in my face.

Without using my fangs, my saliva, or maybe Tatius's ancient body healed his wound quickly. He ripped open his wrist time and again. I hoped it hurt. Nathanial sat ramrod straight on the couch, his eyes locked on us, his expression frayed around the edges.

A knock sounded, and my head shot up as the door opened.

"Not exactly perfect timing," Tatius said, but he smiled at the two women in the doorway.

The first woman bowed to him before backing out of the room. The other, dressed as—a whore, perhaps?—strolled forward. Tatius's blood was already warming my limbs, so I wasn't starving by a long shot, but with the taste of blood still on my lips, I was hyper aware of all the pale skin her skimpy outfit displayed. She was human. I could tell by the way she moved, the pounding of her heart, or maybe just by the fact she registered as food.

Crap. I dropped my gaze to the thick carpet, trying to concentrate on a scorch mark where one of the candelabras must have fallen. I was looking up again before I realized it.

Tatius stepped around me to greet the woman. "Tiffany, thank you for joining us." He dipped at the waist and kissed her hand. She giggled like a school girl, blood rushing to fill her cheeks as she blushed.

I ripped my eyes away. *What's wrong with me?* I'd been around more humans earlier in the night and hadn't experienced this many issues. Then again, I hadn't had the taste of blood to wake my hunger.

Tatius slid an arm around her waist and steered her toward me. "This is Kita. She's new and having a little trouble."

Her gaze swept over me. The playfulness fled from her face. I pinpointed the second she decided I was competition—for *what*, I wasn't sure. She cocked her hip and stared down her nose at me. It was obvious: she didn't like me. Then Tatius leaned in and stage whispered, "I was hoping you wouldn't mind giving her a small donation," and her whole demeanor changed.

She reexamined me, everything in her face softening, turning up with interest. Her heartbeat, already pounding in my ears, beat harder as her pulse jumped. *Fear or excitement?* Based on the lustful shine in her eyes, I was betting on excitement. Okay, she had serious issues. *Does she understand what Tatius is suggesting?*

He extended his hand toward me and I shook my head. Oh no, I wasn't playing this game. Willing dinner or not, I was on a strictly 'no human' diet.

My refusal earned me a frown.

I tried not to let my eyes travel to the woman, really I did, but they found their way there anyway. She noticed, and bit her lip, smiling.

Is she flirting with me? I'd heard of flirting with death before, but this was ridiculous. I took a step closer to Nathanial. His mask was back in place, but he wouldn't meet my eyes. Tatius would, though his gaze threatened to burn through the top layer of my skin.

"Kita, willingly or unwillingly, you will do what I tell you," he said. "Now come here."

I shook my head, and took another step toward the couch and Nathanial. "I can't. We don't know what will happen." I was the only shifter in the mages' records to ever successfully complete the change to a vampire. No one knew if I could tag humans by drinking from them or not. I wasn't handing the judge a reason to revoke my protected status.

I was less than a step from the couch when my body froze. One foot dangled in the air as time hung on a moment of puzzlement. Then my legs strolled forward of their own volition. Tatius held out his hand, and my arm reached for him.

What the hell? I tried to jerk away, to back up. My body didn't listen. My brain told me I was struggling, but my body passively let Tatius lead me to the brunette woman.

Tiffany slipped out of her heels, and leaned in, exposing her throat. I lifted onto the balls of my feet.

No!

My body wasn't listening. My arms slid around her and she quivered. *Run.* I didn't. Only my eyes were still under my control, and I shot a frantic glance at Tatius. He smiled, crossing his arms over his chest.

I tried to struggle, but the best I could do was roll my eyes. *Stop.* I couldn't. My body moved without my permission, drawing Tiffany closer to me. *I have to fight. To run. I have to—*

I blinked. My vision filled with the sight of ghost-like red cords lifting in the air around Tiffany. I'd have gasped if I could. I'd seen similar half-there shapes only once before. That had been when I'd been starving and my vamp powers had kicked into high gear. I'd accidentally used the power to feed from a hunter before erasing his memories. Scary, if admittedly useful, but unless my mezmer ability could get me out of this mess—and I didn't think it could—I did *not* need freaky vampire abilities acting up right now.

Not that I had any choice in the matter. The red coils slithered around me, unseen to any eye but mine, and as they wound around my skin, I could taste Tiffany's need. She wanted me to bite her. Wanted it more than anything else.

I screamed, or I tried to, but instead my fangs sank into Tiffany's throat.

She moaned, her arms sliding around my waist, her manicured nails clenching my hips. She pressed her body against mine, and her small gasps fluttered along my skin. Warmth and life flowed down my throat, sweetly perfumed by her ecstasy. Then her mind opened and I rushed into her memories.

I glance around the bar, glasses of liquor I know the vamp can't drink clutched in my hands. But the man at the table is a vamp. I know he is. I knew them all by sight.

He doesn't even glance at me as I place his and his date's drinks down. He knows it's only been a week for me. I can't donate again so soon. That's Tatius's rule. But three weeks? Why do I always have to wait three weeks? I have too much blood under my skin. I can feel it. The vamps need it. Why won't anyone take it?

God it feels good when they bite me.

Someone notice me. Someone touch me. I want to feel it. I don't need to wait three weeks to recover between bites. Please . . .

My fangs retracted, pulling my mind free of her thoughts. My tongue darted out between my lips, sealing the wound on her throat, and she swayed in my arms. Her head lolled to the side, a contented sound slipping from her barely conscious body. *Did I take too much?* My body, still moving without my control, leaned down and scooped Tiffany's legs off the floor, lifting the taller woman without difficulty.

A slick layer of sweat clung to her skin. She smelled of exertion and endorphins. The vampire who had escorted Tiffany into the room appeared at my side, or maybe she'd moved there while I'd been caught up in the human's mind, either way, my body handed off the mortal burden. The other vampire carried Tiffany out of the room.

The door slid shut, and my body turned to face Tatius. Something snapped inside me, and my legs crumpled, dropping me to the floor.

"What the hell—?" I could speak again! I lifted my hands, wiggled my trembling fingers. I could move.

I pushed off the floor, rolling to my feet, and Tatius took a step toward me. He offered me his hand, and I tried to stand and jump back at the same time. The result was an awkward scramble that dumped me on my ass. I crab walked, half scooting half crawling, toward the couch.

"Help. Help me." The mewling words tumbled out of my mouth. Pathetic. I couldn't call them back.

My back hit the couch with a thump. Nathanial's hands slid under my arms and he lifted me to my feet, tugging me against his chest. I drank down his familiar scent, clung to the silky fabric of his jacket. My cheeks were damp, though I couldn't remember when I'd started crying. The moisture soaked into Nathanial's jacket, but he just held onto me tighter, like his arms could keep my body from shattering.

"What happened?" I whispered.

"Tatius is known as the Puppet Master." He leaned in so the words were pressed into my hair.

I shivered. A puppet? Yes, someone else pulling my strings accurately described what had happened. I'd had no control. Just my eyes and my thoughts. Nothing else.

That woman, Tiffany, she'd wanted me to bite her, was addicted to the bite, but had I taken too much? She'd been carried out nearly unconscious. Tatius had controlled that. Had made me drink.

I shivered again, remembering the ecstasy in her mind, the feel of her pounding pulse. I hadn't wanted to stop. The thought had never occurred to me once my fangs were in her throat. In truth, if Tatius hadn't been controlling my body, she would have died. That was a frightening thought. My trembling ratcheted up to near violence, like I could shake the thoughts and memories loose. Nathanial held me tighter and brushed a kiss into my hair. I wasn't the only one shaking.

"Stop coddling her," Tatius said.

Nathanial's body jerked as the larger man grabbed his shoulder, turning us both.

"Release her," Tatius commanded.

For a single heartbeat, Nathanial's arms tightened, pressing me against his chest hard enough to hurt. Then his hands fell from me, his arms hanging limp by his sides. He stepped back. He was only an arm's length away, but I was alone. Exposed.

I hugged myself, willing my trembling to cease. I didn't look up, didn't meet Tatius's eyes, though I could feel his gaze boring into my skin. His hand appeared in my peripheral, but I concentrated on the toes of my sneakers.

"I think you'll do what I ask now, won't you?" The threat was clear in his voice.

Without looking up, I laid the tips of two fingers in his palm. His hand closed around my fingers like a Venus fly trap, and he tugged me forward. I let him.

His free hand shot out, swiping the neckline of my sweater off my shoulder. I jumped. I couldn't help it. I'm not sure what I was expecting, but him attacking my clothes wasn't on the list. He leaned down, staring at the lacerations from the hare. I rocked onto my heels, not stepping away, but putting a little more distance between us.

His hand moved to my collarbone, and I flinched, expecting pain, but his touch was gentle. "A human would have needed stitches."

"I've never been human."

He grinned at that. "True."

He was close enough I could feel his breath on my skin with the word, and I squeezed my eyes closed. I had a sinking suspicion I knew what he planned to do. Another warm breath gliding over my collarbone confirmed my suspicions a second before his tongue ran over the jagged skin.

He was gentle, so remarkably gentle my eyes flew open to confirm it was truly the same vampire who'd taunted and threatened me only moments before. It was. Despite Tatius's care, my skin still burned as his tongue dipped deeper into the wound. The pain only lasted a few heartbeats, then a tingling warmth spread around his mouth as his saliva closed the wound. Then even that ceased, and I knew the wound was sealed. Healed.

Tatius's lips trailed from where the jagged scratches had been and crawled along my collarbone. Feather light, his lips traveled up my shoulder, toward my throat. I stepped back, I couldn't help it—I probably should have tried harder. His fingers curled in my hair, and he forced my head to the side, baring my neck.

I expected him to bite me, expected pain, but one moment his breath touched my throat, and the next he was gone. I hadn't realized I'd closed my eyes, but I must have because I had to open them. Nathanial stood directly behind Tatius, his hand on the other vampire's arm, his knuckles white.

Tatius craned his head around but didn't release me. "You're the one who decided not to leave, Hermit."

The skin over Nathanial's knuckles stretched as his grip tightened. His fangs were exposed, bearing into his lower lip with the force of his clenched jaw, but his eyes held uncertainty. There was no hope for me to latch onto in those eyes. I swallowed hard, my neck aching where Tatius still bared my throat.

"Nathanial," Tatius said. It was the first time I'd heard any of the vampires use his real name.

Nathanial blinked, his gaze dropping from mine. His hand fell from Tatius's arm.

"Good. Now sit down or get out," Tatius said. Then he turned back to me. "Where were we?"

He leaned forward, his mouth parted. A fluttering sensation erupted in my stomach, not all of it fear. His breath danced over my pulse, and the flutters turned frantic—I wanted him to bite me.

No.

What was I thinking? I didn't want him to bite me. But Tiffany would have. And I had her memories.

Her need, her addiction, whirled in my mind, ignited my skin. Blunt human teeth grazed the flesh over my pulse, and I gasped. It would feel good. I didn't need Tiffany's memories to tell me that. I had personal experience.

Tatius's fangs pressed against my throat, not yet piercing the vein. Fire flushed my skin and a gasp escaped my lips. The sound made him chuckle, his amusement rumbling against my body where we touched.

I gritted my teeth, willing my reactions silent, but as his hand played across my stomach, trailed down to cup my hip, my breath hitched. My skin felt hyper-sensitive, overly aware of the heat of his body. He nicked my throat, not actually biting, and I trembled.

I couldn't take anymore.

"If you're going to bite me, get it over with." My voice sounded thick, breathless in my ears, but Tatius went still. My words were apparently not what he expected.

"So much spirit," he whispered. Then he stopped playing, and his fangs slid into my throat.

A flash of pain shot through me, then there was only the liquid heat of his mouth. A heat that expanded, spread, and spiraled to my center, building into a giddy current. Electricity ignited inside me, rushing through my body, reducing the world to static and heat. A wave of pleasure crashed through me, knocked my knees out from under me. There was no time to recover as a second and then third wave crashed.

Tatius pulled back, and I sagged in his arms. Someone was breathing hard, gasping for breath. It was me. I swallowed, trying to focus my blinking eyes, but nothing felt real. Nothing but the warm arms around my waist, the broad chest against my cheek. A rumble built in my chest, and I realized I was purring.

Well, why wouldn't I be? I felt good, content. I snuggled against the chest cradling me. Hadn't I been panicked earlier? It seemed like I had, but it must not have been important. I drew in a deep breath, cataloguing the base scent of the man holding me.

Stone dust. Hot metal. Sea Salt.

I blinked. I didn't know those scents. At least not as belonging to anyone I trusted. My head snapped back, and I wiggled in Tatius's arms, inching away from his chest. I stepped back, still caught in his arms, and it was those arms that kept me standing when my knees wobbled. I swallowed and concentrated on standing upright. Just standing on my own would be an accomplishment.

"Let go," I whispered.

He looked at me, just looked at me, his green eyes sparkling with amusement. "You'll fall."

"Let go."

He did.

My legs buckled, refusing to support my weight, and I collapsed to my knees. Tatius, not touching me, moved with me, and I realized my fingers were tangled in his mesh shirt. I didn't remember grabbing him. Forcing my stiff fingers to uncurl, I dropped my arms to the floor. I stayed like that a moment, on all fours, on the floor, just breathing. Then I pushed to my feet. My legs wobbled, but held my weight.

Tatius watched me, his green-eyed gaze blistering, searing my skin until a flush crawled to my cheeks. *What's wrong with me?* I needed to be more on the ball than this. *One little bite and I turn into a simpering idiot?* Hell no.

I lifted my chin and I looked around. Nathanial was on the couch again, but his gaze was on the floor. He didn't look up. Didn't look at me.

I didn't blame him.

"Happy now?" I asked Tatius, forcing every last bit of bravado hiding in my body into my voice.

He didn't look fooled as he smiled down at me. "Not yet. But closer." His arm wrapped around my waist, and he turned me, tucking me against his hip so we were standing side by side. "You'll be on my arm tonight. Hermit, are you coming? We have an appointment with the Collector."

Nathanial's head shot up. I'd seen him rage once before, and it had been a terrifying thing to behold. It was no less frightening to see his full lips thinned in anger, his gray eyes wide and hurt. He stared at me and I was the one to drop my gaze this time.

"Get a hold of yourself," Tatius chided. "We will present a unified front, with all of my council backing the fact my companion had nothing to do with the albino's demise."

"Your companion?" Nathanial's words were hardly more than a broken scratching sound issuing from his throat. He looked at Tatius. The rage had thinned in his face, a sharp edge of fear taking its place. I'd seen similar expressions on animals before. The question in their eyes wasn't an indication they were beaten—it was the panic of being backed into a corner. A cornered animal was deadly.

Tatius stroked my hair. "Yes, *my* companion."

A statement. No question. No room to argue.

I tried to push free. "No."

He cocked a dyed eyebrow. "No? My dear, you get no say in this matter. You are a novelty, a child, a commodity. And now you are mine."

Chapter Seven

His?

Like hell. I didn't belong to anyone. Least of all to Tatius.

My effort to detangle myself from Tatius's arms redoubled, and Nathanial was suddenly in the space before us. I hadn't seen him move, hadn't heard him. His hand shot out, ripping me from Tatius's grasp, pulling me behind him.

My legs still weren't steady, and I stumbled, falling to my knees. I rolled with it, letting the momentum turn me. Then I shot back to my feet. My vision filled with black dots. That didn't stop me. I slid into a defensive crouch, my fists clenching. One heartbeat pounded behind my blind eyes. Two.

I couldn't hear the fight. Couldn't tell who was winning.

The darkness gave way to a gray washed world. I caught a glimpse of Nathanial's back, his hands locked with Tatius's as the two of them grappled. The gray parted. Nathanial crumpled to his knees, his arms going slack.

Shsssk. The dagger slid from Tatius's thigh hilt.

Nathanial didn't move. Didn't twitch.

The dagger angled toward his throat, and I threw myself forward, knocking Nathanial to the floor. I expected pain to slice through my back, across my unprotected shoulders. It didn't. I chanced a glance up.

Tatius glared down at me, his arms crossed over his broad chest and the dagger tapping his forearm. "You're both fools. Get up."

Nathanial rose smoothly before turning and offering me a hand. I wouldn't normally have accepted the help, but it had been a hell of a night. I took his hand, glad for it as I realized I was shaking again.

"Come," Tatius said, holding out his arm for me to take. Apparently we were picking back up where we were before Nathanial's outburst.

"No," Nathanial stepped in front of me, blocking me from Tatius's sight with his own body. "No. She is my companion. I brought her here in good faith. She will not be presented on your arm."

I could just make out Tatius around Nathanial's shoulder. He shook his head, his expression turning dark. He lifted the blade, and it glimmered in the candlelight. The orange glow made the surface look like it was already coated in blood.

"Is that the position you are choosing to take, Hermit?" The threat was clear in his voice, and if not his voice, then in the glinting blade.

Nathanial spun. His arms locked around my waist and lifted me from the floor in one movement. I gasped as the ceiling rushed toward us and he hugged me tighter to his chest.

"Shhhh," he hissed in my ear.

I held my breath, willing my heart to stop its deafening banging. It didn't obey. I caught my reflection in a mirror. I hated the frightened look carved across my face, my too wide eyes. My reflection looked away. I blinked. *What the—?*

There was no mirror.

Doppelgangers hung in the air around us, each an exact copy of Nathanial and me. *How?*

Nathanial. One of his powers was to create illusions. He used it to make himself invisible when he flew, and once he'd changed my appearance, but I'd never realized he could do anything so . . . elaborate.

Half a dozen doppelgangers filled the small room. The Kita-copies all looked stricken as they stared at each other. Two red dots decorated each of their throats. *The bite*—Tatius hadn't closed it. The Nathanial-copies stared at Tatius, brows creased with strain, pupils expanded until their gray irises were eradicated.

"This is foolish, Nate," Tatius said, crossing his arms over his chest. "And deadly."

He sounded at ease, bored even, as his gaze moved over the half dozen copies, but his pupils had also expanded, only the thinnest sliver of green left.

Nate? It was a very un-Nathanial like nickname. Was Tatius's use of the nickname supposed to engender trust? To remind Nathanial of some shared past—or possibly to remind himself?

Nathanial floated us toward the door as the doppelgangers dashed in front of us. They dipped as they flew, switching places like a street magician's sleight of hand trick. Which cup is the quarter under? Which Nathanial and Kita are real? The audience rarely guessed correctly, and Nathanial was more than a street magician—he was an old vampire with a gift for illusion.

But Tatius was ancient.

We glided toward the door, invisible, undetectable. The doppelgangers were mere distractions. They darted closer to Tatius, feigning attacks, drawing his attention. We couldn't fight Tatius and win—that had already been proven. But maybe we could still run.

Under my hands, I felt the strain tingling along Nathanial's skin, the tension stiffening his shoulders. He'd told me once that he couldn't maintain a moving illusion more than a few feet. We were now yards from the darting copies of ourselves. One of the feigned attackers dashed at Tatius's back. Tatius spun, his dagger disappearing into the fake Nathanial's chest. The real Nathanial shuddered, his arms tensing around me. The impaled copy vanished.

Tatius whirled and planted the dagger in another illusionary chest. Another doppelganger disappeared. Only four remained. Our slow glide toward the door picked up speed. Tatius spun. The dagger flew through the air, straight at us. Nathanial careened sideways, the dagger slicing through the material of his tux before burying itself halfway to the hilt in the door.

Found you, Tatius's smug voice said *inside* my head.

I swallowed hard, clinging tighter to Nathanial. Tatius lifted his hand, not even the smallest bit of green left in his eyes. He ignored the illusions darting at him, his intense gaze fixed on us. Nathanial's fangs flashed, his pupils expanded, turned his eyes black.

The doppelgangers disappeared. Nathanial's flight path changed. He was pouring all of his energy into making us invisible, but Tatius's eyes tracked our movement.

A smirk twisted Tatius's lips, and he clenched his fist as if snatching a butterfly out of the air. Nathanial froze. Then the ground jutted toward us as we dropped.

I crouched, absorbing the impact, but Nathanial hit the carpet hard, his body crumpling like a boneless doll—or like a puppet with limp strings.

Horror twisted my stomach as Tatius strolled across the room, casual-like, to retrieve his dagger. Nathanial never moved. My hands trembled as I reached down and lifted him under the arms. His pulse pounded against my palms, so he was alive, but he was dead weight. Only his eyes, wide and locked on me, showed he was conscious.

Dammit.

He couldn't move. He would have if he could. Tatius had control of his body. And speaking of, Tatius was almost upon us. I looked around. I was strong and fast, but Nathanial hadn't been a match for Tatius, and Nathanial could kick my ass while reading a book. *Think of something, dammit.*

Nothing emerged from my panicking mind. Which meant I was winging it or dying. *Maybe both.*

I lowered Nathanial and he slumped forward like a rag-doll. Tatius, still strolling, was less than a yard away, his dagger flashing in the candlelight. I stepped between him and Nathanial.

"Move," he said, stepping into my personal bubble.

"You made your point," I said between gritted teeth. "You've reestablished yourself as the biggest badass around. We get it."

He lifted an eyebrow. "Move."

I didn't.

I wasn't familiar with vampire society, but I knew 'ruled by the fittest' structure. In Firth I'd been named *Dyre*, destined to take my father's place as *Torin*, but if I'd stepped up as *Torin*, my position would have been challenged, hard. I'd left before I was old enough to be opposed, but if I'd have stayed, I'd have needed a deadly reputation to survive.

Tatius was no kitten amongst lions, but I had no doubt he had a reputation to maintain. With my issues with authority, you'd think I'd have appeasement tactics down. Instead I'd spent much of my life thankful I healed quickly. Not an option currently. If I didn't diffuse this situation, one of us wasn't walking out of the room alive.

I kept my gaze locked with Tatius's but sank to my knees. I was still in his path, still blocking him, but in a much more placating position. His eyes moved from my face to my neck. No, not just my neck, but to his bite marks in my throat. I brushed aside my hair, giving him a better view of the wound.

"You made your point," I said again. "There were no witnesses. There's nothing more to prove." Because what happened behind closed doors was always easier to forgive.

"Are you bargaining for your master's life?" Tatius frowned at me, but a rim of green appeared around his pupils. "What do you have to bargain with?"

Damn. I mentally cast about, but I had nothing. Nothing to offer or trade. Whatever my face revealed made Tatius smirk, a small, self-satisfied twist of his mouth. He crouched in front of me and reached out, his hand hovering over the bite in my throat.

I winced and my tongue dried and stuck to the roof of my mouth. I *knew* what I had available to trade. My lips cracked as they parted, as if they were the last defense trying to keep the words from leaving my mouth. I spoke anyway. "Me? I mean, my companion bond?"

His smirk turned crueler. "An awful big opinion of yourself for a runt with no manners or feminine wiles. Besides, I can already take your bond. As you said, I proved my point and our sad little Hermit cannot deny me. Offer me something else."

I swallowed around my thick tongue. *What else did I have?* I seriously doubted he'd want the marbles or other knickknacks I'd collected. All I had was myself to offer.

"No resistance," I whispered.

"What?"

He'd heard me, I knew he had, but I cleared my throat, speaking louder anyway. "My cooperation. That's what I have on the table."

His fingers, still hovering over my throat, dropped the inch to my skin. They landed ever so lightly above my pulse then trailed downward in a smooth stroke over the bite mark he'd left open. My back arched as a maddening mix of pain and pleasure shot from my throat and pooled in my center. I gasped. My vision blanked.

Then the sensation passed.

What the hell was that?

I swallowed, shaking as my breath tumbled out of me. When my vision cleared, Tatius's nose was less than an inch from mine, his face filling my awareness.

"You couldn't resist me," he whispered, his breath passing the words over my lips.

Every instinct in my body urged me to pull back, to run away. I was more than flirting with death, I was presenting myself to him as a cheap whore. I swallowed down the need to flee, forcing it into a bottle deep inside, knowing the next time I examined that corner of my psyche I would probably end up screaming.

"Take it or leave it," I said. And here I'd thought I'd exhausted my bravado.

Tatius stood, sheathing his dagger in one smooth movement. "I do like your spirit."

Was that acceptance?

I rose slowly, my knees unsteady as I pushed to my feet. Behind me, I heard Nathanial move as well.

"Kita?"

Just my name, carried with so much uncertainty, I almost didn't recognize it from Nathanial's mouth. I could feel him staring at me, the weight of his gaze prickly against my back.

I didn't turn. I couldn't.

"Let's get this over with," I said to Tatius.

"So anxious?" He held out his hand, and I gritted my teeth but obediently took it, letting him pull me closer. He lifted his wrist and bit deep. "His life is in your hands. Drink."

"I feel a slight sense of déjà vu," I said, but leaned over his bleeding wound.

His fingers trailed through my hair as I drew from his wrist. He didn't tell me not to bite him this time, but I guessed as much. Besides, I was well fed, and even with blood running over my tongue, my fangs didn't descend.

He opened his wrist twice more before he nodded. "That will suffice, for now. We three have a date with the Collector."

Chapter Eight

The council chamber was empty when we left the sitting room. Tatius walked through it without comment. Then he led me through so many corridors and stairways I couldn't have guessed where we were.

Nathanial followed behind us. He hadn't said a word since I made my deal with Tatius, but I could feel his gaze on my back. I didn't turn around. I didn't know what to say to him. Sorry? You're welcome? I'd done what I had to do, and we'd both survived. So far, at least.

Tatius finally stopped outside of a large door, but he didn't enter. Instead he turned, his gaze assessing as he looked me over. He didn't look completely pleased with what he saw.

We'll have to do something about your wardrobe, his voice said inside my head as he reached out, straightening the collar of my old gray coat.

After swiping my hair over my shoulder so the bite he'd left on my neck was unobstructed, he nodded as if satisfied, took my arm, and turned toward the door again. Then he just stood there. He didn't seem inclined to open the door for himself, so I reached out. *Companion and servant, lucky me.*

Tatius stopped me with a gentle jerk back, and the door peeled open. A vampire I didn't recognize blinked at me, her baby blues wide as she looked from my arm locked in the crook of Tatius's to his mark on my throat. Surprised or not, she didn't falter as she stepped aside. Her head dipped to Tatius as we passed, a small but intentional movement. *A sign of respect?* I hadn't noticed the other vampires bowing before, but as we passed, each vampire paused to tip their heads, some touching the tips of their fingers to their foreheads. *Am I expected to do that?*

Three council members sat at a large dark wood table in the center of the room, two additional seats had been left open. One was for Tatius, and now that Nathanial was on the council, the other must have been meant for him. *Where the hell am I supposed to go?*

I glanced around. The non-council vampires, who had been scattered around the room, were now congregating along the far wall.

The setup looked exactly like the council room we'd been in earlier, down to the fabric draping the walls.

"Should I . . . ?" I nodded to the line of vampires.

Tatius smirked, his green eyes glowing with the candlelight. "Companions remain with their masters."

He tugged me toward the table—and the too few chairs. Slouching into the centermost seat, he slapped his thigh.

Oh, he has to be kidding.

He wasn't.

Gritting my teeth, I perched on the edge of his leg, my back straight as I continued to hold most of my own weight. He didn't let me get away with that. Wrapping an arm around my waist, he dragged me further into his lap.

Now smile at my vampires, his voice said in my head.

Oh hell, I wasn't going to be able to keep this bargain. Not at this rate. I chanced a glance at Nathanial. He was staring straight ahead—which meant he was the only person in the room not watching Tatius's little show. Taking a deep breath, I flashed my teeth at the vampires gathered along the wall.

Tatius nodded. *See, that wasn't so hard.*

Says him. "I thought you wanted me to keep a low profile," I whispered.

Questioning me already? he asked inside my head, and I dropped my gaze. I didn't want to put Nathanial or myself in danger over one stupid question. Tatius's hand flexed on my hip. *Other master's companions are not important enough to acknowledge with more than feigned interest, particularly when they are displaying an overt amount of affection for their masters. It would be rude. Now, work on that affection.*

Rude? I looked around and realized none of the vampires present were staring anymore. In fact, now that they had gotten over the surprise of seeing me enter on Tatius's arm, they were very pointedly *not* looking. *I have a lot to learn about vampire politics.* And I had the feeling I'd be getting a crash course soon. *Goody.*

Aloud Tatius said, "I've sent for the Collector."

The atmosphere in the room, which had been thick with curiosity, turned restless at his words. Boots scuffed the ground as the vampires along the wall shuffled, and Nuri, who sat to Tatius's side, smoothed her small hands along her pleated skirt.

Tatius propped a booted foot on the table and held up a hand. The vampires stilled, silence engulfing the room. I wanted to stand, or at least squirm, but Tatius's hand around my waist kept me still.

I waited. We all waited.

The doors swung open, revealing the dark hallway beyond. The air rushed out of the room as every undead creature in the room sucked in one anticipatory breath.

A man stepped into the doorway. Actually, he ducked under the door frame—and it wasn't a low threshold. I blinked as he straightened, his head nearly brushing the nine foot ceiling. The giant Nathanial had spoken to earlier still wore the maroon frock coat, frilly lace spilling from his cuffs and collar, but he'd discarded his masquerade mask, and his shoulder length auburn hair now hung loose around his blocky face. Elizabeth, the vampire the Collector had called on to 'assist' Nuri, walked in at the giant's side. She'd also abandoned her mask, leaving her face as stark and pale as a porcelain figurine with dashes of color brushed on her eyes and cheeks.

The giant's strides were tight, not like he was making an effort to walk slowly, but like it was habit for him to match his steps to hers. He inclined his head when he reached the center of the room, and Elizabeth curtseyed deeply, spreading her dress in a display of white lace. From the corner of my eye, I saw Tatius nod to them, then they turned, their gazes going back to the door.

Two men entered next. They faced slightly away from each other, and from us, so that their shoulders were turned toward the corners of the room and the back of their hips touched. Their blond hair glowed slightly orange in the flickering candlelight as they walked in a strange synchronized manner, their sides still pressed together. No, not pressed, joined. *Conjoined twins?* I stared, I couldn't help it, as they approached the council table and spun slightly so first one and then the other could bow to Tatius. Then they joined the giant and Elizabeth, and all eyes migrated to the doorway.

A lone woman entered next. *The Collector.* Her face was full of severe lines, as if smiling would have made her crumble. She'd removed every trace of her festive masquerade costume. Her hair was pulled back in a tight, no-nonsense bun, and her gold-trimmed gown had been traded for a dress made of thick gray material which neither accentuated nor hid her figure. I thought at first she was in her late forties—or had been when she'd been turned—but as she drew closer, I realized her smooth hands, loosely clasped in front of her body, and her wrinkle-less face belonged to a younger woman, maybe someone closer to my age. Her eyes though, brown with no warmth, were old.

Very old.

As she walked across the room, her steps slow but assured, several other people slipped into the room. They moved quickly, heads down as they gathered along the opposite wall from the non-council Haven vampires.

The Collector stopped before the council table, her back straight, her chin firm. Tatius was the one to move first. Just the slightest inclination of his head, smaller even than the giant had made.

"I bid you welcome, Collector," he said, his foot still propped on the polished wood table.

"I confess to feeling less than welcomed, Puppet Master." Her eyes traveled over the council, me in Tatius's lap, his booted foot, and then moved on. "It has been several hours since the body of a member of my entourage was found, and I have seen no results, no recompense."

"I assure you my people have done everything in our power to discover how your woman came to lose her head. We have found no fault among those we've questioned, including this *child* "—he jostled me—"who discovered the body. But, as requested, I have brought her for you to examine."

I tried not to flinch at the word 'examine', really I did, but a twitch jumped through my hands anyway, made my shoulders jerk. I could almost feel the Collector's gaze drawn to me, but it flickered away as quickly as it landed.

"Bring our guest a comfortable seat," Tatius commanded, and one of the vampires along the wall slipped out of the room.

He returned immediately, balancing an unadorned chair over his shoulder. It must have been on hand. Was it hospitality that Tatius offered her the chair . . . or a power play that he'd made her wait for it?

The vampire set the chair in the center of the room, his gaze never lifting higher than the floor. Then he scurried back to his spot on the wall, leaning against the draped stone like he could sap strength from the rock.

The Collector lowered herself onto the chair as if it were a gilded throne. The giant moved to her side, but even his massive height didn't dwarf the plain-looking vampire's presence. She drew all attention while appearing perfectly drab, unassuming. Elizabeth knelt beside the giant, her small head leaning against his leg, and the twins moved behind the chair. The arrangement could have been posed by a photographer. A strange family portrait, with all members gathered around their matriarch.

Tatius lifted his foot from the table and gave my hip a gentle squeeze before he started to stand. I jumped to my feet.

"At the time your human's body was found," he said to the Collector, "every vampire in this room was present, but only one was close enough to touch." He nodded in my direction. "I have examined her and determined her without fault. It is only because I guaranteed your people safe passage and my hospitality that I grant you the opportunity to examine her."

He held his hand out to me. I seriously didn't want to take it. Turning around and running out of the room sounded like a much better idea. Not that I'd get far. My legs stiffened with dread, but I laid my fingers against his palm.

I think my lack of resistance surprised him, because an honest smile peeked out behind his smirk. It probably wouldn't have been a bad smile under different circumstances. Even under these, the smile made something inside me flutter, a fluttering that streamed down from the bite in my throat.

Vampire tricks. I *hated* vamp tricks.

Whatever he saw in my face changed his expression, and he turned back toward the Collector. "On the condition that no harm comes to her during your investigation, I present to you my companion."

The Collector considered me from her seat as Tatius escorted me around the table, his arm sliding around my waist. It was possessive, but with the Collector's cold gaze tracking my steps, I found myself glad I didn't have to make the short walk alone.

As we moved, two vampires left the wall where the Collector's people had gathered. They approached the group without a word, standing slightly off to one side like sentinels. Both had hard eyes, their gazes assessing and constantly moving. Guards, I'd bet my tail on it. Hired muscle had a look, and *loyal* muscle an even stronger one.

We were two yards from the group when I ground to a halt. Tatius's smirk never slipped, but he turned, the eyebrow the Collector couldn't see arched, his eyes burning with warning. I swallowed and sucked down another breath. The taste of the air sliding down my throat was familiar and unmistakable. After all, how many bodies had I found tonight? It wasn't like I'd forget the victim's scent.

Walk, Tatius's voice demanded inside my head.

I frowned at him. Could he read my thoughts as well as yell in my mind? *I recognize the scent,* I thought at him.

His expression didn't change, didn't reveal he'd heard. *Walk, or I move you.*

Crap. I really didn't want to be a puppet. Not again. But the scent . . . I glanced back at Nathanial. His face was blank, unhelpful, but his fingers swept through the air as if he were shooing a fly—or urging me to keep moving.

I shuffled forward, three steps that equaled only one, and sucked down another lungful of air. My nose hadn't been as good since I became a vampire, and the scent was already growing faint, my olfactory glands exhausting.

"Is there an issue?" The Collector asked, looking at Tatius, not me.

"She's shy." Tatius made the last short word suggestive, his voice reaching across the space between us, playing on the open bite on my throat. A shiver ran over my skin, exploded as heat in my middle. My breath tumbled out. Not a gasp, at least, not quite.

I stumbled back a step.

I *hated* vampires.

I jerked my hand out of his, curling it in a fist by my side. "One of her people fed from the victim tonight." I forced the words through my clenched teeth. They came out without a hitch.

Tatius's mocking expression froze, and the air in the room vanished.

The Collector shoved up from her chair.

"What?" The word was a whisper that crackled around the room like a firework fuse, ready to blow.

Rude or not in vampire society, everyone was staring now, the weight of their gazes smothering me. I sucked down another lungful of the explosive air.

"The headless woman. One of them fed from her. Tonight." I nodded at the cluster of vampires in front of me.

I wasn't close enough to know which vamp had sucked on the victim, and with my nose giving out, I'd probably have to draw the scent right off their skin to tell. I took a step forward.

Stop. Do not move. Do not speak.

I flinched as Tatius's words cut through my brain. I had the urge to throw my hands over my ears, but the action wouldn't have accomplished anything. Well, anything but pissing Tatius off more.

"Is your companion unwell?" Elizabeth asked, managing to sound both concerned and offended simultaneously.

"Elizabeth," the Collector said, but her voice was empty, no warning or emotion left in it. She turned to Tatius. "Puppet Master, what is the meaning of this?"

"I would call it an interesting development," he said, hooking his thumbs in his studded belt. "Kita, continue," he commanded without looking at me, then followed the words with his voice slicing into my mind again. *You better have something to follow that little announcement. Keep it simple and short. Lives are on the line. Quite definitely yours.*

Well, crap.

"It's the scent," I said, staring at the woven belt at the Collector's waist. "Someone is carrying the base scent of the harlequin under their skin. That only happens when blood is exchanged."

Someone? Tatius's voice asked inside my head, his annoyance clear in the mental touch though his expression never changed. Aloud he said, "Most intriguing, wouldn't you say, Collector?"

"Are you making an accusation?" Her voice was low again, the edge of anger cutting the end of her sentence. "I remind you, Puppet Master, my human was killed after we'd been granted safe passage in your city." The implied fact that it was *his* honor being called into question went unsaid.

Tatius rolled his shoulders in a casual shrug. "Not one vampire I've questioned saw the woman alive. Knowing who saw her last could be helpful."

And that actually sounded reasonable.

The Collector tilted her head, but didn't turn to face her people. "Did one of you drink from Luna tonight?" No one answered and a smile spread like creeping frost across her face. "As I thought."

Tatius's eye flicked toward me, only a momentary glance. *You're sure?*

Was I seriously supposed to answer a question only I had heard?

I took a step forward, trying to catch the victim's scent again, and the two bodyguards moved to intercept me. They were fast, faster than I'd ever seen Nathanial move. One moment they were standing off to one side, and the next they were in my personal space, blocking my path.

I stumbled back. The bulkier of the two crossed arms thicker than my thighs over his chest—right at my eye level and not a foot from my nose. The other man was smaller, wiry, and all sharp angles with little squinty eyes. He wasn't much taller than me, and I was short. He sneered, his lip curling, the gleam of fang escaping a cruel mouth. He took another step closer, exaggerating the two or so inches of height he had on me.

I flashed him a little of my own teeth then froze. This close, his scent lifted off him with the heat of his body. And I knew that scent.

I backpedaled, my shoulders slamming into Tatius's chest. *When had he moved behind me?* It didn't matter. His hand slipped around my waist and I pointed at the wiry guard.

"Him."

Pressed as close to Tatius as I was, I felt the stillness overtake his body. Felt the exaggerated moment as no one spoke. His fingertips ground against my hip. Finally Tatius's chest rose as he drew in breath.

"Well?" he asked, his voice betraying none of the strain I felt in his body.

"Jomar?" The name resounded around room, as if the stillness of every vampire present gave the Collector's voice buoyancy. The short guard jerked. Then he turned and bowed in one swift motion.

"Mistress," he said without looking up.

"Who did you feed from tonight?"

"Selene. I swear to you."

The Collector nodded, and the giant turned. Addressing one of the vampires on the wall, he said, "Summon Selene and Chandra."

Tatius's grip on my hip tightened. I looked up at him, hoping my eyes conveyed my absolute certainty. He searched my face, searing my flesh, but I didn't dare look away. I was right. I knew I was. My nose wasn't as strong as it used to be, but it didn't lie.

You'd better be correct. His hand loosened.

The Collector sank back into her chair, crossing her leg over her knee. Then she leaned forward. "I had not heard you sired a companion, Puppet Master. She is very young." Her gaze swept idly over me before returning to Tatius. "But then you are very old. What ability is this she is manifesting?"

Tatius shrugged, but the movement wasn't completely smooth. "A rather unusual one."

"I have observed that. I assume it has been formally tested?"

"Of course," Tatius said without pause, and I worked hard at keeping my face blank. What I wouldn't give to have the control Nathanial had over his face.

"While we wait for . . . corroboration, why don't we take care of the true purpose of this impromptu gathering." She didn't wait for

Tatius to agree, but twitched a finger at the doll-like vampire by the giant's feet. "Elizabeth."

The giant leaned down, touching the top of the woman's pile of dark hair. She smiled at him, and then drew herself up, rising in a foam of silk and lace as if something other than muscle and bone were under the dress. She curtseyed before the Collector, the movement so deep the lacy dress collar fell forward, brushing the stone floor.

"Child, come forward," the Collector said, looking at me once more.

I didn't want to. I really, really didn't want another vampire biting me tonight—or ever.

Offer your wrist, Tatius's voice demanded.

No. No, no, no . . . I lifted my arm, realized my fist was clinched. I sucked in more air, letting the pressure of filling my lungs travel down my body, flow into the soles of my feet. One by one, I coaxed my fingers to uncurl from the knot of my hand. Another deep breath, and I extended my wrist.

Elizabeth smelled of old cloth and a flowery scent I didn't recognize, but was so sweet, it made me think of poisonous plants. As for the giant beside her—I froze.

What now? Annoyance shined through Tatius's projected thought.

My gaze traveled up, and up, until my neck hinged at a ninety degree angle and I could see the giant's face. My senses were sharper now that I'd fed, but I couldn't believe I'd failed to notice such a bizarre thing when I'd first met the giant at the party. "He has no scent," I whispered.

Which wasn't possible. Everything had a scent. I wasn't aware of Tatius's scent currently because we'd swapped blood, but I could still smell the chemicals his clothing had been washed with, the astringent scent of his hair dye. Elizabeth had a variety of smells beyond her base scent, but from the giant I smelled nothing. Not his scent, not his clothing, not wind caught in his hair—nothing. *It's like he's not here at all.*

"He's not," the Collector said, and I realized I'd spoken the last thought aloud. She was standing again, those cold, calculating eyes on me. "This is my second in command. He is known as the Traveler due to his ability to project a corporeal body from a distance." She turned to Tatius, her hands moving to her hips. "Your companion most assuredly demonstrates an . . . unusual talent. It is a shame she doesn't also demonstrate any discipline. Or are all the least significant members of your city allowed to speak out of turn? No wonder your guarantee of safe passage was so easily disregarded."

The room went as silent as if I'd been sucked into the void between worlds again. I stiffened, expecting an explosive response from Tatius. She'd just insulted not only him, but also his ability to run his city. But instead of a roar of anger, laughter escaped Tatius's chest.

"We all show favoritism from time to time, do we not?" he said aloud, but in my mind he warned, *No more outbursts or I'll cut your wagging tongue free of your pretty little mouth. Every night. For a year. Now concentrate on the memory of finding that damned harlequin and get this over with.*

Right. I bit my lips together. I'd rather keep my tongue in my head. I nodded, catching the motion mid-movement and freezing, which probably brought even more attention to the fact I'd responded to a command not given out loud. Swallowing another breath of air oddly not scented with the Traveler's presence, I held out my wrist.

Elizabeth's fingers slipped around my arm. She stepped forward, her fangs flashing. My breath caught, but not in fear. *Damn Tiffany and her vampire-bite addiction.* I shoved the reaction away just in time for Elizabeth's fangs to break skin. Warmth rushed up my arm, the blaze filling my body, my mind. On my other side, Tatius's hand on my arm was like a cool oasis. I groped for his fingers, locking mine around his, pressing the long side of my body along his, and the fire in my body calmed enough I could still see, still think.

Cool.

Leaning against Tatius's shoulder, I focused on the memory of the party, of seeing the open couch and escaping to it. Of smelling the blood. I tried not to think about the head spilling forward, but of course by not thinking about it, the memory sharpened.

Elizabeth pulled back. Her pupils had filled her eyes, not even a trace of blue left. A drop of my blood filled the crease of her lips, and her small tongue darted out as she blinked at me.

"Well?" the Collector asked, tapping her fingers on the chair arm.

"Everything happened as she described," Elizabeth said. "But she's . . . " Elizabeth glanced at the Traveler then back to the Collector. " . . . odd. Not human. Never human."

Crap. So much for the idea that concentrating on the memory would keep her out of my secrets. The Collector looked at me again. No, not again. She'd looked in my direction a few times before, but this was the first time she was actually *looking* at me. Her evaluating glance trailed over my tri-colored hair, my more-yellow-than-green eyes, and then lingered on the wound in my throat.

"What is your companion, Puppet Master?" Her voice made it sound like an idle question, but her eyes . . . her eyes betrayed her.

"Vampire, of course." Tatius's arm slid around my waist, drawing me closer even as he rocked onto one hip, striking a pose of nonchalance.

Games. All of it. Both of them. And little ol' me, I didn't even rank as high as a pawn. A pawn, sacrificial as it might be, could at least take another piece.

"Come here child, I wish a peek into your mind." The Collector held out her open palm, beckoning me forward.

Tatius's grip around my waist tightened.

"I granted you a chance to view what she saw of your human, not free reign in the memories of my people. You have what I promised you. Be satisfied with it."

"Of course." She smiled, the demure gesture looking too genuine to be true. "I believe Selene has arrived."

She held up her hand, summoning the two women standing in the doorway. Their heads hung as they trudged across the room. Identical falls of pure white hair covered their downcast faces like veils. They shuffled around the chair, stopping directly beside me before dipping simultaneously into curtsies. They straightened slowly as if every upward inch stung.

I expected them to be old, but young faces were revealed when they looked up. Young, colorless faces. I'd never seen skin so pale—the only color was a glimpse of snaking veins under their skin. Both wore sunglasses as if the flickering candlelight were too much for their eyes.

Albinos. And twins at that. Identical.

I blinked at them. Twins with terribly familiar scents. They had to be related to the dead woman.

Triplet albinos?

I inhaled slowly, tasting their scents. I was well fed, but they were human, and my pulse picked up from being so close, from my nearly intimate dissection of their scents. Theirs were similar, oh so similar, to the harlequin. More alive, of course, fresher, but the same combination of damp darkness with a hint of sweet sunscreen. But under that, each woman had a slightly different scent. Subtle, but definitely different. The headless woman had smelled of wind in the moonlight, and only the guard shared that particular combination.

The Collector steepled her hands, looking between the two

women. "Selene, child, who did you feed tonight?"

The twin closest to me started. "I—No one," she whispered.

Jomar whirled around. "But—"

The Collector held up a hand to silence him. "No one?"

A long strand of colorless hair brushed against my arm as she shook her head. "I was supposed to. It was my turn." Her shoulders heaved, a small, soundless, hiccup of a movement. Then they did it again. "Luna took my place." Her voice quivered, and her shoulders jerked again, as if someone had tied a string around her torso and tugged.

The other twin wrapped her arms around her sister. "It wasn't your fault," she whispered, which only made Selene's trembling more violent. A wet sob tore from her throat.

I shuffled my feet. I needed to get away from the twins. I was too close. Much too close to a pair of strangers who had just lost their sister. Tatius's arm tightened around my waist, as if he sensed how close I was to bolting.

Jomar watched the twins with emerging horror written on his face. As another sob sliced the air, he fell to his knees. Then he lowered himself completely prostrate before the Collector.

"I didn't know. I swear to you. I thought she was Selene. Luna was alive when I left her."

"Silence!" The Collector's voice boomed through the room, and for the first time her composure cracked. The look she gave her prostrate guard verged on homicidal, but then she cleared her throat and smoothed the front of her skirt. When she looked back up, her eyes were once again calm, her mouth unemotive. She nodded to Tatius. "Your companion was correct. Can her inhuman nose tell us anything else?"

Tatius smiled at her, and it was an oily, smug tilting of his lips. "It is a shame about the disobedience in your bloodstock, Collector. You might need to question them further. My companion," he looked at me, lifting an eyebrow. I tilted my head back, searching the scents in the room, but a yawn caught me unexpectedly and cracked across my face. "Is quite exhausted, as you can see. Dawn draws near. We should conclude this discussion before we retire for the day."

The Collector nodded, but her eyes were on me. Watching. Analyzing. I pressed three fingers over my mouth, covering my yawn as I stared back at her, knowing that, at least at the moment, my face betrayed nothing, particularly not interest. Returning her stare probably wasn't exactly respectful, but I'd spent a good deal of my life as a cat, and every cat, everywhere, has mastered the disinterested stare. Her bottom lip twitched, like she'd suppressed a frown or some other disapproving expression, then her gaze slid away, dismissing me.

"This has been a most unenlightening investigation. Should I assume you will compensate me for the loss of one of my collectables?" she asked, her voice deceptively bored, as if she could barely be troubled to look into Luna's death any longer.

"Of course," Tatius said, flashing teeth without smiling. "That is, if fault is found in my people."

I blinked, trying to push back the exhaustion suddenly pressing down on me. Tatius hadn't been lying about dawn approaching.

Time for good kittens to be in bed, I suppose. Tatius's voice said inside my head.

"Excuse us," he said aloud. He crooked a finger, and a female vampire pushed off the wall. "Take Kita to our chambers," he told her when she was only half across the room.

I stiffened at the words. *Our* chambers?

"I—" I didn't get a chance to finish, or even start. My jaw snapped closed, blocking off my words. I felt an alien smile crawl over my lips as my body moved on its own. Great, one kitten-puppet, made to order.

Tatius leaned down, pressing a kiss against my mouth. A surprisingly chaste kiss. Maybe it just wasn't fun to control his partner in a kiss—kind of like a teenager making out with a mirror.

Go with Samantha. I'll be there as soon as I finish here. And use that nose of yours as you pass the Collector's vampires. With that, he dismissed me and turned back to the Collector.

I glanced at Nathanial. He was staring at me, his mask perfect everywhere but his eyes. And when those lost eyes met mine, he squeezed them shut, looked away. I wished I could have closed my eyes too. Made the vampires all disappear. But I'd made my choice, given my word. Nathanial and I were alive. And I guess I was now going to learn where exactly Tatius and my 'chambers' were.

❧ • ❧

I paced across the main room in Tatius's underground suite. I had no idea if I was still somewhere under Death's Angel or if these underground hallways had taken me halfway across the city. Samantha had shown me to my new 'chambers' which, like most other rooms in this place, were mostly cloth draped stone.

Dawn pressed against me, making each step I took heavier, but I had to keep moving. If I stopped, I'd fall asleep. *I will fall down if I do not lie down soon,* I thought, but the thought sounded like Nathanial's gentle chiding in my head. Not him broadcasting directly in my brain like Tatius, obviously, but it sounded like something he'd say.

I forced my legs to lift, my knees to bend. My chin hit my chest in mid-motion, but I lifted it again. I really did have to find somewhere to sleep soon because sleep was unavoidable. Every heartbeat was slower, dawn imminent. I dragged my feet, stumbling.

I needed to close my eyes.

The suite had only three rooms: the sitting chamber where I currently paced, a bedroom, and a bathroom full of every color of hair dye on the market—the vampire should have owned stock in a hair-color company, or maybe he did. No second bedroom was present, and certainly no second bed. I'd agreed to be Tatius's companion, not his whore.

Shuffling to the furthest corner of the sitting room, I sank against the wall and slid down. I wasn't going to his bed, but I had to sleep.

Drawing my knees to my chest, I closed my eyes and surrendered to oblivion.

Chapter Nine

Something blocked my vision.

I blinked, my eyelashes brushing against something solid, yellow, and covering my face.

What the hell? I reached up, jerking at the thing over my eyes. It crinkled in my grasp. *Paper?*

I pulled the thin sheet of paper, my eyes misting at the sharp sting as the tape securing the paper to my forehead ripped free. I sat up, silky crimson sheets falling around me. *Where am I?*

I glanced at the note and its large, flowing script.

"We sleep in the bed. Not on the floor."

Oh crap. I was in Tatius's bed.

I scrambled from the mattress, nearly tripping as I tried to kick free of the sheets. My feet hit the plush carpet, and I took inventory. I was barefoot, but still dressed in my jeans and sweater, so while he'd moved me out of the sitting room and into his bed, he hadn't undressed me. Well, except for my coat. I glanced around but didn't see the familiar gray material. I also didn't see Tatius.

Thank the moon.

Clothes had been laid out in a chair by the bed, another yellow note taped to the stack. I crept over, recognizing the flowing script as the same as had been taped to my forehead.

"Get dressed. Sam will assist you."

Great.

I looked over the clothing. There was a short—a very, very short—black dress made out of a shiny black vinyl, a stringy corset that looked like a torture device, fishnets, and black boots made out of the same material as the dress. *Yeah, I think not.* I dropped the 'clothes' back on the chair. There had to be something else to wear in the place.

I headed for the door, but the knob turned under my fingers. I jumped back as the door opened. A tall woman with straight, black hair and a tight, red dress that showed more than it concealed stepped into the room.

"Good, you're awake," she said, smiling at me. "Now let's get you dressed, deary, so I can do your hair and get you to the council room."

"Samantha?" I asked, remembering the name on Tatius's note. The woman who'd brought me to Tatius's room last night had also been a Samantha, but this wasn't the same woman. Hell, if this was another Samantha, she was the third vampire by that name I'd met in Haven.

Her smile slipped an inch, and she tapped a finger against her cheek, her black polished nail pressing against a small red birthmark. "That's right," she said. "You're new. You wouldn't know. Well, let's get this over with."

She strolled further in the room. Turning, she gave me a wink. "Ready?"

Ready for what? I didn't have time to ask.

Her appearance rippled, and like one image unfolding to reveal another, changed. Her long dark hair flowed into blond, her makeup brightened, and her body rounded out to voluptuous curves. Even her dress changed from a revealing red to clinging silver sequins. The only thing that didn't change was the small red birthmark on her cheek.

"More familiar now?" she asked, twirling and making the edge of her skirt lift.

I blinked, my jaw going slack. I most definitely recognized her now. I'd met her during my first visit to Death's Angel. She was probably also the redhead who'd brought me here last night. *But how did she . . .* "An Illusion?" I asked.

"Like the Hermit?" She shook head and her appearance rippled again, changing back to the dark-haired woman who'd first entered the room. "I'm called the Chameleon. I'm a master soldier."

She said it like that should mean something to me. I just stared at her. "Soldier?"

"A soldier vampire as opposed to a psychic vamp," she said, and then, looking at my expression, laughed and shook her head. "Deary, you really are new. It's a blood-line title. Us solider vamps are stronger, faster, and we can turn humans easier than you psychic vamps, but we don't have the euphoric bite or the mental powers. Hasn't the Hermit taught you *anything?*" She didn't give me a chance to answer. "Well, don't worry. Tatius will take good care of you. Now let's get you in that dress."

An hour later, I was fully dressed—in a manner of speaking—my hair was piled artfully atop my head, and Sam had attacked my face with half a dozen cosmetic brushes. She stepped back, pursing her lips, but she nodded.

"That should do it, deary. Why don't you take a look?" She pointed to the full-length mirror on the other side of the room.

I stumbled over, my ankles wobbling in the spike-heeled boots. When I reached the mirror, I scowled at the stranger inside. The corset was indeed a torture device, which Sam had pulled tight enough that I was lucky I didn't actually need to breathe. It tugged my waist in, making my non-existent hips look rounder and pushing up my chest, exposing maximum amounts of my small cleavage. It could have been a good look. After all, the shiny black dress and thigh high boots transformed me into someone who'd belong on Tatius's arm. But the woman in the mirror looked uncomfortable, fake.

I turned my back on the mirror.

Samantha stood several steps behind, admiring her handy work. "I think you're ready. We should get you to Tatius."

Of course. She walked out of the room. I started to follow, but as I reached the doorway, a tingle of magic rushed over my skin, and I froze. *Oh no. Gil wouldn't seriously show up here, would she?*

An unmistakable *pop* sounded from further in the bedroom. Magic filled the air.

Dammit. Not now. I couldn't let Samantha see Gil.

"I, uh, forgot something," I said, grabbing the doorknob.

Samantha looked back over her shoulder. "Wha—"

"Be right back." I jerked the bedroom door shut.

A fist pounded on the door from the other side. "Kita, what's going on?"

The knob jiggled in my grasp. *Crap.*

I whirled around to face Gil and mouthed the words "Go. Get out."

"Just five minutes," the mage said. A bristly wave of magic washed over me, and I fell into blackness that wasn't true darkness.

🙰 • 🙠

I screamed. The darkness absorbed the sound before it could escape my throat. A moment? An eternity? I fell through the space between worlds. Or maybe I didn't fall. But I sure as hell wasn't standing. I *hated* the void. I was *so* going to hurt Gil.

I swallowed hard. I might hurt Gil, but if Tatius discovered I was gone, he would *kill* Nathanial. I'd bargained for Nathanial's life with my cooperation. Tatius would definitely consider my disappearance as reneging on that promise. I couldn't let that happen.

68

I had to get back to Death's Angel.

I'd no sooner had the thought than the empty darkness shattered. Light and color exploded around me in a chaotic jumble. I saw stars, literally. Hundreds of pinpricks of light filled my vision.

I squeezed my eyes shut and doubled over as a wave of nausea slammed into me.

"Dammit, Gil. How much time passed?" I gasped the question. The world was too solid, too *real* after the void. But I couldn't stay wherever she'd taken me. Pushing away from the grass beneath me, I wrenched my eyes open. "You have to get me back to Death's Angel. Now."

"This will just take a—"

"Now!"

In my still blurry vision, the pink-coated Gil-ish blob backed up. Then it stopped and little pink arms crossed in front of it.

"No."

"Gil, I don't have time for this. Nathanial and I have a situation on our hands. If I don't get back before Tatius realizes I'm gone—"

"No, Kita Nekai of Firth," she said, her voice firmer than I'd ever heard it. "No. Have you forgotten the Judge's mark on your back? He's out there, searching for proof you are too dangerous to be allowed to live. You told me yourself that you scratched several men when they attacked you months ago. We know Tyler was tagged and became a dangerous rogue. What if one of the others was tagged as well? What if the judge finds him? The judge will blame *you*. I'm doing this to keep you alive, so you should be more appreciative *and helpful.*" She turned and marched past a stone mausoleum.

My fingers moved reflexively to the small of my back, where, under all the layers of vinyl, the Judge's mark coiled, the tattoo-like snakes twisting and slithering in the shape of a Celtic knot. Gil was right. I needed to find out if there were any other tagged shifters. *But if Tatius thinks I've broken our agreement . . . .Nathanial . . . .* I looked around. Gil had disappeared around the corner of a crypt. *She said five minutes.* Hopefully Tatius wouldn't notice if I was gone for just five minutes. I hurried after Gil.

Or at least I tried to.

It had rained recently, and the ground was moist, soft—not a good thing for four-inch spike heels, especially when I could barely walk in the damn things to start with. The heels sank with every other step, stopping me, making me work to get free again. Then one of the heels snapped. *Dammit!*

I rolled the boots down and stepped out of them. Grabbing the boots and the broken heel, I marched in my fishnets across the damp grass. I finally caught up with Gil in front of a cast-iron gate blocking the doorway to a small mausoleum. A thick chain and padlock ensured the deceased beyond rested in peace.

Great. *Helpful* apparently translated into heavy lifting and lock-picking—nice to be useful.

"Hold onto these." I shoved the broken boots at Gil, and she made them vanish. Then I reached for my pockets only to remember I was wearing a tight black dress, not my familiar gray duster. "Uh, Gil," I said, flashing my empty hands. "No lock picks."

Her dark brows merged into one across her forehead. "Can't you snap the chain or something?"

I gave the chain, the links as thick as my wrist, a doubtful glance. Oh yeah, I could just *flick* that apart. No problem. *Riiight.*

"Well, if not the chain, maybe the padlock?" she asked.

I lifted the darkened lock and a whisper of magic ran up my fingers. *What the—?* I jerked back. "You tried to magic this open already?"

Gil's gaze dropped to her plastic rain boots as she nodded.

Great. I glanced over the lock. Even if I'd had my picks, Gil's botched spell had melted part of the locking mechanism. Unfortunately, the spell hadn't damaged the lock's integrity, and my attempt to jerk the lock open accomplished nothing.

I dropped the lock. "There's no way in. Take me back to Death's Angel."

"There has to be a way." Gil tugged at her sleeves. "I've already set off the magical tripwires. We have to get in tonight. Can you break down the gate?"

I blinked at her. "Uh, no."

She just frowned at me, and I sighed, glancing at the mausoleum entrance. It was old, the stone façade weathered and blackened, the iron gate red with rust. Old hinges too—real old, pin-type hinges. *Maybe I can . . .*

I grabbed the gate, and, bracing with my knees, lifted upward. Rust whispered like dry husks rubbing together, red flakes showering the stone steps, but the hinges lifted. I twisted, setting the heavy gate down crooked. It was still connected to the one side of the mausoleum by the chain, but the opening on the hinged side of the gate left plenty of room for Gil and me to squeeze inside.

"Excellent." Gil clapped her hands as she slid past me. She really shouldn't have looked so excited about breaking into a tomb. I probably should have asked her to explain, but I wasn't sure I wanted to know. *No, sir, Judge, sir. I have no idea why she brought me here.*

Inside, a stained glass window depicting an angel dominated the wall opposite the door. In the thin moonlight streaming in, she looked over the pairs of sarcophagi lining the side walls. Gil summoned a small purple light to her palm. It twinkled softly, floating to her shoulder, creating quivering shadows around the tomb.

She walked to the closest sarcophagus, the little globe of light following her. "This should be it. Open it up."

I glanced at the sarcophagus's hundred-year-old inscription. *Bartholomew Mattholm.*

Let's get this over with. The night before, I'd had to shove the stone lid aside. Tonight I was better fed, and when I slid my fingers under the lip and pulled, the stone lifted. I hefted it open a good foot from the base and peeked inside. I expected bones and rags, but inside the sarcophagus, a perfectly preserved corpse rested on decaying linen. A blaze of strawberry blond curls framed the strongly masculine face of a man who must have died in his early thirties. He looked like he could have been sleeping, but my hunger didn't react to him—his heart wasn't beating. *Dead, and unappetizing.*

"Well?" Gil asked, bouncing from foot to foot behind me.

"He certainly looks good for a man dead over a hundred years."

The corpse opened a pair of blue eyes. "Why thank you. I was considered quite handsome once."

I backpedaled, dropping the sarcophagus lid. *What mooncursed manner of—*

The sarcophagus shook. Then the large slab of granite slid aside enough for the corpse to crawl out.

"Well, that was totally bogus," he said, brushing grave dust from his denim jacket. "You wake me up and then drop a big piece of rock on me? Where were you raised?"

I stared at him. "But . . . you're dead."

The corpse looked at me, blue eyes twinkling in the moonlight. "I don't think you're in much of a position to discriminate based on mortality, babe."

Okay, he had me there. But . . . *he* had no heartbeat. No warmth. He was dead.

Dead, dead. Like, way *more* dead than me. At least vampires had a pulse.

I didn't realize I was backing away until I fell against one of the other sarcophagi.

"Sorry about that," Gil said, stepping up to him with a beaming smile and holding out her hand empathetically. "I'm Gil, a scholar-trainee from Sabin. That's Kita."

The corpse eyed her fingers but shoved his hands in the pockets of his tight black jeans. "A Sabinite, huh? Last time I was awake it was illegal to so much as *talk* to a necromancer." His eyes moved past her and landed on me. "So, an undead babe. Totally excellent. Been a while since I saw one." He drew a shimmering glyph in the air, and magic, like a cold wind, tried to settle into my skin.

Magic had never felt cold before.

I glared at him. "Whatever you're doing, stop," I straightened to my full height. I was still a foot shorter than him, but I didn't want him to think I was cowering. Cowardly creatures were prey. I wasn't.

"You're sensitive, for a vampire." He turned back to Gil, reassessing her with his gaze. "You have a vampire-familiar?"

"Me? No, I didn't mark her."

Wait a minute. Did he say *familiar*? Like a witch's *familiar*? I bore the Judge's mark, but this was the first I'd heard anything about being a familiar.

The corpse cocked his head. "Did the High Assembly dissolve or something?"

Gil shook her head. "Nope, they're still the ruling power in Sabin, and before you ask, yes necromancy is still illegal."

"Then what the hell is going on here?" He made a sweeping motion that included both Gil and me. "I've got a scholar-trainee seeking me out in the company of someone else's vampire-familiar?"

"Well," Gil shuffled her feet. "We need a favor."

Chapter Ten

"Wait!" Gil yelled, running after the dead man as his long strides took him across the cemetery grass. "You haven't even let me explain what we want! Where are you going?"

I trudged after them. "He's a walking corpse, where could he go?"

He stopped, the short red curls fluttering before settling around his face. "First of all, Little Miss Undead, I'm the *living* dead, not a walking corpse." He swung a hand at the grave markers around us. "If I raise a couple of these rotting blokes around us *then* you get the walking dead. But me? I'm animated by my own power. Got it?"

He crossed his arms over his chest, glaring at me. "Secondly, I've been asleep for twenty years. I want a look around. See what's changed. And before you ask, no. The mortals won't notice a thing. They only ever see what they *think* is in front of them. You should know." Then he turned to face Gil. "And thirdly, it doesn't matter what you want, babe. You can't afford my services."

Gil's face flushed, but she held out her hand. A clear orb, no bigger than a cat's toy, floated an inch above her palm, a small wisp of blue smoke caught in the center. "I have this."

"Is that what I think it is?" He leaned closer. "How did a scholar-trainee get her hands on a Last Breath?"

"I captured it myself." Gil managed to sound both proud and defensive simultaneously.

"Is it from someone who died of natural causes?"

"No." She shuffled her feet. "Will it be enough?"

"Maybe." He walked over to a free-standing sarcophagus and leaned against it. "Let's talk business. What is it you want?"

Gil tugged on her sleeves. "Well, we need information from someone who sort-of died."

"Uh-huh, keep talking. You want me to raise you a zombie with its memories intact? That's pricey. An unnatural last breath will be cutting it close on the trade scale." He pushed away from the sarcophagus. "But I've never been able to resist a couple of babes in need. You can call me Avin. This sort-of dead guy? Where is his body buried?"

"He isn't exactly *buried*." Gil pulled a skull out of the void. How much stuff did she store in that place? And how come I never saw any of it when she tossed *me* into the void?

Avin took the skull from her, frowning. "You didn't tell me all you had was the skull. That changes everything."

"According to my research, the skull should be enough. Do you know another necromancer who would be able to animate a skull?"

"Hold on now, I didn't say I couldn't do it. I said it changed everything. Making a zombie that can remember who it was when it lived is tricky and requires a fresh body. It takes highly controlled magic to reconnect the synapses in the brain so the stupid creature will play back its life like a record." He examined the skull. Then he balanced it on one of the headstones so the empty eye sockets watched us. "But you don't have a body. All you have is a bit of bone. That means I have to create a ritual to find this bloke's spirit, *if* he left enough behind to find, and then I thrust it into this skull; which, let me tell you, spirits don't tend to like. It will be *big* magic. Complicated."

I groaned. "In other words, expensive." I turned to Gil. "He's not going to do it. Let's go. We'll find someone else." Okay, that last bit was a bluff. Gil had obviously been researching a while to find this necromancer, but he couldn't know that.

Avin stepped between Gil and me, his hands up, palms out. "Don't run off just yet. I didn't say I wouldn't do it. We just need to negotiate a price. I'm thinking you give me, one, the Last Breath, and two, your true name." He pointed at Gil, and she went pale. Then he turned to me. "And I want a favor from you, to be determined at a later date."

A favor? "Like an errand or something?"

He titled his head as if considering the question, and then smiled, nodding. "Yeah, like an errand. Or something."

Not the most reassuring response. "Nothing life-threatening," I said, and his smile spread.

"Deal." He glanced at Gil. "How about it? Your name?"

She was still pale, but she handed over the bauble containing the Last Breath. "Gildamina."

Avin acknowledged her name with a nod as he took the globe. Holding it up in the moonlight, he studied it. "This is really well-captured. You said you did it yourself?"

Gil nodded.

He made the Last Breath disappear before focusing his attention back on her. "You're not wearing a family ring. It used to be rare for a commoner from Undin to make it to a Sabin academy. I doubt things have changed much. Hmmm?"

She didn't meet his eye, but studied her funky purple boots like she'd never seen them before. He went on, ignoring her obvious discomfort. "In fact, an Undinite would have to test off the scale in magical potential for the old Sabin families to let her in an academy— way more potential than someone destined to become a scholar. No one *chooses* to be a scholar. It is the career that rich Sabin brats get stuck in if they show no promise in any other magical disciplines."

Gil's face flushed from pink to crimson. "I gave you the payment you asked for. You made the bargain, now animate the skull so we can get out of here by dawn."

Dawn? "Gil, you said five minutes." Which had already passed, but I'd thought we were closer to getting answers. But *dawn?* Hell no. "Take me back to Death's Angel. Now."

Her head shot up. "What? But we haven't—"

"I don't care. We can come back later," I said over her protest. "I need to be at Death's Angel before Tatius—"

"Hey!" Avin shouted, and he must have magically enhanced his voice, because it boomed over us, making me flinch. Both Gil and I turned. He smiled. "Enough shouting, babes. This is the resting place of the dead. Show a little respect. Now"—he turned and pressed the tips of his fingers against the skull—"Neither one of you can leave. I need you for the ritual. But as I was saying, an Undinite doesn't get to the academy and become a scholar unless something goes wrong." He glanced at Gil. "I bet you excelled at all your basic courses but then couldn't test into a discipline. There is *one* they didn't test you for, though. *Wouldn't* test you for."

Gil shook her head. "I'm not having this conversation."

"You hang with vampires, you sought out a necromancer, and you study topics that could get you a death sentence—because, I know, any book containing a spell to capture a Last Breath in it is on more than just the banned reading list. You're a natural-born necromancer."

"I said I wasn't having this conversation." Gil tugged at her coat sleeves, but the movements were more violent than her normal twitchy actions. "Can't you just do the job we paid you for?"

"I'm getting to it." He set the skull on the ground.

Summoning a long blade from thin air, Avin used the point to draw a circle around the skull. Outside the circle he drew several twisting symbols. I was surprised Gil wasn't taking notes. After tugging on her sleeves a couple more times, she finally caved, pulled out a scroll, and started scribbling.

"See, you're fascinated. You can't help it," Avin said, vanishing the blade again.

"She does that all the time." I said, leaning against a statue. "Gil's a natural-born scholar."

She gave me a death glare, and I frowned. *What'd I say?*

"I was just trying to help," I muttered under my breath. Louder I asked, "How long is this ritual?"

Both mages ignored me. Avin summoned four candles and placed them around the circle he'd drawn. A flick of his wrist and small flames consumed the candle wicks. I couldn't see what he placed between the skull's teeth, but with another flick of his wrist, spicy smelling smoke rolled out of the skull's empty eye sockets and mouth.

"Come here," he said without looking up from his work. "Tonight you babes will be playing the connection between the living and the dead."

Uh . . . I didn't like the sound of that. Still, cooperation would get me back to Death's Angel faster.

I trudged over as Avin summoned his knife from the void, again. He pressed the tip of the blade into Gil's index finger, and she flinched but let him coax blood from the wound onto the knife. He then anointed the skull with the blood before moving to me. He lifted the blade to my finger the same way he had for Gil, but as the metal touched my skin, a stinging chill that had nothing to do with magic shot through my flesh.

I jerked back. "That's a *silver* knife."

"It's a ceremonial tool."

He reached for my hand again and I shook my head. I might not be able to shift anymore, but my silver allergy persisted. "Use a different knife."

"I don't have one. Now give me your hand, it will only hurt for a moment."

I glanced over my shoulder, hoping Gil would help, but she was busy jotting something in her scroll—probably about me, the lab rat. Holding out my hand again, I squeezed my eyes shut as the knife bit into my flesh. At the touch of silver, first my finger, then my entire hand went numb. The drop of blood from my finger fell on the skull's forehead, and I felt the pulse of magic in Avin's circle. Hugging my numb hand to my chest, I retreated to the company of a stone angel.

Avin sat down cross-legged in front of the skull and bowed his head. His voice lifted in a low, sing-song chant, the words foreign but commanding. The candlelight flickered. Once. Twice. Then the smoke stopped billowing out of the skull and, twisting in midair, it turned and flowed *downward* back into the sockets.

Avin opened his eyes.

A scream issued from the skull.

"Kill you!" the skull shrieked, enunciating surprisingly well for something with no lips. "I'll kill you. You can't kill *me* this time."

I gasped. I recognized the voice. "Bryant?"

In life, Bryant had been an average-Joe human until he was tagged by Tyler. A hyena spirit took up residence inside his body, breaking his mind and sense of self, and, under the tutelage of Tyler, he'd turned into a vicious predator. Human turned shapeshifter in the hands of a psycho? Not a good combo.

I frowned at Gil. "It's Bryant's skull?"

"Obviously. The other rogue ended up a pancake on the sidewalk. I couldn't salvage anything from *him*."

The skull turned on its base so the smoke-filled sockets glared at me.

"Monster," Bryant's skull yelled. "Monster! Kill her!" Then it gave out a blood-curdling howl. Apparently he and the hyena were still bound together—and just as insane—in death. It made me wonder anew what had happened to my cat-self after I became a vampire.

"Shuddup. You're a talking skull." Avin rapped the skull on its cranium. "This thing wasn't human. What did you have me bring back?"

"Rogue shape-shifter," I said, staring at the angry skull.

Bryant's skull went on shrieking. Nights ago, when Gil had mentioned she was working on a way for us to question the dead rogue about his accomplices, I'd thought she'd meant Tyler, not Bryant. Two rogues had gone on a killing spree, but only one of them, Tyler, had been tagged directly by me. I'd stopped them both, but the monster I'd accidentally created when I defended myself with my claws had been Tyler, the one to tag Bryant. Tyler would have been far more useful.

Still, the two rogues had traveled and killed together for several months. Bryant could know something important.

If the skull would just stop bellowing long enough for us to question it.

"Can't you make it stop screaming?" I asked, pressing my hands over my ears, which did little to dampen my hyper-sensitive hearing.

Avin hit the skull again, but it kept howling. "You neglected to mention you killed this dude-thing."

"I didn't think that was an important detail," Gil said, shuffling her feet. The skull turned to yell at her again. She ignored it. "Can we question him now?"

Avin shrugged. "Knock yourself out. Don't know how helpful he'll be. Spirits don't tend to like the people who sent them to the incorporeal world."

"But *you* can make him answer. I've read that a necromancer should be able to control a rampaging spirit."

" 'Course I can. For a price."

"We don't have anything more to offer—"

Avin interrupted her, "I want to test your aptitude for necromancy, and if what I suspect is true, I want to train you to use your potential. That's it. That's my price."

Gil's lips parted as her jaw fell crooked. She glanced my way, her eyes a little too wide. I shrugged. It wouldn't be the first thing she'd done that went against Sabin's laws.

"Okay," she nodded, and I couldn't tell if I heard fear or excitement in her voice. *Probably both.*

Avin closed his eyes again. Bryant suddenly stopped yelling obscenities at us and contented himself to hiss quietly between his teeth.

Without opening his eyes, Avin said, "Try your questions now."

Gil leaned toward the skull. "How many humans were tagged and became shifters?" she asked. The skull hissed at her. She repeated her question.

"Just me," the skull finally said. "Me and Tyler, monsters, partying all the way to hell."

"He's lying." Gil's expression scrunched up, her lips twisting. "I thought he wasn't supposed to be able to lie."

Avin raised an eyebrow, eyes still closed. "He can't lie."

"He *has* to be lying."

I waved a hand. "Uh . . . " I happened to have it on good authority that Bryant's skull *wasn't* lying—I'd seen inside his mind before he died.

But, while I was willing to cooperate with Gil's whole, Kita-is-my-lab-rat thing, telling Gil I had bits and pieces of *two* homicidal rogues traipsing through my head wasn't something I was ready to share. Not yet, at least. Maybe not ever.

"Gil, he's not lying," I said, pushing away from the angel statue and creeping closer to the skull. The chill of Avin's magic crawled over my skin as I approached his circle. "Bryant wasn't one of the attackers from the street. He was tagged by Tyler."

Gil's brows knit together as she digested this. "By the *other* rogue? I got the wrong skull?"

"Bryant might still know something. What about any other 'monsters?'" I asked him. "Did you see any others? Did Tyler ever mention any?"

"You!" Bryant's skull yelled. "*You're* a monster. Monster."

Not helpful.

Gil huffed. "Did Tyler ever mention family? Friends?" she asked. "His last name?"

The skull managed to look contemplative. "No."

"Did Tyler tell you how he became a shifter?"

I knew intimately how Tyler had been tagged, but maybe, if he'd told the story to Bryant, he'd mentioned the names of his companions that night.

The skull's bony jaw clicked. "Yeah, he said the devil called his name and gave him the power."

The devil? Right. This was going nowhere. I bit my lip and tried to examine the memories I'd siphoned from Tyler.

He'd been thinking about killing when we'd fought and I bit him and dived into his mind. In particular, he'd been thinking about killing *me*, but the thought had opened paths to memories of his other kills. In my mind's eye, flesh parted, screams echoed, and the taste of raw meat, of human meat, filled my mouth. *So many women.* Even the ones who hadn't survived were familiar to my mind's eye now.

But I didn't need to see his victims. I needed his companions. I found a memory of myself through his eyes, of the night I'd inadvertently tagged him. His companions' faces floated into view, but no names. I could only focus on the memories I'd taken from his mind before his death.

I had enough of his sadistic memories to supply a lifetime of nightmares, but not enough to find the other men who'd jumped me. I'd defended myself, but in the process, I'd accidentally tagged Tyler. And possibly his friends. Thinking of the attack brought the memories full circle, filling me with what he'd planned to do to me, what he'd wanted. Screams ripped through my mind again, and I shivered, shoving the memories back in the dark hole I'd made for them.

Opening my eyes, I frowned at Avin. "You might as well make Bryant's skull stop talking. There's no point. It doesn't know the answers we need."

"Wait," Gil said. She stepped in front of me, blocking my view of the skull. "We can ask him other questions. This is the perfect time to study why humans who turn shifter go insane. Not to mention how the two spirits are tied together and to the memory of the body—"

"Study later. If I don't get to Death's Angel before Tatius discovers I'm gone, it's Nathanial who will pay." I glanced at the sky. How long had I been gone? Had Samantha reported my defection to Tatius? "Get me back to the club."

"But—" Gil started.

"You're going to be my apprentice, remember, babe?" Avin smiled at Gil. "Trust me, you'll have plenty of opportunities to study the dead."

She frowned but nodded. "All right. I'll come back after I take Kita home."

Avin made a slight nod goodbye.

And for the first time, I waited anxiously to be thrown into the void.

Chapter Eleven

Snow crunched under me, the dampness clinging to my fishnets. "Gil, this is not where you picked me up."

"It's close." She shuffled in the snow. "I've read about these clubs. No one should notice you coming and going."

My teeth clenched in an effort to ward off a scream of frustration. I needed to be back in Tatius's room, pretending like I'd never left. Walking in through the front door of Death's Angel and winding my way through the lower levels was bound to draw attention. My jaw cracked as I forced my teeth apart. Gil took one look at my face and backed up before I uttered a word.

"Uh, you probably need these." My ruined boots appeared in her hands, and she dropped them between us. "I should, uh, go. Lots to learn."

She vanished.

Great. Just great.

Leaning down, I snatched the broken boots from the snow then padded around the side of the building. I'd been led underground twice since becoming a vampire. I *should* be able to make my way to the lower levels. Now finding Tatius's suite, that was another matter. *I'll deal with it when I get to it.*

If I even made it that far.

Getting into the club wasn't a problem, nor was taking the staff-only halls through to the VIP area, but that was where my luck ended. A huge metal door blocked my path to the stairs leading underground. I'd forgotten about it. A keypad was inlaid into the wall beside the door, but I didn't have the code. A fingerprint reader rested above the keypad, and I pressed my left thumb to the panel. The small machine made a noise as it scanned, then the light flashed red.

The door didn't unlock.

Crap.

Behind me, in the VIP room, an unseen door crashed open. I jumped. *Did I trip an alarm?*

I glanced around for somewhere to hide, but the short hallway held nothing but the door I couldn't get past and the one I'd just entered from. Another door banged open, this one closer. With nowhere to hide, I leaned on the metal door to the underground and crossed my arms over my chest, forcing a relaxed pose.

The door across from me flew open, and three large men poured into the small hallway, moving fast—inhumanly fast. My arms over my chest tightened, my muscles tensing. Otherwise I didn't move—where could I really go with the locked door at my back?

The men stopped in the middle of the hall, still several yards away. Two wore more straps and chains than anything resembling clothing, but the third wore black jeans and a muscle shirt. He was the one who held up his hand, stopping the other two. His head cocked to the side, his chocolate-colored eyes pinching quizzically as they slid over me.

"You're the Hermit's companion, aren't you?"

That was a complicated subject, and at least one of Tatius's vampires could see through lies, so I let him believe what he liked. Cocking my head to the side, I jerked my thumb at the door.

"I got locked out."

I smiled as I said it, but he only frowned at me, his eyes sliding over my—probably very expensive—water-stained dress, the broken boots dangling from my grip, and my torn and grass-stained fishnets. Then he nodded at the other men. They turned without a word, strolling out of the hall and back the way they'd come. He remained.

I shifted my weight between my feet, and his eyes snapped back to me. He stared at me long enough that the urge to squirm traveled all the way up my spine. Then he marched to the door and pressed his thumb to the scanner. A green light flashed as a loud *click* resounded in the short hall.

"I'm Liam," he said, hauling open the door.

"Kita." I stepped around him, hurrying into the stairwell beyond the door.

I expected him to escort me down—probably all the way down to the council room, but he stayed at the doorway. "Don't wander the city. With all the shit going on with the Collector's visit, pandemonium is one drop from spilling over all the lesser vampires." Then he slammed the door, the large lock snapping back in place.

I blinked at the door for a long heartbeat. A friendly warning? A dire one? Turning, I hurried down the stairs. The waiting room was empty, thank the stars, but now I had to find the door. With all the walls draped behind heavy layers of fabric, that was easier said than done, but after a moment of flailing with the drapes, I located the hidden door and slipped into the hall beyond.

Now all I have to worry about is finding Tatius's suite.

"Where the hell have you been?" an annoyed female voice whispered as I turned a corner in the hall.

Okay, apparently I didn't have to worry about navigating the underground labyrinth after all.

Samantha closed the space between us. Her hand shot out, her polished nails digging into my bicep as her fingers locked around my arm. "Are you trying to tangle us both in Tatius's wrath?"

"There was a misunderstanding and . . . well . . . I'm here now." Oh yeah, that was pathetic.

Her eyes slid down me, taking in the damage my wardrobe had already suffered tonight. "Saints alive," she hissed in an exasperated whisper. "The dress will have to do. Lose the stockings and the boots. We don't have time to find replacements."

She released my arm and stepped back. Her nails clicked together like claws as she waited for me to shuck the ruined fishnets. I hadn't thought much of the stockings while I wore them, but once they were off, the short dress felt all that much more revealing.

"What do I . . . ?" I looked around for a place to put the fishnets and boots.

Samantha snatched them out of my hands. "Come on. Do you think you can keep him waiting all night?"

I didn't have to ask who *he* was.

I followed Samantha as her heels tapped an angry staccato down the hall. She took me on the same path Tatius had led me and Nathanial the night before. We ended back in front of the council room where we'd met with the Collector. Samantha jerked open the door, and her posture changed, her movements became smoother so that she swayed as she sashayed into the room.

It was a wasted effort—the council wasn't inside. A couple of vampires were moving chaises into a circle in the center of the room, but the council table was empty. No council meant no Nathanial. I still didn't know if he was okay.

Samantha smoothed her gown with a jerky movement that betrayed her annoyance and held up a hand, motioning me to stay. She marched to the closest vampire, her whispered words too soft for me to catch in the cavernous room. The other vamp set down the chaise he'd balanced over his shoulder and pointed toward the ceiling.

Samantha nodded. Then she made her way back to me, shutting the door behind us as she led me into the hall.

"You could have told me Tatius wasn't down here," she said.

I blinked at her. "How would I know?"

She frowned, her full lips dragging down her cheeks. "Well, if your bond with Tatius isn't tight enough for you to feel his location yet, you could have told me Nathanial wasn't here, either. Obviously, they'll be together."

I tried not to gape as Samantha's slanted eyes drilled into me. *Feel Nathanial's location?* I had never had any woo-woo sense of where he was. Not once.

But he always knew where I was.

I swallowed. Gil had told me that I was the first shifter to become a vampire and that the effects of the change were unknown. Apparently this whole *sensing* thing was something I'd missed.

Not wanting Samantha to realize I was deficient in vamp powers, I smiled weakly and said, "Right. Sorry." Then I lifted a finger to the ceiling like I'd seen the other vamp do. "He's upstairs?"

Samantha's frown twisted harder, but she nodded. Turning on her heel, she stormed down the hall.

❧ • ❧

We emerged from the underground halls into a large, walk-in freezer, through which Samantha led me into a bustling restaurant kitchen.

"Where are we?" I whispered as a waiter in a dark waistcoat scurried by.

"*Crimson.* Another of Tatius's investments." Samantha glanced around the kitchen. "You there, you're a manager, right?"

A woman in a sleek black dress looked up from her conversation with a cook and placed one hand on her hip. "Yes. Is there something Tatius needs?"

"Your shoes," Samantha said, holding out her hand.

The manager blinked, but when Samantha just stood there, waiting, the woman leaned down and pulled off her simple black pumps. She handed them over, and Samantha shoved the shoes at me.

"Put these on and hurry up."

I shoved my feet in the pumps—two sizes too big—and then hobbled after Samantha as she pushed open a swinging door. The chaos of the kitchen faded as we entered a dimly lit dining room. A harpist sat in one corner, her fingers pulling ethereal sounds from a harp as tall as me. The soft music drifted around the room, mingling with the hushed conversations of the diners. Candles flickered on top of tables covered with pressed white table cloths and gleaming with real silver.

This did *not* look like Tatius's kind of place.

Speaking of Tatius, I didn't see him, Nathanial, or the rest of the council anywhere. Samantha, who had been scanning the room, turned toward me and lifted one of her well-shaped eyebrows. "Well?"

Damn, guess that meant I was supposed to be able to *feel* them or some other vampire nonsense. "Uh . . . " I searched the room. Women in evening gowns and cocktail dresses peered across tables, laughed with wine glasses held aloft, or concentrated on pushing food around their plates. Men in tuxes, and a few in suits, laughed good-naturedly, cut into steaks, or puffed on spicy smelling cigars. My heartbeat kicked up a notch, my breath rushing out in a gasp. I hadn't realized how hungry I was until I was surrounded by humans. I pressed my lips closed, worried my fangs might slip, but my teeth were flat, no burn in my jaw. Hungry—*not starved.*

Holding my breath, I forced my gaze around the room again. Just people. The height of society, no doubt, but humans. No vampires. No council.

I let out the breath, ready to confess I was missing this extra vamp sense, when Nathanial stood from a table in the middle of the room. My lips parted. *He's okay.*

Relief bubbled up in my chest, and I felt the smile unfold across my face. He didn't return my smile, but as he nodded, the movement drawn out, his gray eyes remained locked on mine. For a moment, I forgot anyone else was in the room. But if he was here, the rest of the council would be, too. I blinked, dropping my gaze.

The council sat around a large, unset table in the center of the room. *How did I miss that?* Frowning, I walked toward them, trying to remember the patrons I'd seen before Nathanial had stood. Hadn't a group of businessmen been gathered around that table?

An illusion? If so, it was an elaborate one. Nathanial's eyes were pinched ever so slightly around the edges, his lips thinner than normal—evidentially, maintaining the illusion on the entire table was taxing him. *Why didn't they find a private place for this conversation?*

That would have made more sense . . . unless Tatius was forcing Nathanial to maintain the illusion as some sort of punishment. Nathanial *had* used his ability against Tatius, in an attempt to conceal me.

There were no empty chairs at the table, but as I approached, Nathanial gestured for me to take his. He had been sitting between Mama Neda, the old crone who'd taken care of me just after I'd been turned, and a blonde, male vampire. Nathanial scooted the chair closer to the old woman before holding it for me. I sat, but when Nathanial turned to steal another chair, the blonde hooked his foot in the bottom rung of my chair and dragged me closer to him.

I frowned, recognizing the sharp planes of Tatius's face. *Blonde? Seriously?* His hair hung in long, pale strands, nearly glowing against the dark material of his tux. Either he'd done one hell of a dye job tonight, or he hadn't dyed it at all—for once. He looked different without the punk hair style and assortment of piercings. He looked less mocking, more intense. And he was already intense enough. *How come he's wearing a tux and I'm stuck in a vinyl dress and a corset?*

Nathanial said nothing when he returned with the chair. He just placed it in the spot beside Mama Neda and fixed his attention on the table.

"Continue," Tatius said, making a sweeping gesture with his hand.

Nuri, dressed in a midnight blue dress that fit her undeveloped, pre-teen form like a glove, nodded and cleared her throat. "As I was saying, I have now examined every local vampire except Magritte and Gareth. I've sent enforcers to look for both, but I have no reason to believe their absence is unusual or connected to the human's death."

Nuri looked up, as if to measure Tatius's response to her words. He nodded, motioning her to continue. He even looked interested in her report. *Does he actually listen to his council?* Nathanial had once called it a puppet council, and I'd been under the impression Tatius was a tyrant. Well, maybe not a complete tyrant. His actions in public *were* different from those in private—if that weren't true, Nathanial would be dead. But I hadn't anticipated that he'd be the kind of leader who'd listen to his advisors.

Nuri continued, her hands flat on the table in front of her. "I have now also interviewed all of the Collector's vampires. None interacted with the woman in the hours before her death. A few recall seeing her, or possibly one of her sisters, but otherwise, no one noticed her before her body was found."

Tatius nodded again. Then his gaze swiveled as the front door of the restaurant opened. The large, plain-clothed vampire who'd caught me sneaking into Death's Angel bustled into the room, sidestepping the hostess who stood to greet him. Liam's eyes scanned the diners, probably seeing only the same upper class crowd I'd seen when I first entered. Then he froze, his eyes narrowing. He gave one sharp nod, as if answering some unheard question—actually, that was probably exactly what he was doing.

I glanced at Tatius. *Can he read thoughts as well as project them?* I had no idea. He gave no indication either, but turned to Nathanial, who stood. Liam blinked as his eyes landed on our table, clearly seeing through the illusion. He nearly ran over a server in his haste to reach us.

Tatius cocked his head to the side. "Yes?"

The large vampire doubled over, bowing deep. Then Liam held out a squat black cylinder. "We just found this."

Tatius's gaze cut across the table to Nuri, who slid out of her seat and retrieved the small canister. It looked like an old 35 mm film container. The contents rattled as Nuri lifted the cylinder from Liam's hand, the soft *plink* sound marking whatever was inside as much smaller than a film cartridge. Nuri popped the plastic lid free, and her expression froze. She went still, too still to be mistaken for anything fully alive.

"What is it?" The balding council member, dressed in tweed once again tonight, asked.

Without a word, Nuri tipped the canister and two off-white objects rolled across the tablecloth. The small objects, neither longer than the last digit of my pinky, were pointed on one end, and a flaky, rust-colored substance covered the other. I caught a whiff of old blood and reeled back. Sliding closer to Nathanial, I wrapped my arms over my chest.

"Teeth." My whisper barely carried in the low lit dining room.

"Fangs." Nathanial's voice was flat, no emotion, no inflection, but that one word seemed to break the spell holding the council suspended.

Everyone began speaking at once.

"Where did you find this?"

"Do we know who they belong to?"

"Mama Neda has never seen nothing like this before."

"Which vampires are unaccounted for?"

"Silence." Tatius didn't yell—he didn't have to.

The council members fell silent, and even the din from the other patrons fell away. He reached forward, lifting one of the fangs. He rolled it through his fingers, staring at it as if the fang could tell him to whom it had belonged.

"Is there anything else in the tube?" he asked after several seconds passed.

Nuri looked down, then using two small fingers, fished something flat out of the tube. She unfolded what looked like a thick piece of paper about the size of my palm. As she passed it to Tatius, I leaned in, peering around his shoulder at the creased photograph.

A body dominated the image, as if the photographer had focused on the bare butt and muscular back of his subject. Male, definitely. And headless.

I swallowed against the flutter of panic threatening to crawl up my throat. The image was black and white—or at least mostly monochromatic. Someone had taken the time to hand-tint the blood pooling around the body.

Another headless corpse? This one was different, though. Luna had been drained, her body posed and left to find. This victim had blood to spare, but his body was missing and only a photograph announced his death.

Tatius placed the photo on the table in front of him. He smoothed a hand over it like he could press out the creases. "How did you acquire this, Liam?"

The question was quiet. Dangerously so. The other vampire shuffled, his shoulders slumping forward. He was a big guy, but his fear was palpable in the air. "It was left in one of our tip jars at Death's Angel."

"When?"

Liam winced, shaking his head. "Sometime in the last hour. I brought it here as soon as I saw it."

"Did anyone see who placed it there?" Tatius asked, and Liam shook his head again. "Answer aloud."

The other vampire cringed so hard he actually stepped backward. "I didn't take a lot of time to question everyone, but none of the bartenders saw who left it."

Tatius's gaze slid off Liam to land on Nuri. Her eyes had gone black again. At her nod, Tatius turned back to Liam.

"Did anything else unusual happen tonight? Any unexpected guests? Patrons who didn't fit in?"

Liam opened his mouth. Closed it. His gaze slid to me. Then he shook his head. "The Hermit's companion tripped security trying to go downstairs, but otherwise the crowd in the club is typical and traffic has been fairly low tonight."

I went still before Liam finished speaking. Around the table, eyes locked onto me, but the intense green gaze I expected to turn on me, to freeze me in place, didn't come. In fact, Tatius didn't even blink at the mention of my failed attempt to sneak into Death's Angel.

He tapped his finger against the edge of the photograph, but his gaze was further off, his thoughts elsewhere. No one spoke. No one at the table even breathed. Liam shuffled his feet and Tatius's head snapped up.

"Was there anything else?" The question was a demand and dismissal at the same time.

Liam took it as such. "No, my lord." He bowed low then turned and high-tailed it out of Crimson.

I stared at the contents of the canister he'd delivered. Somewhere in Haven, a vampire was dead. Someone wanted the council to know about it. The question was, *Who?*

Chapter Twelve

The table remained quiet several heartbeats after Liam left. Then Tatius pushed the photograph forward.

"Does anyone recognize him?"

The balding council member lifted the photo from the table and stared at it several seconds before shaking his head and passing it to Nuri. She bit her bottom lip, studying the black and white image.

"It could be Gareth, I suppose," she said, her thin eyebrows drawing together in sideways question marks.

Mama Neda's gnarled fingers shot out, snatching the photo. She studied it, scratching her lopsided bun and pressing her wrinkled lips together. "Mama Neda won't complain about the view, but she can't recognize this ass from another. Where is the little stud's head, she'd like to know?"

And wasn't that the question *everyone* wanted answered?

Mama Neda passed the photo to Nathanial next. He glanced over the image, shaking his head before passing it back to Tatius. After one more glance at the gray body floating in a sea of crimson, Tatius re-folded the image with deliberately slow movements, as if quick movements would tear the image to shreds. Then he tucked the photo back into the canister and dropped the disembodied fangs in with it, before sealing the lid.

Nuri cleared her throat in a single, feminine cough. "Sire, may I suggest once again that you cancel tonight's meeting until this"—her long fingers swept through the air, indicating the canister still clutched in Tatius's hand, "—is resolved."

"Not an option. I cannot show weakness."

Her dark eyes narrowed. "Then let me put extra enforcers in the room."

Tatius hesitated. "Nothing obvious."

The ancient pre-teen vampire smiled as she ducked her head in acquiescence. I had the distinct feeling her idea of *obvious* and Tatius's would differ. She'd put as many enforcers in the room as she could rationalize.

Tatius stared at the dark canister a moment more. Then he pushed away from the table. His chair scraped the floor as he stood. "Cormac, spread the word, everyone is to roost in the sanctuary night and day. No exceptions. I don't want a single vampire of mine on the streets until after the Collector and her entourage have left town. Nuri, increase security at all the entrances to the sanctuary. Then head to Death's Angel and find out if anyone saw anything. Anything at all."

Cormac, the balding vampire, and Nuri both nodded, and I clenched my hands at my sides, waiting for someone to disagree. No one did. Tatius shoved his chair under the table and turned away.

I looked around. Everyone was getting up. Even Nathanial stood and pushed his chair under the table.

"But . . ."

Nearly half a dozen gazes slammed into me. Nuri looked annoyed, Cormac irritated, Mama Neda—well, she just looked crazy, like always. Nathanial gave me a worried look, almost a warning one. *As if I don't realize silence is smarter.* Still . . .

I ignored all of them as I turned to Tatius. I didn't meet his gaze, but stared at his shoulder as I grasped for the most diplomatic way of saying what was on my mind. "If you gather your vampires and increase your display of militant force, won't the Collector see your actions as hostile?"

I'd seen a similar situation occur in Firth once. A misunderstanding had turned into a bloody feud between two clans because both assumed the other was about to invade their lands. My father had been one of the *Torins* the elders assigned to clean up the aftermath and negotiate communication. He'd described it as a messy and unnecessary waste of life.

Tatius didn't move, but the air around me might have well turned solid, unbreathable. I looked down, biting my tongue—too late, of course.

"She might be right," Nuri said, startling me enough that I jumped. "As the Collector already considers herself the injured party, she would be over sensitive to an increase of hostile activity." She sounded irritated to agree with me, but I gave her points for seeing past the fact I was a 'baby vampire' and actually considering my idea.

Tatius, on the other hand, scowled. "Then gather everyone quietly. I won't have my people at risk on the streets until I believe the danger has passed. And if I need an army around me, I want my vampires here, at the heart of the city, ready to defend my territory.

Now go." He turned away from them.

Nuri lowered her gaze. "Yes, sire."

"Should Mama Neda alert the Collector of when Tatius wants to see her?" Mama Neda asked, oblivious to the mounting tension.

Tatius paused without turning back to the table. "No. You and Nathanial go ensure the room and entertainment is prepared. I have something to do before I join you." He took several steps from the table, and I'd just begun to relax in my chair when his voice drifted back toward me. "Aren't you supposed to be following?"

I cringed, sinking lower in the chair. *Don't be talking to me.*

Do I have to move you? Tatius's voice asked in my head.

I jumped to my feet, knocking over my chair in my haste. It crashed to the floor. The dining room went silent.

Eyes turned to our table, and Nathanial's brow creased, obviously fighting the strain of so much attention focusing on his illusion. I reached for the fallen chair, but Tatius was already there, righting it. Once the chair was on all four legs, Tatius's hand closed around my bicep, his grip vice-like, his fingers pinching my bare skin. "We have unfinished business."

With that said, he set a quick pace away from the table with me in tow.

❧ • ☙

The door to Tatius's suite closed behind us, and I rubbed my palms on my dress. I had the feeling this had something to do with feeding and that whole I-need-master's-blood-nightly thing. I'd seriously been hoping he'd forget.

The candles, which had been dark when I woke, now sputtered to life. Tatius crossed the room without comment on the sudden appearance of the flames. He opened the door to his bedroom, and I swallowed hard. *He doesn't think I'll* . . .

I shook my head, and his eyes narrowed. I stepped back, the movement completely involuntary. I did *not* want to go to his bedroom. Sharing blood was intimate enough. My gaze shot around the sitting room, looking for some way out of this. I'd never been alone with Tatius before, at least not while I was conscious. I couldn't follow him into that room. I just couldn't.

I have to.

My fists clenched at my sides, but I knew it was true. I had to follow him. If I didn't walk on my own, he would move me. Wrapping my arms across my chest so he wouldn't see my hands trembling, I ducked my head and trudged across the room and through the open door.

I stopped in the center of the bedroom and just stood there, uncertain. The door clicked closed behind me. I waited. I didn't turn around. It was easier that way. I felt the heat from Tatius's body fill the air behind me, and I held my breath.

His hands landed on my shoulders, and I jumped. Then I closed my eyes as his heat pressed along my back.

"You're trouble," he whispered, his lips inches from my ear.

I expected him to bite me, some small part of me even wanted him to, but one moment he was filling all my senses, and the next the world spun around me. Tatius whirled me around, strands of my hair flying free with the motion. My back slammed into the wall on the far side of the room, knocking the air out of me, and something hard pressed against my throat.

I swallowed—a reflex—and the sharp blade of Tatius's dagger bit into my throat. A trickle of heat slid down my skin as the nick drew blood. Tatius didn't pull back.

"Where did you go?" His voice was rough, demanding. It matched his eyes, which were hot. Not with passion. With rage.

"I didn't—" I didn't get a chance to tell him I hadn't meant to leave. That it hadn't been my choice.

He pressed the dagger deeper, cutting me off. "Don't lie to me. I might not have fully bound you, but I can feel you. Where did you go?"

I didn't dare breathe. How could I answer? I didn't know what I could say to appease him. *A mage dragged me off to a graveyard?* I didn't even know where we'd gone. It was south, somewhere without snow. That was the extent of what I knew.

Somehow I didn't think that would satisfy him.

Nothing I said was likely to help me. I hadn't planned to leave. Hadn't even meant to. But, I didn't know how to convince him of that fact.

Or maybe I did.

"Look." I whispered the suggestion, trying to speak without driving the dagger deeper. "Bite me and look." I hated the idea of his fangs in me, but he'd have to see then that I hadn't wanted to leave. Besides, he would bite me eventually anyway.

He stared at me, his intense gaze assessing. Then, in one movement, the dagger withdrew and his fangs pierced my throat.

He'd been gentle, almost teasing, last night. He wasn't gentle now. My back arched, my chest pressing into his as he tore into my flesh. Then the first deceptive wave of pleasure rode through my body. I shuddered and tried to remember to think about Gil, about her throwing me in the void and magicking me away to that cemetery, but it was hard to think about anything except the heat rushing through my body, pooling in my abdomen. Tatius's hands, which had been pinning me against the wall, slid down the curve of my back, lifted me, pressed me against his body.

I gasped as he drew back. His tongue circled the bite wounds, but he didn't close them—again. Then his hand slid into my hair, drew my head back. His tongue traced the shallow cut from the dagger. That wound he sealed.

I was still breathing heavily when he straightened. He didn't release me, which was good. I couldn't have stood on my own. I hated it, but it was true. *Vamp tricks.* I *hated* vamp tricks.

He bit his wrist and held it before my nose. In that moment, as shaky and unreal as I felt, the cloying scent of his blood was beyond my ability to resist. I closed my lips around the wound without being told and drew hard. His blood flowed faster tonight, the consistency not as syrupy thick as before. It was still as potent. I could feel the strength flowing into my limbs, feel the world sharpen around me. My legs turned solid under me, and I sealed the wound.

He frowned as I drew back, but he didn't reopen the bite. With a nod, he stepped away and I scooted around him. He could cross the room before I could blink, could slam me into the wall again before I could react. I *knew* that. But distance still made me feel better. And it was a hell of a lot better to not be cornered.

"Now what?" My voice came out steadier than I expected, and I gave myself points. I could have been discussing the weather for all my tone revealed.

His eyes roved over me, but they were calmer now. "There's no time to find you a new dress."

"Er . . . okay?" I glanced down. The corset strings were a little damp, and there were dried water-stains from the snow on the vinyl, but it wasn't like I'd ripped it or anything. At least if he was worried about the dress he wasn't planning on killing me.

Tatius stepped forward. He circled me twice. Then he reached out and pulled a clump of my hair free of the ornate up-do Samantha had labored over. Nodding, he tugged at the plunging neck of my dress, but not like he was pulling it into place, more *out* of place.

I jumped back. "What are you doing?" I asked, as I attempted to twist the dress back into what felt straight.

He swatted my hands away and rearranged the garment incorrectly again. "If you're going to look unkempt, you will look like the reason is for something more interesting than wandering around a cemetery with a couple of mages. Now stay still."

I blinked. *A couple of mages?* He said it so casually, as if it were no big surprise. I'd found out a couple of weeks ago about Sabin and the existence of mages, but the idea still hadn't become expected. "You *know* about the mages? I mean, before you were in my mind, you knew they existed?"

His very old, very heavy gaze cut down to meet my eyes. Then he shrugged. "Don't look so shocked. The mages haven't always been as secretive as they are now."

"But Nathanial . . ." Nathanial hadn't known. I knew he hadn't. He'd been as shocked as I had, though he'd admittedly handled the revelation better than me.

"Nathanial is powerful, but he is young," Tatius said, pulling more pins from my hair.

I tried not to let my dismay at his words show in my face. Nathanial was over four-hundred years old. That was not *young*—not by any definition I could think of. *Exactly how old is Tatius?*

The question must have been clear in my expression. "I am ancient," he said. "And I am master of this city. I am privy to secrets my subjects are not. You'll do good to remember that secrets are meant to be kept quiet."

I nodded. The judge had bound a certain amount of silence into my very skin when he'd marked me, so I wasn't about to go blabbing about what I'd seen recently. If I could have forgotten all about mages and vampires, I would have—life had been simpler when shifters were the only supernaturals I knew about.

That thought touched something deeper.

"Did you know about my . . . that is, shifters?" I asked, almost afraid of the answer.

"You ask too many questions." He finished releasing my hair from the elaborate up-do and ran his hands through it. "That will suffice," he said, once I looked like I'd been rolling around in a bed.

"I—"

He didn't give me a chance to protest but wrapped his arm around my waist and dragged me out of the room. "Spirited or not, the only thing I expect your mouth to do tonight is smile. Now, we've a date with the Collector."

Chapter Thirteen

I fidgeted in my spot on the overstuffed chaise, and Tatius's hand slid down the curve of my body, making all my muscles lock in response—I also stopped fidgeting, which was probably his intention. Heat from his body pressed along my back where we were touching, sharing a chaise in such a way a permanent blush burned across my cheeks.

Concentrating on relaxing in my position—because if I got too stiff, Tatius would slide into my mind and force my body to relax—I tuned back into the conversation. So far the Collector and Tatius had engaged only in small talk, a tense dance of gossip about vampire business around the country. I'd spent most of my time ignoring them.

"This is all well and good, but surely more brings you to Haven," Tatius said.

Thank the moon. Maybe this conversation would finally get somewhere and we could get out of here.

The Collector drew herself up in her chair. It was only a small shift of weight, but it marked the end of the casual conversation. "Too true, Puppet Master. But I fear my purpose might have changed since arriving."

"And what was your purpose, pray tell?"

"I had heard of the strength you've gained in recent centuries, and what a prosperous and well-managed city Haven has become." She tilted her head slightly as if considering something, but the movement was measured, all show. "In light of recent events, I find myself . . . unimpressed."

Tatius's fingers stiffened where they cupped my hipbone, but his voice, when he spoke, betrayed none of the tension pressed against my body.

"I suppose I won't be asked to join your esteemed council of city masters then, will I?" The amusement lacing his voice was a whisker twitch from disrespectful, but the Collector's smile only widened—until she flashed enough teeth to rival a shark.

"I suppose *you* will not."

A council of cities? If she was assembling a council of city masters, all as strong as Tatius or stronger, that would be a scary group of vampires. The fact that her words indicated Tatius was expendable? Downright terrifying.

I glanced at Nathanial, looking for a sign I was interpreting the situation correctly. With his emotional mask firmly in place, he looked attentive, if aloof, as he watched the proceedings, but his gaze flickered toward me. When he saw me watching him, his gaze snapped away from me.

I sighed. *Is he mad I made a deal with Tatius? For the moon's sake!* I'd saved his life. It wasn't like we'd had a lot of options.

Frowning, I focused forward again. The china doll, Elizabeth, watched me, a small smile creeping across her face, like she'd uncovered a secret. Then she leaned her head down and rested her cheek on the giant's knees. The Traveler's hand moved absently to her hair, stroking her loose curls.

"So," Tatius said, leaning forward enough I could feel the muscles in his chest press hard against my back, "should I plan a goodbye celebration for you later tonight?"

The Collector steepled her hands. "That would be appropriate. I expect to move my retinue beyond your city lines before first light." She paused and shot a meaningful glance over her shoulder. "But first, I've yet to present the entertainment I prepared."

She lifted a hand, and a small cluster of her people hustled forward. They gathered in front of Tatius and dipped into deep, formal bows. There were seven women and four men, all dressed in elaborate kimonos. Something inside me registered the group as food, which meant they were human, but they tempted me no more than a gazelle tempts a well-fed lioness. Once Tatius acknowledged them, half moved to the side and picked up musical instruments; the men took small drums, one woman cradled a strange, stringed instrument, and another lifted a bamboo flute.

The remaining five women formed a single-file line directly in front of Tatius, one behind the other. As they assembled, a scent that didn't belong caught my nose, and I stiffened.

Tatius must have felt the change. *What?* his mental voice demanded as he turned my face to his like he would kiss me.

I wasn't sure about the whole psychic mind communication, so I mouthed the words 'not human.' His gaze flickered over my shoulder to the women a moment before returning to me. Gently, he lifted my chin and pressed a chaste kiss on my mouth. I didn't move, didn't pull back—the kiss was a follow-through of Tatius's ruse. He released me without comment and I turned back to face the 'entertainment.'

For a moment, I thought all but one of the women had returned to the wall. Then I realized they'd lined up so perfectly that, from my perspective, all disappeared behind the first. The other council members must have had a less illusionistic view.

"What is this you've arranged for us?" Tatius asked.

"My most recent acquisition: Akane, and her troupe of performers." The Collector lifted her hands and clapped once. "Begin."

The drums tapped out a slow, two-part beat. On the strongest beat, the woman at the front of the line took a sliding step forward and clicked her fan. She turned, and on the next strong beat took another slow, measured step toward my right. Her fan clicked. No, she wasn't the only one moving. Two Kimono clad dancers stepped toward my right, two to my left. Their fans clicked. Their slow, deliberate steps took them away from the center line, opening a chasm between the two groups by mere inches at a time.

It wasn't like any dancing I'd ever seen, but ever so slowly, the movement revealed a fifth woman. Unlike the other dancers, who all wore red kimonos, the final dancer wore a gold-trimmed blue kimono. She didn't move from her stiff pose until the other dancers had opened a narrow path before her. Then the dancers in red turned and froze in a deep bow to the dancer in blue—Akane, most likely. She used painfully slow steps to cross the path, her constrained movements bringing her within a yard of our chaise. The drums sounded their loudest beat then fell silent as she bowed before Tatius.

The musky, inhuman scent met my nose again, and for a brief moment, her dark eyes met mine, shock clear in her features. She covered the look quickly, but she missed the first step of her dance as the flute and the strange stringed instrument sounded their first delicate notes. The music rose in a lyrical melody and Akane's movements turned fluid; the slow sway of her body both suggestive and hypnotic.

One of the red dancers moved toward Akane, and without disrupting the serpentine dance, untied Akane's sash and unwrapped yard after yard of material. The next dancer helped Akane out of the kimono, leaving her in only a gauzy undergarment. A third dancer approached and slid the thin fabric from Akane's shoulders. Akane's naked back faced our chaise, and as the garment slipped away, it revealed a thick tattoo running from over her right shoulder, down her back and legs, and ending around her ankles. In the flickering candlelight, Akane's gyrating movements caused the intricate snakeskin design to mimic life.

Turning, she never broke the gently coiling dance. The tattoo ended with the snake's fangs piercing her bare breast. She beckoned the last dancer, and the girl hurried over with an ornate wooden box. Akane threw open the lid and removed a large snakeskin—the largest snakeskin I'd ever seen. I shivered. *Wouldn't want to meet the snake that shed that. It could swallow a cougar whole.*

Akane tossed the tail of the skin over her shoulder. Then she pressed the head of the snakeskin to the tattooed snake head. When she pulled the skin away, the tattoo vanished. The snakeskin expanded as she lifted it over her head like a hood. As she pulled the two sides to meet in the front, the skin knit together seamlessly, and suddenly not a woman in snakeskin but a five foot snake stood on its tail in front of us. Then the snake unbunched, flowing forward to triple its length and half its width.

As the enormous snake coiled itself in the center of the room, the skin along my spine tingled. If I'd been in cat form at that moment, all my hair would have stood on end.

"She's magnificent, is she not?" the Collector asked, the stunned silence filling the room.

Tatius said nothing, and I wrinkled my nose. The snake smelled of reptilian musk, a chilly serpent smell that assaulted my senses. The way her head darted, her tongue tasting the air as she swung to face me, I had the feeling she didn't like my scent any better.

"Your collection is world-renowned. Your newest acquisition is . . . unique," Tatius finally said, a note of boredom clear in his voice.

Boredom he couldn't have possibly felt.

I'd never seen anything like her. *Is she from Firth?* I'd never heard of shifters who stored their skin. It was different. Strange. She slid closer, and I reeled back, plastering myself against Tatius's chest.

"Your companion has quite a unique background herself, Puppet Master," the Collector said, as the snake's head swayed a few feet in front of me. "I wonder if I could convince you to part with her. She would make a lovely complement to my collection. I would compensate you generously."

My heart stuttered to a stop, my whole body tensing. I shot a desperate glance at Nathanial. His gaze crawled to mine, and he shook his head, just a small movement, but it lacked his normal confidence, and I wasn't sure if it was directed at me or Tatius.

Tatius wouldn't . . . Honestly, I had no idea *what* Tatius would and wouldn't do.

"I'm quite fond of my companion. I think I'll keep her." Tatius announced, and the breath I'd been holding tumbled out.

My muscles all but melted in the rush of relief that washed through my body, and there was no holding back the smile I felt slide over my face. Nathanial's body also relaxed, releasing tension I wouldn't have believed was there if I hadn't watched it dissipate.

Dragging my gaze back toward the Collector, I forced my face to what I hoped was blank. My eyes tripped over Elizabeth. She wore a small, I-know-a-secret smile again. She delicately pushed off the ground and sauntered to the Collector's side. She curtseyed, then, at the Collector's nod, leaned in and whispered something in a lyrical language I couldn't follow.

By the time she finished, the Collector was also smiling. Her eyes sparkled as she glanced at me. Then they went black.

The room slipped away in darkness—the darkness I'd seen in her eyes. *What*—? I tried to look around, but there was nothing, no one, just blackness. *The void?* But it wasn't. The void was oppressive in its vast nothingness. This, this was darkness filled with a presence. The presence so close, so all encompassing, that I felt like I was suffocating. *Vamp powers.* It had to be.

"Return to your true master, child," a voice in the darkness commanded.

The words seeped under my skin. Urged me to move. To go. The darkness pulled back, revealing ghost-like silhouettes around me. Nathanial stood out more clearly than the other gray shapes. I had to go to him. I *needed* to.

Springing to my feet, I reached for him, but I couldn't move. Something held me back, held me still. I frowned. I had to move. Had to go. I glanced back. A gray ghost of Tatius clung to my arm. Gray light glowed in the center of his face, growing lighter, brighter until green burst through the obscuring fog. *His eyes.*

The light he generated reached for my flesh and his control slipped over my body. I couldn't move, but I still wanted to. The world remained gray except Tatius's eyes and glimpses of Nathanial.

"Do you think you can hold her? Can fight me?" the voice in the darkness asked, and the fog grew thicker, the suffocating presence heavier.

The fog billowed around Tatius. The brilliant green light faded. My body became mine again. I tugged my arm from Tatius's grasp and ran for Nathanial. His ghost accepted me with open arms, pulling me against his chest.

Color poured over the world in a dizzying kaleidoscope. I blinked. Nathanial's familiar scent surrounded me.

Oh crap. The Collector had vamped out, had done something to me. It wasn't my fault. But would that matter to Tatius? I pushed against Nathanial until he released me enough I could move. Then I twisted so I could face the room.

"As I suspected," the Collector said, her eyes brown again. Shaking her head, she stood and walked toward me. I cringed from her hand as she reached for my face, but I had nowhere to go with Nathanial's body behind me. She touched my cheek only briefly with her cool fingertips before turning to face Tatius. "Dear boy, you who have stolen so many companions but never sired one of your own, you could not possibly understand what a master goes through when their companion is taken from them." She gave him a sad smile, and his face darkened.

"I—" Tatius started.

"Silence," she snapped, and turned her back on him.

She gave him her back? Trust or . . . dismissal? *Definitely* dismissal. She'd just declared Tatius not a threat. Over her shoulder, I saw him bristle. His anger wrapped around him, and the candlelight flickered, each tiny flame shivering in the rising tension.

The Collector didn't seem to notice.

"Hermit," she said, "I have a proposition for you. Come to my city, bring your companion, and I promise no one will take her away from you."

I swallowed and glanced at Nathanial. His face was carefully empty as his gaze traveled from me to Tatius then back to me again. The Collector watched him with a growing smile.

"You need not decide on the spot, Hermit. But soon, very soon." She gestured to the Traveler, and he and Elizabeth hurried to her side.

Tatius strolled across the room, his stance casual, and yet the fluidity of his movements spoke of a predator prepared to pounce. He stepped between the Collector and me, knocking Nathanial's hand from my waist as almost an afterthought.

"How dare you come into my city and cause such disruption." He crossed his arms over his chest, and though he loomed over the Collector, she managed to stare down her nose at him. He stepped forward, into her space. "You've made allegations, insulted my hospitality, and now you are trying to fracture my council? I want you out of my city."

She laughed, a mirthless sound. "You don't have the power to back up that command if I choose to stay. You couldn't even hold onto an infant vampire you'd already begun to bind."

Nathanial stepped around me, blocking me from the rest of the room as the other council members surged to their feet, responding to the Collector's blatant threat. The vampires lining the walls on both sides of the room straightened. Neck ties were loosened. Knuckles were cracked. The possibility of violence saturated the air. Filled it until I was afraid any movement might ignite bloodshed.

Someone yelled, and every gaze in the room locked on the hall's door as it swung open. The beefy enforcer the Collector had brought with her the night before stormed into the room. He carried a box with him, innocuous enough in appearance, but the scent of old blood, of death, reached me across the room. My fingers dug into the sides of Nathanial's tux, and his hands moved to cover mine.

"Something dead," I whispered, as quietly as possible, and heads swiveled my direction.

The enforcer knelt before the Collector, his head bowed over the box. "Forgive the interruption, Mistress. This was just delivered." He opened the box and held it out for her inspection.

Her eyes rounded like the dots on exclamation points, and for once, I didn't think her display of emotion was measured or feigned. Her fingers shook as she reached into the box.

Her hand emerged with her fingers twisted in short brown tuffs of hair attached to the death-slackened head of a stranger. His jaw hung open, revealing two gaps in his top gums. *Gaps where his fangs had been removed.*

"What is the meaning of this, Puppet Master?" The Collector's voice trembled slightly, but I couldn't tell if it was shock or anger. Probably both.

Tatius glanced around his court, then his gaze landed on Nuri. She shook her head and he turned back to the Collector. "I'm at a loss."

"At a loss? At a *loss?*" Her voice lifted from her regular tenor. "First one of my collection is murdered and now one of my enforcers?

Are you behind this? I believe you are starting a war!"

Nathanial's hands, still cupping mine, had turned so stiff he might have been made from stone. Tatius leaned back, hooking his thumbs in his belt loops and striking a casual pose that was so at odds with the fine tux he wore that it almost looked blasphemous. He was posing, I felt it in my bones. I barely knew him, and if it was obvious to me, it must have been clear to everyone. He was stalling, trying to remain in control of the situation—at least in appearance.

"My people were thoroughly questioned. No one knew anything about your albino's death. I would gamble that no one will have knowledge of your enforcer's murder either." He cocked his head to the side. "Are you cleaning out your own ranks? Doing it in my territory so you can move against me and my city and justify your actions as retribution?"

I grimaced. He was reaching.

The swish of scales on cement sounded behind me, and I realized I'd been hearing it for quite some time. The scent of snake musk grew stronger, and I ripped my gaze away from the center of the room and the master vampires about to erupt in what I could only guess would be a bloody war.

Akane, still in the form of a giant, eight-foot serpent, drew herself up behind me. Her V-shaped head darted forward, flashing fangs as large as my fingers. I reeled back, my shoulder crashing into Nathanial's back and bouncing off like he was a stone wall. I was vaguely aware of him whirling around as the snake latched itself to my left bicep.

Pain tore through my arm, pulsed down to my fingers, up over my shoulders. A scream ripped from my throat, tasting of equal parts fear and fury.

Nathanial grabbed the snake. He tried to rip her free but only managed to jerk me forward. I lost feeling in my left arm. The numb tingling rushed over my shoulder, spreading fast. I screamed again and pain shot through my right hand. The joints in my knuckles snapped, bent backward, and the skin at my fingertips split as my claws burst free.

I didn't wonder. I didn't hesitate. I just struck.

My claws slid through Akane's thick scales, opening four large gashes. The snake jerked, her fangs taking a chunk of my skin with them. She slithered backward as I pressed my clawed hand over the gaping bite.

The snake bunched, drawing herself in until she was the length of a five-foot woman again. Then the skin down her belly split, and a woman tumbled out, the cast-off skin once again just the shed hide of a reptile. Blood dripped down her back from four gashes in her shoulder. A stream of foreign words spilled from her mouth.

"Is this your declaration of war?" Tatius asked the Collector, his voice a quiet blade that cut through the tension and heralded worse violence. Nuri, Cormac, and Mama Neda had moved forward sometime during the attack to cover Tatius's sides and back. "You've accused my people without proof, but your snake undeniably attacked my companion."

"No." There was true franticness in the Collector's voice now. She threw her arms out, her palms parallel to the floor. "Back down, all of you."

The numbness in my arm spread across my shoulder blade, and my ribcage tightened in a vise of tingles. Dark blotches filled my peripheral vision and blocked out the vampires on either wall. Nathanial was an arm's length from me, and I forced my suddenly leaden feet to lift. I stumbled on the first step as darkness crawled across my vision.

Arms wrapped around me, keeping me from falling. The silky material of Nathanial's tux brushed my cheek, and I clung to him. My vision cleared enough that I could read the concern written on his face when he tipped my head back.

"Is she well?" Tatius's voice was closer than I expected.

I jumped and regretted the motion immediately as the numbness traveled to my legs—which promptly gave out beneath me. Only Nathanial's arms kept me upright.

"I feel . . . " I shook my head, pressing my face harder against Nathanial's chest. His heat barely reached me—or maybe my cheek was going numb. "Poison?"

"Impossible," the Collector said, or at least, I thought it was her, but her voice sounded far off. "Vampires are immune to intravenous poisons."

I blinked, trying to clear my vision, but it was dark. *Immune? Maybe to normal poisons, but what about supernatural poison?* I had the feeling I'd be the first to find out.

"Hermit." Tatius's voice sounded like he was yelling from deep inside a cave. "Take her to my—"

It was all I heard before the suffocating darkness pressed down on me, and the world vanished.

Chapter Fourteen

I was having one of those dreams where I thought I was awake but I wasn't. Or at least, I *hoped* it was a dream.

A woman I didn't know knelt beside me, intently darning something out of my view. She'd killed what looked like a seal and wore the skin around her shoulders like a hooded cape. So intent on her work, she didn't notice me studying her, and I watched as she pulled a wickedly large needle up and straightened the crimson thread.

"Who are you?" I mumbled, my lips too cracked, too thick, to form the words.

The woman jumped. "She's lucid."

Who is she talking to? I tried to turn and see, but my head lolled uselessly to the side. A hand caught my chin and Nathanial's face snapped into focus. Strands of his long hair had fallen loose of his ponytail and hung chaotically around his face. Blood stained the once-white tuxedo shirt.

"You okay?" I asked.

Some of the tension lines between his eyes eased as he leaned down and kissed my forehead.

I tried to pull away. "Stop that."

"You are most definitely yourself again," he whispered into my hair. Then he straightened enough to give me a haggard smile. "Drink this."

Nathanial lifted a large thermos to my lips. I tried to take it from him but couldn't figure where my hands were. *Okay, now* that's *disturbing.* Nathanial ignored my distress as he upended the thermos. Room-temperature blood poured into my mouth.

I coughed, nearly choking on the wash of blood. "Who did you kill?"

"It is from a blood bank. Drink it."

He lifted the thermos for me again and I swallowed another mouthful. It was terrible: lukewarm and full of chemicals. *Anticoagulant?* Maybe. I swallowed another mouthful and gagged. *Like drinking pond sludge.*

I forced myself to swallow another mouthful. *What is going on? Where am I?* The last thing I remembered was the snake woman. She bit me. *Poisoned me.*

I twisted away from the thermos. "What happened? After?"

"Do not worry about it right now. Drink."

I shook my head and tried to push the thermos away. Or I would have, if either of my arms would have worked. *What the—*

I looked down. I was in a large, freestanding tub. Thick ropes bound my right arm to a metal handrail. The seamstress leaned over my left. I paled, gawking at the slit she was stitching that ran from my armpit to my wrist. And I was wrong—she wasn't a seamstress.

"What are you doing? Who are you?"

The skin-clad woman looked up from her work. "You can call me Biana. Gil asked me to help." She noticed me looking around the room and shrugged. "She got a little green when things got bloody. Once I'm finished I'll fetch her."

Biana didn't have a drop of blood on anything other than her hands, but I was certainly bloody. My dress was a mess: the vinyl stretched, torn, and covered in gore. The corset was missing completely. Blood covered my legs and coated the base of the blue tub.

There were also splashes of blood on the tiled bathroom floor. I frowned. A bathroom I didn't recognize, but the design was familiar enough. The large tub took up most of the room, leaving just enough space to comfortably walk around the rim. A walk-in shower stood recessed in one wall. There was no toilet or light fixture. A small, floating globe over Biana's shoulder provided the light she sewed by. I'd never seen the room before, but it bore Nathanial's taste preferences—not Tatius's.

"Where are we?"

"How much do you remember?" Nathanial asked, opening another bag of blood.

"Akane attacked me." The only memories I had after that were vague flashes of fear and rage. *A nightmare?* Nathanial didn't say anything, and I frowned at him. "You look like you've been through a fight. Did the Collector attack? What happened? Why am I sitting here in my own blood like a butchered pig?"

Biana and Nathanial exchanged a glance. Neither answered me. *Okay.* Gritting my teeth against the pain, I attempted to lift my mangled arm. My fingers flexed, but the twitchy movement was all I could accomplish—too much muscle and tendon damage.

"Don't squirm," Biana snapped without looking up from her work.

Nathanial forced the thermos at me again. I drank as much as I could stomach. *This is ridiculous.* "If you aren't going to tell me anything, can you at least untie my good arm?"

Nathanial nodded as Biana knotted her thread. She backed away a little too quickly. "I'll fetch Gil." She all but ran from the room, letting the bathroom door slam behind her.

I frowned after her, but Nathanial didn't comment. As he leaned over me to undo the rope, I stared at his ruined tux. *Is all that blood mine?* This close I could smell the blood clinging to him. Most of it smelled acrid, like the snake woman, but a warmer, fresher scent also reached my nose.

"You're bleeding," I whispered.

Nathanial cut his eyes toward me, his agile fingers still fighting the rope. "Not badly."

"What the hell happened, Nathanial?"

The bathroom door cracked open and Gil peeked into the room. "Are you sure she won't go psychotic again?"

Psychotic?

"Kita will be fine." Nathanial sent Gil a cold look. "Come in or out."

Gil and Biana crept into the room, but they lingered around the door. The air filled with tension as the rope fell to the floor. What? Did they expect me to jump up and attack them? Nathanial's fingers massaged the skin the rope had bitten, and feeling returned in tingles of pins and needles. Still no one answered my questions. I growled under my breath, and Gil and Biana took a step back.

"Is anyone going to tell me what happened?"

"You were poisoned by a *hebi no josei*," Biana said.

Oh yeah, that clears everything up. "A *what?*"

"A *hebi no josei*. We thought they were extinct."

I frowned at her. "You're a scholar like Gil, aren't you?"

Biana cocked her head to the side and shrugged one shoulder. "Gil is a scholar-trainee; I'm a scholar. I graduated from the university a hundred years ago. I specialize in studying skinwalkers." At my blank look she fingered the seal-skin around her shoulders. "There is little known about the skinwalkers, and they are quite rare. Some myths exist in human tales. Have you heard of selkies?" I shook my head, and she stroked her fur cape again. "Well, the point is that you were poisoned. A single drop of the *hebi no josei's* poison is lethal to most living things. If you were mortal, you would be well and truly dead."

"Okay, but I'm not mortal. I just passed out."

"Your heart stopped." Biana smiled a mouthful of needle pointed teeth. "We were forced to remove all the blood from your body."

"You what?" I felt the blood drain from my face, and black dots filled the edges of my vision. I blinked them away. "My arm?"

"Held the highest concentration of poison, but it had spread through your body."

"So you sliced open my arm?"

She shrugged again. "You'll heal."

She'd butchered my arm, but, hey, I'd heal. Okay, my first impression of Biana wasn't too shiny.

My feet drew paths through the blood coating the tub as I tried to get my legs under me. The effort made me dizzy, and I collapsed back into the tub with a sticky crash. Nathanial poured another bag of blood into the thermos.

I shook my head when he held the metal container out to me. "I've had enough of that stuff."

"Drink it. You need your strength."

"Didn't you tell me once that I only needed a pint of blood a night to survive?"

Nathanial sighed, but he didn't put down the thermos. "First of all, we are replenishing your base blood supply. Secondly, this is processed plasma. It offers you only a fraction of what you need. Now drink."

I took the thermos. The chemical taste clung to the back of my tongue, and my stomach quivered as the tepid liquid hit, but slowly warmth crawled to my skin. I balanced the still half-full thermos on the edge of the tub.

"So what happened after I passed out? Was Akane *ordered* to attack me? Was poisoning me some part of the Collector's plan? Maybe she has an antidote?"

"There is no antidote for a *hebi no josei's* poison," Biana said. "The poison is typically fatal within minutes, but the effect of the poison on a vampire has never been studied." She sighed. "I suppose this means I'll need to write another boring paper the university students will have to read."

"I'll write it," Gil said cheerfully, her scroll in hand and quill poised to take notes.

Biana looked thoughtful for a moment, then nodded. "That will fulfill your debt for my help, but my name better be on it, not *yours*. I can use the paper to apply for a new grant."

Disappointment played across Gil's face, but she didn't argue. I drained the remainder of the thermos and stared at my working hand. My claws were still out. I flexed the fingers, trying to retract the claws. A wave of dizziness crashed over me from the effort.

My claws. This was the second time the claws had extended since I became a vampire. *Will I shapeshift again? Is this proof I will?* There was no one to answer. No one knew. While being the only shifter-turned-vampire had the fringe benefit of protecting me from the judge, the fact I couldn't turn to anyone sucked. Everything was trial and error. So all I could do was try to retract my claws again, but it was no more effective than all the nights I'd tried to extend them. Both times my claws had appeared I'd been in danger.

Screw meditation, apparently my cat only surfaces during near-death experiences. If nearly dying was what it took to make just my *claws* appear, would I survive the kind of danger that provoked me to shift into cat-form again?

I pushed the thought aside. I needed to wash off the blood drying on my skin. If I didn't want to be sitting in the gore, the shower was the way to go. *Now just to get everyone to leave and to make it across the room.* I shoved against the side of the tub, but I couldn't get my feet under me. Nathanial put a hand on my shoulder, stilling me.

I frowned at him. "No matter how weak the bagged blood is, haven't I drunk enough that I should be able to stand?"

"Remember what Tatius said about *vampire* blood?" Nathanial whispered. He held his wrist under my nose.

I grimaced. *Right, I need master vamp blood.* I didn't like the idea, but as weak as I felt despite the quantity of bagged blood, I knew he was right. And I'd take his blood this time. I would. Just . . . not with an audience. I shot a meaningful glance toward the two mages. Nathanial's gaze followed mine, and he turned to Biana and Gil.

"Thank you for your help," he said tilting his head. "May I have a few minutes alone with Kita?"

Gil looked offended by the dismissal, but Biana stepped closer to the tub and shot us another smile. *Did she alter her appearance?* She certainly couldn't pass for human, like Gil. Biana's pointed teeth and greasy, clumped hair reminded me of human stories of wild children raised by wolves. Of course I'd met plenty of people raised by wolves, hell, *I'd* been raised mostly by shapeshifting mountain lions, and I didn't look like a wild child.

No, right now I just look like a field-dressed rabbit.

"A moment to discuss payment for my assistance." Biana stroked the seal cloak again and stared at me with pupil-less eyes.

Great, I had to pay her for butchering my arm.

"Let me guess, you require an 'unnamed favor to be called upon on a future date,'" I said, and her smile grew.

"I see you are accustomed to working with Sabinites."

"I'm learning that favors are the acceptable currency for most supernaturals."

She nodded. "Well, my payment is nothing so vague. If you encounter the *hebi no josei* again and can determine where she hides her skin, steal it. I *want* that skin."

"Why? Can you use the skin to shapeshift?"

"Each skin is unique to the skinwalker born with it, but with the right magic, it can be used." She stood and fingered her sealskin cape again.

"Does a selkie turn into a seal?"

She flashed another smile. "Tell Gil if you acquire that snake skin. She knows how to find me."

Magic coursed through the room, and Biana disappeared. I glanced at Gil.

She shrugged. "I'll be in the other room," she said, letting herself out.

And then I was alone with Nathanial.

He raised a hand to cup the side of my face, but hesitated before he reached my skin. When his fingers finally landed, the touch was tentative, as if a butterfly had landed on my cheek. "Tatius doesn't know where we are."

That was all he said. But it was all the things he *didn't* say that flashed in my mind. If Tatius didn't know where we were, Nathanial must have taken me and left. Just left.

I'd heard Tatius command Nathanial to take me . . . somewhere. I assumed Tatius's chambers. But if Tatius didn't know where Nathanial had taken me . . . . I shivered, remembering the press of Tatius's knife in my throat. *He'll kill us.* When he found us. And he *would* find us. I knew he would.

Tatius had known I'd left the sanctuary before. He'd told me he'd 'felt' me. I was missing that weird vampire sense but Nathanial always found me. So what would stop Tatius?

"He'll follow the bond," I whispered, knowing my eyes were wide, knowing they showed fear I wished they wouldn't.

Nathanial shook his head. "No. We replaced your blood base, Kitten. All of it. His blood is no longer in you. He has no bond to you."

"Oh." That changed everything, didn't it? No, because if we were in the city, Tatius *would* find us, eventually. He had enforcers, agents, spies. And he could pierce Nathanial's illusions—he'd proven that. We couldn't hide. "Now what? Do we run?"

"I do not know." Nathanial sank to the floor behind me.

He leaned against the edge of the tub, and with him sitting outside the tub and me in it, we were the same height. The sides of our heads touched. I leaned against him, felt him do the same. We sat like that, in silence. *Companions in uncertainty.*

That thought made me stiffen. If Tatius's influence had been drained from my body with my blood . . . "So my bond to you is broken, too?"

I heard Nathanial sigh, which was an unusually human gesture for him. "No," he said after a moment. "My blood remade you when you became a vampire. It is a part of what you are. To fully bind you, Tatius would have to have given you enough blood to remake you again. He did not have that opportunity."

So, Tatius's influence had been drained away, and now I was Nathanial's companion again. Just Nathanial's. A fluttering sensation attacked my stomach, made my heart beat too fast.

"Besides," he said. "You would not be cognizant if you completely lacked master blood. I gave you some while you were still . . . unaware. But you need more to regain your strength."

Right. This conversation was getting a little too surreal. I needed out of the tub. I needed a shower. Clean clothes. Something akin to normal. I struggled to stand, and suddenly Nathanial's hands were on me.

He lifted me by the underarms. I balanced on my feet for a breath. Then my knees buckled and only Nathanial's hands kept me upright. *This is ridiculous.* I had plenty of blood in my system; my stomach felt tight with all the plasma Nathanial had forced on me. I was cold, but nothing unmanageable. *I can at least stand on my own. Clean off the blood.*

Concentrating, I managed a step forward before sagging in Nathanial's arms again. He pulled me out of the tub then held me in a tight embrace, which wasn't necessary to help me stand, but it was obvious I wasn't walking anywhere on my own. Not any time soon, at least.

"Can you drop me off in the shower?" I asked, knowing that would mean he'd have to come get me again later.

I reached up, intending to wrap my uninjured arm around his neck, but as my palm slid over his shoulder, liquid warmth seeped against my skin. I froze. *Blood?* I pulled back, and careful of my claws, pushed the shredded material of Nathanial's dress shirt aside. Four deep lacerations—that looked suspiciously like claw marks—decorated his skin.

"How did this happen?"

He shrugged my hand away and bent to lift my legs. I frowned at him. Oh no. I wasn't dissuaded that easily. "Gil said I went psychotic. Did I . . . attack you?"

"It was my fault, Kitten. Biana said we needed to drain the poison. You were unconscious, seemingly dead. I was . . . not myself. I did not stop to consider the fact that once we drained the blood and you woke, you would be beyond conscious control."

I blinked at him. Nathanial considered *everything*. If he hadn't considered what would happen when they drained me of blood . . . . He must have been frantic. *About me.* I looked away. And how, exactly, was I supposed to apologize for going crazy and clawing open someone's shoulder? *Sorry* didn't really cover that.

Nathanial carried me to the recessed shower in the corner of the room and set me on my feet. When my knees gave out he lowered me gently to the tile. He turned, sliding the glass shower door closed.

Closed, with him still in the shower. With me.

"What are you doing?" He couldn't be in here. He needed to leave. Like now.

He didn't.

He adjusted the shower knobs, and streams of water jetted from the walls and the shower head. "We are both covered in blood, Kitten. It needs to be washed off." As if to illustrate his point, he drew a finger through the tacky mess drying on my shoulder.

"Right, shower. Got that part. But you have to get out."

"Can you stand?" he asked and I frowned at him. "Then you need my help."

I growled under my breath but didn't argue. After all, he had a point—we both needed the shower. *It's efficient.* The fluttering in my stomach didn't agree.

Still, I raised my arms, indicating I was ready to accept his help. His mouth quirked, but he didn't say anything as he leaned down. He gathered me in his arms and lifted me until only the tips of my toes touched the ground.

Water poured over me, turning pink as it rinsed blood from my dress and skin. I blinked away the water running into my eyes, and Nathanial turned us so I wasn't directly under the shower head. The jets of water from the walls beat against my back, but it wasn't an unpleasant feeling. The already blood-sodden dress grew heavier as the lining soaked in water, the ruined material stretching with the weight.

"Drink," Nathanial said. I expected him to hold out his wrist. Instead he tilted his head, baring his throat.

"Uh . . . " I'd have rather taken from his wrist. The neck was more intimate. Much more. This was already weird enough. "Nathanial, I don't think . . . "

"It is not an option. Not anymore." There was more force, more command, than I'd ever heard in his voice. His tone made my teeth grit, made me want to struggle, to fight, but at the same time, the fluttering grew frantic in my abdomen, my instincts reacting to the power lacing his words, to the strength in the arms holding me still.

"Drink," he said, the word both demanding and compelling.

He lifted me higher. My toes left the floor and slid across the tops of his dress shoes. His throat was so close. My heart crashed against the front of my ribcage like it was trying to break through my skin, to join Nathanial's, where I felt his heart beating against my body.

My fingers trembled as I peeled away the collar of Nathanial's shirt. Then I hesitated. A fresh bite decorated his throat, the edges torn in a jagged line down to his collarbone. I touched the puncture marks with my knuckles, not trusting my claws in such a delicate area. Nathanial drew a sharp breath, and I dropped my hand.

"I did this?"

"You were not yourself."

No. No, I wasn't. And maybe I wasn't myself now, either. I dropped my gaze.

"Put me down. Let me shower."

He drew me tighter against him, tight enough to verge on pain. "No," he whispered. "No. I almost lost you. Again. I need you strong. Healthy. Take from me, Kitten. Please." The *please* was a frayed whisper, like his heart was breaking with the word.

As confused as I felt, I knew one thing: I did *not* want the heart pounding against me to break.

My lips parted, and my mouth sealed over the pulse in his neck. His arms convulsed around me as my fangs slid into his skin. A wave of tension flowed between our bodies. Then I lost myself as my consciousness dove into his mind.

For a single heartbeat, I was so deep inside his mind that I felt my teeth in his throat as if it were *my* throat. The woman in my arms was small, so very small and fragile, and I was so very frightened for her. The world shifted, his mind pushing me away. I fell into his memories.

Tatius holds her and she quivers in his arms. Her lips part as she gazes at him, wraps her small fingers in his mesh shirt. No. She is supposed to be mine. I found her. Turned her. He has no right.

She leans into his chest, content, sated. No, not quite content. Yes, remember who you are, Kitten. Remember you are mine.

Like a door being slammed in my face, Nathanial expelled my mind from the memory and I slipped into another.

Tatius stands in the center of the room, blood dripping from his torn frock coat and from the daggers in his hands. Bodies litter his wake, bodies of people I've known since I was a child. He turns, his gaze falling on me as he considers whether I will live or die. He lifts the dagger—

Nathanial's mind hurled me from the memory. I slid through the darkness of his past, looking for an open door, until I found myself in the memory of him teaching a class. The memory was empty of emotion and completely uninteresting.

Safe.

I wasn't sure if it was my thought, or his.

I pulled back and sealed the wound on his neck. His memories still flashed through my mind. His anger moving under my skin. His hope. I blinked, seeing myself through his memory. Feeling his hopelessness when he could do nothing but watch me in Tatius's arms. Confused emotions tangled at the edge of my mind.

Does he know what I saw? Did I even understand everything I saw? Did I want to? I needed something else to think about. To focus on. My gaze landed on the other bite on his neck. *I can heal that.* I flicked my tongue over the torn flesh.

Nathanial jerked his head back. His eyes were still cloudy from my bite, but they cleared as he studied my face. "That is the equivalent to a kiss in Firth, is it not?"

"What? No, I was only—" My eyes flew open as his hands slid

under the short dress to my mostly bare bottom. He lifted me higher, pressing against me, and flattening my back against the shower tile. "What are you—" but the words stalled as he leaned forward and ran the tip of his tongue along my collar bone. My breath hitched, caught in my throat, stuck around unspoken words.

Words I couldn't remember. Couldn't think about. I didn't want to think right now, anyway. My legs rose, folded, hugged him. I locked them around his waist.

Nathanial nuzzled my cheek with his—not a human gesture, but one that set my skin ablaze. His tongue flicked against the edge of my chin, and my heart fluttered. A purr thrummed deep in my chest. My good hand went to his hair, my claws breaking the pony grip that held it. His hair fell around me like a black silk curtain, and he leaned down. The sigh that escaped his lips danced over my earlobe and sent shivers down my spine.

I'd waited so long to feel his hair between my fingers, but the lethal tips of my claws were in the way. I growled in frustration, and a spasm ran through my hand. My joints popped back into normal alignment as my claws retracted. I had only a moment to be amazed before Nathanial's fangs nicked my throat.

I gasped, shivering in his arms. A dark sound tumbled from his throat, something between a growl and a moan, and he pressed harder against me, his hips grinding against mine. My fingers trailed through his water-soaked hair, following the strands down to where they plastered to his chest, exposed below his torn shirt. I ripped the material further so I could feel more of the hard planes of his smooth flesh.

His mouth locked on mine.

I froze.

The tips of his fangs pressed against my lower lip, making me squirm, but the heat gathering in my body chilled. I tried to move away, but there was nowhere to go with my back against the wall. I pushed at his chest, my palm bearing into the wounds near his shoulder.

Nathanial pulled back, crystal eyes swimming with heat. I looked down, away from his gaze, and he groaned.

"Kitten," he whispered, leaning forward to rest his face on the tile behind me. Our bodies were still pressed together, and I felt the shaky breaths he took, acutely aware that mine matched.

I had to get out of there. Away from him. Away from the

tumbling of my heart. He made me feel crazy, like my skin wasn't big enough to hold all the chaotic emotions whirling through me. I couldn't stay. *If he hadn't kissed me . . .*

Animals didn't kiss, not by locking lips, at least. Neither did shifters. *And what am I?* I didn't know anymore.

I shivered, my skin burning from all the touches before the kiss. Nathanial's body went still against mine.

"Elizabeth's master is the one called the Traveler," he said without looking at me. "She is older than I am and has been a master at least as long."

I frowned. *What does that have to do with anything?* Maybe it didn't. Maybe he was just trying to distract himself. I could use the distraction.

I asked the first coherent question that came to mind. "Why does she remain his companion if she is a master?"

He pulled back. "Why do you think?" He studied my face, watching for something. Something my face apparently didn't give him. "I thought that perhaps, after some time, you would . . . " He squeezed his eyes closed and lowered me to my feet.

My legs shook but held. *His blood.* He'd been right. His blood had helped. A lot.

I took an experimental step, and Nathanial's fingers flew down the few surviving buttons on his shirt. He slipped it off his shoulders. I tried not to stare, but I'd never seen Nathanial in anything less than a casual suit. He looked good in a suit.

He looked better out of it.

My fingers had felt the hard planes of his chest, but my brain hadn't translated that tactile information yet, and my eyes drank in what my skin already knew. Sleek muscles accented his chest and arms, and I stared at his lack of hair, so different from the shifter males I'd become accustomed to seeing while growing up. Water ran down his skin. A blush crawled to my cheeks, and I turned away, stared at my toes.

"What are you doing?" I cringed at how breathy and unsure my voice sounded.

"Showering."

"But . . . . " No argument came to my mind. But I couldn't stay. Not now. Not after nearly . . .

Grinding my teeth, I slid open the door and retreated from the shower. Some part of me wanted to glance back as I heard Nathanial's pants hit the ground, but I suppressed the urge. Leaving a wet trail behind me, I fled.

Chapter Fifteen

I ran into Gil in the hallway, her purple mage light floating over her shoulder. She gawked at me—not all that surprising considering I was still streaked with blood and the vinyl dress had taken more damage in the shower and now barely hung to my body.

"Clothes?" I asked.

She just shook her head, still staring.

Great. Stoked with Nathanial's blood, I was hyper-aware, but I couldn't hear anyone in the house besides Gil. *At least I don't have to worry about running into anyone else.* Still, it took opening three doors before I finally stumbled on a bedroom.

Slamming the door behind me, I ransacked the dresser. Slight though he might be, Nathanial's clothes were too big for me. I shucked what remained of the dress and pulled a plain white undershirt over my head. It turned translucent as it clung to the water soaking my body. *Of all the mooncursed luck!* I walked over to the closet and pulled out the first colored dress shirt I found. It was an odd shade of deep blue that probably looked amazing with Nathanial's dark hair and gave color to his eyes.

I frowned at the shirt and shoved it back in the closet.

The next shirt I found was a simple brown, and I shrugged it on over the undershirt. I had to fight to get my useless arm through the sleeve, and I couldn't work the buttons with only one hand, but it hung to my mid-thigh and kept me from looking completely indecent. As I fought with the sleeves, trying to roll them so they didn't cover my hands, the door opened behind me.

"Later, Gil," I said as mage-light filled the open doorway. The door closed, blocking out the light. *Well, at least she didn't argue.* Giving up on the sleeves, I turned and almost jumped out of my skin.

Nathanial stood just inside the door, his long hair streaming over his shoulders and chest until it blended with the black towel wrapped around his waist. Whatever expression he read on my face made him raise an eyebrow, but as he strode across the room toward me, he kept his features carefully empty.

He stopped an arm's length from me and reached forward. Gulping, I stumbled back in a confusion of tangled feet. That earned me a frown, but he stepped into the space I'd vacated.

Normally he didn't push things. Tonight obviously wasn't a normal night.

He reached out again, and I held my breath as his fingers closed on the shirt. He buttoned two of the buttons in the center of the shirt, and then rolled the sleeves to my elbows. I stared at anything in the room other then the wall of bare chest in front of me. Once the sleeves were even, he stepped around me without a word and walked to the wardrobe.

That's it? He fixed my clothes and went on about his business? I whirled around.

His back was facing me, but he'd pulled off the towel and wrapped it around his hair. The full length of his body was on display like a pale marble statue. And it was . . . my mouth went dry, and I shook myself, tearing my gaze away. *I really must be going crazy.* I'd seen naked men all my life. Hell, lots of shifters rarely wore clothing, even in human form. Why should this be any different?

Because I'd never seen Nathanial naked before.

He glanced over his shoulder and studied my face. A small smile lifted the edge of his lips. *He thinks this is funny?* No, I realized. This was a show. *Damn vampire.*

Fine. If he wanted an audience, I'd give him an audience. I wrenched open the door. "Hey, Gil. Come here a moment."

I glanced back before she reached the door and found Nathanial staring at me, fully dressed. Or, at least, he *looked* fully dressed, but he'd gotten that way too fast for his clothes to be anything but an illusion. *Show's over.* I flashed him some teeth and left.

⇛ • ⇚

"I've already answered that question. Twice."

Gil tapped her pen on the scroll and frowned at me. "I need to make sure I have all the facts straight. I've read that when vampires are low on blood they lose control, but I was under the impression they remembered what happened afterward. You're sure you don't remember anything?"

I glared at her in response. We'd already been through this. I understood that she had to write Biana's paper, and I was thankful she'd brought in Biana to help, but enough was enough. I crossed my arm over my chest and glanced at Nathanial—who was, thankfully,

fully dressed.

He sat in a chair at the other end of the coffee table. His elbows were propped on the arms, the tips of his fingers pressed together in front of him. He leaned forward as if intent on something, but his gaze was distant, unfocused. And definitely not focused on Gil's and my conversation. No help was coming from him.

Gil gave me a petulant look and tapped her scroll again.

With a sigh I said, "I don't remember anything between passing out in the council session and waking to Biana sewing my arm." She looked on the verge of interrupting so I held up my hand, silencing her before she asked the next inevitable question. I could guess it anyway. "I've told you everything I know about the *hebi* thing. And don't even ask me what the poison felt like again."

Gil's mouth opened then snapped shut, her teeth clicking with the force. She vanished her scroll. "I swear, if you and this study weren't going to make me famous . . . " She shook her head. "Fine. We're done. I'll write the report from the little bit of information you've given me. The very little bit." Her bottom lip extended in a pout. Then she vanished.

I leaned back against the couch, rubbing my eyes with my good palm. It felt late—or early, depending on how you looked at it. *How long was I . . .* 'unconscious' was the first word that came to mind, but apparently that hadn't been true for the entire block of time missing from my memories.

Pulling my knees onto the cushion, I settled into a more comfortable position and watched Nathanial. His expression hadn't changed when Gil vanished, and I wasn't sure he'd noticed she had left. His hair was still damp—and still loose, falling around his shoulders in heavy black strands.

Even as still and deep in thought as he appeared, there was something about him that looked more on edge, more . . . uncontrolled than I was used to. Heat crawled to my face, remembering what had happened earlier, and I dropped my gaze, forcing myself to look around, at the abstract paintings on the wall, at the bronze figure in the corner, at the bookshelves around the fireplace—anywhere but at the vampire in the room with me. Not that he noticed my distraction.

"So, where are we?" I asked.

Nathanial continued staring into space.

"Nathanial?"

His head lifted, but his eyes didn't focus. Scooting off the couch, I stepped around the coffee table and waved my fingers in front of his face.

He blinked. I wasn't convinced I had his attention yet, but that appeared about as good as I was getting.

"Where are we?" I asked again, waving a hand to indicate the room.

He looked around as if he didn't remember, and the corners of his mouth dipped. "A home I own."

"Yeah, I assumed that." *Terribly helpful, isn't he?* "Are we still in Haven?"

He nodded. "The very heart of the city. This house . . . no one knows I own this house. Not even Tatius."

At the mention of Tatius's name, the worry I'd been ignoring clawed its way to the front of my mind. I sank back onto the couch. "So, are we staying here?" In the heart of the city? Right under Tatius's nose?

He nodded. "Tonight."

But not tomorrow? We were running. I sighed. Nathanial's home had been mine since he'd turned me—only two weeks ago, though it seemed like forever—but now we'd be on the street again. I pushed aside the unexpected disappointment. How was running now any different from the past five years? Well, except the whole sunlight-restriction thing, and the addiction to blood. Oh, and let's not forget the Judge's mark, and . . . Okay, so things were more complicated now. But I'd made it on the run before. I'd do it again.

"What is our next move?" I asked, wishing I had my gray coat with me. It had been with me a while. We'd gone through a lot.

Nathanial didn't answer. He stared into space again. *He's planning.* I wasn't much of a planner while on the run. I was much more a stowaway-on-a-train-and-see-where-I-end-up kind of stray. Of course, that was how I'd ended up in Haven in the first place.

I pushed away from the couch and paced in front of it. I needed to call Bobby. I'd never made it back to the cabin last night, and I obviously wasn't headed there tonight. *Or possibly ever again.* Running was like that. You didn't look back. You didn't get attached.

But I'd disappeared on Bobby once before. I didn't want to do it again. As for notifying Gil, she had no trouble tracking me down, so no need to let *her* know we were leaving. I glanced down at the shirt I'd misappropriated from Nathanial's closet. *I'll need some different clothes to blend in. Nathanial will also have to—*

My mental packing ground to an abrupt halt. I'd never been on the run *with* someone else, but I'd added him to my mental to-do list without thinking about it. *It's just until I become a master vampire. Once I don't need his blood anymore, we'll go our separate ways.*

How long would that take, anyway? I had no idea.

"So now what?" Good to get the question out there as many times as it took for Nathanial to actually answer.

Nathanial leaned back in his chair and crossed an ankle over his knee. "I can appeal to Tatius, though since everyone in attendance heard him tell me to take you to his chambers, they will know I did the exact opposite of what he commanded. He is unlikely to forgive such a public display of disregard for his authority anytime soon. We can keep a low profile until I find another city willing to take us in, but time is against us. Remaining in Haven increases the risk Tatius will find us." His frown deepened, cutting into his face. "There is the Collector's offer?" His voice sounded like he was considering it, but he shook his head. "You would grow to hate me."

"You think I don't already?" I asked, trying to make my voice light, a joke. He'd told me once that no matter how fond I was of saying it, I couldn't hate him.

He didn't smile. Maybe he didn't even hear.

"So what do you—" I cut off, my body going stiff. Tilting my head, I breathed deep. "Do you smell that?"

I know that scent. I breathed in again. The clanless. I'd encountered the clanless shifter several times during my hunt for the rogues, but I hadn't seen him since. *Why am I catching his scent now? Here?* I looked around, trying to decide which direction the scent was coming from before my nose gave out.

I crossed to the windows, but the scent grew fainter as I moved. I crept back, moving to a door that led deeper into the house. Nathanial followed, his steps silent behind me.

The scent was stronger in the hall, and I crept all the way to the end. *Was the scent here earlier?* As I reached for the doorknob, Nathanial grabbed my wrist. He pressed a finger over his lips and stepped around me before flinging open the door.

The room beyond was dark. Dust sheets covered the minimal furniture, but the air wasn't stale. A light breeze made the drapes flutter. *An open window? In the middle of winter? In a vampire's secret house?*

Not likely.

Nathanial crossed the room in less than a heartbeat. When my eyes caught up with him, he was jerking something out from behind a gray sheet. No, not something. Someone.

Nathanial lifted the much larger man by the front of his coat and slammed the man's back into the wall hard enough to send two framed photos crashing to the floor. Nathanial drew his head back, his fangs glimmering in the street light filtering through the grimy window. His mouth descended on the man's neck.

"Nathanial, don't!" I dashed across the room. Nathanial fed on criminals and this man certainly qualified, having just broken into Nathanial's house. But he wasn't just some random burglar. I knew him.

My good hand landed on Nathanial's shoulder. He'd already broken skin, I could smell the blood. But under my fingers, I felt the tension leak out of him. He lifted his head, glaring at the man he still held against the wall.

The clanless smelled of sweat and fear, and the thrum of energy spilling in the air betrayed the fact his wolf was close to the surface. But he smiled at Nathanial, one side of his mouth lopsided from the scars branded into his right cheek.

"I recognize you," he said as his hand lifted to his throat, which bore no mark—Nathanial had sealed the bite. "This might explain a lot." His gaze moved to me. "Ah, my *Dyre* enigma. I should have guessed I'd find you here." He tilted his head forward, though being pinned to a wall limited his ability to pantomime lifting an imaginary hat.

"Clanless," I said, the word sour on my tongue.

His lopsided smile froze. "Degan."

"What?"

"My name. It's Degan." He didn't identify what clan he'd once been part of—not that I would have expected him to. Hell, I hadn't expected him to tell me his name at all. He hadn't offered it any of the last three times we'd run across each other.

I hesitated, but finally said, "Kita." Then I turned to Nathanial. "What do we do with him?"

The clanless—Degan—had tried to subdue me for reasons unknown the first two times I'd met him, but the last, we'd had the common goal of wanting a murderous rogue captured. We also had a mutual distrust of each other. During my battle with Bryant and Tyler he'd backed off, giving me a chance to deal with the rogues myself, but threatening that he'd deal with them and me if I failed. I'd dealt with them.

Nathanial lowered the clanless to his feet but didn't back off. Degan was taller, but Nathanial gave off more menace. "Why are you here?"

Degan ran his hands down the front of his worn coat. The movement was nonchalant, but his nostrils flared. *He's buying time to sift through scents?*

I switched my weight. If he lunged, he wouldn't get past Nathanial, but my good hand curled into a fist anyway.

He seemed to reach some decision, because his shoulders rolled back, and he shoved his hands in his pockets. I tensed, ready for him to pull out that damned silver chain he carried, but he just leaned against the wall—a mockery of calmness his racing pulse disputed.

"I picked up a strange scent. But it isn't either of you."

"Do you break into houses every time you smell something you don't recognize?" I asked, letting my skepticism show in my voice. All my life I'd heard that the clanless were not to be trusted but Degan had kept his word the last time I'd met him. From what I understood, he hunted rogues and investigated suspicious deaths in Haven, mostly just to keep the hunters from sniffing around what he considered his territory. But, regardless of his reason, he appeared to be one of the good guys. Not that I'd turn my back on him.

"Do I break into houses to track strange scents?" He gave me an incredulous look. "When it is the same scent I found on a headless corpse? Yes. I do."

I froze. My pulse rushed in my ears. In what felt like slow motion, I turned toward Nathanial. His back betrayed his tension. He'd gone into statue mode.

He had to breathe to speak and his draw of air was sharp in the stillness. "You found a decapitated body? Where?"

Degan shrugged, but the movement was stiff. "Let me sniff out the source here, and maybe I'll lead you to the body."

Nathanial shook his head. "No."

I touched Nathanial's arm, drawing his attention to me. "Let him look. If there is a scent here that is unusual and similar to the body . . . " I could only think of one scent that would lead Degan to this house, and I was guessing his nose would lead him to the tub I woke in.

Nathanial's brows knit together, but he didn't say anything as he studied my face. I tried to show confidence and curiosity in my expression but my stomach twisted at the idea of a clanless in my territory—even a temporary territory such as Nathanial's secret home. *Well, not quite as secret now.*

Still, I wanted to know. If the scent I thought had led him here truly had . . . I shivered, remembering the numbness sinking into my body as Akane's poison spread. A connection between the snake woman and a headless body would be valuable information and my father always said information put the bearer in a powerful bargaining position. Nathanial and I could use some bargaining power on our side.

Nathanial's lips thinned as his eyes swept over my face, but he nodded and stepped back. "Fine. Search out the scent."

Degan's gaze moved between Nathanial and me as he pushed himself away from the wall. I cringed as he stepped forward, and he paused, his weight shifting back, becoming more defensive.

I forced my muscles to relax, and he responded in kind. Backing up, I gave him a wide berth to pass me. He slipped almost silently out of the room. I tried to trail behind him, but Nathanial stopped me, motioned me behind him. Right. I needed my vampire meat shield. I rolled my eyes but didn't hesitate to let him in front of me.

Degan stood in the center of the hall, his body leaning forward, intent. He tipped his head back, his nose working. Then he took a few steps and repeated the exercise. I tried to catch the misplaced scent, but all I could smell was the old house, the dusty books sitting on the bookcases distributed at even points in the wide hall, and the prickly scent of Degan, a wolf-in-human-skin, pacing between the doors.

In front of a blank patch of wall, Degan stopped, pressing his nose to the paint. Moving again, he walked to the next door and stuck his head inside. After a moment, he doubled back and tried the door on the other side of the patch of wall which seemed to interest him. That door he slammed, stalking back to the wall. He ran his fingers along the dark paint, his features bunched in concentration.

His fists clenched, and heated energy bled through the room. *He's going to shift?* I found myself stumbling back a step, but Degan's skin didn't slip. Instead, the front of his face elongated, and his nose widened, becoming thicker, shinier.

I stared. He'd changed his nose into a wolf's nose. Just his nose. *Like I can change just my hands into claws.* I'd seen both my father and the *Torin* for one of the bear clans extend claws in human form, but I'd never before seen a shifter change their *nose* without going through a full shift.

Degan pressed his new, hyper-sensitive nose against the wall. He sniffed. Walked a step. Sniffed again.

"There is another room here." It wasn't a question, more like he was thinking aloud.

In front of me, Nathanial tensed.

I knew why. Somewhere along that wall would be a passage to the lightproof portion of the house. It wasn't exactly a public area. Considering I fell asleep just before dawn and didn't wake again until after full dark no matter what happened, I certainly wasn't thrilled with the idea that a potential enemy would know where I spent my most vulnerable hours.

Degan looked up, and Nathanial shrugged. "There are only three doors on this wall," the vampire said.

Degan huffed. "Three?" Then he drew in a surprised breath, and I bit my tongue to keep from showing my shock.

There were indeed three doors on the wall now. Nathanial had created an illusion. He must have. It was the only way to explain the door's sudden appearance. Illusion or not, as he walked over and twisted the knob on a door that wasn't there, I couldn't tell the difference.

The door opened to a dark hall I recognized from earlier. Degan scowled as he stepped through the threshold, but he didn't question it. I followed, and in the darkness, I caught the faint hint of dried, sour blood. My fingers tapped nervously against my thigh as I walked. I was sure I knew *exactly* what had drawn Degan here, but I needed him to confirm my theory.

Degan raced down the hall like a dog on a fresh trail. He threw open the bathroom door, and by the time Nathanial and I reached the room, he was already leaning over the tub where I'd woken. He pressed a finger to the base of the tub and lifted it to his nose.

Energy radiated off his skin, his wolf close enough to the surface that I could feel the nearness of his shift from across the room. He looked up, his dark eyes fixing on me.

"Who did you bleed here?" he asked, prickly wolf energy rolling off him.

Crap, he's going to shift. Completely, this time. And he'd only shift if he planned to attack.

My back hunched, the hair on my neck lifting in reaction to the buzz of pissed-off wolf in the room. I stumbled back, barely realizing I was backing up until I hit the wall. *Cornered.* A spasm shot through my hand. Blood ran between my fingers as my claws forced their way through my fingertips.

Degan's eyes moved to my hand, and his coat slid to the floor, his knees bending as he prepared to shift. *Crap.*

Nathanial flowed in front of me. Where Degan radiated his anger, his intent to do violence, Nathanial was the eye of the storm—still, calm, and about to destroy the clanless without mercy. I had to defuse this situation. Fast.

I waved my clawed hand. "Stop!"

Neither man looked at me.

"Mooncursed luck. Nobody died here, Degan."

He didn't seem to hear me. The pitch of energy turned up a notch. *Wolf.* Fear jumped up my throat. My feet urged me to run.

I didn't run.

My instincts told me Degan was one of the good guys. *I have to stop this fight.*

Nathanial continued to stand between Degan and me, deceptively still as he responded not only to Degan's threat, but to my fear of wolves. I swallowed. *I can't just cower.* I pushed away from the wall and looked around. *How am I supposed to convince Degan no one died when the room is filled with the scent of blood?*

Well there was one way.

I darted around Nathanial and jerked at the buttons on my shirt, but one arm hung useless at my side and my claws made it hard to operate the buttons. Degan's skin split over his back. I was out of time. With a frustrated growl, I ripped the shirt, rending both layers I wore. Pain tore over me as I jerked the fabric off my body. I swallowed back a curse and stepped around Nathanial.

"It's *my* blood." I dropped the shredded shirts to the floor, revealing the jagged suture marks running the length of my arm. "My blood."

Degan's human bones were already reshaping into a wolf's form, his muscles making wet sounds as his joints popped. *He's too far gone.* His eyes were clear, though. He watched me, and I saw the alarm in the still mostly human-shaped face. Then his skin sealed back around his body.

His human skin.

I blinked in surprise. I wouldn't have been able to reverse a shift that advanced. He was powerful, a lot more powerful than I would have guessed. But lethal energy still rolled off him, enough energy that he could have shifted again. Immediately, if needed. I gulped, feeling very vulnerable, standing half-naked and injured in front of this fallen *Torin.*

My instincts better be right.

Degan stalked across the room, his nose flaring as he moved into my personal space. Nathanial was suddenly there, between us. He threw only one punch, and the clanless shifter crashed into the wall. The thud shook the room, but Degan rolled to his feet. Stood. I wrapped a hand around Nathanial's bicep before he could move forward to continue the attack.

"Don't. He wasn't going to hurt me." Or at least, I didn't think he'd planned to.

Degan rolled his shoulders back, but while his stance was defensive, he ducked his head. It was an apologetic, almost submissive gesture. "I should have announced my intentions. I wish only to analyze your mate's scent," he said, nodding at Nathanial.

"He's not—" My teeth snapped shut before I finished the sentence. In Firth, a male shifter would never touch a mated female without her mate's permission. Nathanial and I had shared blood, which had mingled our scents. My cheeks burned. With our merged scent—mating was a logical assumption. Denying it would damage my credibility. *Besides, after what almost happened in this room . . .* I didn't finish that thought. Dropping my gaze to the floor, I muttered, "It's complicated. Nathanial?"

He was staring at me again, as if he was trying to figure out my thoughts but couldn't follow them. I didn't have a great track record for good decisions. I could only hope I was making one now. If my poison-tainted blood was what had drawn Degan here, there were only two explanations as to how I could have picked up the scent of the murder victim. One was when I shared blood with Tatius. The other was Akane's venom. I was betting on the latter. If we knew who killed the Collector's vampire, we'd have one very powerful bargaining chip.

Slowly Nathanial nodded, but his eyes revealed how unhappy he was with the situation. He unbuttoned his shirt and slid out of it before holding it out to me. I accepted his help into the shirt, which hung halfway to my knees, and let him button it for me. I guessed Degan didn't give a damn about the fact I'd been nearly nude—most shifters didn't, but covering myself seemed to make Nathanial feel better, so I did.

Once Nathanial stepped back, Degan approached slowly, as if giving the vampire time to protest. It was a very polite action, very much something I'd expect of a well-bred shifter—not one I anticipated from a shifter severed from his clan, branded criminal and untrustworthy. Of course, maybe he was just trying to save his own skin.

He didn't touch me when he crossed into my space, he simply leaned down, his nose within an inch of my skin. Air moved through my hair and across my throat as he inhaled. A shiver threatened to tremble up my spine. Part fear, as the scent of wolf enveloped me. Part not-fear, as his breath touched my throat. *Geez, a couple vampire bites and Tatius has already programmed a response into me.* The thought pissed me off, but there was no denying the truth.

Degan stepped back, his features drawn in as much confused skepticism as when Nathanial had made an empty wall turn into a door. "Your blood is in that tub, but your confusing, convoluted scent isn't the only one. And you have no hint of the tainted smell I'm tracking."

That last bit was actually relieving. *Biana drew out all the poison. Good to know.* But, as Degan backed away, his confusion became the prickly heat of his wolf. He was confused, and until he figured it out, we were enemies. I could see his reasoning, could even understand it.

"I was poisoned. By . . . " I wasn't sure how to explain Akane. "A foreign snake shifter. The blood is from drawing out the poison."

"A snake?" He tilted his head back, his nostrils flaring.

He breathed in again, and his beast subsided, his energy sliding back under his skin. I nearly sighed with relief. He believed me. I mean, it was true—mostly—but I hadn't been sure he'd believe me.

A smile cracked across his face again as he shook his head. "Nothing's been sane since you came to my city." Then, scooping his battered coat from the tile, he shrugged it on and headed for the door. "Come on. I'll take you to the corpse I found."

Chapter Sixteen

Wind tickled my face as Nathanial carried me soundlessly through the air. We trailed the clanless from just above streetlight level, wrapped in the tightest illusion Nathanial could command. Being on the street increased the danger of being caught, but Tatius was the only Haven vampire strong enough to break Nathanial's illusion. With any luck, he was still preoccupied with the Collector. But he might not be. He might be out searching. It was a chance we had to take. Nathanial agreed with me, knowing more about the decapitated body could help us.

So far, there was a human body with a missing head, and a vampire head with a missing body. We were either about to see the enforcer's body, or there had been another murder.

The towering buildings rushed by on either side of us and made the flight more nerve racking than normal—or maybe that was because I could only cling to Nathanial with one arm. Nathanial had fashioned a makeshift brace for my butchered arm and buttoned a borrowed coat over me. The nervousness could also have something to do with being wrapped in the warm circle of Nathanial's arms again, but Nathanial was completely focused on his illusion and on trailing Degan.

If his thumb didn't occasionally trace a line along my spine, I'd have thought he'd forgotten I was even pressed up against him. There was no hint of the heat that had been between us earlier. I hated the twinge of disappointment I felt at that fact.

Nathanial's secret home was close to Sydney Park, but Degan's path led us to a busier, more nightlife-oriented area of town. I tensed as we flew past Death's Angel, but no legion of vampires burst through the door determined to drag us back. Soon its black lights faded behind us. We were only three streets from the club when Degan ducked into an alley and stopped.

The clanless shifter hadn't looked behind him for the entire trip—Nathanial had told him he wouldn't be able to see us following—but now his gaze roved the street, trying to find us.

Nathanial landed behind Degan. Snow crunched under my bare

feet as Nathanial lowered me to the ground, and Degan spun around, energy leaking into the night. His eyes narrowed, but he only nodded in greeting, not voicing the agitation I could feel swirling around him. I didn't hold it against him—predators get cranky when you startle them.

"This way," he said, moving beside the boarded windows of a closed nightclub.

A hint of acrid smoke clung to the building, offering a clue as to why it looked condemned, while the rest of the area hosted a thriving nightlife. Degan shoved his fingers under a large piece of plywood and pulled it aside easily. Too easy, even for someone with a shifter's strength. *Clearly this has been used before.* The question was whether Degan had made the makeshift entrance or if he'd just stumbled over it. He disappeared into the dark opening, and I moved to follow, but Nathanial held up a hand, stalling me.

"In case this is a trick," he whispered. Then slipped around the crooked slab of wood.

I gave Nathanial a five-second head start—it had taken him mere seconds to subdue Degan earlier—then I pulled the wood aside with my good hand and slid inside.

The hint of smoke had merely tainted the alley, but inside the damaged building it threatened to overwhelm my senses. I wrinkled my nose.

Come on. Sift past the fire stink.

I drew another breath. Under the acrid smell of burnt wood I caught dried blood and the sour scent of something foreign. A foreign scent that did smell a hell of a lot like the blood Biana had drained from me.

My vampire eyes adjusted immediately to the inky darkness of the inside of the club, but besides Degan and Nathanial, there wasn't much to see. Charred wood, barely recognizable as tables and chairs, littered the large room. A darkened, hulking mass took up half the space, and I guessed it had been a bar at one time. Support beams, fallen from the floor above, broke the space as if a designer had decided to decorate with a post-apocalyptic theme. A few bottom steps remained from a wooden staircase, but the fire had consumed the rest.

I walked to the center of the room and turned a full circle. "No body." No blood pool either.

Degan pointed up, and I glanced at the dark, half-fallen ceiling. *Okay. Second floor.* But the stairs were burned to a crisp. Nathanial could fly us up, but unless Degan had climbed up via one of the fallen support beams, I didn't see how he'd found the body in the first place.

The clanless stayed by the entrance, watching me. *What, am I supposed to figure it out myself?* I glanced at Nathanial. He looked up, and then he was in the air. Degan started, his hand reaching for something in his pocket. He stared at Nathanial, who hung in midair between the two floors. Degan had known, in theory, that Nathanial could fly, but accepting something as possible and seeing the proof were very different things. I felt for him; we were throwing a lot at him, and all and all, he was taking it well.

"The body is up there," Nathanial said, landing beside me. He reached out, like he would pick me up.

I stepped back. "I'll find my own way." After all, if Degan could do it, so could I. Besides, unless the victim—or possibly the killer—could fly, they had to have found an alternate route upstairs as well.

I traced my steps back to the boarded window and knelt. Charred bits of wood and ash covered the floor, clearly marking the outline of footprints. Lots of footprints. The boxy, dress-shoe prints were Nathanial's and stopped right inside the entrance. The barefoot tracks were mine. There were also three sneaker impressions—one that left zigzagged impressions in the ash, one with diamond-shaped impressions, and one that was missing large sections of the impression, like the sneakers were worn. Occasionally I caught sight of another track, this one smaller, with a pointed-toe, but the person with the diamond-treaded sneakers had walked through those smaller prints, obscuring them.

Two of the sneaker impressions, and the small, pointed-toe impression, all walked a direct path like they knew where they were going. The person leaving the zigzagged sneaker marks had wandered the room, the tracks crossing themselves at times. I glanced at Degan.

"Let me see the sole of your shoes."

He frowned, but lifted his feet. His shoes were old, the rubber missing from the sole in some places. *So he's the worn impression.* He'd followed the direct route. I traced his steps.

The prints lead into a tiny alcove I hadn't noticed earlier. A cast-iron spiral staircase hugged the corner, hidden from view if you weren't standing in the alcove. *Well, that answers the 'how to get upstairs' question.*

I glanced back at Degan. "You walked straight to this stairwell. How did you know it was here?"

"Same way you did. Tracks."

Fair enough. We'd both been raised in Firth, and, at least in my clan, tracking was taught as soon as we could crawl. I doubted whichever clan Degan had been thrust out of had been much different.

I took the stairs one at the time, using my good hand to support me. Nathanial glided up through the wreckage, settling somewhere in the darkness of the second floor. Once I reached the floor myself, it was easy to spot him. He wasn't far from me, and neither was the nude body from the photo.

Nathanial knelt over the headless corpse—the second one in as many days. It was face down, that is, if it had still had a face. He lifted the man's hand, examining it briefly before lowering it back in the dried blood surrounding the body. Degan followed me up the stairs but stood off to one side, watching silently. The floor felt precarious under me, the fire-weakened wood threatening to crumble under our steps, but it had held the vampire and his killer, surely it would hold us.

Nathanial stood as I approached. "What do you smell?"

I tilted my head back. The scent of rotting blood was stronger on this floor, but it couldn't contend with the scent of smoke that coated the back of my throat. Under that, though, was another scent. Something sour and *wrong*.

I knelt beside the body, leaning close, and drew in a slow breath. "Degan's right. The blood Biana drained from me and this body both smell tainted."

Degan shook his head. He pulled a handkerchief from his pocket. The same handkerchief he'd used to collect a scent sample of my blood from the bathtub. He sniffed it. Then he knelt by the blood pool and compared the scents. "Not completely the same." He held out the stained cloth to me.

I took it, obediently inhaling the scent. I smelled oiled metal, which reminded me instantly of Tatius and was probably part of the base scent I'd temporarily adopted from him; a trace of lavender clung to the back of my tongue—which was likely part of whomever Tatius had fed from. Another jumble of scents rolled through my senses, some of which were part of my own base scent. Over it all hung a sour, musky scent thick enough to swallow. The smell made my tongue curl in disgust, but Degan was right. The scents were similar, but there was something slightly different about the blood drying around the body. Something extra, something more bitter than the scent in my blood.

I related all of this, and Nathanial nodded before returning to his perusal of the body. After parting the man's thighs and examining the insides of his legs, he flipped him. Nathanial was strong enough to roll the large man, but it was still an awkward amount of weight. One of the corpse's hands flopped to the side, falling against the floor with a sick plop.

"What are you looking for?" I asked as Nathanial continued his search along the front of the man's body.

"He has no marks on him. No fang punctures, no cuts, no indication he struggled with his attacker at all." Nathanial waved at the man's hands.

The corpse's nails were long for a male, but they were all unbroken and clean—no skin or blood under them that I could see. We couldn't be certain about the wounds to the head that had been delivered to the Collector, but we had the rest of the body. A body with absolutely no defensive wounds.

I stood and walked a small circle around the body. "So, what, he just stood there and let someone cut off his head?"

"His heart wasn't beating when his head was removed," Degan said, sidling closer.

"How do you know?"

"You've hunted wild game," he said, crossing his thick arms over his chest. "What happens when you cut a major artery?"

I frowned. "It sprays blood." I glanced at the blackened but low ceiling over us, then at the floor around the body.

There was no spray—just the pool around the body, which had clearly flowed out of the neck. The blood pool wasn't large enough to have covered all evidence of arterial spray during a beheading.

Degan was right. The vamp's heart hadn't been beating.

"Could he have been sleeping at the time he was killed?" I asked, looking at Nathanial. Vampires fell into a type of stasis during the day. The saying 'dead to the world' was a pretty good one. No movement, no consciousness, and very little in the way of a pulse. If the vamp's heart had slowed enough, there might not have been enough pressure to cause a spray.

Nathanial shook his head and pointed to the wall. "The windows are not boarded on this level. During the day, sunlight will stream inside."

"He could have been brought here. In a coffin maybe? If he was brought before full dark but while he still slept?"

Again Nathanial shook his head. "I know of this vampire. He was a master soldier. He was old enough and powerful enough to have woken long before dusk." He bent over the body again. "Look at this."

I moved to his side, but didn't see what had interested him. He pointed to a spot just below the corpse's hip, and I leaned closer.

Nathanial pointed to a small hole, not much bigger than a large pore. But vampires don't have pores. "A needle mark?"

Nathanial said nothing as he leaned closer to the wound. I pushed to my feet. "You searched this place, did you find anything?" I asked, looking at Degan.

He pointed to a spot in the corner. "His clothes."

I walked over and stared at the small stack of clothing. A stack of *folded* clothing. Complete with a pair of size-eleven sneakers on the bottom. *What is the likelihood the killer undressed him after beheading him, then proceeded to fold the clothes and leave them in the corner?* I grabbed the tee-shirt on the top of the stack and shook it out.

No blood. Not even a drop.

Well, if the vamp's heart had stopped, there was a chance the killer had taken the time to undress him before lopping off his head. I glanced back at the vamp and picked up the sneakers. The sole was made up of a diamond pattern. *Just like the prints downstairs, the ones that went straight to the stairs.*

I walked back to the dead vamp and glanced at the soles of his feet. Smudges of burnt wood and ash covered the pads. He'd walked barefoot, and quite possibly undressed himself. *What the hell had he been doing here?* I thought back to the prints downstairs, of the mostly obscured, small, pointed-shoe impressions.

Small enough to be a woman's.

"Okay," I said, looking between the dead vamp and the stack of clothes in the corner. "So this vamp and likely a woman came here. One of them knew how to find the stairs. They came up to the second floor and he, at the very least, undressed. Was this a romantic encounter gone wrong?" I frowned at the neat stack of clothing. "But he took time to fold his clothes? Not a lot of heat in that. I mean, Nathanial you and—" I cut off, heat rushing to my face. *You and I nearly shredded each other's clothing earlier,* was what I nearly said, and the knowing look Nathanial gave me made my blush burn hotter.

As the silence made it clear I wasn't going to continue, Degan said, "So, then we need to know if the woman is the killer or if she's another victim."

None of us had an answer for that. I turned to Nathanial. "Now what?"

"Now I get you home before dawn." He strolled across the crisp boards and wrapped his arms around my waist.

Degan frowned at us. "I suppose that leaves me to get rid of the body."

"Leave it," Nathanial said as our feet left the scorched boards. "Dawn will destroy the remains."

∾ • ∿

"What do we do now?" I asked as I trudged into the living room of Nathanial's secret house.

"I need to consider our options," he said, which pretty much meant he wasn't sure if he would take the information we'd found to Tatius or not. Or maybe it meant we hadn't learned enough.

I sank onto the large green couch. As far as I was concerned, the presence of snake venom in the victim's blood was a damning fact, but vampires couldn't smell it, which complicated things. My chin touched my chest and my eyelids fluttered as I fought dawn and sleep.

Nathanial's scent filled my world as he scooped me off the couch. "Best not to sleep in a room with windows," he whispered, his lips pressing against my hair. Even this close to dawn, the sensation sent a tingle of electricity across my skin.

"Will it be safe to go to Tatius?" I asked, struggling to keep my eyes open. "What if he acts first and asks questions later?"

"I do not think Tatius will hurt me."

I frowned. My brain was turning sluggish, but he made it sound like Tatius wouldn't hurt him, in particular. "Why? Because you are on the council now?" That hadn't seemed like much protection when Tatius had tried to pin him to a door.

"No," Nathanial whispered as my eyes drifted closed. His lips trailed down my forehead, over the tip of my nose until his breath brushed my mouth. "No. He will listen because I am his brother."

Chapter Seventeen

I woke to the sensation of tongues of fire crawling under my skin. Jumping from the bed, I flung myself to the floor, swatting at my arms.

There was no fire. The room was quiet, empty.

I looked down. My arms were both whole, healed and unharmed. The creepy sensation didn't dissipate. In fact, it grew worse, as if something too warm for comfort had slithered into my body.

What the hell? I stripped off Nathanial's shirt and rubbed my hands over my bare arms, thighs, stomach. The feeling of flames licking my flesh only increased. It was more of an irritation than a pain, a prickle of *wrongness*.

The poison? I hadn't felt this way when I fell asleep.

All but running to the bathroom, I turned the shower on full blast and stepped under the jets of water. It didn't help. I couldn't stand still long enough to wash my hair.

I climbed out of the shower without turning off the water and left a wet trail behind as I stalked back to the bedroom. I raided Nathanial's dresser and stole another undershirt. Then I grabbed the coat I'd worn the night before and tugged it over the thin shirt. The coat's hem clung to my ankles as I left the light-safe portion of the house.

I searched each room I came across, but Nathanial wasn't in any of them. *Did he decide to see Tatius? Without me?* I paced around the living room couch, rubbing my arms through the thick coat. The tiny tongues of fire creeping under my skin sped up, prickling, pinching.

I paced faster. Moving helped.

I have to get out of here.

The thought barely had time to register before I found myself springing down the front steps, the door slamming behind me. I walked barefoot in the darkness, through the snow, across the yard, through the gate, and onto the icy sidewalk. I didn't pause to consider which direction to walk. The moving mattered, not the destination.

As I walked, the burning dulled, and then faded until it was only a minor annoyance. I turned down another street and stopped.

What the hell am I doing? Trying to get caught? I turned, starting back the way I'd come. The licks of flames along my skin rushed back with a vengeance. More than irritation. More than pain. It struck with agony.

I gasped and dropped to my knees.

"Stars above, what the hell is it?" I whispered, blinking at the snow under my nose.

Pushing to my feet, I hobbled forward, my vision red with pain. I didn't pay attention to where I walked. I didn't care. I shouldered through a wooden gate, and the pain fell away.

I almost collapsed from the sudden relief. *But where am I?* I looked around. Under the blanket of snow I could just make out the enormous shape of a slide.

A playground?

My footprints left a lonely trail through the snow as I walked toward a play fort shaped like a miniature pirate ship. A set of snow covered swings hung beside the monkey-bars; apparently the kids didn't play here during the winter. The first swing hung loose on one chain, but I knocked the snow off the other and sat.

Something slammed into my back, catapulting me out of the swing. *What the*— I landed on my feet and twisted, my hands balling into fists. A bundled figure stood just behind the swing, his arms still extended from where he'd shoved me. I dropped my weight onto my back leg, lifting my fists as the figure knocked the swing aside.

"Hey, babe, don't get all defensive. I didn't mean to send you into the snow. Just thought you needed a push."

I recognized that voice. "Avin?"

"In the flesh."

"What are you doing here?" Of all places and people, why would I run into a necromancer in a playground?

"Waiting on you, babe. You sure took your sweet time answering my call."

Call? When I blinked at him, he held up a gloved hand. Opening it, he showed me a marble sized globe floating above his palm. A small crimson dot hung suspended in the globe's core. I might not have known much about magic, but I knew blood when I saw it. I reached forward, and Avin snapped his fist shut.

"I've come to collect my favor."

"Already?"

"Well, I had planned to hold out for something special, but I had a bad day." He pushed back his hood.

I could only stare.

His red hair was gone, and without it, his head looked misshapen. Actually, maybe it *was* misshapen. If he'd told me someone had given him a makeover with a hammer, I wouldn't have been surprised. Cuts decorated his face, several gaping wide enough to reveal bone. His lopsided jaw hung slack. He shot me a feeble smile. Most of his teeth were missing.

"A regular monsterpiece, aren't I?" He chuckled and lifted a hand to his face. "Compliments of some street thugs. I tell you, babe, this world got a lot more dangerous since the last time I was awake."

It took effort to wrench my gaze from his mutilated features. I stared at a spot over his left shoulder. "Can . . ." I cleared my throat. "Can you heal that?"

"Nah, this body's dead. I can possess it and preserve it, but I can't heal it. That's where the favor you owe me comes in."

I cringed, already not liking the direction of this conversation. Avin didn't notice.

"I need a new body. You're going to get me one."

He has to be kidding. The destroyed features betrayed no jest. *Mooncursed. That's what I am. Totally mooncursed.*

I sank into the swing and shook my head. "So what, you want me to dig up a corpse for you? Sneak into a morgue?"

"I just came from a morgue and have no intention of visiting one again anytime soon. I swear, a guy can't even rest in this world without people assuming he's a murder victim. I'm sure I livened up the crime lab's life though. They couldn't figure out how I died, but were even more puzzled as to why someone did this," he pointed to his face, "post-mortem. I'm sure they must be losing their minds now that my 'corpse' is missing." He shot me a disturbing, toothless smile again. "But I'm way off topic. I want a *fresh* corpse to *quicken*. No one dead long enough to make it to the morgue. Would *you* want to live in a body that's already started decaying? Also, embalming is a disgusting habit, knocks out half my senses."

"Okay, so I have to snatch a dead body before it makes it to the embalming table."

He wrinkled his crooked nose. "Bodies begin decaying fast, and the ritual needed to jump from one host body to another is long. It can't be so random as snatching a chance body. I need to be ready and waiting as they die."

"No." He was suggesting I kill someone for him. I wasn't doing it.

"We agreed on nothing life-threatening."

"Yeah, see, you have to be careful with your word choice, babe. 'Life-threatening' means dangerous for you, and draining a human isn't. So, run off on your 'errand' now."

"No."

"Really? You can't renege on your bargain. You owe me a favor. I'm cashing in on it." He held out his hand and opened his fist to show me the bauble again. A flash like lightning ran through the globe. The fiery pain crashed into me again. It turned the world white. Knocked me out of the swing.

I smothered the scream clawing up my throat. When the last tremor of pain finally subsided, I was on my knees, the coat hanging open around me.

"Nice legs, babe. I forgot you undead can't feel the cold."

I glared at him as I pulled the coat closed and picked myself up off the ground. His lopsided smile wasn't frightening anymore—it was inviting me to help further rearrange his face. I balled my hand into a fist. Jerked my arm back.

The blow didn't have time to land.

Avin's eyes flicked to my fist, and lightning flashed through the globe again. The torrent of pain slammed into me. Fire roared over my skin, ignited my insides, melted my knees.

"Now be nice," he said, smiling as my legs buckled. "I might have forgotten to mention it, but vampires are close enough to death to be affected by necromancers, especially when a necromancer has collected a sample of said vampire's blood." He shook the bauble, and the world spun.

Blood?

The knife.

That damn ceremony. He must have taken my blood from the blade after the ritual. *And Bryant's answers were useless.*

None of that mattered now. I couldn't change the past. Right now, all that mattered was that damned globe and the fact Avin wanted me to kill someone for him.

"You're a big powerful mage, why don't you collect your own body?"

"My specialty is with things already dead." He shrugged and closed his fist over the globe. "If *I* kill my new host, he'll show signs of violence. That makes blending in with humans hard. But you vampires, you create beautiful corpses. You drain the blood, seal the wound, and my new host dies in perfect condition."

"You've done this before."

"Of course. How did you think I acquired this beautiful body?"

I stared at him.

"Well, it *was* beautiful," he said with a grimace. "That's a requirement, you know. I want a good-looking body. Young. Attractive. No one famous, though. I don't need to be hiding from wardens and the paparazzi."

One night I was going to wake up and things would make sense. Be normal. Tonight sure as hell wasn't that night. I pressed my palms over my eyes, willing Avin to be gone when I looked up.

He wasn't. *Of course.* He continued casually describing the type of person he wanted me to pull off the street and slaughter.

"You listening, babe?" He stepped closer, his uneven shoulders looming over me. "I'm in kind of a hurry, so I want to make sure you know what you're looking for. Oh. I almost forgot. You'll need this." He held out a small ring that glimmered in the pale moonlight.

I didn't reach for it. "That's silver."

"What's with you and telling me what metal my stuff is made from? Take the damn thing. It's not like it's an engagement ring. You wear it, you call my name when you find a suitable body, and I'll show up and prepare the ritual before you make the kill. Easy as that." He pushed the ring toward me.

Reluctantly, I held out my hand. Pain shot through my flesh as he dropped it in my palm. Numbness spread through my fingers, up my arm. *Perfect.* I shoved the ring in my pocket. *How do I get myself into these things?*

"Tomorrow night, midnight, should be a sufficient amount of time for you to locate an appropriate body, don't you think?" he asked, and my jaw dropped.

"Tomorrow?" I cast around for some way to stall. "I can't—"

I didn't get a chance to finish. Avin lifted the globe. Light flashed through it and unseen flames attacked me.

"You promised me an unnamed favor, babe. I get to set the rules. Attractive body. Tomorrow. By midnight. Call me if you finish early. Don't tell a living, or unliving, soul." He pulled up his hood, stepping closer, filling my personal space. "And remember—"

Movement blurred in front of me, and I never found out what I was supposed to remember. Nathanial appeared between Avin and me. I caught a glimpse of his coat, his shoulders, but he flowed into motion again before gravity caught up with his dark hair. He moved fast, faster than I could follow, and Avin slid through the snow.

The mage didn't waste time getting to his feet, didn't try to fight the angry master vampire. He just looked at me and said, "Tomorrow, babe."

Then he vanished.

Chapter Eighteen

The chill of magic pressed against my skin even after Avin disappeared, and I stared at my bare feet as Nathanial turned.

"I can explain," I muttered. But I couldn't. Not completely. Not why I'd left the house. Not who Avin was. *"Don't tell a living or unliving soul,"* he'd said. And I'd felt the twinge of magic that made it stick. *How did I mess things up this badly?*

I'd struck a deal with a bad guy. That's what I'd done. *And he wants me to kill someone.* Someone who likely didn't deserve to die.

Not that I hadn't killed before.

I'd fought and killed two rogues only weeks ago. But they'd been insane. Murderers. In the end, it had come down to more than my responsibility as the one who tagged Tyler, more than preventing any more women from dying, more than self preservation—Nathanial and Bobby's lives had been on the line, too. This was different. Hugging my arms across my chest, I sank into the snow.

Nathanial was suddenly there, filling my senses. His arms wrapped around my waist and pulled me against his chest. His familiar spicy scent encircled me.

"What happened?" he whispered.

No accusation. No demand. The question was calm, his voice offering comfort as his warm arms buffered me from the world.

Comfort I didn't deserve. After all, I'd gotten myself in this mess. Drinking down one last lungful of his scent, I stepped out of the protective circle of his arms. I dug the ring out of my pocket and stared at it as it burned into my palm. Welts formed around the gleaming silver edges.

I won't do it. I won't kill for Avin. Consequences be damned.

I hurled the ring, using all the supernatural strength I'd gained from becoming a vampire. The ring flew, twinkling like a star in the night. I didn't watch where it landed, but turned to Nathanial.

"How did it go with Tatius?" I tried to keep my tone even, to not betray how much I wanted to know the answer. I failed.

Nathanial shook his head. "I left unexpectedly, so we did not conclude our negotiations. Kita, do not change the subject. Who was that man? A mage, I am assuming."

Again, no accusation, but the questions were more demanding. What went unsaid was that the unexpected interruption of his negotiations had been me. He must have felt my fear through the bond. I doubted Tatius approved of the sudden recess.

Hanging my head, I studied the trampled snow beneath my feet. Pain shot through my hand. *What the—*

The silver ring rested snugly around my pointer finger.

I stared at it a full heartbeat before ripping the damn thing off, ready to toss it again. Further this time, if I could. Then I lowered my hand. *No use.* Avin must have ensured I couldn't lose the damn thing. Gritting my teeth, I dropped the mooncursed loop of silver back into my pocket.

"So now what do we—" I cut off as the gate creaked behind me.

I whirled around as Nathanial stepped between me and the sound. The gate swung on its hinges, but no one was there. The gateway stood empty.

I tilted my head back, breathing deep and searching the wind. Nothing. Just normal city scents. And the only nearby sounds were the creaking gate hinge and a swing swaying in the breeze. Nothing else moved.

"Perhaps we should move somewhere less open," Nathanial said as he turned toward me. He sounded relaxed, but he took to the air as soon as his arms slipped around my waist.

We were a couple yards over the snow when I caught sight of movement. Not on the ground below. No. Above.

A star winked out, blocked by a dark body.

"Nathanial there's—" Something heavy and metallic fell over us, cutting me off.

Chains?

A chain net.

Nathanial picked up speed, ignoring the heavy net clattering around us. I untangled an arm from behind his head and struggled with the chains. Each link was as thick as my wrist. I was strong, but I had no leverage in the air. My effort to heave the net off us only tangled me further.

The vampire who'd dropped the net dove toward us. He grabbed a corner of the net and was joined by three more vampires, each taking one corner. Gravity played for their side, weighing us down.

Our ascent slowed.

Stopped.

I couldn't move, couldn't even struggle. Nathanial fought to lift the chains, to defy gravity.

He didn't win.

We hit the ground with a thud. My knees buckled under the impact, but though grounded, Nathanial didn't stay down. He rose in the air as far as the net would allow, staring at our captors, his calm face a contrast to the tension I felt running through his muscles.

The four vampires flashed their fangs and staked down the corners of the net.

One of the vamps pulled a cell phone from his pocket and pressed a button. "We've got them," he said to the male voice that answered on the other side.

"Do you?" Nathanial arched an eyebrow and stared down at the vampire on the phone.

We were inside a damn chain net, but the vampire took a step back, his adam's apple bobbing in his throat as he swallowed. But all he said was, "I'll send the coordinates now." He pulled the phone from his ear, his fingers skimming over the flat screen.

Outside the gate, a car rumbled around the corner. Slowed. Stopped. Gravel crunched under the tires of a second car. The sound of two engines idling rolled through the park.

Four men and two women dashed around the wooden gate. Scratch that. Six vampires.

They joined the four vamps around the net. Ten against two? *And we're as trapped as a fox in a snare*—only we couldn't chew off a leg for freedom.

One of the female vamps stepped forward, her gaze locked on Nathanial's face. "You will come with us peacefully, yes?"

Nathanial said nothing, his expression never changing.

"We are going to release you now," she said, waving a hand at her companions.

The four original vamps pulled crowbars out of stars knew where and pried the stakes free. I forced my body still and focused on keeping my fists from clenching as they hauled up the edges of the chain.

The net reached the level of my knees. I dropped, rolling under the edge of the chain in one movement and springing to my feet in the next.

Not that I made it far.

The Collector's beefy bodyguard grabbed my arm, pulling my stride short.

"Lookie what I caught . . . a collectable," he said, his tongue darting out to wet thick lips.

"Doesn't look like much to me, Ronco," Jomar, the rat faced guard who'd fed on Luna, said.

Oh no, I wasn't caught that easily. If there was one thing I'd learned being the smallest shifter, it was that sometimes being big wasn't an advantage. I twisted, pulling against Ronco's oversized meat hooks. At the same time, I slammed my knee into his groin. He made an *oolf* and I wiggled free of his grip.

I ducked, but his fist snagged my coat, dragging me back.

Dammit!

I shrugged free of the coat and ran. Nathanial had escaped the net, too. I had to reach him. But a group of vamps circled Nathanial. One vamp, braver—or stupider—than the rest, broke the formation. He charged forward, his arm already cocked for a punch.

The blow never landed.

Nathanial was in front of the vamp one moment and behind him the next. The vamp had no time to turn. Nathanial tilted, unleashing a strong and fast kick from the hip. The vamp flew forward, the sound of his spine snapping following in his wake. His body slammed into another vamp and they both crashed to the ground.

It happened fast, faster than two of my running strides. Then Nathanial straightened. His eyes found me. I was almost to him. *We'll make it out of this.*

Jomar was only a step behind me. I pressed my legs for more speed. If I was good at anything, I was good at running.

But Jomar caught up.

He dove into my path. I lashed out, and he caught my wrist. He twisted my arm, jerking it behind me as he kicked my knees out from under me. I went down, hard. Snow crunched under my bare knees. My shoulder screamed as Jomar jerked my arm higher.

"Stand down, Hermit, or I start breaking your companion's bones," he threatened.

Nathanial froze. He lifted his hands, palms up. Surrender.

"No," I yelled, then yelped as Jomar jerked again. Pain tore at my shoulder and arm.

"Kita, be still," Nathanial said, his eyes begging me to cooperate. I gritted my teeth. I wasn't about to make that promise.

Near the gate, a delicate throat cleared. The china doll, Elizabeth, stood just inside the park, her little ballet slippers soaking up snow.

"Please join us in the car," she said. Then she turned and disappeared beyond the gate.

Jomar hauled me to my feet and shoved me forward, almost sending me to my knees again. Only his grip on my arm kept me standing, and that came with the price of a new wave of pain rushing down my shoulder. But as I stumbled forward, a new pain surged through me, this one a stinging numbness originating in my finger. Avin's ring. I'd left it with the coat, the spell must have triggered when I got too far away. I didn't have time to worry about it right now.

Digging my heels into the frozen ground, I gritted my teeth against the pain in my arm and refused to be budged. Jomar growled and the vamps surrounding Nathanial looked at him.

"We will go. Willingly." Nathanial looked at me with the last word. "Bring her coat."

Ronco, my coat still wrapped in his fist, stepped forward and tossed the coat haphazardly over the front of my shoulders. Nathanial nodded and placidly followed his captors.

Well, it looked like I didn't have any choice but to go along with this. Without a word, I clung to my coat and let Jomar march me across the snow.

Nathanial slipped inside a dark limo as I rounded the gate. Jomar pushed me in after him, intentionally knocking my head against the car as he shoved me though the door. He dumped me in the seat beside Nathanial, directly across from the Collector. Elizabeth sat beside the Collector, the conjoined twins catty-corner beside her. The Traveler was nowhere in sight.

As Jomar slid into the seat beside me, the Collector waved her hand in a shooing motion. "Thank you, Jomar. That will be all."

Jomar's grip on my arm tightened. "She's a lively one, Mistress. Shouldn't I—"

"I dismissed you."

He bowed as well as he could while already crouched in a car. Then he dropped my arm. My shoulder ached with relief, and I pulled my arm around me, hugging it to my chest. Pain radiated down my hand as feeling rushed back. The skin on my ring finger was red and swollen around Avin's silver ring. I ripped the ring off and dropped it in the coat pocket as the beefier guard leaned down, sticking his head in the open door. He didn't ask anything, just looked at the Collector. She gave him a sharp nod, and he squeezed his bulk onto the seat beside me. Outside the car, Jomar's squinty eyes glared.

Someone's fallen out of favor.

Jomar slammed the door, and the car engine roared to life. My already tense muscles locked in response. I *hated* cars. Nathanial slid closer, his hand reaching for mine as the car jutted forward.

Seat belt, seat belt. Where is that damn—

I caught sight of the canvas strap sticking out from under the bulky guard beside me. I jerked at the belt, and the large vampire blinked at me in surprise. When I tugged harder, he shifted his legs until the belt slid free. The car took a turn and I yelped, every muscle in my body locking tighter, making my sore shoulder throb. My hands shook as I grabbed the metallic end of the belt, and I fumbled with the buckle until Nathanial took it away and snapped it for me.

"I apologize if my men were rough. They tend to get carried away," the Collector said as the city blocks slid by the window. "But, no matter how little your companion was wearing, them stripping her was most uncalled for. I shall have words with them."

My face burned at her double-edged apology. The coat had fallen to the floorboards as I fought with the seat belt, and I was showing a lot of thigh under the thin white under shirt—a whole lot of thigh. But it wasn't like I was *naked*. Nathanial leaned down, scooping my coat from the floorboard. He handed it to me, and I hesitated a moment before draping it over my lap.

Hesitated because I was trying to decide if I should acknowledge the Collector's jibe by covering myself. After all, what she hadn't apologized for was pulling us off the street. *Which she sure as hell had no right to do. What do I care how about her opinion of how I'm dressed?* In the end I relented only because I knew Nathanial was the one navigating these political waters, and I didn't want to make things any harder on him.

As I smoothed the coat over my lap, Nathanial's fingers slipped around mine. He squeezed lightly, which I interpreted as a silent 'thank you'. I sank lower in my seat. Surely I wasn't so difficult that such a little thing got a thanks. Was I?

"You have gone through a lot of trouble for this conversation," Nathanial said, not acknowledging the lackluster quality of the Collector's apology. "Tatius was informed you had already left Haven."

"Clearly he was misinformed. Have you considered my offer?" Her eyes bled to black as she watched him. "Tell me your thoughts,

Hermit," she paused, "or Illusionist, as you should be called."

"I am fine with my title." Nathanial's voice held no emotion, but his hand tightened around mine. "You should be informed that Kita, my companion, lost the ability to do the things the Traveler's companion saw. Those abilities did not survive her turn. She can no longer shift."

Glassy black eyes studied him, probably seeking a lie, and the ice queen demeanor the Collector had displayed in Tatius's court surfaced in her features. Her hands folded in her lap, her fingers forming a steeple before her chest.

"Akane had a twin sister. I commanded one of my servants to turn her. The conditions were perfect, but she died during the turn in an agony I have never seen matched. These others," she made a vague hand gesture to include me, "are perhaps resilient to turning. More so than humans. Still, abilities surviving or not, your companion interests me."

Nathanial said nothing. The sound of the tires on the pavement and the low rumble of the engine filled the car in the absence of conversation. The car made a turn, picking up speed. Then it merged onto the freeway, the ride became smoother. Still, no one spoke.

The silence grated on me. My stomach lurched with every move of the vehicle, but the weight of the silence was worse than even my fear of being in the moving limo.

"What do you want?" I asked, unable to take the silence a moment longer.

The Collector regarded me with a look most people reserved for bothersome flies. That was as much of her attention she spared before her gaze returned to Nathanial.

He freed his hand from mine and slid his arm around my shoulders. It was a casual pose, but his fingers pressed against my skin, and I wasn't sure if he was silencing me or if his nerves were showing.

"Tatius is unlikely to be pleased with our abduction." He made the statement sound off-handed, unimportant.

It wasn't.

"Abduction?" The Collector's smile widened. "You and your companion are my honored guests. I intend only to show you what you will be gaining when you accept my offer. You have not left Tatius's little tract of land in centuries; since a time when tribes of savages were your only meal choice. The world has grown and changed, and while Haven is an impressive city, it is hardly a culture capital. I think you will enjoy the finer arts my cities can offer."

The Collector nodded at Elizabeth, and the small doll of a vampire reached under her seat. She pulled out a large, manila envelope and handed it to Nathanial.

He accepted it, opening the envelope slowly, as if cautious of what might be inside. Considering the last two packages vampires had received, I didn't blame him. But I didn't smell any blood, and when he reached inside, all he pulled out were colorful booklets. I frowned. *Travel guides?*

"My council members are each a master of a city. Please, pay attention to the earmarked attractions." The Collector waved her hand to indicate the guides. "Surely there is somewhere you've always longed to travel."

Nathanial shuffled through roughly a dozen books. *How big is her council?* Tatius had been afraid of any war or grudge she brought to his territory. I could understand why. With so many allies at the Collector's call, the Haven vampires would be more than just outnumbered.

I recognized some of the city names, but one guide in particular caught my attention. *A guide to the nightlife in Demur?* I snatched the guide from Nathanial's hand.

"You have connections in Demur?" I asked, flipping the guide over, looking for a map. There was probably more than one city in the country named Demur, but . . . The rogue I'd tagged had come from Demur. If I wanted to make sure there were no other men I'd accidentally tagged—or that Tyler had tagged during his deranged period as a shifter—Demur was where I needed to go.

The Collector ignored me. I was supposed to be seen and not heard.

Nathanial lifted the guide from my fingers. "As guests, I imagine we are guaranteed certain courtesies?"

"Of course. I am a hospitable hostess. All of your needs will be seen to."

"And our blood?" he asked.

"Off-limits. As long as you are guests."

Nathanial nodded. "In that case, Demur would be my preference."

Chapter Nineteen

Several hours, a private jet—which was a brand new type of hell—and another limo ride later, we were ushered through the front door of a Victorian mansion. During the period I'd survived by posing as a stray cat, I'd been taken home by many kinds of people and thus ended up in many interesting houses.

But I'd never ended up in a house that included tall, tower-like turrets, large, sweeping staircases, or crystal chandlers that hung fifty feet over my head. I tugged the coat closed tighter around me and stared at my bare feet on the polished marble entry.

"The Mistress is in the drawing room," the man who'd answered the door said as he bowed to the Collector.

She swept by him without a word, Elizabeth and the twins following. The man didn't straighten from his bow, but he looked up, and his lips curled in a sneer as he watched their retreating backs. Okay, apparently the Collector wasn't all that welcomed of a guest, even in cities she considered her own. That or the vamp didn't appreciate the lack of acknowledgement. Hard to tell. Not that I had time to puzzle over it. Nathanial was already walking down the hall, following the Collector. I trudged behind him.

I was the last to file into the drawing room. Unfortunately, I wasn't too late to miss the show. A blonde woman, wearing a dress gauzy enough to be seen through, sat in the center of a plush, red-velvet couch. A tanned man wearing only silk shorts and oil swayed on his knees in front of her, his body tilted forward, his head craned to expose one side of his throat, his eyes squeezed shut, and his hands moving over the lump in his black shorts. A thin trail of blood escaped around her brightly painted lips where they were locked on his throat. Another man, dressed identically to the first, lay sprawled across her lap, his eyes dazed.

She took her time amidst the tangle of male bodies, letting us watch from the doorway as her dinner began to tremble. I shuffled my feet, moving closer to Nathanial. He scowled at the scene, but his pupils were more dilated than the brightly lit room required. I'd taken a lot of blood from him the night before. Had he had time to hunt since then? I wasn't sure I liked how he watched the stream of blood trailing down the man's neck, but at least watching Nathanial's reaction helped me ignore my own rising hunger.

The man cried out, drawing my attention again. His hands stilled and the woman pulled back. She let him sag to the floor as she stood. The limp man on her lap slid to the floor as well. Then she stepped over their prone figures.

She touched a manicured finger to the side of her mouth and sauntered forward. "Collector, you honor my city with your presence. I trust your trip was a pleasant one?"

Her city? *This* was the Master of Demur. *Well, crap.* Weren't there *normal* vampires anywhere in the country?

The Collector frowned at the woman. "Actually, the last few nights have been trying. Has Aaric arrived yet?"

"Shortly before you did," a booming voice said from the doorway, and I jumped.

The Traveler ducked under the threshold, his long stride setting a path toward the Collector. I stiffened as he stepped around me. Unlike when I'd seen him in Haven, he had a scent now. He smelled of spongy wood, old cotton, and tanned leather. *Not a vamp-powered projection this time.* Elizabeth rushed forward to greet him, but his attention was focused on the Collector as he bowed.

The Collector nodded at her second-in-command. Then she turned back to the Master of Demur. "Have my guests shown to a room," she said before walking out with the Traveler. At the door she paused, turning to lift a finger at me. "And find some appropriate clothes for that one."

Of all the— I gritted my teeth to block the string of words threatening to pour out of my mouth. *I'm sure as hell wearing more clothing than the Master of Demur and her two snacks.* Not that I wanted to be compared to them. Shoving my hands in my pockets, I stared after the Collector's retinue as they filed out of the room. Nathanial didn't move to follow, so apparently we were waiting on the hospitality of our hostess.

The blonde woman stared at the doorway. No color lifted to her cheeks, but it might as well have—the anger coalescing in the air was all but palpable. I shifted my weight from one foot to another. Once the Collector vanished deeper into the house, the blonde turned back to Nathanial and me, her eyes assessing.

"And you would be who?" she asked, crossing her arms and tapping her long, red lacquered fingernails on her elbows.

Nathanial gave her a small bow from the waist. "I am known as the Hermit."

Her full lips puckered as her eyes roved over him, but it wasn't a hungry look and certainly not sexual. No, this vampire's gaze held measuring scales.

Nathanial smiled at her. It was a dazzling smile that softened the sharp angles of his face. It was also fake. He held out his hand. "And you must be the radiant Aphrodite, Master of Demur. The reputation of your beauty has reached me even in my seclusion."

Whatever scales she'd been measuring him by shifted, the balance weighing in his favor. She dropped her crossed arms, one hand moving to her hip, which she jutted out, exaggerating her hourglass shape. The other hand she slipped into Nathanial's. He kissed her knuckles lightly.

"You're not as old as your power feels," she said, and it was a statement, not a question. "Yes, I am Aphrodite. You and your companion are welcome in my city, Hermit." She turned, gesturing to one of the young men sprawled on the floor. He lifted his head groggily. "Daniel, show them to a guest room."

o • o

"Wait! Be careful what you say. Someone might be listening."

The other side of the phone line was so quiet, I thought Bobby might have hung up. Hell, I was surprised he'd answered in the first place. The phone had never rung while I'd been at Nathanial's house, and it had taken Nathanial two tries before he'd remembered his own phone number.

"Where are you?" Bobby finally asked.

"Does your hunter clearance allow you to leave the city?"

I could practically hear his frown through the phone. "I'll see what I can do. Where are you?"

"The city our trouble started in."

"You mean D—"

I cut him off. "Just try to make it here. Gil will meet you once you do." Or at least, I hoped she would. I hadn't talked to her yet.

"What's going on, Kita?"

"I—You're just going to have to trust me, Bobby. Oh, and Nathanial wants you to board Regan. The vet's number is on the fridge. I have to go." I hung up without saying goodbye.

Nathanial watched me from the edge of the king-sized bed that dominated the small room where we'd been escorted. He'd said little since we arrived, and had warned me to watch what I said. As if I didn't know our 'guest' status was more along the lines of 'prisoners.' I'd been held in worse places—chained to a mattress in Mama Neda's basement directly after Nathanial turned me came to mind—but there was no doubt in my mind that we were both trapped and under observation.

The mostly glass French doors and the vast array of decorative mirrors guaranteed we could be seen anywhere in the room. The massive bed included gauzy, cream-colored curtains tied back with gold ropes, but while the curtains matched the comforter and the mound of cream and gold pillows, they were translucent, providing little privacy.

The only place that might have been 'safe' was a small bathroom tucked away in the corner. It was a pointless amenity for Nathanial and me, but it was stocked with soap and toilet paper, so maybe humans used this room on occasion. It also had a door, which made it the most private spot available.

I dropped the phone back in the cradle and dragged my bare feet through the thick carpet. Dawn was drawing dangerously close, but I had to talk to Gil before sunrise. The bathroom was about the only place I could chance calling her. I didn't hear Nathanial slide off the bed, but suddenly his arms wrapped around my shoulders.

"This scheming is dangerous," he whispered into my hair. "Come to bed."

I shot a disparaging glance at the bed. The bed, *singular*—as in only one in the room. Then I glanced at the mostly glass doors.

"We're practically a zoo exhibit in here," I whispered, turning to face him.

I shouldn't have turned. With his arms around my shoulders, turning brought us chest to chest, and with the invisible eyes I imagined watching us, it was too close, too intimate. But he didn't appear to have any intention of letting me go. Instead, he leaned closer, bringing his lips near my ear.

When he spoke, his words were only for me. "We are guests. Vampires take hospitality very seriously. As long as we retain our guest status, we will be treated cordially and will be guaranteed safe passage. While the room lacks a measure of privacy, our room will be our sanctuary during our stay. That said, very little can be kept private in a house full of vampires. Even if they do not intentionally eavesdrop, careless words can be overheard. I imagine Aphrodite has sound proof rooms for her sensitive business discussions, but this is most definitely not one of them. Stop scheming. Let us go to bed."

I shrugged out of his arms. Safe passage sounded good, as did sanctuary and the idea we might not be under constant observation. "I'll be quick," I said, slipping into the bathroom. At the disapproving look he gave me, I added, "and quiet."

I would have shut him out if I could have closed the door fast enough. I was just a little too slow. The bathroom wasn't made for two, and it sure as hell wasn't made for three. *Hopefully Gil has enough room to join us*. I didn't even want to think about what would happen if she popped into the bedroom where stars-knew-who was watching.

Nathanial leaned against the wall as I turned the sink on full blast. Then I moved to the tub, turning it on as well. The roar of water made the small space even more uncomfortable, but it created a nice blanket of sound.

"Gildamina," I whispered. Nothing happened.

"What are you doing?" Nathanial asked.

I waved him into silence. *It worked before*. It had pissed her off. But it had worked.

I said her name again. Then I repeated it a third time.

Magic crackled in the air and Gil appeared, standing in the tub basin. Well, good thing she always wore rain-boots.

"You better have a really import—" she started.

I threw my hands over her mouth, smothering the words. "Keep your voice down," I whispered, looking around as if I could spot the unseen ears that might be listening.

Gils eyes widened, anger flushing her cheeks. "I told you not to use my name!"

I cringed. "I know. I know. Sorry, okay? I didn't have a choice. Listen, I don't have time for the long version of what's going on. It involves vampires kidnapping us, but the important thing is that we're in Demur."

The anger fell from her face, and Gil's eyes widened as she looked around. "Demur? That's where the—"

"Yeah. I need you to find Bobby. Set up a meeting place for tomorrow night, but don't tell me where, and whatever you do, don't show up unless I call. Okay?"

Someone knocked on the French doors. *Of all the mooncursed timing.* Of course, there was a good chance the knock had nothing to do with timing and everything to do with Nathanial and I being out of sight. Or with Gil's yelling.

Nathanial pressed a finger over his lips in the classic sign for silence before slipping out of the bathroom wordlessly. Gil and I just stared at each other as we listened through the door. I didn't recognize the male voice that asked Nathanial where I was.

Dammit. Now what?

A knock sounded on the bathroom door, and I made a shooing motion at Gil. Her brows knit together but she disappeared.

Nathanial stood on the other side of the door, a small stack of folded clothes in his hands. Right, the Collector had told Aphrodite to send some up. Whoever had delivered the clothing was now gone. I grabbed the stack from Nathanial and retreated back into the bathroom.

My first assessment that the stack contained clothes had been a little over optimistic. Aphrodite had sent me a thin, cream-colored slip trimmed in lace, and a gold satin robe. *Gee, I'll match the bed.* The robe had a small pocket, and I moved Avin's silver ring to it so the damn thing didn't magically jump to my finger again. Wearing my new finery, I turned the water off and dropped my coat and shirt over the tub ledge. I let myself out of the bathroom, ignoring Nathanial's intense scrutiny. Another knock sounded on the bedroom door.

"The Mistress said you needed a snack before dawn," a man in his mid-twenties said as he let himself into the bedroom. He wore only a pair of tight jeans, leaving his well-muscled chest bare. Like the other human men who served Aphrodite, he had a rich, unseasonable tan, but the slightly orange tint indicated his came from a bottle.

Oh hell. A snack. He meant *him.*

I wasn't desperate for blood, but I couldn't hold out forever. At the same time, since I was still a shifter deep-down, each human I bit might have the possibility of being tagged and then shifting when the gate to Firth opened. I couldn't leave a trail of city-shifters and rogues in my wake. Not only would it earn me a fast death sentence when the judge discovered I'd created more predators, but it would be wrong.

I could drink from Nathanial, he'd already been exposed to both my fangs and claws. When the gate to Firth opened, he might shift, but that damage had already been done. It couldn't be helped. But no more humans. The chance I might tag more humans was too great to risk.

I opened my mouth to tell the man to leave, but he reached out a hand and rubbed his thumb along my bottom lip. His excited heartbeat filled my ears, pressed against my skin. My fangs slid out. I couldn't help it. Couldn't stop it. He leaned in, his mouth inches from mine.

One moment the man's ragged breath tumbled over my lips, and the next, the air in front of me was empty. I blinked, snapping out of the blood daze as the man spun, and judging by the lack of grace, not fully of his own volition.

Nathanial stood only a foot from him, his arms crossed over his chest. "Your services will not be required."

"But the mistress said—"

Nathanial flicked a hand through the air. "You misunderstood her command. You are not required."

The man shoved his hands in his pockets. "I was told to—"

"Leave," Nathanial said. "Or I will remove you."

The man opened his mouth like he was going to protest. He took a good look at Nathanial and his jaw snapped closed. Slumping, he dragged his feet out of the room. The door closed behind him before I turned to Nathanial.

"Thanks." *I think.*

He didn't acknowledge my statement. He didn't even look at me. I stepped closer and realized he was breathing. He rarely breathed. But not only was he breathing, he was breathing fast.

"Nathanial?"

"While we are here, take the blood you need from me. Only me." His words were so quiet, I barely heard them. He lifted his hand, but his fingers stopped short of touching me. He turned away.

I frowned as he meandered to the other side of the room. He moved too calmly for me to accuse him of running away, but he was. Very slowly, but he was running. *Isn't that supposed to be my job?*

I followed, but not close, giving him space. Giving us both space. While he might be a *safe* blood source, biting him was definitely not without risk. Not for my emotional health, at least, and I didn't like the possessiveness in his voice when he said I should drink *only* from him.

He stopped to inspect a large painting of a nude woman riding an open shell over sea foam. A woman who looked an awful lot like the Master of Demur.

I gaped at the painting. "I've heard the name Aphrodite before. Isn't she some beauty goddess from—"

"Ancient Greece." Nathanial nodded. "Our hostess is not old enough to be the inspiration for those myths, though she was clearly the model for this. A Botticelli, I believe."

"How can you tell?"

"Look at the resemblance."

"No, I mean that she isn't old enough to have inspired the original myths?"

Nathanial frowned at me. "Kita, when you meet a new vampire, what do you notice first?"

I shrugged. "I don't know. First I have to notice them at all. I still haven't figured out a good 'tell' for identifying vampires." Shifters typically had unusual hair or eye colorations they shared with their beast, even in human form, but unless I was hyper-aware and could see that vampire flesh lacked pores, vamps looked indistinguishable from humans to me. "I guess the only consistent similarity I've noticed is that vampires don't register as food." Though admittedly, neither did mages or shifters—unless I was starving or they were bleeding.

I surfaced from my introspection and realized Nathanial was staring at me. *What did I say?* I returned his frown. "Is there something I should notice?"

"When you are near another vampire, you do not sense the weight and depth of their power? You cannot guess their age?"

I meant to shake my head, but the muscles in my neck locked. Nathanial already knew I couldn't feel his emotions the way he could feel mine. I hadn't yet told him I couldn't track him through our bond. And now, here was something else I was supposed to be able to do, but couldn't. *Not only have I lost my cat, but I'm a broken vampire.*

That thought caught like a barb in my chest. I'd been a pathetic excuse for a shifter, being a six-pound cat surrounded by lions and tigers. I hadn't chosen to become a vampire, but why should I have expected to be anything better than pathetic?

I don't know what Nathanial saw on my face, or maybe he used the emotional barometer part of our bond I was too head-blind to access, but he closed the distance between us. His arms slid around my waist, warm and sheltering. His lips brushed my forehead.

I closed my eyes, letting his heat surround me, his spicy scent envelope me, and for a moment, I almost felt like I belonged. Almost. Then the moment passed and turned awkward as I stood there. Nathanial's arms became heavy against my satin robe. I shrugged away.

"You should feed and go to bed," he whispered.

Feed, as in from him. I shook my head, but when I opened my mouth, a yawn broke free. Nathanial ignored my protest. He walked over and let down the canopy curtains around the bed—I was right, they were so translucent they might as well have been see-through. I still hadn't moved by the time he finished. He frowned. Then, walking back over, he took my hand and tugged me toward the bed.

I stumbled over my own feet as I nodded off between blinks. Okay, so he was right—I could barely hold my own eyes open.

Nathanial sat on the edge of the bed and pulled me down beside him. "Drink," he whispered, holding up his wrist.

Dawn was too close and I was too tired to fight. He clutched me tighter to his side as my fangs pierced his flesh. His fingers slid along my hip, and the skin over my stomach tightened. My mind fell into his, but the approaching dawn made my own thoughts too slow, too muddled, to follow his memories. Contented warmth spread through me, and I pulled back, sealing the wound.

Nathanial guided me down to the mattress. The lace pillowcase my face landed on felt rough and scratchy, but the down pillow it covered was blissfully soft.

"Sleep," he whispered as his fingers combed through my hair, and I fell asleep in a strange house, filled with strange vampires, yet feeling warm and safe for the first time in years.

Chapter Twenty

"This is boring," I whispered, squirming in my seat.

Nathanial glanced at me long enough to disapprove of my fidgeting. Then his attention returned to the stage.

Not that there was anything to *see* on the stage. The Collector had raved about the view from her private box, but it overlooked the same musicians who'd been playing for the last half hour. A singer might have livened things up a bit, but it was just one instrumental piece after another.

I squirmed again, and Nathanial lifted a white-gloved finger to his lips, not even looking at me this time. His eyes closed, and his fingers twitched a pattern to the music as if he were the conductor. *He* obviously enjoyed the symphony. Hell, he was damn near enraptured by it.

I sighed, blowing a loose strand of hair out of my face and fidgeting with the small pouch where I'd stashed Avin's ring. *In all his rapture, Nathanial better remember we're not staying in Demur.* The Collector might "encourage each of her cities to grow into a cultural apex" as she put it, but I sure as hell wasn't joining her sideshow so Nathanial could attend symphonies.

I slouched in my seat and picked at the satin gloves that matched my scarlet gown. By the time the last note faded, I'd pulled apart the inside seam of my right glove. I balled my hand in a fist, hiding the glove's damage as the audience burst into applause.

As the lights came up, the Traveler, who I'd been trying to ignore through the performance, turned toward me. "You seem restless, child. I take it absolute music does not agree with you?"

"No. I mean, it was great and . . . loud."

He stifled a laugh. "I must say, this is the first time I've heard the adjective 'loud' as a principle description of Beethoven's Sixth Symphony." He turned and regarded Elizabeth on his other side, "What did you think, my dear?"

"The orchestra as a whole captured the expression of feeling in an enchanting way, but the piccolo in the fourth movement did seem off."

"My dear you always say that." The Traveler leaned closer to me and whispered, "She was at the *Theater an der Wien* when the Sixth premiered. All and all an under-rehearsed mess from what I heard, but she loves to remind me of my absence that night."

I stared at him blankly as he laughed at what was obviously a long-running conversation. The boisterous sound echoed around our box, and his eyes sparkled merrily by the time he turned back to Elizabeth.

"Come along, Hermit," the Collector said, sweeping by our seats. "Demur's elite are gathered here for the gala. There is a reception in the hall, and it is a time to see and be seen."

Oh goody. Mingling.

Aphrodite, her eye-candy, and her council accompanied the Collector out. The twins, the Traveler, and Elizabeth rose to follow, and Nathanial held his hand out to me. I reached out, remembering too late about the gaping hole in my glove. He lifted an eyebrow, staring at the ruined glove.

Oops. I winced, stripping off the gloves. I looked around for somewhere to stash them before anyone else saw the damage I'd done. There was nowhere. *Oh well, can't be helped.* I tossed the balled up gloves over the balcony ledge.

Nathanial stared at me like I'd just sprouted whiskers, and I flashed him a sheepish smile. Shaking his head, he took my now bare hand and led me from the box.

"You like it here," I whispered as we made our way to the reception hall.

He shrugged. "The orchestra was quite talented."

That wasn't what I meant. I bet he knew it, too.

The small hallway from our box emptied into a room filled with Demur's rich and powerful. I scanned the crowd of tuxes and gowns—no one was wearing leather. Or chains. Or electrical tape. Even in its elaborate up-do, my tri-colored hair stood out, but Nathanial fit right in. The Collector and Aphrodite stood amid a crowd of humans, both holding glasses of champagne they couldn't drink. Nathanial joined the group, and the smile that touched his lips was more genuine than his typical masked expression as he joined the conversation.

"While it is incontrovertible that Beethoven's early works were influenced by Haydn and Mozart, his later—"

I backed away as Nathanial spoke. I couldn't contribute to the conversation—hell, I couldn't even follow it.

My feet itched to pace, and the skin on the back of my neck felt too tight, like someone was staring at me. *I need to get out of here.* Except there was nowhere to go. Avoiding both the vamps and the highbrow humans, I stopped in front of a painting, pretending to study it.

"An interesting commentary on society, don't you agree?" a male voice asked behind me. Aphrodite's second in command, the General, stepped closer, pointing at the painting. "See how the child in white is the only civilized person at the luncheon?"

Right. "Excuse me."

I grabbed two fistfuls of my full skirt, and lifting it from the ground, negotiated my way to one of the alcoves in the corner of the room. The alcove wasn't large, maybe two feet deep and only partially shadowed, but it separated me from the mingling peacocks and penguins.

I leaned into the darkest corner, pulling the skirt of my dress in so the shadows covered me. I needed to talk to Gil. We needed to plan how to search for evidence of tagged humans, or 'city-shifters,' as the hunters called them. I was considering whether I had room to call Gil without anyone noticing, when a man backed into the alcove and stumbled into me.

"Hey!"

He jumped. "Oh, sorry. I didn't know this hiding spot was taken."

"I'm not hiding," I mumbled, pushing off the wall.

The look of polite apology on his face warmed as I stepped out of the shadow. "Of course you're not hiding," he said, running his fingers through his perfectly styled hair. He was around my age, and dimples appeared in his cheeks when he flashed me a wolfish grin. "I hate these events too. My father always insists I come. He has since I turned eighteen. This is my usual alcove, when I don't just sneak out. If this arch could talk . . . " He shook his head, chuckling at some memory. "I'm Justin."

He held out a hand, rolling his shoulders back so his already wide chest became more prominent. *Preening and posing like a bird.*

I accepted his handshake reluctantly, and even though I was well fed, my pulse raced to match his at his touch. "Kita," I said, retrieving my hand before my instincts decided it was snack time.

Justin was attractive, but I'd spent the last few weeks with carved-from-marble-gorgeous Nathanial and ruggedly handsome Bobby. Heck, then there was Tatius with his intense eyes and the power that practically leaked out of him, and all of Aphrodite's fawning male eye candy, who ran around her mansion half naked. I was at the saturation point for attractive men, and Justin just didn't measure up to the competition. That fact must have shown on my face, because Justin's dimples faded.

"That's Justin Morgan, by the way," he said, propping one elbow against the arch. "As in Morgan Suites, the national hotel chain."

I'd never heard of it, but I nodded anyway. The skin along my spine tingled, the sensation irritating enough I had to resist the urge to massage my neck. It was like someone was staring—except I was in an alcove with my back to the wall. No one could be staring.

"Right." Justin straightened, dropping his arm. His sudden awkwardness as he backed up a step made him look even younger. "Nice meeting you. Guess I'll sequester a different alcove."

"Wait." I tried to shake off the unnerving feeling as I focused on Justin again. "You said you sneak out sometimes? Is there a way to come and go without notice?" If I could sneak away long enough to have a couple minutes to talk to Gil without the danger of being overheard . . .

Justin paused. "Yeah, but you have to know how to disarm the alarm. Which," he raised his shoulders, his hands sliding into his pockets. "I happen to know how to do. Are we getting out of here?" The last was said with a smile, his earlier confidence restored.

We? I glanced around the edge of the arched wall. Nathanial still stood amid a crowd, his smile real as he inclined his head, conceding a point to the woman speaking. The Collector and Aphrodite stood beside him, animatedly involved with the conversations if their body language was any indication, but I saw the Collector's accessing glance sweep over Nathanial, the smugness pinching her lips. *They'll be at that a while.* No one would notice if I disappeared for half an hour.

Besides, the feeling of wrongness crawling down my back had turned incessant, and the need to move and do something, *anything*, had me rocking on my toes. I smiled at Justin.

"Yes, let's go."

"Are you here with someone we need to avoid being seen by?" he asked as he led me out of the alcove..

"Several, actually."

"Blood red isn't the sneakiest color. You couldn't have worn a black gown, could you?"

I didn't have any response to that one. What looked like just another alcove turned out to be a stairwell. He pushed open the door, ushering me in quickly. Then he led me down six flights of stairs—with me in a ball gown. And heels. At the bottom of the stairs waited a fire exit. The red bar across the door proclaimed that an alarm would sound if opened, but Justin turned to a keypad beside the door and punched in a code. Then he took a deep breath and shoved the bar.

No alarm sounded, and Justin's relieved breath rush out of him.

"See. I'm a pro," he said, his confident smile at odds with the excited race of his heart I could almost feel crashing against his chest in the small stairwell. He gave a small bow, holding open the door. "Your freedom awaits, my lady."

I rushed by him, taking the frozen outside steps two at a time.

"Hey, wait up," he called behind me. Not that it took him long to catch up.

The steps led to an alley behind the concert hall. I could hear traffic on the street, but the alley was quiet, deserted. It would be the perfect place to call Gil. If Justin weren't present.

"So, you never told me your full name," he said, as we reached the bottom of the stairs.

"Katrina Deaton." The name Nathanial had given me still felt weird, but I gave it to Justin anyway as I glanced around the narrow alley. Nothing moved, but . . . It didn't feel as empty as I'd first thought.

"Deaton? The name doesn't ring any bells. Not a regular mover or shaker here in Demur, are you?"

"I hope not." The last time I'd been to Demur I'd accidentally created a rogue—which I'm sure had shaken quite a few things up. Now I just had to make sure I hadn't created more than the one. First I had to ditch Justin.

"Listen, thank you, but I have—" I cut off as heavy material landed on my shoulders, and I glanced at the tux jacket Justin tugged around me.

"You must be freezing," he said, stepping closer.

"You really shouldn't— "

He waved away my argument.

"You hang onto it. I'll be warm enough," he said, but undermined the statement by blowing on his hands. His breath fogged in the cold air. Mine didn't. "There's a nice little diner down the block. How about I buy you a coffee?"

I was barely listening anymore. There was something at the end of the alley. I was sure of it. And I couldn't seem to look away. My dress dragged in puddles of dissolved snow and street-salt as I walked toward the back corner of the building.

"Hey, wrong way. The diner's in the other direction."

I didn't response. Something in the darkness moved, but even my vampire eyes couldn't make sense of the shadows. I took another step closer. Justin grabbed my arm, stopping me. The tingling exploded along my spine like small tongues of fire. *That* I'd felt before. *Oh crap.*

I pushed Justin back, my eyes flying wide. "Get out of here."

"What the hell—"

Justin hadn't finished the sentence when Avin stepped out from the shadows of the building, his deformed figure hidden in a dark trench coat.

"This one is perfect, Kita," he said, shuffling toward us.

No. No. No. I tried to shove Justin out of the alley. He didn't move. *Dammit.*

"What's going on?" he asked, his eyes flicking from me to the decrepit figure shambling forward.

"Run, you idiot!"

Justin backed up a step. But he didn't run. I stepped between him and Avin.

"Kita, behave," Avin chided. Something flashed in his hand.

A globe. Lightning. I fell to my knees.

Pain roared through me like liquid lava coursing through my veins. My fangs exploded from the roof of my mouth, but I strangled my scream. The pain only lasted a second. Then I fell forward onto all fours.

"Stop." My whisper came out hoarse.

"Then give me my payment." Avin was right in front of me now.

Justin still stood beside me, eyes wide and uncomprehending.

"I'm calling the cops," Justin warned, but he fumbled pulling the phone out of his pocket, and it hit the snow by his feet.

Avin ignored him. I pushed off the ground. My legs trembled under me, but held. Snow clung to the front of my dress. Turned the scarlet a deeper red as it melted.

"He's Justin Morgan of the Morgan Suites fortune. He would be missed." *Let him recognize the name.*

"An heir? Dammit, that won't work." Avin turned away, cursing under his breath. "Get rid of him."

I grabbed Justin by the arm, dragging him from the alley, but my feet didn't seem to be working right, my movements jerky and uneven as I tried to run.

"Not you, babe," Avin called after me, and pain roared through me again, stopping me in my tracks.

"Run," I yelled at Justin.

He didn't hesitate this time. "I'll get help," he called over his shoulder as he rounded the corner.

Now it was just me and Avin.

I whirled around and he pulled back the hood, revealing the monstrous features left of his face.

"It's after midnight. I don't see my new body. Do you know what happens to oath breakers?"

Energy crackled through the air. If I thought the pain was bad before, it was nothing compared to this. Fire ate me from the inside out as my skin flaked off in charred layers. There was no holding back my scream this time. It ripped from my throat. The pain built, the fire all consuming.

Time froze. Stopped. The pain ended.

I blinked away snow. I was face down in the dirty alley. My mouth tasted of blood, but the fire in my skin had passed. My flesh wasn't charred. I pushed away from the ground.

Avin squatted beside me. "It's no fun if you black out, babe. You owe me a body, and you don't seem to be doing anything to acquire one for me."

"I got kidnapped." I spat out the words. They were moist, filled with my own blood and terror. My fingers jerked violently as I gestured to the alley. "Look around, this isn't my city."

"That's not my problem. My problem is that I look like Frankenstein's monster." He stood and pulled the hood over his head. "If you don't call me by the end of the night with a body, expect me to be there when you wake at sunset. If you know what's good for you, babe, you don't want that." Magic danced through the air, and he vanished.

Chapter Twenty-One

I stumbled up the concert hall steps as the door flew open. Nathanial rushed out. His frantic eyes swept over my ruined dress, my tousled hair, the blood I'd tried to wipe from my face. Then he pulled me into his arms.

"What hurt you, Kita?"

I didn't answer or pull away. I just leaned against his chest and breathed in his scent. My hands trembled where I clutched them by my sides. I couldn't make the shaking stop. I'd tried. The tremble stayed.

"I'm cold," I whispered into the front of Nathanial's tux. His arms wrapped tighter around me, but his warmth offered me no comfort. The only warmth in my body was building behind my eyes. The first tear tripped down my cheek.

Nathanial took a step back and examined my face.

"You are in shock. What happened?" When I didn't answer, he went on, "I felt your fear, but I did not realize you had left the hall. What happened?"

I scrubbed the tear off my cheek but another slipped free to blaze its own bloody trail. The harder I fought not to cry, the more the searing pressure behind my eyes built, the more bloody tears slipped free. Vampire tears. I drew in a deep breath. It was supposed to be calming. Instead it was ragged, tasting of blood and fear.

Dammit. I hated this. I hated the fear. I hated the tears. I hated the whole damn situation. I was stuck in one shape, in a strange place with creepy vampires who wanted to show me off as a freak, and I had an insane necromancer who wanted me to find him a new body.

But at least no one's trying to kill me.

Yet.

A laugh slithered up my throat. I convulsed with it, fresh tears burning their way free. Nathanial pulled me against him again, as if his arms could shield me from the hysteria shredding me. I wrapped my hands in the front of his tux. Held on.

I took another breath. It still shook, still cut through me with violence, but it was cleaner than the last. Stronger. Nathanial held me.

Kept me in one piece. I still hadn't told him about Avin. I wasn't sure what would happen if I tried, but I was at the point I'd risk the consequences. I opened my mouth to begin, but my gaze landed on the Collector and her retinue as they walked out of the concert hall. I couldn't tell him. Not here. Not with so many ears around.

"I need to talk to you," I whispered, and Nathanial's arms tightened around me.

"Well, no one's stopping you," Aphrodite said, snapping a pair of gold opera glasses closed. "So the missing fledgling has been found all safe and sound. Are we returning to the gala?"

"No." The Collector strolled down to stairs. "I believe this will end the night. Hermit, it is time we had a talk." She turned to Jomar. "Summon the cars."

I pushed away from Nathanial. A light tremor still shook through me, but it was inside, not evident in my limbs. Just to be sure, I hugged my arms across my chest, tucking my fists into my armpits. I walked to the bottom step, trying to find some distance from the vamps.

It didn't work.

Elizabeth broke from the Traveler and daintily made her way into my flimsy bubble of solitude. She remained on the last step, giving her a height advantage as she looked down her small nose at me. "If you insist on sneaking about, you should choose better chaperones than Justin Morgan. He will never amount to anything."

"I wasn't sneaking anywhere. And I don't need a chaperone."

She sniffed. "It's disgraceful and no way for a companion to act. I'm surprised the Hermit tolerates it."

She's lecturing me on proper companion etiquette? I so couldn't deal with this right now. I walked to the curb.

All I wanted in that moment was to tuck my tail and find a nice, small cat-sized hole to hide in and lick my wounds. Not like that was an option, but even fading into the background proved futile as the Collector strolled down the steps. She stopped far enough away that her location could have been misconstrued as impatience as she waited for the limos.

I wasn't fooled. She'd moved closer to me, which she proved when the chill of her gaze landed on my bare shoulders.

"I suppose you slipped away in an attempt to meet that boy, Bobby," she said.

So they had been listening to my call. I wasn't surprised. Based on the way the Collector studied me, I probably should have pretended to be.

But my nerves were too raw, too close to the surface, to lie with my reactions.

"Now, this 'Bobby,' is he a shapeshifter?" She stepped closer. "I would very much like to meet him if he is. I could be very generous if someone were to capture a functioning shapeshifter for me."

Her eyes had bled to black, and I dropped my gaze. She'd bespelled me once before with just a glance in her eyes. I wasn't going to hand her the opportunity to do it again. *Can she compel me to reveal other shifters to her?* A shiver ran down my spine.

I couldn't let that happen. I wouldn't.

She flicked her wrist at her side, the movement meant to draw attention. "Where are you meeting your friend?"

I shrugged, not looking up, not meeting her eyes. Still my vision went dark. A stifling presence weighed down on me in the blackness.

"Answer my questions truthfully," her disembodied voice said from the darkness. "Where are you meeting your friend?"

"I don't know," I heard myself reply, though I hadn't meant to say anything.

"Then how will you find him?" she asked. I bit my tongue hard, concentrating on not saying anything. She clicked her tongue. "Answer me."

"A mutual friend."

"This friend is a shapeshifter?"

"No."

"What is he?"

"She is a scholar." I gave myself a mental pat on the back for restraining from saying mage.

"And where is this scholar?"

"I don't know."

"Then how will you find her?"

"I'll call her."

"What is her phone number?"

"I don't know."

The darkness around me buzzed with irritation, and an agitated sound escaped the Collector's throat. "What *do* you know?"

Oooh, an open-ended question. "I know that sunlight prompts the brain to produce happy chemicals, and so it is my belief that older vampires are grouchy due to light deprivation."

The darkness surrounding me retreated with a snap. The street fell into focus. I swayed, disoriented. The Collector's icy—and completely unamused—eyes dominated my vision. My hand ached, and I realized Nathanial held my fingers in a death grip. I looked at our hands. *When did he*—? Hell, what did it matter?

"You are a most frustrating creature," the Collector snapped. Then she turned. "Jomar! Where are those limos?"

The squinty faced guard shuffled his feet. "There appears to be a problem, Mistress. One of the drivers is missing. I've sent for another. But until then, there is only one car."

I couldn't see her face, but it must have been fierce because Jomar stumbled back. He growled something into his cell phone, and Nathanial tugged on my hand, drawing me several steps away. When we were several yards from the other vampires, Nathanial's arms slid around my waist. He pulled me against his chest.

I stiffened. "Nathanial, I—"

"Shhh, Kitten. Listen to me," he whispered, his lips so close they brushed my ear as he spoke and I still scarcely heard.

And if I could scarcely hear him—*No one else could.* I settled against his chest, and he let out a sigh as if he'd expected me to put up a fight. I frowned. This wasn't the first time he'd acted surprised when I didn't fight him. He clearly considered contrariness my default mode. I huffed out my breath. *Okay, so maybe I'm a little difficult at times, but I'm not completely unreasonable.* If this was the only way to have a somewhat private conversation, so be it.

"I know you need to search for the unaccounted-for members of Tyler's gang, and I will help you when I can, but you must be careful."

Like I don't know that. "Trust me, it is not on my to-do list to get Bobby and Gil added to the Collector's zoo."

"Kita, there is more at stake than that. We are walking a precarious line with vampire laws of hospitality. Right now she is trying to seduce us with grandeur—"

"You. She is trying to seduce *you.*"

I felt his lip twitch, just a small movement against my cheek. A frown? A smile? I wasn't sure. After a moment, he continued, "She is splitting hairs with our laws. You are a companion, so she cannot separate you from me by force unless we are in her territory."

"We *are* in her territory."

"That is why we must be careful. For now we are guests, but if we break her rules or disobey her, we could be seen as hostile. That would be a very bad situation to find ourselves in."

And more than likely, she'd consider my sneaky behavior and

smart mouth a violation. "She promised you we wouldn't be separated if you joined her."

"I remain Tatius's subject and only a visiting master unless I petition her for a place in her city. If I am deemed hostile or a threat, she could execute me without penalty. You would then be masterless."

And I'd already learned that masterless meant 'anyone's meat.'

We had been whispering for too long. I pushed away from Nathanial, and he didn't fight me. Rocking back on my heels, I considered our dilemma.

"How long are we visitors?" I asked. The other vamps might be able to hear, if they were straining to listen, but what did it matter? I was getting the abridged version of vampiric law, I'm sure they already knew it.

"Our timeline is dictated by Tatius. Though I am a master vampire, I must still answer to the master of my city. As Tatius's subject, I am protected. But if I disobey him while out of his territory, I effectively disclaim him and am without protection. He is no fool. By now he has surely confirmed we are missing. We cannot know if he believes we left willingly or not, but when he finds our location, he will demand our return. I think the Collector is counting on his move. When he sends for us, time will be up and a choice must be made."

A choice? Like joining the Collector's menagerie was an option? Of course, Tatius had to be well and truly pissed by now, and if he believed Nathanial took the Collector up on her offer . . . Returning to Haven might not be possible. Moving to another master's city meant Nathanial would have to negotiate our safe travel, which would be hard to do while we were under lock and key as the Collector's guests.

"We're so screwed."

Nathanial winced. "Charming vernacular, but accurate enough."

"So what do we do?"

Nathanial drew me into his arms again. "We play by her rules. She owns many cities. If we are not forced into an urgent decision, I may be able to negotiate a permanent relocation for us. One which will limit how she displays you."

Limit being the key word. "I hate vampires."

"I know." He brushed a kiss across my forehead. "And I know the urgency in which we need to untangle . . . that other issue." His thumb trailed over the Judge's mark, indicating which other issue he meant. "But for now, it would perhaps be more appropriate if you attempted to behave like Elizabeth." He nodded to the porcelain doll where she clung to the Traveler's hand, her body leaning against his.

My teeth gritted. *I can't believe he just suggested*— "There is more going on," I whispered, the words hot with anger. "There is the necro—"

My jaw snapped shut as twin currents of first fire and then ice ripped through me. *Avin warned me not to tell.* I squeezed my eyes shut as I swayed. When I opened them again, I was clinging to Nathanial, his worried face filling my vision.

"Kita, what happened? What was that?" As he spoke, a single white limousine rounded the corner.

I shook my head as the limo pulled to the corner. I'd have to find a way to tell him. Somehow. But later.

The Collector turned toward us. "I trust you have finished your gossiping?" It wasn't a question. She strolled toward the limo. "Aphrodite, you appear to have a personnel issue with your drivers. I suggest you fix it." She gave the blonde woman a tight smile. Which was not returned. "You and your council can wait for the backup car. *My* council will be returning to the mansion. Hermit, come. We have much to discuss."

❧ • ❦

At the mansion, I left Nathanial in Aphrodite's drawing room, with the Collector. My fate was being decided in that room, but I wasn't allowed to speak, so there wasn't any reason for me to be there.

Well, actually, I thought there was plenty of reason. But after the Collector expressed her 'plans'—she wanted me to do the grand tour, letting each and every master vampire she wished to impress take a bite out of me—and I lost my temper and told her where she could shove her offer, I was kicked out.

I hated vampires.

Stupid, selfish, power hungry—

I lingered outside the drawing room door for a few moments, but the damn room was sound proof. I couldn't hear a word. Now all I could do was trust Nathanial to negotiate a better deal. *If he can.*

I sighed and took the steps of the sweeping staircase two at a time. Mine and Nathanial's bedroom was the last on the second floor. I didn't pay any attention to the doors I passed on my way, until one opened. The sour smell of snake musk preceded a kimono-clad figure into the hall.

Akane.

She glared at me, stepping into my path. Then she unsheathed a

174

gleaming blade. *Crap.*

The only Japanese sword I knew was the *katana*, and her sword was much too short to be one. No doubt it could still do damage. *If she knew how to use it.*

Her body language promised that she knew *exactly* what she was doing.

"You smell foul," she spat. "You make the whole house stink."

"Nice to see you again, too. How about putting away the pointy sword?"

She didn't. Spreading her stance, she lifted the sword, angling it toward my throat. *Not good.* I backed up a step and gripped the folds of my gown. *Come on, now would be a good time for claws.* I pushed energy at my hands, my fingers. A spasm shot up my arms.

Thank the moon!

Another spasm hit, a pop sounded. Then a wave of dizziness rushed over me. I staggered and Akane charged.

Crap. I flung myself back, lifting my hands. The spasms had stopped, but instead of claws, *I had paws.*

I wasn't sure what her reach was with the sword, but it was definitely longer than mine, especially since at the moment my only natural weapons were fangs. She blocked the path to the stairs. Screaming for help wouldn't do a whole hell of a lot of good with Nathanial holed up in a sound-proof room. My choices came down to an out-matched fight or barricading myself in my room.

I ran.

Akane followed, her wooden Japanese shoes making soft clicks on the carpet. I rounded the corner. The glass doors to my room were only yards away. I just had to reach them.

Air hissed around Akane's blade as she swung, and I dropped. The sword swished through the air, but I was fast enough to dodge. Or at least, I thought I was, until Akane's foot slammed into my back, sending me sprawling forward.

I twisted as I hit the ground, trying to get my legs under me. Too late.

Akane's next kick knocked me to my back. Her foot ground into my chest, and she pressed the blade against my throat. Warm heat ran down my neck.

"See what you did, beast." She pulled open the collar of her kimono and exposed angry red grooves running over her shoulder— my claw marks. They hadn't healed.

"You poisoned me."

Not the response she wanted.

Her blade bit deeper into my throat. I swallowed. Losing my head wasn't on the top of my to-do list.

Reaching out, I grabbed the foot planted on my chest and twisted, hard. Something popped. Akane screamed.

The sword pulled back, and I rolled. Just in time.

The arc of her sword sliced through a clump of my hair. But not my neck. I threw my weight at the leg still supporting her, and she crashed backward. The sword flew from her grip.

"What's going on here?" someone yelled from the direction of the stairs. Footsteps ran toward us.

I pushed myself off the floor, one paw-like hand pressed against my bleeding throat. Akane tried to stand, but her leg bent at an unnatural angle. It didn't hold her weight. She glared at me, a steady stream of melodic but pissed-off words flowing from her. I didn't know the language, but I could guess what she meant.

"Not this time, worm," I said, kicking the sword further away.

Three figures rounded the corner, rushing toward us.

"What did you do?" a familiar, squinty faced guard asked as he charged toward me.

Jomar grabbed me before I could backpedal. He wrenched my hand away from my throat and twisted my arm, jerking it behind my back. Oh, now this was familiar.

"Let go. She's the one who tried to decapitate *me*."

He jerked my arm harder, turning me around in the process. Then his hand shot out. The back of his hand slammed into my cheek, made my vision turn red.

"That was for the disrespect," he said. Then he pushed me away, turning back to the other two enforcers with him.

Pain pulsed upward to my eye, but I didn't touch my face. I wasn't going to give him that satisfaction.

"What should we do, sir?" a vampire I'd never seen before asked, as he attempted to help Akane stand.

Jomar looked from where Akane hobbled in the vampire's arms to the blood trickling down the front of my dress. "Ronco, escort her," he pointed at me, "back to her room and make sure she stays there. Sean, we'll carry Akane back to her room."

Ronco took me by the arm, and his eyes went from my throat, to my misshapen hands, and then back again. "She's losing a lot of blood.

Shouldn't we seal the wound or send for her master?"

"I'm not touching that unnatural *thing*," Jomar said, sneering. "Knock yourself out if you want to, but the mistress should be done with her master soon."

Ronco reached his thick fingers toward my throat and I took a step back. Oh no, he wasn't putting his mouth on me.

"It's fine," I growled.

He shrugged and encircled my wrist with one giant hand before leading me down the hall to the room Nathanial and I shared. After depositing me inside, he leaned against the French doors, effectively blocking the only exit. *Jerk.*

I headed directly to the bathroom.

I studied my neck in the mirror. The cut looked superficial, and the trickle of blood was slowing. I searched the bathroom cabinets, but there were no medical supplies. I did find a washcloth, and used it to rinse away as much of the blood from my skin as I could. I blotted at the tacky blood clinging to the bodice of my dress, but it was a lost cause—the gown was beyond ruined.

I turned the faucets on full blast and peeked out the bathroom door. Ronco still had his back to the room, not paying attention. *Good.* After shutting and locking the door, I backed to the corner of the bathroom and whispered Gil's true name. On the third repetition, magic tinted the air and she popped into the tub. Her eyes scanned first me and then the small room before she spoke.

"Took you long enough," she whispered. "Bobby gave up waiting hours ago. He's been combing the city looking for you."

"Well it's a good thing he didn't find me. I never thought I'd ask this, but throw me in the void and get me the hell out of here."

She blinked at me in surprise. "You realize how close it is to dawn?" she asked. At my nod, she frowned. "Where's Nathanial?"

"Busy. Let's go."

She didn't hesitate again, but laid a hand on my shoulder. Then the world dropped away.

કે • ન્ક

My eyes hadn't adjusted to the light in the alley before Bobby captured me in a tight embrace. I pushed away from him, not only because he had a mate who wasn't me, but because he smelled awfully good. Not sexy man good, but juicy steak good. I must have lost more blood than I thought.

"What happened? Where have you been? Are you okay?" Bobby

demanded, not releasing me. His gaze landed on my hands and the other questions died on his tongue. "You have *paws?*"

I frowned. "I'm too weak to change them right now."

Gil stepped closer, staring. "You can change them at will now? When did this happen?" She pulled her scroll out of the air.

"It's new, completely irrelevant, and not necessarily at will." I hid my paw-like hands in the folds of my gown. "We need to make a plan on how to search out the other men I might have tagged. I'm not sure when I'll be able to get away again and—"

"I found one already."

I stopped, my mouth still stuck in the shape of the next word as I turned and stared at Bobby. "What?"

"I found one of the shifters. He isn't a hunter. The scent isn't from Firth. It's like the rouges we chased before. A city-shifter."

I blinked at him. So there *were* more. And he'd found one. Which was great. *I think.* "Did you . . . ?"

"Kill him?" Bobby shook his head. "We don't know if he turned rogue or not. I scouted the area and waited to see if he would move from his hidey-hole, but he hadn't emerged by the time I left to meet Gil."

He beamed at me, bright eyes sparkling in the dim street light. He was clearly thrilled to be the source of good news. And this was good news. Right? I mean, we didn't have to go out and hunt the shifter, we already knew where he was.

Too easy. Nothing ever came easy without a catch.

I tried to share Bobby's optimism, but I just didn't have it in me. I flashed him a weak smile and stared at the night sky. It was still dark, without a hint of predawn light, but I could feel the dawn coming like a gradually increasing weight around my neck. It had been a long night already, and Avin still expected me to turn a body over to him by dawn. Oh, and the vamps were at the mansion discussing whether I would be a side-show attraction. It was definitely a night I'd like to have a 'do-over' button for. *But if we find the city-shifter . . . .* At least the night wouldn't be a total loss.

"How far?" I asked.

Bobby's gaze followed mine. "We will have to hurry."

Chapter Twenty-Two

I stared at the twisted razor wire ringing the fence around the junkyard.

"You're sure?" I asked, glancing back at Bobby. He didn't answer. He didn't have to. I had caught a hint of city-shifter. He was right.

Bobby hauled the edges of the chain link up, making a gap for me to slip under. The dress caught as I crawled under the gate and tore as I jerked it free. Well, it was already ruined anyway. Standing, I grabbed the bottom links of the gate, holding it for Bobby.

Gil watched. Then she vanished, reappearing a moment later at my side. She smiled, and a small ball of purple mage-light appeared over her shoulder.

Show off.

"So where in here is he?" Gil asked, her bubble of light reflecting off mountains of twisted and rusted metal.

Vehicles smashed beyond recognition, cars missing their doors and interior, and scraps of parts were thrown into towering piles. The carnage gave me a whole new reason not to trust cars. But it didn't tell us where our shifter was.

I tilted my head, scenting the air. I could catch hints of the city-shifter on the wind, but my nose told me only that he was somewhere further ahead. I glanced at Bobby, and he nodded. *Okay, time to search.*

At one point, there had been a trail around the gutted cars, but busted glass and rusty parts now littered the path. And I was in heels.

I picked my way along the jagged path carefully. Not quite careful enough. My skirt snagged on the rusted end of a muffler half buried in the snow. I jerked it free and the material gave way with an awful sound. I glanced at the large 'V' shaped rip. *Let's see just how many holes I can get in this damn thing.* I hauled the skirt up to my knees. It didn't help. I tripped over a snow-covered fender.

I growled in frustration, and a growl answered.

I froze. Gil's mage light flickered out, leaving me blind in the sudden darkness. *The city-shifter?* If it was, he didn't sound happy.

Another growl sounded. I swung around, peering through the

dark at the skeletal body of a Jeep. Nothing moved. My heart thudded in my chest. Bobby crept closer. The growl sounded again. Still nothing moved.

Until something did.

A huge body lumbered out of the Jeep. Not a shifter. A Rottweiler.

Moonlight twinkled off the spikes in its leather collar. I stumbled back. My shoe ground into shattered glass hidden in the snow. Another growl rumbled behind me. Closer. I twisted. Another massive canine emerged around a crushed truck.

Crap.

A small voice in the back of my head reminded me to stay very still.

The rest of me didn't listen.

I was two sprints into a run when a pair of strong hands jerked me to a stop. Bobby dragged me back. Held me still. Gil was nowhere in sight, but the dogs were almost on us. Closing fast.

My mouth went dry. My tongue plastered itself to the roof of my mouth. I couldn't yell.

"They're just guard dogs," Bobby whispered, releasing my arms. He stepped beside me and lifted his fists.

There was no time left to run. The dogs were on us.

I kicked wildly. Missed. The dog's teeth snapped shut on my skirt. He shredded the hem. My next kick caught him in the jaw. *Dogs. Why does it always have to be dogs?*

Bobby knocked the dog sideways. It yelped, but immediately climbed to its feet again, lip curled. Both dogs growled, and Bobby answered. His beast was near the surface, energy pouring off his skin and prickling along mine. The dogs paused, just out of reach of my swinging foot. They circled. Flanked us. In unison they crouched, prepared to lunge.

Bobby's energy rolled over my body. Like a rising scream, a hot, animal energy answered under my skin. It burst from my core, spread outward.

The Rottweilers fell flat, their nubby tails tucked as they whined. The sharp scent of submissive urination touched the air. Bobby growled again. The two dogs turned and ran, both their heads and butts dragging the ground.

I stared after them. "Crap, Bobby. That was an alpha pulse. How the hell did you do that?"

Bobby turned toward me, not saying anything. I looked at him and found him studying me, a look of awe on his face. He shook his head. "Not me. *We* did it. You're my *Dyre*."

I frowned at him as the tingly feel of magic laced over my skin. Gil appeared in the empty space beside me, her scroll already in hand.

"Interesting," she said, scribbling down a note, "can you explain exactly what you did?"

I scowled at her. "You could've helped."

"I've read several books about the strength of vampires. You surely didn't need my help with a pair of dogs. Now answer this . . . ."

I ignored Gil's incessant questions about how we'd intimidated the dogs and returned to navigating the path of dead cars. I also made a point not to acknowledge the hopeful grin that lit Bobby's eyes every time he looked at me. I couldn't acknowledge it. I was too busy trying to ignore my own spark of hope.

I stumbled over my leaden feet and pretended I'd tripped over a rearview mirror sticking out of the snow. I was weaker than before. More so than could be explained by the approaching dawn. *But my cat . . .* I pushed my attention deep inside and touched the frozen core where my cat had once resided. Did it feel slightly warmer now, slightly less knotted?

The coil was quiet. Cold. Dead.

But . . .

I stared at my half shifted hands. *Did we really create that dominant energy surge?* In Firth, *Torins* and *Dyres* could borrow energy from their clan members. My father wouldn't have needed to siphon energy from another shifter to create one small alpha pulse—he could dominate shifter or beast by his will alone. *But his cat's not a dead coil like mine.*

"*We did it. You're my Dyre.*" Damn Bobby. Why did he have to say that? It gave me hope, but that hope was deceptive.

Snow crunched ahead of me. I stopped mid-step. The city-shifter's scent was stronger now. It saturated the air around us. *He's close.*

Bobby stilled behind me, obviously equally aware of the newcomer. But Gil was oblivious. I pressed a finger over my lips, trying to quiet her. She didn't notice. She hadn't summoned her light and she was concentrating hard on her footing instead of me. She tripped over something in the shadows and squealed as she fell, her butt landing in the snow with a thump.

Well, there goes any element of surprise—which we'd probably already lost, but still.

Bobby turned to help Gil, and I crept into the shadow of the nearby junk-pile. The mountain of metal beside me released a slight creaking sound. A soft curse drifted to me from the other side. Then snow crunched under heavy boots.

I pressed deeper in the shadows as the shifter rounded the corner. He marched past my hiding spot, a metal pipe clutched behind his back. Gil barely had her feet under her, and Bobby moved to barricade her body with his as the city-shifter stopped a few yards in front of them.

"Get outta here," the city-shifter yelled, the pipe still hidden behind his back.

Bobby frowned. His gaze drifted past the city-shifter to the spot I'd been standing earlier, and then across the shadows. The astringent scent of fear reached me. Not from my companions. From the city-shifter. He followed Bobby's gaze, stepping sideways so he could keep Bobby in his peripheral vision as his eyes darted nervously in my direction.

I held my breath, going statue still the way only a vampire could be still. *Come on, Bobby, don't give away my position.*

As if he heard the thought—which I knew he couldn't have— Bobby's gaze snapped back to the city-shifter, but the damage was done. The city-shifter had the idea someone else might be in the wreck-yard. Shifters have superb night vision, but unlike vampires, they can't see into dark shadows like the one where I was crouched. As he searched the darkness, I caught my first clear view of the city-shifter's face. Recognition slammed into me.

I saw him from Tyler's memory. The city-shifter was smiling. Younger. Cleaner. He passed a cigarette, joking about something. I squeezed my eyes shut and tried to shove Tyler back into the depths of my mind as ghost images pressed the sides of my vision.

"Get lost tag-along. This isn't the place for little boys."

"Shove it, Tyler. Danny's no older than me."

"Yeah, but you don't have the stomach for it." He didn't. I knew he didn't. He never would. And I'd prove it to him, too. "Fine. Come along. We'll have some fun. See the chick over there. The one with the stupid streaks—"

The image of myself in the memory snapped me back to the present. I'd lived parts of that memory before, but I'd never noticed the seconds before Tyler pointed to me. Before he made me a target.

I'd been distracted for several crucial seconds while lost in Tyler's memories. The city-shifter had pulled his pipe. He growled, slapping it against his palm. The pipe splintered in a shower of red rust flakes, and I crept soundlessly from my hiding spot.

"We, uh . . ." Bobby stammered, but the shifter brandished the broken pipe, cutting him off.

"I don't care what you were doing. Get out. Get out now!" He lunged forward, and Bobby jumped to the side, dragging Gil with him. A crazed laugh trickled from the city-shifter's throat. "Too late. Too late."

He ran at them, swinging the pipe in a wide arc. Gil's hands flew into motion, and a purple haze filled the air in front of her and Bobby. *Her barrier.* The semi-translucent wall solidified, separating them from the city-shifter. He slammed into it, bounced back, and a smile spread across Gil's face.

A premature smile. I could feel the tingle of magic in the air growing, building.

Then the barrier exploded.

Three bodies flew in opposite directions, joined by a shower of displaced snow and spare car parts. I pushed out of my shadow, ignoring the clumps of snow and bits of rusted metal raining down around me. Bobby and the city-shifter climbed to their feet, staring at each other. Gil moved slower.

My skirt rustled as I stepped forward, and Bobby's gaze snapped to me. I shook my head, willing him to look away. Too late.

The city-shifter glanced over his shoulder. Not like he meant to, but like a reflex. His gaze landed on me. The reek of fear poured off him. He whirled around. He'd managed to hold onto the pipe, and he swung at me.

Great.

I hid my deformed hands in my skirt.

"Drop the pipe," I said in as even a voice as I could. He didn't. A name floated up from the pit I kept Tyler's memories in, so I used it. "Steven, drop the pipe."

The shifter jumped at his name, and the arc of his swinging pipe slowed, but he still clutched the weapon. He chewed at his bottom lip, a lip chapped and scabbed like chewing at it was a habit. His eyes grew wide as he stared at me, the whites overpowering the expanded pupils.

"Oh god, you're her," he said, backing up until his back pressed against the side of a junked SUV.

The pipe slid from his fingers. He fell down after it, his hands groping blindly, his gaze stuck on me. "You're *her*."

Bobby kicked the pipe further from him, but Steven didn't notice. He just kept staring at me. I stepped closer and his mouth dropped, his tongue darting out to wet his cracked lips. Something else—something too desperate to be hope—mixed with the fear in his gaze.

"Please, take it back." His words were barely audible as he fell forward onto the ground. He groveled at my feet in the churned snow. "I swear, I'll never do it again. Please take the curse back."

Bobby glanced from the prone shifter to me. I'd asked Nathanial the same thing once—to take back the curse. I'd been talking about vampirism, but it was the same request. *Make me what I was.*

But I couldn't. Just like Nathanial couldn't. Steven was a shifter now. *But is he a sane one?*

I stared at the cowering man. Hair that would have been light brown if it were clean hung in heavy, tangled clumps halfway to his shoulders. A light covering of coarse whiskers covered his chin—not thick enough to be called a beard. He hadn't had either in Tyler's memory. I frowned. He wouldn't be filthy if he'd been shifting.

I tilted my head back, sniffed the air. There was no doubt. He'd been tagged. *But he's not shifting?* How many days would a shifter have to go between changes to get so dirty?

"Stand up, Tag-along," I said. Then I winced, realizing I'd used Tyler's sarcastic name for him without meaning to.

He also flinched at the name, his shoulders nearly touching his ears. A fine tremble shook his body, but he pushed off the ground. Stood. This time he kept his gaze down.

I searched his face, searched for signs of insanity. *And exactly what does that look like?* Steven just looked scared. Tired. And young. Way too young.

"It's not a curse," I finally said. "You'll be a shifter until you die."

Which wouldn't be by my hand, if I had anything to say about it. I'd send him back to Firth with Bobby. Hopefully one of the clans would take him in. Teach him how to be a shifter. How to accept the new animal soul sharing his body.

He looked up then. His green eyes wide. "No," he whispered. "No. You have to take it back. You have to. You don't know what it's made me do!"

Bobby growled and spat in the snow. "Your beast doesn't *make* you *do* anything."

Steven cringed again, and I frowned at Bobby. A month ago, I would have whole-heartedly agreed with him, but now I had the memories of a pair of tagged shifters. I knew from those memories that the human mind was too confused to curb the beast's instincts during their first shift. Humans who were intentionally tagged were guided through their first shifts to help them adjust, but even then the insanity rates were high. I had no doubt Steven believed his beast controlled him.

Bryant had, too.

But Bryant had shown no remorse for his actions. He'd given into his every impulse and then compartmentalized the guilt by believing he had no control over his beast. That was why Bryant was dead.

"What did it make you do?" I asked, ignoring the shocked look Bobby gave me.

Steven didn't answer. He stared at the ground. Gil moved closer to me, her shoulder brushing mine. The touch sent a thrill of body heat through me. I swallowed. I had way too little blood in me to be rubbing elbows with anyone. *Oh yeah, I understand impulses.*

Scuttling away from Gil put me closer to Steven. Even stronger than the scent of unwashed body was the reek of fear still pouring off him. Around the edges of my vision, I thought I saw faint yellow outlines twisting around him. Ghostly yellow lines that looked a hell of a lot like what I saw when my mezmer ability decided to help me hunt. I ignored it. I did *not* need my vamp powers rising to the surface right now.

"What are you waiting for?" Gil asked, her eyes widening and brows lifting to emphasis her words.

I was too busy calming my hunger to follow her meaning, and Gil jerked her chin indiscreetly at Steven. *Oh.*

"I don't think he's rogue," I whispered, though at this distance, Steven probably heard me better than Gil. I turned back toward him. "What did your beast make you do?"

Steven glanced between Gil and me. "You're here to kill me?"

I opened my mouth to deny it, but no words came out. If he were rogue or on the verge of turning rogue, it was true. I had to destroy him. I'd tagged him. He was my responsibility.

"I tried to do it myself," he whispered. "Twice. But both times I woke up as that . . . that *thing* instead."

I shared a glance with Bobby. A suicidal shifter? Antidepressants don't work on shifters—our metabolism's too fast. If he were unstable enough to attempt suicide . . .

"I'm your second. Do you want me to take care of him, Kita?" Bobby asked.

I shook my head. I'd never actually accepted Bobby as my second. Not that he'd care. He'd probably walk right up to the elders and tell them he was ready to accept his share of my punishment when he returned to Firth. *Stubborn bobcat.* According to our laws, a second could execute a tagged shifter in danger of turning rogue. But I didn't want Steven executed. He wasn't rogue—not yet, at least. He was confused. Scared. But why wouldn't he be? He was alone. He just needed a chance. He was so young. And so familiar . . .

"Bobby, I want you to take him to a safe-house until the gate opens."

Bobby stared at me. He opened his mouth. Closed it. Opened it again. "Kita, it would be a mercy kill. You heard him."

"Yeah, and I tried to sunbathe a couple days after becoming a vampire. Do you think someone should have mercy on me, too?"

His jaw dropped. "Kitten, you wouldn't—"

"Can you arrange for the safe-house or not?"

He nodded.

"Then it's settled. Now, Steven, the other men with you the night you attacked me, did any of the others change?"

His sour scent of fear turned sharper at my words—which was not the response I expected. I frowned, and the world went black for a second as my eyelids closed. *Crap.* I pried them back open.

"I think I need to get back," I said.

Then my eyelids fell again and I slipped into darkness as dawn approached.

Chapter Twenty-Three

Consciousness hit with a jolt. My eyes flew open, pain blossoming in my chest as my lungs expanded with my first breath of the night.

The pillow under my cheek smelled like Nathanial. I snuggled against it, breathing in more of the scent before my brain caught up with my actions. Realizing what I was doing, I pushed away from the pillow, and the gold–and–cream-colored sheets slid off me.

Apparently Gil had magicked me back to the mansion before full dawn. I frowned at the pillow and then looked around. The blankets hugged the corners of Nathanial's side of the bed, the comforter not turned down until a couple inches from where it pooled around me. At home, Nathanial always made the bed. But never *before* I got out of it. Either he didn't sleep at all during the day, or . . .

"We have been summoned."

I jumped, my head swinging toward the sound of Nathanial's voice. He'd been so still, I hadn't even noticed him leaning against the wall. *Good survival instincts Kita, don't notice the predator in the room.* I pulled aside the gauzy curtains and met his eyes. His cold glare spoke volumes. None of those volumes happy.

"Sorry about . . . " I waved my hand through the air because I couldn't apologize for leaving out loud. Besides, I wasn't *that* sorry. "We found something."

Nathanial continued to stare, not moving, his arms crossed over his chest. He'd never been mad at me before, not like this, at least. I dropped my gaze, looking for something else, *anything* else, to focus on. My gaze trailed over to the bed. It was my pillow that smelled of him. *Only my pillow.*

"Did you—?"

Nathanial cut me off. "Anaya and Clive arrived with an ambassador from Haven late last night."

"Oh." *Then we're out of time.* "How did your negotiations go?"

Nathanial pushed off the wall. His movements were stiff, lacking their usual casual grace. He grabbed a pair of garment bags from a hook in the bureau and tossed them over the edge of the bed.

"The Collector has requested our presence in the grand parlor. Get dressed."

I raised an eyebrow and frowned at the bag. Nathanial turned his back. *Illusion of privacy, or display of frustration?*

"So now what?" I asked as I unzipped the first garment bag. Nathanial didn't answer as I pulled out an awful, cream-colored skirt covering layer upon layer of tulle. The stiff material practically stood on up on its own. "Uh . . . "

Nathanial glanced over his shoulder as I stared dumbfounded at the skirt-thing. "You wear it under an outer garment," he said.

When I didn't move, he stepped around me and unzipped the second bag. It held a satin emerald gown with enough material on the bottom to use as a tent, but only a small, corset bodice that would leave my chest mostly bare.

"Please get dressed."

"Not like I have much choice," I muttered, gathering the clothes. Appearing before the Collector in only the slip wasn't an option. Speaking of the slip . . . where had the gown I'd worn last night gone? I frowned, but one glance at the stiff set to Nathanial's shoulders told me now was not the time to pick a fight. *When this is all over, we're having a talk on personal boundaries.* With my arms filled with garment bags, I headed for the bathroom. Nathanial caught the door before it shut.

I rounded on him. "I'm not going anywhere," I whispered, the words louder than I meant because of the annoyance bleeding into them. "I'm just dressing."

He didn't say anything. He just looked at me with his carefully empty expression and stepped inside, closing the door behind him. *Oh hell.*

I opened my mouth to protest, and he laid a finger over my lips, silencing me. "I felt you succumb to dawn," he whispered, moving close enough that his body heat filled the space between us, but only his one, silencing finger touched me. "I felt the distance. I had no idea if you were safe. And I could do nothing." His hand dropped. "Nothing."

His expression wasn't empty now. The fear, the worry, the aggravation at feeling helpless—it was all there on the surface, exposed and vulnerable.

"I'm here. I'm safe," I whispered because I couldn't look at him and not say anything. I almost reached for him, almost closed the space between us. But I didn't, and the moment stretched, turned awkward. I looked away. "The Collector's waiting. I should dress."

I struggled into the petticoat, all but swimming through the scratchy layers of tulle. The gown presented the next difficulty. By the time I put on the corset, I was ready to search for fire and burn the damn dress. I fought with the lacing, and warm hands slipped over mine, taking the cords and undoing the mess I'd made. Nathanial's long fingers worked methodically, gently tightening the corset as he moved toward the center of my back.

Once he tied it, his hands slipped over my shoulder-blades and moved into my hair. He plaited my hair with practiced movements, and I watched as he piled the tri-colored braid atop my head. He didn't say anything.

"Did you reach a compromise with the Collector?" I asked as the silence stretched sharp enough to abrade my skin.

Nathanial met my gaze through the mirror as he grabbed bobby-pins from the sink. "Not an acceptable one."

Okay, that was probably bad. But Tatius had sent an ambassador, not just demanded we return. "The ambassador's presence means Tatius understands we might not have had a choice, right? Returning to Haven might be an option?"

His gaze dropped. "I do not know."

"You want to stay."

"I do not want you unhappy."

That could have meant anything. I frowned at his reflection, but he didn't look up and he didn't elaborate. Once my hair was sprayed and pinned to the point I would probably have to shear it if I ever wanted to wear any other hairstyle, Nathanial took a step back to look over his work. I tried to turn, but he caught my shoulders. We stared at each other through the mirror.

The damned awkward silence was back, and I shuffled my feet, but I didn't look away. "Legend says vampires cast no reflection," I said, because I had to say something.

Nathanial's reflection smiled at me. "Legend says mirrors reflect a person's soul. Our souls are not missing. You said you found something?"

"More like *someone*," I whispered, casting a leery glance at the walls around us. How could we be sure no one was listening?

Nathanial's right hand trailed from my shoulder to trace the curve of my neck. His fingers left a trail of blessed warmth in their wake, and I forgot all about the possibility of being overheard. He leaned in, his lips touching the flesh where his fingers had been. A shiver ran across my skin.

"Show me." His lips brushed the words over my pulse.

I'd forgotten to breathe sometime between his fingers and his lips reaching my throat, so when I opened my mouth, the only sound that came out was a gasp. My reflection looked surprised at the sound, and Nathanial's eyes pooled with heat.

The glint of his fangs flashed pale against my skin. Broke the flesh. The pinch of pain immediately burned away as his mouth turned blistering hot and my eyelids fluttered. His gaze still held me in the mirror.

I knew I was supposed to remember something. There were things he needed to know. The thoughts escaped me. There was only his mouth. His hands sliding over my body. Those warm gray eyes.

Then I lost all that. Lost all sense. I was just feeling. Just pleasure. Ripped apart. Remade. Spinning. Dying. Burning. Living.

The sensations could have lasted a moment or a million years. I couldn't tell. Couldn't care. But, as the waves of pleasure faded, I was left with twitching nerves and the utter feeling of darkness inside, as if I'd held the sun but it had been taken away.

I blinked. Someone was breathing hard. Making soft noises in the dark.

My vision cleared. Nathanial's eyes—no reflection this time— were inches from mine, his mouth poised only a breath away. I could smell my blood on his lips.

"I should sit down." The words came out husky.

The edge of Nathanial's mouth twitched. He was so close I could only focus on one feature of his face at a time. Too close. Some part of me refused to pull away. Or maybe that was due to the fact the floor tiles were under my head. *Apparently a little too late to try sitting.*

Nathanial was leaning over me. Close. So close. But not touching.

I wanted to be touching.

His eyes studied mine like he thought they would reveal an answer he desperately wanted. He exhaled, his breath washing his scent over me. His mouth followed the breath until his lips pressed against mine.

His palms, pressed against the tile on either side of my head, held his weight. Our lips were the only place our bodies touched. The world narrowed as I surrendered my mouth to his.

Firm but soft, his tongue parted my lips and filled me with the taste of familiar spices. I closed my eyes, yielding to my other senses as

Nathanial's tongue slowly traced the teeth between my fangs. He shifted his weight, breaking contact as he slipped a hand behind my head. My own hands, suddenly restless, moved to his arms, traced his biceps through his dinner jacket.

I thought he would kiss me again. I wanted him to. *Needed* him to. But his brows creased as he studied my face.

"Are you really you?" he asked.

I lifted to meet his mouth.

Surprise flashed through his eyes. Then his fingers tightened behind my head. His lips pressed firmer against mine, his tongue demanding. I froze.

I don't know how to kiss.

Nathanial must have felt my hesitance. He eased back, not pulling away, but no longer demanding. He nipped at my lower lip.

A startled sound escaped my throat. Nathanial's lips pressed a smile against mine, and he nipped again, harder this time. Then he drank down my gasp. The kiss turned gentler, less desperate. His tongue flicked to touch mine before withdrawing. Teasing. Taunting.

Tentatively, I ran the tip of my tongue along his front teeth and discovered the impossibly smooth skin on the inside of his lips. Nathanial moaned into my mouth and my heart skipped a beat.

The next heartbeat crashed loud in my ears. Nathanial jerked back, leaving me cold and floundering until I realized the sound hadn't been my heart but the door banging open.

The newcomer stood inside the doorway, but my eyes refused to focus on him. He was a shadow against darker shadows. Nathanial had moved away, but even in the dark, I knew where he was. Not by his smell or any other sense I could pin-point. I just knew.

The newcomer huffed under his breath. "The Mistress summons you, and you decide to make out on the bathroom floor?"

I knew that smarmy voice—Jomar. I growled, annoyed by his presence. No, not just annoyed. Angry. An anger so complete, it filled me. Filled every sense. There was no one source for the anger. It was like it filtered into me from outside. Baring my fangs, I hissed at him.

"Hermit, you drained your own companion?"

Nathanial stepped in front of me. "Get out," he said, his voice deep, dark.

I reached for him as he moved, smiling as he glanced at me. I couldn't see his features, but I could tell he wasn't happy. No. No, that wasn't good. I didn't want him unhappy.

I pushed to my feet. My legs were shaky, and I swayed as I rose, but I kept my feet. I thought that should have made Nathanial happy—it sure as hell felt like a big accomplishment to me—but as I wrapped my arms around his waist, he stiffened.

"You enthralled her?" the Jomar shadow asked.

Nathanial jumped at the sound of Jomar's voice, his body sliding out of my embrace.

I turned toward the Jomar shadow. *Damn him.* Everything had gone wrong since he showed up.

Without Nathanial's body near mine, without his heat, his presence, cold saturated my skin. I shook.

So cold.

So empty.

So . . . hungry.

Color bled into my vision. Instead of a shadow, Jomar was a red shape, pulsing with warmth.

Warmth I wanted.

I lunged, my fangs extended. I didn't land. Didn't get a chance. Arms wrapped around me. Jerked me back. The door slammed.

"Drink," Nathanial instructed, leaning over me, extending his wrist.

I didn't hesitate. My fangs sank into his flesh. The first mouthful of blessed heat filled me.

Then I fell into his mind. I blinked, confused, as I stared down at the top of *my* head where I bent over Nathanial's wrist.

Too deep, a voice whispered, drawing me away from the confusion.

Emotions tugged at me even as pleasure ripped through me from the fangs in my wrist—*not my wrist?* Guilt twisted through my body. Fear.

Would she understand I had not meant to do it? Would she resent me more?

She who? She me?

My throat convulsed, my fangs retracting. The connection to Nathanial's mind snapped. I was warm. Sated.

And everything was wrong.

What was I thinking? What did I do? Why did I—? I backpedaled, scooting away from Nathanial's crouched body. My back hit the wall. I pressed myself against it. I hadn't been thinking. I hadn't been *me.*

I looked at Nathanial. Colors swirled around his head. Strings of emotions coalesced around him. Emotions turned visual by my mezmer ability. So many colors, so many threads, but Nathanial's face was blank, his hands loose by his side.

"Kita?" he whispered, but he made no move toward me. The colors around him dampened, not fading, but becoming too discouraged to shine in bright hues. Only a single, sickly yellow strand kept its color.

I swallowed. The memory of his thoughts tugged at me. But the memory of his flesh, of his breath against my skin, of his lips, tugged harder. Heat rose to my cheeks. I attempted to hug my legs against my chest. The thick tulle got in the way. I beat at it, taking my confusion out on the layers of material.

"Do you remember?" Nathanial asked.

Did I remember what? Him kissing me? Or me kissing him back? Me reaching for him? Needing him? Did I remember that for a few minutes my world revolved around whether he wanted me? Whether he was happy with me? My teeth ground together. What had Jomar called it? *Enthralling?*

"What did you do?" My voice cracked, the words ragged. *Vamp tricks. He used vamp tricks on me.* But even as the thought sliced through my mind, I knew, I knew with my gut, with my whole body, that he hadn't intended to. The question was, did that matter? *And can I trust my gut?* "That wasn't me. You had to know, that wasn't me."

The muted colors around Nathanial's head blanched. Then they filled with darkness. He shoved away from the floor, not looking at me. "Of course. It could not have been you. How dare I believe you would feel anything, particularly for me."

He turned and the door slammed as he left. My stomach twisted. I wanted to follow.

I suppressed the urge.

Is it even my urge? My want?

Burrowing my head in the mounds of green satin covering my knees, I trembled. The memory of the echoed thought in Nathanial's mind came back to me. *"Would she understand I had not meant to do it?"*

I understood. And I believed him. I might be a mooncursed idiot, but I believed him. What I couldn't believe was me.

A knock sounded on the door. I didn't move.

"We are late." Nathanial's voice held no inflection. No emotion.

I leaned my head against the hard tiled wall. *I can't do this.*

"I'm not going," I whispered, knowing he would hear.

No response came from the other side of the door.

I sighed. "Go without me. They don't need me."

A soft bump sounded, as if Nathanial had leaned his head against the door. "Kita."

Just my name. Nothing else.

I squeezed my eyes closed. I *wanted* to go to him. I *wanted* my name to never sound so lost on his lips. But I couldn't trust it. I couldn't trust myself to be me.

Tatius had used vamp tricks on me. Nothing I felt around him was real. But with Nathanial, I thought . . .

I was wrong. Nothing since I became a vampire made sense. My instincts were off, and now my very emotions were circumspect. A tear hit the tile beside my hand. I stared at the red drop, feeling another trail down my cheek in the same path.

"I'll meet you downstairs." My voice sounded broken, like it was trying to squeeze out of a too-tight throat. Wiping my cheeks with the back of my hand, I sat up straighter. I drew in a deep breath. Held it. "Just give me a couple minutes alone. Please. I'll meet you downstairs. I promise."

Nathanial didn't answer. I waited, slumping against the wall, hugging my knees.

Several heartbeats passed. Then the French doors closed, and I released the breath I'd been holding. It sagged out, shaky, and I did it again. And again.

Once my breathing steadied, I pushed off the floor and examined myself in the mirror. My hair had survived crawling around on the floor, only a couple strands escaping the trap of pins. The dressed had not done as well. Creases and wrinkles marred the skirt, and the bodice was twisted, uncomfortable. I shook the skirt, trying to dislodge the wrinkles as well as I could, but there wasn't much to be done.

Sighing in defeat, I swept out of the bathroom. The bedroom was, thankfully, empty. I considered crawling back into bed. Starting the night over.

I couldn't.

I was expected downstairs. I had to face the Collector, and Tatius's emissaries, and I had to face Nathanial.

Chapter Twenty-Four

"Why aren't you in the parlor already?" a chime-like voice demanded as I trudged down the stairs.

I looked up. Elizabeth stood just inside the main door. *Is she waiting on me?*

"I, uh . . . " I really didn't have a good answer, and I sure as hell wasn't going to tell *her* what had happened upstairs. Jomar had seen enough that the Collector probably already knew more than I was comfortable with.

Elizabeth tapped one dainty foot on the marble floor. "Well, hurry up. You've been missed."

I doubt that. But I did take the stairs a little faster. She led me to the double doors of the parlor and pushed a small button. Ronco opened the door a crack.

"I found her dawdling in the stairwell," she said in a whisper loud enough every vampire in the room could hear.

Great. I glared at her back as Ronco admitted us. Elizabeth sauntered to the Traveler's side, but I loitered in the doorway. Nathanial sat alone on a couch in the center of the room. The Collector sat across from him, her back straight, her posture perfect without looking tense. The Traveler and the twins sat on a couch beside her chair. The third couch was taken by a small figure with dark dreadlocks, who had her back to me. Anaya and Clive stood behind her. *Nuri?* Nathanial had said an ambassador arrived, but Nuri appeared to be Tatius's right-hand vampire. Him sending her had to be a good sign of his intentions. *Or a really bad sign.*

Nathanial inclined his head toward me, indicating the spot beside him on the couch.

"Do sit down so we can continue," the Collector said, sparing me a moment of her cold glare, though she didn't wait for me to comply before resuming the conversation about political obligations she must have been having before I entered.

I sat on the furthest cushion I could and still be on the same couch as Nathanial. Then I squirmed. The skin along my back was tight, uncomfortable. I ignored it. Avin was calling me. I was sure of it. Not that the illogical need to move was easy to ignore. I forced myself to focus on Nuri.

She sprawled on the couch, looking as laid back and unconcerned as Tatius himself might have if he were in the room. I frowned. I'd met Nuri only a few times, but she never *sprawled*. I studied her as casually as I could. A small red, hand-shaped birthmark decorated her golden cheek. *Samantha?*

I looked down, afraid my expression would betray me. *What the hell is going on?* I chanced a glance at Nathanial. *Surely he's noticed?*

"The Puppet Master appreciates the hospitality you've shown his council member, Collector, but it is time for—" Samantha-in-Nuri's-face made it no further as the parlor doors burst open.

Aphrodite, her blond hair foaming around her like a mantle, stormed into the center of the room. Three of her council members and half dozen of her enforcers followed. The enforcers fanned out around the room. Three moved behind my couch, and I cringed, twisting to keep them in view.

"Where is the rest of him?" Aphrodite demanded, her song-like voice shrill as she looked first at the Collector and then Nathanial.

I jumped to my feet, responding to the waves of tension filling the air. I wasn't the only one. In fact, only the Collector kept her chair. She looked at the fuming city master, her face cold, impassive.

"Calm yourself," she commanded, her voice blanketing the rising tempers in the room. "Now, where is the rest of whom?"

Aphrodite's blue eyes flared. "Don't think me a fool, Collector. My memory is not so short. It was only a century ago you brought me here and supported my conquest of this city, and merely a decade ago you supported the ousting of the old master of New Brennan. You may have found a new pet in the Hermit, but I will not be cowed. I have the power to back up my claim to this city."

She thought the Collector was setting Nathanial up to be Master of Demur? I glanced at him, raising an eyebrow. He shook his head, his face carefully empty. No. He didn't know anything about what was going on.

The Collector rose to her feet. "I'm sure I have no idea of what you are speaking. Perhaps we should have this conversation somewhere more pri—"

"No. We're having it here." Aphrodite turned and a vampire carried a silver platter into the room.

In the center of the platter was the head of the General. His blond hair, dark with dried blood, spilled over the sides of the tray, and as the vampire carried the platter closer, the scent of old blood reached my nose. Old blood soured with snake venom.

"The servants discovered this," Aphrodite pointed at the platter, "in the kitchen. I want Gordon's body. And I want it now."

Her gaze speared the Collector, who stared at the platter and its grisly contents.

Another decapitated head. *And more venom.*

"What game is this?" the Collector whispered so quietly I wasn't sure she was aware she'd said it aloud. Then her eyes narrowed. She turned, her gaze landing on Samantha-Nuri. "Your arrival was perhaps too convenient. Your diplomatic immunity just expired." She lifted her hand. "Elizabeth, I think it is time to truth-seek the Truthseeker."

A cruel smile cut across the china doll's face as she stepped forward. Samantha's eyes flew wide. They sought out Nathanial, her expression begging help.

He looked away.

"Wait," I said.

The Collector turned, her gaze slamming into me, her eyes vamp-black. Darkness filled my vision.

"Silence," a voice commanded. I had no choice but obey. Then the darkness retreated as the Collector's attention moved back to Samantha.

"Do you have something to hide, Truthseeker?" One of the twins asked, his arms crossed over his chest, his brother mirroring the position. "If you've nothing to hide, you've nothing to fear."

Samantha glanced at Anaya and Clive. Anaya smiled, but it wasn't a happy look. She grabbed her companion's hand and they vanished.

"Take the Truthseeker," Aphrodite yelled. Her enforcers surged forward.

Samantha never stood a chance. Nathanial never moved.

They held Samantha as Elizabeth grabbed her wrist. Dainty fangs tore into her skin. Samantha ceased struggling.

"She's a pretender," Elizabeth proclaimed, pulling back. "A chameleon. The Mad Hag masked her psyche and powers."

"The Puppet Master's Chameleon?" the Collector repeated. "And the bodies? What does she know of them?"

Elizabeth shook her head. "I see nothing."

A frown stretched across the Collector's face. "Fine. Lock her away." She turned back to Nathanial. "The Puppet Master sent three disposable soldiers to retrieve two psychic vampires, one a member of his own council. Do you think he is a fool, or does he simply not value you, Hermit?"

It was a dig at Nathanial as well as Tatius.

"Think on my words, Hermit. And my offer." She turned away and lifted a hand toward the Traveler. "Aaric, attend me."

The giant moved to her side and offered his arm. She shook her head. Her steps were stiff, her back straight, but as she walked toward the door, there was something slightly off balance to her movements. Something her commanding words and icy eyes didn't reveal, but it was there, in the way she moved.

"We are not done, Collector," Aphrodite said, her lithe arms crossing her chest.

"We are," the Collector said without looking at her.

The offhanded dismissal made color sprout in Aphrodite's pale cheeks. "My second's body is still missing. If the Puppet Master's Chameleon knows nothing of it, it is unlikely he was involved. The guilt falls to your retinue or your new pet. I demand his body and recompense."

The Collector stopped. "I will not continue to ignore your temper, child. Do not push me for I am in a most foul mood."

"As am I." Aphrodite's eyes bled to black. She lifted her hand as if reaching for something in front of her. "I see your fear. I can almost taste it." She closed her fist. "Are you afraid of me, Collector? Or of your schemes unraveling?"

Aphrodite's power surged through the room. It burst from her like an alpha-pulse, crashing over the vampires present and feeling oh so familiar. It called to me. Called to my energy. But no, my first impression was wrong. The power was nothing like an alpha-pulse. The energy filling the room didn't resonate of Firth. It was all vampire. *She's a mezmer.*

And so was I.

I felt my pupils expand and knew my eyes turned vamp-black. I couldn't help it. Couldn't stop it. My ability rose to the surface, answering her surge of energy.

Where a moment before it had looked like Aphrodite gestured in empty air, I now saw the thin yellow strand of emotion that had trailed in the Collector's wake. Aphrodite tightened her grip on the thread, and her power filled the room. The sickly yellow line grew thicker, knotted around the Collector's torso.

Fear.

I knew it. I could almost taste the sourness of it. Aphrodite threw more power into the strand, and the Collector sagged, the fear constricting like a giant serpent.

"Yield to me," Aphrodite commanded, binding the words, her will, with the tendril.

"You're a fool." The Collector's voice caught on the edge of panic, feeding the fear around her, but her eyes went wide, wild. And vampire black.

A glimmer of yellow circled Aphrodite, her own fear rising to the surface. But, she didn't release the Collector's strand. The air turned thick with power. Vampires backed away, yellow fear dripping like sweat from their bodies. Nathanial tugged my shoulders, but I couldn't move. Couldn't look away. I held my breath. Watching.

Aphrodite screamed. A black tendril of rage reached for the Collector, fueling Aphrodite's power.

It wasn't enough.

"To your knees," the Collector commanded, her voice soft but full of steel.

Aphrodite's struggle splashed in a dozen colors around her. Her muscles locked, her teeth gritting as she fought the command.

She lost.

Her knees collapsed beneath her. Darkness spilled from her, until I couldn't see her blond hair beneath it. The tendril of fear slipped from her fingers and shrank, vanishing. Aphrodite's hands sank to the floor by her knees. Her head hung downward, her eyes on the thick carpet.

"Good. Now, stay like that. Edlin, Alion," the Collector said, turning to the twins. "Compile a list of vampires suitable to take over as the new Master of Demur." Then, without another word, the Collector stormed out of the room.

Chapter Twenty-Five

Stunned silence followed in the Collector's wake. Aphrodite remained pressed to the floor, stuck, unable to disobey. *A duel of wills.* And she'd lost.

Her remaining council looked around, clearly uncertain where they fell. The master of their city had just been dethroned. *Will they scatter, or climb over their fallen?* None seemed certain as they milled about. Several excused themselves. The only thing all the vamps appeared to agree on was that none would help Aphrodite.

Nathanial's arm slid around my shoulders, tugging me toward one corner. I hesitated at his touch but let him lead me out of the center of the room. The need to move, to pace pressed on me. Made my skin itch.

Maybe I can just . . . I froze, realizing I was looking for the easiest way out. I didn't *need* to pace. *Damn, Avin's call.*

Wrapping my arms around my chest, I leaned on the wall next to Nathanial and concentrated on being still. If I could ignore the burning need to move, maybe he'd call back later—like next lifetime. *Yeah, and maybe I'm a Labrador.* If I didn't respond to his urge to move, he'd send pain. I knew he would. I could already feel small pinches of fire, like a dozen burning ants crawled over my arms. It was only a matter of time before his patience waned.

I rocked from my heels to my toes, looking around the room, searching for a distraction. The Twins sat on the love seat, reading a newspaper. They were close enough—and my eyesight was good enough—that I could read the headlines from where I was standing. Unfortunately, they were sharing the sports section. Basketball scores couldn't hold my attention. My gaze moved on.

The rest of the newspaper sat on the coffee table in front of the twins. The angle was awkward, but I could just make out the headline *Morgan Heir Found Slain.*

Oh no. I pushed off the wall. I wasn't sure how many heirs Demur boasted, but I'd met a Morgan last night. Snatching the paper off the coffee table, I stared at the vaguely familiar face smiling from the photograph dominating the front page.

Justin Morgan.

I skimmed the article, dread growing in my stomach with each word. Morgan was last seen leaving a symphony with a young woman in her early twenties with tri-colored hair. *Crap.* Authorities were searching for any further information, and a hefty reward was being offered for any tips that led to the arrest of any persons involved in Morgan's death.

The article continued on another page, and I flipped to it. The second page included more information about the man, his family, and his life. No details on his death. I closed the paper and folded it. Morgan's face smiled up at me from above the fold.

You were alive when you ran from that alley.

So what happened after that?

I tossed the paper on the table. The desire to move was nearly a tangible force around me. And not only because of Avin's summoning now. I wrapped my arms over my chest and forced my legs still, my feet planted.

I was so intent on keeping myself together, I barely noticed when a pair of small hands picked up the discarded newspaper.

Elizabeth made a soft sound in her throat. "Wasn't this the man you left the gala with?"

Her face was earnest, but her tone betrayed the fact the question was fake. She knew damn well that I'd left with Morgan.

The twins, arguably the highest-ranking vampires in the room now that the Collector and the Traveler were gone, and with Aphrodite prostrate under a dominance command, took the paper from Elizabeth. They scanned the article, and then looked up. Four brown eyes evaluated me.

"What do you think?" Edlin or maybe it was Alion—I didn't know which—asked.

The question wasn't directed toward me.

His brother shrugged. "Early twenties with tri-colored hair? I say we confine Kita to her room until the Collector can determine her guilt."

Crap. And now I was accused of murder.

৵ • ๖

I paced the narrow area between the bed and the French doors, my fingers rubbing my bare arms. Avin's call was growing worse, but I had plenty else to concentrate on. *How did Morgan die?*

Would Avin have tracked him after I left? But why would he? He couldn't use the body, and if Justin had been "found slain" there was definitely a body.

But what's the likelihood he's a random victim and I just happened to have the bad luck of being the last person seen with him while he was alive? I had a black cat's luck, but really, this latest bombshell was too much. *And there are too many bodies.*

The General's head showing up on a silver platter proved that whoever had been killing in Haven had traveled to Demur with us. *And I know someone with plenty of venom and a nice sharp sword.* The question was, could I prove Akane was behind the killings? *And does she have help?*

Luna had been drained. That indicated a vampire was involved. I frowned, picking up my pace. I needed out of this room. A closer look—and sniff—of the General's head would be useful. Maybe I'd find something that would prove who'd killed him. Hell, too bad I couldn't call in Bobby, or better yet Degan. With his nose, Degan probably could find the General's body. According to the guards, the General's powers revolved around healing. He was supposed to be nearly indestructible unless he was dismembered and his parts scattered. Maybe if we could locate his body and get his head back on, he could tell us what happened to him. Not a lot we could do while he was just a head.

I stopped.

I *did* know someone who could make a head talk. Avin. Of course, I still owed him for the last skull he'd animated—and I had no intention of paying him. He wasn't likely to help me out of the goodness of his dead, non-beating heart.

I paced faster. The Collector was on edge over the murders. What would she give to find the murderer? Would she grant Nathanial and me our freedom? Would she give him Demur? *Would he even want that?* At least it would solve our Tatius issue. *But can he hold a city?*

I had no idea.

I glanced at him. While I couldn't stay still, Nathanial had gone to near statue mode. He sat in the armchair in the corner, his nose in a book. He didn't look up as I studied him. Actually, he hadn't looked at me since we'd reached the room.

I should have been thankful, I suppose. He wasn't pushing me. He was giving me space. But I knew, from being in his thoughts, he was afraid I was going to run.

And I didn't know what to tell him.

Not at all. I didn't even know what I felt. And right now, I was too anxious to figure it out.

A large portion of that anxiety was Avin's spell, I knew that, but the knowledge didn't make it any easier to ignore. Instead it pissed me off, made me want to bust my way through the wall, or fight the vamps for my freedom. Not that either was an acceptable option.

Something crashed in the bathroom, followed by a familiar yelp. I froze. In what felt like slow motion, I turned toward the door and my guards. They were staring at me, having obviously heard the commotion. I hitched my shoulders and flashed them a sheepish smile. They glanced at each other, and Ronco shook his head before they both turned back around. *Thank the moon.*

I didn't run across the room, not quite, at least. I forced myself to slow before I reached the bathroom.

Nathanial stood as I reached the door. His eyes narrowed and the line of his lips all but screamed at me to be cautious. After a moment, he said, "The house of cards I am building us is tenuous at best, particularly considering recent events."

Right, negotiations weren't going well. I knew that, and I'd be careful, but if I didn't go in to see what Gil needed, she might just come out of the bathroom looking for me. I flashed Nathanial the same smile I'd given the guards. Then I slipped inside, shutting the door behind me. He didn't stop me.

Gil was sprawled inside the tub, her legs in the air and the trash can attached to one foot. I twisted the sink faucets on as I passed and then grabbed the aluminum can, tugging it—and Gil's plastic rain boot—off.

"What are you doing here?"

She twisted, trying to push herself up in the base of the tub, but she ended up flailing more than righting herself. I offered a hand and tugged her to her feet.

"The rogue attacked Bobby this afternoon."

I nearly dropped the trash can. "Is Bobby okay?"

"He's fine. He has the rogue contained," she said, trying to untangle a luffa from her dark curls.

I frowned. If Steven had turned rogue, Bobby would have done more than 'contain' him.

Gil continued without noticing my frown. "Bobby wants you to come spend some time with him. He said that a *Torin's* influence can often help stabilize tagged shifters." Her scroll appeared in her hand. "How would that work?"

It worked the same way an alpha-pulse did. It was will and energy used to dominate beta shifters, but I couldn't exactly go into all that right now. Could the guards hear us? According to Nathanial, our room was supposed to be a sanctuary and they weren't supposed to listen, but did that rule apply now that I was under house arrest and suspected of murder?

"Okay. Take me to him." I doubted I'd be any help to Steven. I wasn't a *Torin*. Hell, no matter what Bobby claimed, I wasn't even *Dyre* anymore. But maybe Gil could do something to help combat Avin's call, and I needed answers about Justin's death before the Collector turned her attention to me. Actually, if Justin had died of suspicious circumstances—as in a supernatural was suspected—the mages were probably already investigating. "I need information about Justin Morgan's death while we're out."

For once, Gil didn't ask. She just nodded and reached for me, but a knock sounded on the door before her hand landed. We both froze.

"Go," I mouthed.

She vanished without me.

I let myself out of the bathroom and found Nathanial standing in the open bedroom doorway, talking to someone I couldn't see. He made a small gesture with his hand which could have either been a 'come here' or a twitch.

I was betting against a twitch.

Moving silently, I joined him at the door. Jomar stood on the other side. His ever-present grimace deepened to a scowl when he saw me.

"The Collector requests your presence," he said adding a small bow to Nathanial out of habit and clearly not because of any respect he held for him. "Both of you."

I didn't get a bow. Not that I expected one. It wasn't a request. It was a summons—she should get in line.

෨ • ෬

The Collector sat ramrod straight in her flat-backed chair, the twins lounging on the loveseat beside her, and the Traveler towering behind her. For the first time, her attention focused on me as we walked into the room. *That can't be good.*

"What, pray tell, is this?" She waved at the table in front of her. A table with the front page of the newspaper spread across it.

"Daily rumor mill?"

She didn't seem to find that funny.

"You were in the presence of Justin Morgan last night, yes?" When I nodded, she continued, "And, after leaving the symphony with him, you returned disheveled and with blood on your dress, yes?"

"That was my blood."

Her eyes flashed black.

I tried to look away, but her power sucked me into those eyes, to a world dominated by her presence. Her will.

"You will answer my questions truthfully." Her power wrapped around me, locking me to her will. In the darkness of her gaze, I forgot to breathe, forgot everything. I just nodded, unable to do anything else.

"Good. When you returned, your appearance showed signs of a struggle and your dress was stained with blood. Yes or no?" Her voice, as sharp as cold steel, cut the air around me.

"Yes, but it was—"

"You killed Justin Morgan." It wasn't a question.

"No."

"Then what happened while you were in the young Morgan's presence?"

I couldn't not answer, and I couldn't lie. Caught in her power, I tried to keep my thoughts ahead of my tongue. "I encountered someone I owed a debt." Which was true. It just wasn't everything.

"And this . . . someone, was a supernatural, yes?"

Crap. "Yes."

"Then what happened?"

"I told Morgan to run. He did. It was the last time I saw him." There was no wiggle room in that one. The Collector clearly realized that as well because the silence stretched.

She'd gotten her information, more than I'd wanted to share, and I expected the darkness to pull back. It didn't. Instead she asked, "What can you tell me about the General?"

The question was so broad, I could technically tell her anything at all I knew. But I gave her what she needed to know and hoped it would win me some favor. "The blood in his hair smells of snake venom."

"The Hermit said you smelled venom in the body you found in Haven as well."

I hadn't known he'd told her about it, but I nodded. "That is true. The scent compared to my own blood after Akane poisoned me."

"But this scent is one only you can smell and therefore not proof."

I gritted my teeth. *She has me caught in a compulsion not to lie, and she still doesn't believe me?*

The swirl of power around me tightened, seeped under my skin.

"You will bring me a shapeshifter."

The command dug into my mind, latched on. *Oh hell no.* But it was an order, a compulsion. I couldn't refuse. Couldn't say no. I couldn't even open my mouth to try.

But I could bargain.

"In exchange, you will grant Nathanial and me permission to leave if we wish."

I felt her shock vibrate in the air before she surprised the hell out of me.

"Done. You are a thorn in my side," the Collector said, as if it were her idea in the first place.

The darkness retreated, leaving me staring at her cold brown eyes, but the compulsion remained. I could feel it twisting inside me. She'd commanded me to bring her a shifter, and I had to do it. I just had to. But the compulsion conflicted with Avin's call. I couldn't answer him while bringing the Collector her shifter, and the two compulsions warred inside me, both fighting for precedence. In the end, while the need to move held me, made my skin itch, the opposing urges balanced and created a type of stasis.

I schooled my face as I realized this. I wasn't about to let the Collector know she'd done me a favor. Besides, if she realized what was happening, she might give me a time limit, and then the balance might shift.

"You are dismissed. Jomar, remove her from my presence," she said, waving her hand.

A familiar grip closed around my bicep and I gritted my teeth. As Jomar steered me toward the door, Nathanial fell in step beside me.

The Collector cleared her throat. "Hermit, I have much to discuss with you yet."

I kept walking. I needed to summon Gil.

Chapter Twenty-Six

"Isn't there a way to back out of the deal or retroactively add conditions?" I asked. The restaurant's table shook with my tapping foot, but I couldn't stay still.

Gil frowned at me. "I haven't seen Avin in days, but if he called in his favor, just do what he asks. You agreed to the price."

Yeah, last unnamed favor I'm ever agreeing to. "Okay. Fine. Just—" I stopped and glanced at the table next to us where Steven sat devouring a stack of pancakes. The opposing compulsions were burning inside me, growing worse. I leaned closer to Gil and Bobby. "Don't let me pick directions or wander. Okay?"

I hated admitting to the weakness. To the fact I couldn't even trust my own actions. But if I wandered I might head straight for Avin, and if I chose the direction, I might inadvertently lead Bobby and Steven to the Collector. I couldn't allow either to happen, so it was better if I just put it out on the table and let one of them decide where we needed to go. Though the idea of following made me want to grind my teeth.

Actually, wait, no. I really was grinding my teeth. That must have been from fighting the compulsion. I forced my jaw to loosen and squirmed in my seat, jerking at the skirt that took up my entire side of the booth.

We made quite a strange group with me way overdressed for a midnight dinner, Gil in her Easter-egg pink coat and big rain boots, and Steven in clothes that hung off his body and obviously belonged to someone twice his size. Bobby, the natural-born shifter who could only achieve fully human form because of the gift locked in his necklace, was the most normal-looking one among us. That had to amuse the hell out of him. At least he'd managed to clean Steven up so it didn't look like we'd dragged in a starving urchin.

"So, did you find anything about Justin Morgan?" I asked, ignoring the stares our two tables gathered.

Gil's scroll appeared in her hand. "Actually, yes. It's strange. He was apparently—"

The diner door opened with the sound of clanging bells. Steven jerked at the sound, dropping his orange juice into his pancakes.

"—beheaded. The investigators in Sabin—"

Steven stared at his ruined meal. A muscle bulged over his jaw. His eyes narrowed.

"—think that—"

Steven swiped the plate off the table, sending it and the orange juice soaked pancakes flying across the diner.

The plate smashed into a wall and Gil yelped, falling silent.

"Hey!" the waitress yelled.

Steven's eyes snapped to her. His jaw clenched but his top lip curled up over his teeth. The waitress faltered.

Crap.

I struggled to free myself from the booth but the damn gown tangled around my legs. Bobby shot to his feet.

"Steven," he said, his voice a low rumble of warning.

The city-shifter ignored him. Steven leaned forward so he could see the waitress around Bobby's body. A growl tumbled from his throat, and his muscles bunched like he would bound out of his seat and after the waitress any moment.

"Quiet," I snapped, finally fighting my way free of the booth.

Steven's eyes tore from the waitress to focus on me. He cringed, his shoulders hunching until they touched his ears. It would have been amusing to see a six-foot man, even an obviously undernourished one, cower in front of little ol' me—except he wasn't acting stable, and I had the unfortunate role of judge, jury, and executioner if he went rogue.

"See," Gil hissed as Bobby hauled the cowering man out of the booth chair.

I frowned at her, and Bobby tossed some money on the table. He all but dragged Steven out of the diner as the city-shifter made pathetic, mewling sounds. I half expected someone to try to stop us, but the patrons—and definitely the staff—appeared happy to see him go.

"He's a little drunk," I whispered to the waitress as I passed her.

She snorted, shaking her head. "Clearly."

Once out of the diner, I turned up the street. Then I stopped. *I'm just walking again.* I couldn't let myself do that. I ran into Avin every time I took off without a direction in mind. I turned to Gil.

"You said Morgan was beheaded?"

She nodded, and Steven stumbled.

His eyes went wide as he stared at me. "What are you talking about?"

I frowned at Steven. If Morgan was beheaded, his death had to be related to the other murders. And I'd bet my tail—if I still had one—that it was no coincidence I was the last person seen with him.

"It's complicated," I said, earning a confused look from the city-shifter. *Oh what the hell. He's a temporary member of my little makeshift clan until Bobby can get him to Firth. No point keeping him in the dark.*

"Gil, take us to the spot the body was found. I think I'm being framed for murder."

ڼ • ۆ

Police tape still marked the alley where Justin Morgan's body had been found, but the crime scene investigators had long since come and gone. All that remained was the tape and a lot of dirty, churned snow.

I looked around. We weren't far from the concert hall. *Was Morgan still alive when I stumbled back up the steps in shock or was he already dead by that point?* The paper hadn't mentioned anything about a frantic 9-1-1 call, so he might have met the killer while I was still blacked out in the snow only a few alleys away.

But how? And why?

Akane hadn't attended the symphony, hadn't been with us. *But one of the limos was missing when we tried to leave.*

It could have been a coincidence—but there were a lot of 'could be a coincidences' stacking up. I tilted my head and searched by scent for evidence of what had happened in the alley. I smelled people, lots of people, and city scents, and under that, old blood. I found nothing I could pinpoint as the killer's scent, and not a clue that Akane had been in the alley. Of course, a day had passed, and there had been a lot of foot traffic. *I could just be missing it.*

I glanced at Bobby. His nostrils also flared as he sifted through the scents on the scene, but the way he paced the edge of the taped line was a good indication that he wasn't finding anything.

Steven rubbed a hand over his nose. "It stinks here."

"You're probably picking up on the old blood," I said, ducking under the crime tape. Steven hadn't been born with a shifter's nose. He probably still got overwhelmed with how much keener his senses were than when he was human.

He wrinkled his nose, following me under the tape. "I know what blood smells like. This is different. Sour. Musky."

I stopped. *Sour musk?* That's what the skinwalker smelled like to me. I tilted my head back again, rolled the scents in the alley through my senses.

No musk.

Frowning, I glanced at Bobby. He shook his head. Then neither of us could smell it. But Bobby and I were cats. Steven was a wolf. His nose would be stronger.

I turned to Steven. "You're sure?"

He cringed, stepping back like my attention hurt him, but he nodded. "I've never smelled anything like it."

So Akane *had* been here. *Now how do I prove that?* It was one thing to prove I didn't kill Justin and another to prove Akane had been a very treacherous serpent. I could take Steven to the Collector. Then it wouldn't just be a 'scent only I could smell'. *That could*—I stopped.

Crap. How could I even consider taking Steven to the Collector? *When you can't even trust yourself . . .*

"Bobby, see if you can help Steven track the scent, but be careful."

Both shifters frowned at me.

Bobby crossed his arms over his chest and rolled his shoulders back. It was a stubborn stance, one ready to argue. "Why does it sound like you're going somewhere?" he asked.

Because I was. I had to get away from Bobby and Steven before I slipped and followed the compulsion to take a shifter to the Collector. As long as I was with them, they were in danger.

"We're splitting up." It was the only way. I turned to Gil. "Think you can get us into the morgue?"

❧ • ❧

An hour later, I'd learned only one thing: Autopsied bodies suck for clues.

Any scents left by his attacker had been washed from the body, and I couldn't tell from looking at the processed corpse if he'd bled out at the scene or been drained beforehand. The only thing seeing his body confirmed was that his head had been severed by a bladed object.

I had Gil drop me off back at our bathroom in the mansion. *Maybe Nathanial will have some ideas.*

The room beyond was silent, which meant Nathanial was still downstairs, in conference with the Collector. *And stars know how long that will last.* I slipped out of the bathroom quietly.

The smell hit me first.

210

Sour musk, cold and reptilian.

Then I saw the movement.

The large snake slithered out from under the bed like an unfolding shadow. It lifted its head, tongue flicking, tasting my scent. Then it lunged.

I'd never realized something without legs could move so fast.

I dove to the side, barely avoiding the strike. I rolled as I hit the ground and concentrated on my hands. *Come on. Come on. I need claws.*

No shift. No spasms.

Crap.

The snake lunged again. And I jumped.

"Back off, Akane."

She didn't.

The snake reared, preparing for another strike. As she lunged, I made a dash for the French doors.

They were locked.

Ronco leaned on the outside of the glass, his girth obstructing the seam and half of both doors. I pounded on the panels as Akane geared for another strike.

"Open the doors!"

Ronco turned. Slow, too slow. He glanced at me then at Akane.

Yes, you big oaf. Look at the big, mooncursed snake attacking me.

He lifted a bushy eyebrow. Then he turned back around. Leaned on the doors again.

Oh crap. They're allies.

Akane struck and I dropped. Cold scales grazed my arm. *Too close.*

I tried to jump to my feet, but the layers of tulle bunched around my legs so I was forced to roll, still tangled in the gown. I pushed up as the snake lunged. Fangs as long as my fingers filled my vision, and my hands shot out, wrapped around the snake's body.

The impact knocked me to the ground, but I dug my fingers in, gripping the cold, scaled body. Holding on. The jaws snapped closed an inch from my nose. *I stopped her.*

Well, I stopped her *head.*

Her clammy coils brushed my waist and circled my body. Crap, I couldn't let her wrap herself around me. She was one huge muscle. She'd crush me.

I also couldn't release her, or I was good as dead.

I screamed, my frustration, anger, terror, everything bursting out of my throat as her body locked around my legs. A tremor shot through my hands. Then another. My fingers spasmed, the skin over my fingertips split, and Akane wiggled forward in my grasp.

I pressed my head back against the carpet. Another transforming spasm shot through my hands. *Come on, I need claws, no paws, like the last time.*

The spasms settled into claws.

I dug into the snake's thick hide. Blood dripped down my fingers. *There has to be a spine in here somewhere.*

Akane hissed, and her coils loosened. She reared back, pulling away. The wash of blood made her neck slick, hard to hold. My grip slipped. My claws took a layer of scales with them as she shrank away.

I tried to roll to my feet, but again the tulle got in the way. I fought my way up, but by the time my legs were under me, Akane was already across the room. She shoved a grate aside and slithered into the open vent. Disappeared.

Dammit.

I looked around. The room was empty. I was alone. Covered in acrid snake blood, but I was unhurt. And I had a fistful of snake scales. *Let's see the Collector doubt this.*

I marched to the doors. Ronco still leaned against the outside, ignoring what I'm sure was meant to be my death. *Well, I have news for you buddy.*

Wrapping a corner of my skirt around my hand, I shoved my fist through one of the large panels. The glass shattered. Ronco leapt forward, whirling around. I smiled at him as I reached through the broken glass and unlocked the door from the outside.

"I need to see the Collector. Now."

Chapter Twenty-Seven

"—Only if you can guarantee Kita will not be subjected to—" Nathanial fell silent as I swept into the parlor. Every eye in the room landed on me as the door clicked closed.

The Collector cocked her head to the side, regarding me with lifted eyebrows. "You come before me covered in blood? Again?"

"I was attacked," I said, then added, "under your roof." After all, she'd made a point of classifying Nathanial and me as *'guests,'* so it was *her* hospitality in question. She'd made a big deal about that with Tatius.

The Collector skewed her lips, and I let my gaze drift to Nathanial. He'd moved to the very edge of his seat, his eyes going black. They darted over me. I nodded to him, confirming I wasn't hurt.

The Collector turned toward me. "What is your claim?"

Walking to the center of the room, I held up my fist, letting everyone see the dark scales. "Your skinwalker attacked me, and your guard ignored the attack."

Ronco rushed forward. "She lies, Mistress."

The Collector's eyes narrowed. "Elizabeth!"

I cringed as the small vampire stepped forward, expecting her to turn toward me. She didn't. Instead she walked over to Ronco and took his wrist. Her fangs flashed.

Now the truth will come out.

Everyone waited. I didn't even breathe. Perhaps I even looked like a real vampire for once. Nathanial rolled to his feet and casually moved to my side.

Elizabeth pulled back, sealing the wound in Ronco's wrist. Then she approached the Collector, curtsying deeply. "There is no memory of an attack in his mind," she said without straightening.

What? I blinked at her. "That's not possible. He looked at me. He looked at me and then turned around."

"There is no memory," Elizabeth repeated.

"A vamp trick." It had to be. It was the only way. "He saw Akane attack me. He must be covering the memory. He—"

"Silence," the Collector snapped. "Hermit, your companion's youth is no excuse for her reckless accusations nor her ignorance. I suggest you keep a tighter leash on her."

Nathanial's hands closed on my shoulders, dragged me back a step. I frowned at him. I wasn't wrong. I knew I wasn't. It had to be a vamp trick.

"But—" I started.

Nathanial shook his head. He leaned in, and my heart jumped as his lips brushed my ear. "Ronco is a soldier vampire. Soldiers are fast and strong, but their minds are as simple as a human's. No soldier has ever developed a psychic ability, and Ronco is not even a master. There is no trick. He has no memory of an attack."

That's not possible. It just wasn't.

Elizabeth watched me from the corner of her eye. Dipping lower in her curtsy, she said, "It appears the Hermit's companion decided to break down the doors of her room. That may explain the blood."

Of all the mooncursed— "And this?" I held up the scales.

The Collector's cold glare burned into me. I didn't back down. Opening my fist, I waved the scrap of flesh. The lights shimmered along the black scales and the dark blood still clinging to my claws.

"Send for Akane," the Collector commanded.

A door opened. Closed. I waited. Nathanial's fingers dug into my shoulders. No one said anything. Then the door opened again, bringing with it a fresh wave of snake musk. My lips curled back as the skinwalker made her way through the room.

She bowed before the Collector. "You summoned me?"

"The Hermit's companion claims that you attacked her. What do you have to say about this accusation?"

"It is false."

Yeah, right.

"I have proof." I tossed the scrap of shredded scales at her feet like I was tossing down a gauntlet.

She stared at the shredded snake skin. "Where did you get that?"

I glared at her. *As if she doesn't know.* "It was caught in my claws. When you attacked me."

Akane turned. Her gaze dropped respectfully as she faced the Collector, but her dark eyes were hard. "Mistress, no," she whispered.

"You deny the accusation?"

"I can prove it false." Her hands moved to the length of cloth securing her kimono. She all but ripped the silk, tearing the material off her body. Naked, she lifted her hair, baring her skin for all the room.

The only wound on her body was the old, healing, claw mark on her right shoulder.

"Impossible." I started forward, but Nathanial tugged me back. How could Akane not have a mark on her? It just wasn't possible.

Unless there are two of them.

"You are dismissed," the Collector said to Akane. Then her gaze slammed into me and Nathanial. "Hermit, your companion has falsely—and publicly—accused *two* of my people. She is also suspected by the human police of murdering a prominent human citizen of Demur. In light of these events, I rescind her guest status. Elizabeth."

A smile stretched across Elizabeth's china-doll face. *Oh crap.*

"No." I stepped back, but Nathanial was still behind me, and he wasn't moving. I glanced over my shoulder, begging him with my eyes.

He shook his head, one sharp movement that sliced through my body. His hands remained locked on my shoulders. His expression might as well have been carved from stone. "Do not make this worse," he whispered. "She will read your memories, nothing more." His face might have given away little, but I could taste the worry in his words.

"Let us see what truly occurred," Elizabeth said, reaching for me.

After one last pleading look at Nathanial—which only confirmed that I had to allow this—I swallowed my panic and lifted my wrist. My arms were still covered in the snake's drying blood, and Elizabeth crinkled her nose, but she said nothing as her fangs pierced my skin.

Nathanial's tight grip on my shoulders kept me anchored as sensation spread from her mouth through my body. I squeezed my eyes shut, fighting the heat building in me. Then it was over.

Elizabeth stepped away. "Mistress, her mind is strange. I saw no attack—"

What? "Tha—"

She continued, lifting her small, chime-like voice over mine. "I also could find no memory of the scales."

The Collector frowned. "You are certain? You are a master of peeling away layers of memories. You saw nothing?"

"Forgive me." Elizabeth ducked, as if the Collector's disappointment in her failure was a physical weight falling on her shoulders. "I looked, but it is like the scales did not exist before she stormed into the room." She paused, a hesitation as if she considered a new thought, but her eyes flickered toward me and the edge of her lips lifted. "Or like it was an illusion."

Crap. Behind me, Nathanial went statue still. I didn't have to look back at him to know what he was thinking. *That little—* She was lying. She'd lied about Ronco's memory, and now she was lying about mine.

The Collector pushed out of her chair. "Remove them from my presence."

Enforcers surged forward.

"Wait," I said.

They didn't.

Jomar rushed at me and I centered my weight. I lifted my hands, flexing my claws.

"Do not fight them," Nathanial whispered.

The hell? If there was ever a time to fight our way out, it was now.

I swiped at Jomar. He dodged, but the vampire beside him wasn't quite as fast. I scored a gouge in that vamp's arm. Not that the injury slowed him. Hands locked around my arms, and I lashed out, kicking, scratching.

"Stop," a pair of masculine voices yelled in unison.

The enforcers fell back.

I crouched. Waiting. Ready.

The twins walked across the room, the enforcers scrambling out of their way as they approached. I flexed my fingers.

"Sleep."

The command crashed through my brain, took me off guard. One minute I was watching them approach, and the next there was only darkness.

❦ • ❧

"No, I—" My eyes flew open. The parlor was gone, replaced by a gauzy golden canopy. *The bed?* Nathanial sat on a chair dragged to the side of the bed. His hands rested on the mattress, as if he'd just released my arm. I frowned at him as I sat up.

"What happened? How long have I been out?"

Nathanial stared at me. His gray eyes were cold, assessing. It wasn't reassuring. "You have slept only a moment."

Then why is he looking at me like that? I glanced at the door. Jomar stood outside the busted frame. He didn't look at us, but I had no doubt he could hear every word spoken. And I wasn't a guest anymore, so no hospitality laws protected me.

"How much danger are we in? Elizabeth lied about—"

Nathanial's eyes showed strain, the corners pinched. "Silence, Kita."

His tone was hard.

Cold.

"What?"

"There is no memory of an attack." He was staring at me like he didn't know me.

Heat rushed to my face. *He doesn't believe me?* "She lied, Nathanial."

He pushed away from the bed, shaking his head.

I followed him. *How could he not believe me?*

"She lied."

He rounded on me. His fingers wrapped round my shoulders, but he kept me at arms distance as he stared at me.

"I looked, Kita. I looked."

Looked? *In my mind.* I glanced down at my wrist. He'd been there, perched over me when I woke. He'd been riffling through my memories. *And he didn't find anything.*

How is that possible?

"Surely you felt the attack? Through our bond. You felt it?"

He released my shoulders. Stepped back. Looked away. "You have been anxious and on edge since dark fell. You have had spikes of panic several times." He shook his head. "I do not know what I felt."

And that was it. *He doesn't believe me.* I'd been fighting conflicting compulsions all night, had been tormented by Avin's call. The attack must have been lost in the mix.

"But the blood and the scales. . . "

He turned his back on me. "I know you called Gil against my wishes."

Something shook loose inside me. I couldn't trust my emotions. I wasn't sure what was real. But I knew I hurt. This hurt. If he'd have looked at me, I would have withered under his cold eyes. But he didn't look at me. And that was worse.

I reached out, touching his elbow. "Nathanial?"

He *knew* me. Hell, sometimes I thought he knew me better than I knew myself. How could he not believe me?

He glanced at my hand on his arm, and then back at me. He didn't say anything, but his face, tight, drawn, it said he *wanted* to believe me. But those eyes. Those eyes that could be both hot and cold, that could look deeper than I wanted. Those eyes looked old for once, worn from the four-hundred years they'd witnessed, and they'd seen lies, and deceptions, and betrayals. He might want to believe me, but he'd believe what he'd seen, or in this case, what he hadn't seen—the memory of an attack.

A throat cleared outside the room. I jumped, my attention snapping to the door.

Elizabeth stood just outside the spray of shattered glass. "Hermit, the Collector commands your presence."

He nodded, and the guards stepped back, letting him pass. He left without another glance at me.

And then I was alone.

Chapter Twenty-Eight

I paced the narrow area in the bathroom as I waited for Gil. She appeared before the last syllable of her name crossed my lips for the third time.

"Stop doing that," she hissed. "Call once. I'll come if I can. Stop summoning me!"

I paused, one foot hanging in the air. *Summoning?* "You can't not come?"

She didn't answer. Instead she focused on smoothing the front of her coat. Then she looked around the small bathroom. "Very little time has passed in this world since I left."

Not much time, but so much bullshit. I didn't even know where to start. Not that I could explain with Jomar only a room away, listening.

I lowered my voice until I was afraid Gil wouldn't be able to hear above the bathroom's running water if I whispered any quieter. "I need to sneak into the skinwalker's room."

"Why would you need me for that? You're the one who can pick locks."

"Because I'm under guard inside this house. Can't you just, I don't know, '*pop*' into the room the same way you appear and disappear all the time?"

"I've never been to her room. In order to work, the spell needs a location I *know*."

"You appeared in Tatius's room. I'm sure you'd never been there before."

Gil lifted one shoulder in a small shrug, but she looked down, not meeting my eyes. "I was able to do that because I put a location spell on you. It sort of . . . acts like an anchor when you're in places I've never been."

More spells being used on me? I forced a breath out between my teeth, making sure that when I spoke, my voice would be level. I wasn't going to over-react about this, really, I wasn't. That didn't mean I wasn't pissed.

"Okay, so you can't magic your way into Akane's room. There is a vamp named Jomar guarding the door. Is there *anything* in your magical arsenal that will get us past him?"

Gil tugged at her coat sleeves. "It's harder to cast spells on supernaturals and . . . " She trailed off.

She'd actually told me that before. But . . . "There are apparently two types of vamps. Jomar is something called a soldier. No mental powers."

Her eyes widened. "I've never read about different lines of vampires. Can you expand on—"

"Later, Gil," I said between clenched teeth. "Do you know a spell that will work or not?"

"I've read about a spell that *might* work."

Might was better than nothing. "Try it." I had to get into Akane's room. This went beyond proving Akane was behind the murders. She'd attacked me. *And Nathanial doesn't believe me.*

Gil nodded. "I'll have to prepare. Get this 'Jomar' inside. I'll be right back." She vanished.

Get him inside? I crept out of the bathroom. Jomar still stood in the hall with his back to the French doors, his hands clasped behind him. *How do I talk him inside?* It wasn't like I could invite him in for tea and scones.

I felt a nearby tingle of magic, and Gil poked her head out of the bathroom. She gave me a thumbs up, then pointed at Jomar and motioned that I should get him into the bathroom.

Great. Not just *inside*, I had to get the nasty-tempered vamp to the tiny bathroom. *How can I convince him*—an idea hit me. I dashed across the room and flung open the door.

"There's a spider."

He gave me a dumbfounded look. "What?"

"A spider. On the ceiling. In the bathroom." I pointed at the closed bathroom door.

"So?"

"So kill it!" I made my voice lift in tone, like I was close to hysteria, but I kept my volume low. I didn't want anyone else coming to find out what was going on. "I have a major phobia about spiders."

Jomar just stared at me. I shuffled my feet. *This isn't going to work.* I shot a quick glance at the bathroom, trying to keep my body language frightened.

Jomar sneered, his lip curling back.

"Fine." He grabbed my arm and marched across the room. "After you," he said, still holding onto me and indicating the bathroom door.

Please let Gil's aim be good with this spell. She didn't have the best reputation with magic. I jerked open the door and walked inside, Jomar following behind me.

He halted. "What the—?"

Magic cut through the air before the door had time to swing shut behind us. He hit the tiled floor with a thud, and Gil grinned so hard her face nearly split.

I glanced down at the vampire sprawled by our feet. He wasn't breathing, but then, vampires didn't need to.

"He's still alive, right?"

"As much as he was before. I think." She stepped around his limp body.

I squatted beside him, listening. It seemed a long time before I heard Jomar's heart beat, but it sounded strong. "How long will he be out?"

"Uh . . ." Gil's smile faded. "I don't actually know. The book wasn't completely clear about that." She sucked her bottom lip in her mouth and stared at the unconscious vampire. "We should probably hurry."

I led the way out of the bedroom and down the hall. When we reached Akane's door I stopped and listened. All was quiet. I didn't knock, I just pushed open the door and ducked inside.

The room was dark. Empty. *Thank the moon.*

Gil followed, and I shut the door behind her. She blinked, her hand groping along the wall.

I grabbed her wrist. "No lights."

"I can't see."

Right, I kept forgetting that just because I had near-perfect night vision, not everyone else did. "Use your magic globe thing."

She glared at me—which she might not have realized I could see. A small purple ball of magic appeared over her palm. She held it up like a lantern and glanced around the room. "What are we looking for?"

"Clues?" I wasn't sure. A blood trail leading out of the ductwork would be good. Or maybe Akane's castoff skin, with a big fist-sized hole in it, ripped by my claws.

Gil headed for the closet as I made my way to a dresser. The drawers were empty, which, considering Akane was part of the

Collector's traveling show and not a member of Aphrodite's city, didn't surprise me. A long case sat atop the dresser, and I dragged it off. Setting the case on the bed, I flipped open the lid.

"Did you find something?" Gil asked, popping her head out of the closet. As she moved, her bubble of light reentered the room, and a purple glow bathed the red-velvet lining of the box.

Nothing was inside.

I shook my head, then stopped. There was nothing in the box currently, but the impression in the lining looked a hell of a lot like a sword. *If she used that sword to decapitate the victims* . . . I leaned forward, all but pressing my nose into the velvet. The box smelled of the wood it was made from, a smoky fragrance like incense, and oil.

No hint of blood.

Frowning, I shut the box and returned it to the dresser. *There has to be something here.*

Gil moved from the closet to the bathroom. Bottles clinked as she sifted through Akane's toiletries. She gave no indication she was finding anything. *If I were Akane, where would I hide something?*

I looked around. There was nothing in the room. Just the dresser and the bed. I dropped to my knees and peered under the bed. A small suitcase was shoved underneath. I squirmed under the bed and dragged it out. Several ornate kimono wrapped in thin paper were inside. Nothing else. *Useless.*

A footstep sounded outside the door. My head snapped up and I listened, hoping whoever it was continued down the hall. They didn't.

Crap.

Gil stepped out of the bathroom just as the doorknob clicked, twisted. I frantically waved her back. She vanished her light and ducked back into the dark bathroom. I crouched beside the bed, watching the door from around the footboard.

Akane stepped into the room, but her hand paused by the light switch. She tilted her head back, her nostrils flaring.

"I smell you, beast," she whispered. She flicked on the light, her dark gaze sweeping the room. "Where are you hiding?"

I held my breath, not moving, as Akane stalked forward. If I could have reached Gil she'd have gotten us both out, but Akane was between me and the bathroom door. She reached under her kimono and drew her sword.

I held my breath. *I can't just huddle here like a treed raccoon—she'll find me the second she steps around the bed.*

I stood, and the skinwalker stopped short. She lifted her sword and dropped into a defensive stance in one fluid movement. I edged around the bed, not moving forward so much as sideways. I was stronger than her, and probably faster, but she had a sword.

We stared at each other, neither moving forward, both waiting, looking for an advantage. If I didn't think of something, she was going to decide *she* had it.

"Why are you killing vampires?" I asked.

"I *hate* vampires." She spat the words, like *vampire* tasted bad in her mouth. "I would rid world of them. But the vampire I hate most, she lives. If I killed, I kill her first."

"The victims have been poisoned."

She flashed teeth at me. It was almost a smile. "I know. I smell the blood."

"You poisoned them."

"No." She stepped forward, testing me. I splayed my clawed fingers and she hesitated. "Not my poison. My sister's."

Her sister's? The Collector had mentioned the fact Akane had a sister—she'd also said the sister had died horribly when her transition to vampire failed.

"She's dead."

Akane nodded. "*Murdered.*" No sorrow in her voice. Just anger.

Is this about revenge? Was she killing to avenge her sister? But she was right, the one vampire who she would have truly wished dead, the one who ordered her sister changed, was still alive. The Collector.

Whatever Akane saw in my face made her tip her head back and laugh, but there was no mirth in the sound. "You made deal with Collector. Agreed to betray your own for your freedom. *You* have no honor. My sister had honor." Akane slid forward another step. "She also made deal, but she sacrificed self. She agreed to become vampire in exchange for *my* freedom. She die. Collector keep me. Now, my sister return. Seek vengeance."

"A ghost?" I rocked back on my heels.

A few weeks ago I wouldn't have believed in ghosts, but now? I'd met vampires, mages, necromancers, demons, and skinwalkers—who was I to dispute the existence of a vengeful ghost?

But I'd fought the snake, and it sure as hell had felt real to me.

Akane's muscles bunched, her center of balance changing, and suddenly she was moving. She leapt forward, her sword swinging in an arc toward my neck.

I dove to the side.

"Gil!"

The scholar popped out of the bathroom as I dodged a second attack. The tingle of her magic washed over the room.

I hit the ground, rolling from Akane. I didn't know what spell Gil planned to use, but her magic didn't always work as intended.

Akane whirled around just as the purple light of Gil's barrier spell lit the room. The spell promptly imploded, and the backlash slammed into the skinwalker. She was hurled into the air, right over my ducked head. Then she crashed into the wall with a hard thud.

Once the purple light died, I looked up. Akane slumped on the floor, breathing, but dazed. Her sword was halfway across the room.

Gil gave me a sheepish look. I could have laughed. "You did that on purpose?"

She shrugged, her smile breaking through. "That stupid spell never works quite right. Always explodes on me."

Akane stirred, and I pushed off the floor. "Let's get out of here."

With a nod, Gil tossed me into the void.

k • k

The moment the dim light in the bathroom broke through the void, I knew something was wrong. The stench of blood coating the air was a big hint.

"Don't go anywhere," I told Gil as I pushed off the tile.

Ignoring my twisting stomach, I shoved the door open a crack. The scent of blood grew stronger. Whatever had happened, someone had been hurt, bad. And there was a sour stink in the blood.

The skinwalker?

I shoved the door open an inch at a time and scanned the room from the vantage point of my low crouch. Nothing moved. I crept out of the bathroom, staying low, making myself a small target. The *thwup* of Gil's rain boots on the carpet followed me.

"Get back," I mouthed at Gil. Something moved in my peripheral.

I whirled back around, my eyes searching. Nothing. Then it moved again. A dark drop of liquid dripped from the bed's sodden coverlet, landed in an expanding pool of blood on the carpet.

Oh no. Forgetting caution, I ran to the edge of the bed.

Jomar's mangled body had been tossed in the center. His severed head sat on the pillows, staring down at the long gashes that had torn open his belly. Dark organs spilled out of the four long gashes. *It looks like an animal attacked him.*

I froze, that thought catching in my chest. His body was in *my* bed, and it looked like someone had eviscerated him with claws.

"Oh crap." This looked bad. Really, really bad. And majorly incriminating.

"What's going on?" a voice yelled.

I jumped and whirled toward the doors. Ronco and the twins were there. Their eyes moved from me to the corpse and gore spread over the bed.

"I, uh—" I could not explain *this*.

Magic surged through the air, and the scene vanished.

"Take me back, Gil!" I yelled into the darkness.

The void didn't answer.

I flailed in the nothingness and light pierced the darkness, making the world spin.

"Take me back," I gasped again, pushing away from the dirty snow of some city alley. My limbs shook, but I climbed to my feet. "You have to take me back to the mansion. Now."

"Kita, that was a dead body. In *your* bed." Gil crossed her arms over her chest. "And those vampires looked none too happy about it. I've officially deemed this situation too dangerous for you."

"And who are *you* to decide that for me?"

Her head snapped up, her chin jutting out. "You might remember that *I* am charged with keeping you from dying inconveniently while you bear the Judge's mark? Besides, if they kill you, I won't be able to finish my study."

Oh, of course. I stormed across the alley, pacing through the slush. I didn't know where we were—I didn't care. Only one thing was important. "They still have Nathanial. What do you think they'll do to him now that I've disappeared?"

She dropped her gaze. "Just stay here. I'll be right back."

Here? While stars-knew-what the Collector and her vamps could be doing to Nathanial? I paced faster, minutes ticking by.

Gil didn't return.

I can't wait any longer. I headed for the mouth of the alley and glanced down the street. I didn't recognize the location. I almost called Gil back, again. *But if she'd gone to help Nathanial . . .* I turned away from the street.

A hulking, misshaped form stepped around the corner at the back of the alley. "Babe, you stood me up."

Avin. Oh, crap.

Chapter Twenty-Nine

"I've been patient, babe. Where's my body?"

Avin lifted his mangled hand, the globe holding a drop of my blood appearing over his palm, and I flashed my fangs at him.

"So, what's your plan?" I asked, bracing my hands on my hips and tapping my claws on the steel boning in the corset. "Are you actually going to kill me or just threaten and torture me?"

His hand paused. Then he pushed back his hood. "Are you goading me? Not smart, babe."

I saw the flash of lightning, knew the pain was coming, but my knees still buckled as it crashed over me. Fire melted my flesh. A scream tore through me. My stomach twisted inside out. The pain dug deeper.

Then it was over.

I blinked. Either I was dead—which, since I considered the option, probably wasn't true—or I'd been right. He had no intention of killing me. I wiped a hand over my mouth and regretted the action immediately. I still had sour snake blood clinging to my skin.

Avin stared at my claws. "What *are* you?"

"You want the long list, or the short one?" I pushed off the sidewalk and summoned all the bravado in me so he wouldn't know my insides shook at the idea of another flash of pain. "Now, if we're done, I have to go see some vamps who *do* intend to kill me, and if I have time, I have to track down a poisonous, shape-shifting snake who may be a vengeful spirit."

Avin blinked at me, and the still-attached side of his mouth turned down. "What the hell are you messed up in?" Then he shook his head. "Never mind. That doesn't matter to me. What matters is—"

"—finding you a new body. I know. I got the message. I can't find you one if I'm dead, now can I?"

"You aren't the only vamp in the world, you know."

I cocked an eyebrow. "You think you're going to be able to trick anyone else into bargaining with you while you look like that?" I swept a hand to encompass his destroyed appearance.

His lopsided shoulders hitched. "You don't seem so inclined to complete our bargain. Here's the way I see it. I need a body, and you're dragging your undead feet." He twisted his hand, letting the globe-o'-pain float over his knuckles. "So, babe, we just became best buds. I'm not letting you out of my sight until I'm wearing a new suit of skin."

"But—"

He cut me off. "Now where would we find a nice-looking sap you can sink your fangs into? Way too late for the local mall. Hell, even most the clubs are shut at this hour."

"I can't just—"

"Yeah, the vamps. You told me." He shook his head. "Do you really think I'm gonna let you run off to a face a bunch of vampires who want to kill you?" A smile tugged across his face, exposing broken teeth. "Like you said, babe, I need you."

"And I need to go. You can't—"

Pain tore through my body. I gritted my teeth, trying to ride out the wave of fire as black dots filled my vision. My claws bit into my palms.

"You're always in such a hurry," Avin said, letting the globe float between his hands. It traveled up his finger and hovered, spinning. "Now, we were talking about where we'll find my body."

I glared at him as I clawed my hair out of my face. It stuck to the moisture on my cheeks.

Avin leaned closer. "What is the crap all over your arms?"

"Ghost-snake blood."

"Babe, ghosts don't bleed." He reached out, and I cringed as first, the chill of his magic, and then, his finger, landed on my skin.

He scraped his nail down the dried blood, leaving a slimy trail of magic on my wrist. Then he stepped back, staring at the flake of blood he'd freed.

"Oh, now this is interesting," he whispered, the tingle of magic around him rising. "Come on. You're going with me."

"What? Where?"

"We're going to find me a body," he said as a small globe of magic materialized around the flake of blood. "And on the way, we're going to track down your *ghost* snake."

☙ • ❧

Avin led me on a winding route through the streets of Demur, stopping occasionally to stare at the floating fleck of snake blood. I tried to slip away. Once. And only once. When I regained consciousness, blood dripped down my neck from my ear. After that, I trudged behind him silently. Avin might not intend to kill me—*at least not until I acquired him a body*—but if I pushed him, he might rip me to pieces from the inside out. I couldn't help Nathanial if Avin incapacitated me and left me to disintegrate in the morning sun.

Not that I know what I can do to help Nathanial.

I couldn't exactly attack the mansion. Any one of the master vamps inside could stop me without lifting a finger. *If we find the snake*... maybe the Collector would listen to me if I brought her proof. Of course, the stars only knew Avin's interest in the snake, and if there'd be anything left for me *to* take to the Collector.

We turned a corner, and the scent of wolf washed over me. Not a Firth wolf. *The city-shifter, Steven.* On my next breath, the wind carried the scent of bobcat to me. *And Bobby.*

I stopped, looking around. They were close. Very close.

"Babe, what's the hold-up? Keep moving," Avin said, letting the globe of my blood flash in his hand.

I winced, falling in step behind him again. But my eyes scanned the street, my nose sifting through the scents. The only living soul we'd run into was a hobo with a bloated nose who was, in Avin's words, *"Too unappealing."* I did *not* want to know what he'd think of Bobby, with his broad shoulders and predator attitude.

But I was out of time to divert Avin.

Bobby and Steven turned the corner at a dead run. I'd last left them tracking the snake from Justin's murder scene—apparently both our trails led here. Bobby's eyes landed on me—how could he miss me in my ridiculously poofy ball gown—and his path veered straight toward me.

"Now, this is more like it," Avin said, drawing up short. "Either of these bodies will suit me fine."

"No."

Avin cocked his misshapen head. "Babe, we've been through this."

I winced as he lifted his hand, but I whispered through gritted teeth, "They're shapeshifters."

"Really?" He turned back to where Bobby and Steven were running toward us. "Well, I'm not prejudiced."

Damn. I'd really hoped the whole not-human thing would discourage him.

As Bobby ran to me his gaze skidded over my posture, the dried blood covering my arms, and the fresh blood dripping from my ear. Then he did what any shifter would do for his *Dyre* or *Torin*. He planted himself between me and Avin. He didn't ask if I needed help. He didn't even take a second look at me. He just moved to my defense. Steven followed, looking bewildered.

Bobby's weight shifted to his back leg as he crouched, preparing to attack. He'd correctly identified the enemy—if only that would help.

Avin's hood slid back as he examined Bobby. Both Bobby and Steven sucked in their breaths at the sight of Avin's mangled face. Not that the living-dead mage appeared to notice. "Oh, this one is perfect." Avin's eyes flickered from Bobby to me. "I'll take him. *Now.*"

Crap.

"Bobby, grab the globe—!"

Pain slammed into me, tore me to pieces. Through the red haze, I saw Bobby turn, but I couldn't hear anything but my own scream ringing in my ears.

Blackness filled my vision as the fire burrowed deeper, filled my lungs. The very air felt like it had combusted, igniting my body, boiling my blood. I couldn't move, couldn't think.

Then it was over.

Calloused hands lifted my shoulders and the world lurched. The hands shook me, the fingers biting into bare skin still remarkably unburned, still attached. My eyes flew open.

Steven's face snapped into focus, and Bobby's coat flashed in my peripheral. I turned in time to see his arm jerk back. His fist landed in Avin's face with a crunch.

The mage hobbled back, and the slimy tingle of his magic filled the air. Bobby had smashed Avin's right eye-socket, so only one, blood-clouded eye swiveled to glare at me. He held up his hand, and something appeared in his fingers. *The globe.* My stomach tightened as I braced for pain, but a crooked smile lifted the corner of Avin's torn lip. Then he vanished.

I squeezed my eyes shut. He still had my blood. He wouldn't be gone long.

Steven shook me again, forcing my attention back to him. "We've got company." He nodded over my shoulder.

I twisted, straining muscles still tight with the memory of pain.

The door to an old warehouse hung open, and a man wearing only dark pants clung to the door frame, his hand extended like he was reaching for something. His dark eyes locked on mine, and a tingle ran down my spine. Magic tinged the air. *Another mage?*

"That's him," Steven whispered. "The musk scent. It's coming from him."

No way. I pushed to my feet. "He's a mage."

Bobby was breathing hard after his fight with Avin, but he appeared unharmed. He tilted his head back, his nostrils flaring, and he nodded. "Steven is right. The smell is coming from that man. He's the skinwalker."

The mage grimaced, his fist closing like he was snatching at smoke. His magic rushed around me, and I tensed, but nothing happened. He jerked as if stung, and his hand dropped. He strolled onto the sidewalk. He never looked away. I rubbed my arms, the sting of both Avin and the mage's magic tainting the air. The stink of snake musk was definitely wafting from the newcomer's direction but . . .

"You feel it, right?" I whispered. "Him using magic?"

Bobby frowned at me, which was answer enough. Only I felt it. *Okay.* I rolled my shoulders. There were three of us and only *one* of him. And if he really was the skinwalker I'd fought in the mansion, he had to be hurt. My claws had done damage.

"Ready?" I whispered, splaying my claws. I centered my weight and waited. I could cross the street in two heartbeats. How fast was the mage?

"What are we doing?" Steven stepped closer to me, right into my personal space.

I bristled. I didn't know Steven well, had never fought beside him, and he was too close. I could smell the stink of sweat under his layers of clothing. Sour sweat that smelled of fear, not exertion. He was scared, and his beast had latched on to me as the resident alpha. *Great, I can't make a dog sit, but I've managed to adopt a city-shifter.* Which meant I was responsible for keeping him out of danger.

"Just stay back," I said, without tearing my eyes away from the mage.

Steven didn't move, but Bobby joined me. "Do we have a plan?"

"Yeah." I said. "Nobody die."

Chapter Thirty

I made it halfway across the street before the mage moved from the doorway. I was fast. He was faster.

Within two of my running strides, he crossed the distance between us. I barely registered the movement. Then he was in front of me, his fist angling toward my face.

I dropped, diving out of the way. In mid-movement, I twisted, swiping with my claws. I grazed his forearm, but he was there one moment and yards away the next. I blinked. Bobby hadn't even reached us yet. A heartbeat, maybe two, had passed.

How can he be that damn fast?

He charged again, and I lashed out. Missed. A blow I didn't see slammed into my chest, knocked me back. I crouched, ignoring the sting spreading across my torso. Bobby reached my side, Steven on his heels.

The mage's movements blurred, and Steven yelped as the mage flung him backward. I didn't have time to turn, to see where Steven landed. I was too busy diving out of the way as the mage focused on me, again.

I ducked under the next blow, lunging forward at the mage's unguarded chest. He darted behind me before my claws reached his skin. Behind me, the crack of a bone snapping sounded, and Bobby grunted in pain.

Dammit. There were three of us fighting him. *How can we be losing?*

I whirled around and aimed my strike too far to the right, while feinting left. The mage plowed into my claws. *Finally.*

He jumped back, hissing. Fangs flashed.

Vampire?

I backpedaled. "What the hell *are* you?" For once it was me asking, not being asked. But really? Magic, snake musk, *and* vamp fangs? *A mage turned vamp and possessing the magic to use a skinwalker's stolen skin?*

"I'm the rightful Master of New Brennan. The Collector and her pathetic freaks stole my city," he said, his voice hissing between his fangs. "and you, freak, are fucking up my revenge." He lunged.

I twisted away, but not fast enough. His fangs tore into my shoulder with a flash of white pain. No pleasure overshadowed the pain. Not a single pulse of anything beyond the average horrific animal bite.

He's a soldier vamp—no mental powers.

"Get off!" I struggled in his grasp, but he was stronger.

His grip tightened, locking my arms to my sides, pinning my claws. I flailed, kicking my feet. My efforts did no good. His fangs ripped deeper, nicking at my shoulder joint. Somewhere, not far away, tires crunched over pavement.

The mage went rigid. He screamed, his head rearing back in agony. His fangs tore from my flesh, and he hurled me away from him. *What?* I'd lost a lot of blood and probably had never reclaimed enough from Nathanial to start with, so my landing lacked any cat-like grace. My feet slid and my arms windmilled. I hit the pavement, but I kept my legs under me.

Bobby stood behind the mage, blood dripping from his knuckles. As the mage turned, I saw why. The hole I'd ripped in the snake's back earlier hadn't healed—it hadn't slowed him down either, but it was a large, seeping wound that now showed evidence of broken ribs, thanks to Bobby. My hunger blossomed. The mage's blood smelled sour, but I was starving.

The mage pulled a large sheath of black scales from the void. A snakeskin identical to Akane's—or likely, her twin sister's actual skin. He wrapped it around himself and expanded into a huge serpent.

"Get back," I yelled at Bobby. *If the mage injected even a drop of poison into Bobby's body . . .*

A vehicle swung around the corner. *Of all the mooncursed luck.* Humans could not be allowed to witness this fight. Imagine their shock: me in bloody tulle, with claws instead of fingers, a giant serpent stretched across the pavement, blood dripping from Bobby's fist, and Steven—I didn't know where Steven was. I glanced around and caught him creeping toward the mage. *Yeah, definitely not a scene for human observers.*

I shouldn't have wasted my concern.

The dark SUV slammed to a stop in the center of the road and the doors flew open. Ronco dashed out of the driver's seat as Elizabeth stepped out of the passenger side.

Why do I get the feeling this isn't the cavalry coming to our rescue?

"Trevin, we'll handle this from here," Elizabeth said as she shook wrinkles from her dress.

The snake's head dipped in agreement, but it didn't retreat. Ronco surged forward, headed not for the serpent, but for *me*. I wasn't surprised. I lifted my claws, keeping one eye on the snake and one on the charging vampire.

The snake lifted its head, its mouth falling open, and a human voice emerged, "The silver, fool."

Silver? *Oh crap.*

"Run!" I turned, taking my own advice. Bobby and Steven did the same.

Not that any of us had a chance.

Ronco tossed something thin and light-weight, and a cord wrapped around my bare neck. My skin went numb, my throat closing, and I stumbled, falling to my knees. Bobby glanced back as I fell. He stopped. Doubled back.

No!

I couldn't speak. Couldn't breathe. I clawed at the silver chain, but my fingers turned numb at the first touch, and my claws dripped with blood as I scratched skin I couldn't feel.

Ronco slammed into Bobby. Another chain of silver glinted in his hands. I had to stop him. I had to . . .

The serpent slithered closer and coiled around my body, constricting. His mouth opened inches from my face. His fangs flashed, dripping poison.

"Trevin, enough." Elizabeth's ballerina slippers made soft sounds as she trudged through the snow toward me. "Don't hurt her."

"Just this one?" Again the snake's voice emerged perfectly clear, as if spoken from a human throat. His head dipped closer.

"No. We couldn't explain her death. Besides, she's much more useful as a decoy. Now go."

The snake's tongue flicked out and danced over my cheek. Then he uncoiled and slithered back toward the warehouse. A scream tore down the street, and I looked up to see Steven fall, thrashing in the silver cords binding him. Bobby was already down. *No.* My stomach twisted. I flailed again with the cord, but the numbness was traveling down my body, making it hard to move. Ronco hauled Steven off the pavement, dragged him toward the SUV.

"Aaric, travel to me," Elizabeth chanted in a sing-song voice, and the Traveler stepped into the space beside her.

He looked around, his thick brows cinching. "Elizabeth, what is the meaning of this? What is going on?"

"Ronco and I followed *her*." She made the word sound distasteful as she jerked her small hand in my direction. "She met with a pair of shapeshifters, and we've captured them. I think the Collector will be pleased." She pressed her forehead against his hand, and his eyes went distant, as if he were talking to someone else without moving his lips.

"She *is* pleased. You will be rewarded," he said as his eyes focused again.

With her face pressed into his hand and tilted toward the ground, the Traveler couldn't see the cruel smile that twisted Elizabeth's lips. I could. But there wasn't a damn thing I could do about it.

The Traveler scanned the bloody street. "The Collector will send a clean-up crew."

"Ronco has already sent for one," Elizabeth said, tilting her head to look at him. Her face was once again pleasant, with no hint of the smile she'd worn a moment ago.

"Very well. Hurry home. Dawn is approaching." He leaned down and kissed his companion lightly. Then he vanished as if he'd never been on the street.

Elizabeth turned back to me. When I'd first left Firth for the human world, I'd been unnerved by the unblinking glass eyes and painted smiles of porcelain dolls. Staring at Elizabeth's perfect but cruelly carved features, I decided that my fear was well justified.

"You can't speak, can you?" she asked, her voice tinny with mock concern. She knelt beside me and rearranged her skirts to keep them off the ground. "Not being able to speak isn't good enough. You must not be able to *share*."

Share? What the hell does that mean? Not that I could ask.

Elizabeth lifted my wrist. I tried to jerk away, to struggle, but my arms were numb. Useless. Her fangs flashed, but instead of biting me, she drew out the moment.

"It's one of my abilities," she whispered. "I lock away memories so no one can find them. And no one knows, except those few who cannot expose my secret. Like you." Then she sank her fangs into my flesh. The first wave of sensation hit me. I could barely feel my body, but the traitorous pleasure? That I could feel. My eyes bulged. When she pulled back, she smiled at me, my blood still staining her teeth. She giggled.

I blinked at her, incapable of doing more. What I wanted to do was rip Elizabeth's throat out so that damned giggling would stop.

Ronco dragged Bobby to the car, the shifter's head lolled to the side. My hearing was too damaged by the silver to know if he was breathing, but if I could have moved, I'd have killed both the vampires or died trying.

A second SUV pulled to a stop behind Elizabeth's, and two vampires jumped out. They hauled a large metal coffin from the back and hefted off the thick lid. Then all eyes turned to me.

No. Oh, hell no. They were *not* putting me in a coffin.

They were.

And there was nothing I could do about it.

As the vampires lowered the lid over me, Elizabeth reached inside and snagged the silver chain from my throat, pulling it free. Feeling slowly returned to my body, so I could feel the tires on the pavement as we drove, feel the coffin sliding as the SUV took a turn too fast. Voices filtered in through the metal walls surrounding me.

"—It's fine. We've improvised," Elizabeth said, and I strained to listen.

"If you hadn't insisted on all the theatrics with the bodies, she never would have stuck her over sensitive nose into this," a raspy voice said. *The snake mage, Trevin?* He was in the car?

"The girl was an unexpected element. But it's fine. I have plans for her." Elizabeth again. Was I 'the girl?' "Besides, it is all working out. Marina's unbalanced, unsure, and her allies are pulling away from her. It won't be long now."

The mage's reply was in a language I didn't know. *Who is Marina?*

"Go. We're almost there," Elizabeth said, and the SUV slowed, the coffin sliding forward as the vehicle braked.

The scream that had been trying to escape finally tore free of my silver-burned throat as the vampires hauled the coffin out of the SUV. I screamed in panic, I screamed in rage, I screamed for help, I screamed for Nathanial. I hated the idea that Elizabeth could be listening, could be smiling at the sound, but I couldn't stop. Once I could feel my hands I clawed at the interior, shredding the satin lining until my claws scraped on ungiving metal.

Then dawn hit. My senses felt it, and retreated. And there was nothing.

Chapter Thirty-One

As night fell a scream burst from my lungs even before my eyes opened to the sight of shredded satin inches from my nose. My own scream filled my senses, competing with the blood rushing through my ears.

Then I heard another sound.

A tremor ran through the coffin lid as something hit it. Metal scraped against metal.

I fell silent, listening. *Rescue or . . . ?*

My hands had shifted back to human form while I slept, leaving me without my claws and way more defenseless than I liked, but the lid was already moving. I slammed my shoulders against it, shoving myself free of the coffin. My fist lifted as I sprung upward. My arm cocked back. Then my gaze landed on crystal gray eyes framed by dark lashes. I froze.

Nathanial.

His arms wrapped around me, dragging me against his chest. The metal lid clattered to one side.

I didn't move at first, too stunned by his presence. After how we'd parted last . . . " You came for me?"

"As soon as I could." His lips pressed the words into my hair, and he held me tight enough it hurt.

My body finally relaxed, and I wrapped my arms around his waist, held him as I let him crush me against his chest.

"My memories—"

"Were altered," Nathanial said before I could finish. "That is the only logical explanation. I should have seen the scales in your memory, but there was nothing, and that cannot be."

I nodded, clinging tighter to him. The fact he believed me, that he believed *in* me again, made something inside me seem to click back into place. I looked up, and his lips pressed ever so lightly against my forehead. My eyes fluttered closed, and I drew in a deep breath, drinking down his spicy scent. But mixed in with the scents I associated with him was the smell of freshly turned dirt and drying blood.

I pulled back. His arms tightened before releasing me, but he didn't stop me from stepping away. Nathanial wore most of last night's tux, but his white shirt was torn and mud-stained. A spray of crimson covered his cuffs. *Not his blood.* My nose told me that much.

He must have seen the questions in my face. He ran a hand through dark hair clumped with wet mud and said, "Gil has poor timing and a unique definition of 'help.'"

There was definitely a story behind *that. And I bet it involves the void.*

Before I could ask, he took my arm, and steered me toward the door. "We have to leave this city. Immediately."

"She has Bobby."

No need to say who 'she' was. Nathanial paused, muscles stiffening along his back, but he didn't say anything as he continued toward the door.

A slumped figure slouched just inside the doorway, a stake protruding from his chest. I blinked, but I didn't ask any questions—the vamp smelled like the blood on Nathanial's cuffs.

"Hermit?" a voice whispered behind me.

The skin between my shoulders tightened, and I whirled around. The room was empty. Or, at least, mostly empty. It was little more than some forgotten cellar, and I hadn't noticed earlier, but the metal coffin I'd been locked in wasn't the only one in the room.

"Hermit, is that you?" The decidedly female voice issued from a box sitting upright against the far wall.

"Stay here," Nathanial said. Then he grabbed the crowbar he'd used on my coffin.

He jimmied the lock off the upright coffin before cramming the crowbar into the seam. As Nathanial pushed aside the lid, Samantha stumbled free. She was no longer disguised as Nuri, but neither did she look like the confident, dark-haired woman she'd been during my last night at Death's Angel.

She lunged for Nathanial, her fangs extended and her thin lips curled back. He didn't dodge, but held up his wrist. She grabbed it, sinking her fangs deep.

"The hell?" I surged forward, ready to rip her off him.

Nathanial held up a hand and motioned me to stop. I did, but my weight remained on my toes, my muscles twitching with the need to yank her away. After a moment, Samantha pulled back. She licked her now full, pink lips.

"Thank you, Hermit," she said, straightening.

Nathanial acknowledged her thanks with a nod. "Chameleon. Did Tatius send a private message for me?"

Samantha pursed her lips, and her appearance changed, melding into a green-haired Tatius. The change was frighteningly accurate, but as this fake Tatius hooked its fingers in the loops of shiny vinyl pants and glanced at me, the eyes held none of the weight of the true Tatius's stare. Using his voice, Samantha said, "We can acknowledge that blood both complicates and engenders loyalty, brother. Your blood runs through Kita, but our blood is the same, and we have history. Return. I will reconsider my position on our companion."

Our companion?

"Those were his exact words?" Nathanial asked.

Samantha shimmered back into her natural, dark-haired appearance. "He made me repeat the message twice."

Nathanial nodded, the movement slow, as if he could buy himself time to think. Then he turned and held out his hand to me. "Back to Haven?"

"Better the devil you know and all that. What about Bobby?" And Steven. I was responsible for the city-shifter as well.

Nathanial frowned, and Samantha's plucked eyebrows pinched together.

"Bobby?" she asked.

"A friend."

"A *mortal* friend?" At my nod, she waved her hand in a dismissive motion. "Mortal lives are short. We should escape while we can."

Yeah, that wasn't an option I was considering. Turning my back on her, I cocked my head, staring at Nathanial.

"We will find him," he said, "but we must hurry."

ல • ல

"Here," I whispered, stopping in front of a door and scenting the air.

Samantha—who had merged her appearance into Ronco, an effective but disturbing disguise—leaned against the wall and inspected her knuckles as I sifted through scents. I definitely thought I could *probably* smell bobcat and wolf. *Damn fickle vampire nose.*

A pair of vamps turned the corner ahead of us, and my muscles tensed, my fists curling. I waited, not even breathing. But, after nodding to us, and receiving a nod from Nathanial in return, they kept walking. I had no idea what illusion Nathanial cloaked us in, but it was working. *As long as we don't run into any of the older psychic vamps.*

Once the pair vanished around the corner, I pulled open the door and slipped inside, Nathanial and Samantha at my heels. The room beyond was large, dark—and filled with the scent of wounded shapeshifters. Nathanial's fingers brushed my shoulder, reaching for me, trying to hold me back. It was too late. I was already running. I dashed across the room, headed straight for the tawny haired form slumped in a chair.

"Hey!" someone yelled behind me.

Crap. Guards.

I didn't slow. Raised voices lifted in my wake, followed by the crunch of bones snapping. Someone grunted. I didn't look back.

"Bobby?" I knelt beside him and he lifted his head.

His eyes were red and swollen as he looked at me, but his skin was pale. Way too pale. He'd been stripped down to just his pants, and the chains binding him to a chair had sunk into his flesh, ugly welts spreading across his bare chest, his arms.

"I'll get you free," I whispered. *But how?* I couldn't touch the silver—losing feeling in my fingers wouldn't help.

Tearing a panel off the bottom of my gown, I wrapped the shiny material around my hands. It protected me from the silver, but the make-shift gloves sabotaged any chance I had of griping the thin silver chains. *Dammit.*

I glanced back at the door. "Nathanial, help."

He hurled one vampire into a second, and both slammed into the wall with a thud. The vamps, dead or unconscious, dropped to the floor, leaving a large, man-shaped indention in the wall. They weren't the only bodies on the floor.

"One got away," Samantha said, her appearance rippling as she shrank down from Ronco's form into her own.

"Then we will have company soon." Nathanial knelt beside me, and I moved over, giving him better access to the chain.

He had to dig into Bobby's bare back to get the end of the chain. He peeled it away from the skin, the silver taking chunks of flesh with it. Bobby squinted his swollen eyes, the muscles in his face twitching, and his lips curling back, but he didn't make a sound as the chain pulled away.

I cupped his large hand in mine and pressed my cheek against his knee, but that was as much comfort as I could offer. There was nothing I could do about the pain, and though the energy of his beast rolled off him in prickly waves, he couldn't shift and heal until the silver was away from his skin.

"We have to hurry," Samantha said, her eyes focused on the door.

"Unwrap Steven," I told her, pointing at the shifter in the other chair. He wasn't moving, his chest barely lifting.

She glared at me, and I thought for a moment she was going to pull the vampire equivalent of rank on me, but then she turned and grabbed the silver chain binding Steven. She yanked, tearing chain and flesh. The shifter screamed and the energy pouring off him filled the room. My skin crawled, feeling too tight for my body.

"Too much," Bobby whispered, the words clumsy from his swollen lips.

"I know." I squeezed his hand. "It's almost over."

"Not me. Steven."

Rogue?

I jumped to my feet just as Samantha jerked the last chain free. Steven lunged from the chair, his body slamming into Samantha. The silver would have weakened him, so it must have been her surprise that allowed him to knock her to the ground. He screamed in her face, his twisted, rage-filled agony turning the scream into a howl.

I surged forward. Before I reached him, the skin down his back split. A glistening spine poked free, muscles bunching, reshaping. I skid to a stop.

"Samantha, get out from under him."

Her eyes were wide, and I wasn't sure she'd heard me as she stared at the man shifting on top of her. I grabbed her arms, pulling her free. You didn't touch shifters mid-change—the magic that reformed a shifter's body could do strange things to anyone who interfered. We couldn't do anything but wait as Steven's joints popped, his organs rearranging.

Wait, and hope he came out of the change sane.

I didn't hold out a lot of hope. A day wrapped in silver could challenge any shifter's sanity, and Steven had already been unstable. Seconds passed, the change progressing agonizingly slow. Tagged shifters were like that, their change sometimes taking several minutes to complete.

"What is the meaning of this?" a cold voice demanded from the doorway.

I whirled around. A group of enforcers poured into the room, Ronco leading the charge. Elizabeth slipped inside as a prim figure in a

cold gray dress stepped through the doorway.
   The Collector had arrived.

Chapter Thirty-Two

"I expected more from you, Hermit. You had so much potential." The Collector shook her head. "Such a waste." Her pupils dilated, her irises disappearing in the expanding darkness.

My heart hammered in my chest, my mouth going dry. Vamp tricks. Of course she went straight to vamp tricks.

My feet itched to slink away, to hide, but I couldn't do that. Steven was in the midst of shifting, and Bobby wasn't free yet. They'd bound him in enough chains to hold ten shifters, and Nathanial was still untangling the mess. Samantha stared at the mess that was Steven, her eyes frozen wide. So that just left me. And I had to do something.

"We had a deal. You have your shifters. Now let us go," I said, ignoring the fact we had obviously been trying to free said shifters.

The Collector's attention slammed into me, and I cringed. Her power snarled at the edges of my mind, swathing my peripheral in darkness. But her concentration wasn't what it usually was. Her gaze darted to Steven's changing form as if she couldn't help herself. Couldn't take her eyes off his shift.

I can work with that.

A cold smile crossed the Collector's face, but she stared at Steven as she said, "My dear, we did not agree on a time frame for your release, and you did not deliver the shapeshifters to me. Elizabeth did."

As she spoke, Nathanial pulled the last inch of silver from Bobby's chest. He dropped the bloody chain, and Bobby stumbled from the chair. His legs collapsed beneath him. I lunged on instinct, grabbing his arm before he hit the floor.

It was the wrong move.

His skin slipped and the energy of his beast washed over me. It stung as it dug into my skin, calling to the beast I no longer appeared to have.

Bobby was no tagged shifter whose change took long minutes. He was natural born, and a fast changer at that. I tried to release him, but his energy tangled around my fingers, gripped my arms. The radiating energy clawed at me. His arm twisted, shifted.

Crap.

I pried my hands away, but they moved too slow, as if the energy had turned solid around me. It clung to me as I backpedaled, and I gritted my teeth against what was both pain and the familiar call of Firth. A call I couldn't answer, now that I was a vampire.

"The silver is effective," the Collector said, tearing her eyes from Steven's slowly shifting shape to focus on Bobby. Her head cocked to one side, her stare an inquisitive but objective observation. I'd seen Gil watch me in similar ways. Very similar. Except Gil wasn't a cold-hearted walking corpse.

At my side, Bobby straightened. Fur cloaked his body, but he stood on two legs, caught in midform—half man, half beast. A warrior's form. Claws curved from his fingers, scythe-like and deadly. A muzzle of carnivore's teeth protruded from his face.

Still the energy of Firth thrummed over my skin—warm, alive. It washed my body in adrenaline. My muscles tensed. My breath rushed out of me. The need to shift battered against my chest and made my skin too tight. But I couldn't shift anymore. The coil deep in my center was still hard. Still cold.

I shoved the energy down to my hands. The joints in my fingers popped, snapped. The skin over my fingertips split. My claws slid free, long enough to make a tiger proud.

Soft, chime-like laughter floated across the room. "You are wonderfully predictable," Elizabeth said, smiling at me like a cat who'd cornered a mouse.

I flexed my claws. I was not a mouse.

"Does this fit in your game?" I asked, goading her. My words came out with a lisp—my fangs had extended.

Elizabeth's smile widened, and she cast a glance at Ronco. "Actually, yes."

She twisted a ring on her finger, and words spilled from her mouth. Words my mind tried and couldn't understand, couldn't remember.

My stomach twisted. I knew of a word that couldn't be heard. A mage's name.

Magic tingled along my skin. The air zinged with power, and a large, black serpent appeared in the center of the room. He reared back, his jaw opening to flash fangs dripping with poison.

The Collector ripped her eyes from Bobby. She glanced at the coiled serpent, a frown stretching over her face. "Elizabeth, what is the meaning of this?"

"This?" the small vampire asked, her face all mock innocence. Then her voice deepened. "This is a coup."

Chapter Thirty-Three

"Now, Trevin," Elizabeth yelled, and the snake lunged.

The Collector didn't flinch. "Ronco, take care of the serpent."

Her bodyguard didn't move—none of her enforcers moved.

Not that I expected them to, but their defection had never entered the Collector's mind. She stood there, assuming they'd jump to her defense.

They didn't.

Surprise flashed through her face as the snake's strike tore into her shoulder. Her eyes flew wide, and she ripped the snake away, hurling the massive serpent across the room. Then her dark glare turned on her enforcers.

"Do not expect lenience, any of you." She pressed a hand to the slowly oozing wound on her shoulder. "This is treason. This—" The Collector took a step forward and her legs buckled beneath her, the poison taking effect. She fell to her knees.

"This is inevitable," Elizabeth finished for her. "Too long my master has catered to your whims. He begs like a dog for your scraps when he should be seated at the head of the table." She curled her small fist in the Collector's hair and jerked, exposing the Collector's throat. "No more. Ronco?"

The large guard unsheathed a dagger and pressed it into her small hand. I glanced at Nathanial. He stood tense at my side, watching, but not interfering. In this situation, the enemy of our enemy was less friend and definitely enemy. It didn't matter who won. All parties involved wanted us dead.

"Goodbye," Elizabeth whispered, and the blade blurred.

The Collector's body crumpled to the floor—her head remained in Elizabeth's hand. Blood splattered onto the skirt of Elizabeth's dress, dark against the white lace. The small vampire lifted the head higher, smiling at the Collector's slack jaw. Then her eyes darted to me.

"Catch." She hurled the head.

It arced across the room, tumbling in the air and slinging blood to the floor, the ceiling. I jumped out of the way, and the enforcers surged into motion. They rushed us, fangs out, fists raised.

I lifted my claws, and Bobby and Nathanial edged in front of me. Samantha's form shimmered, solidifying twice as wide, with bulging muscles and blocky features.

"It is a shame the Collector lost her life in your escape attempt," Elizabeth said, her voice conveying the vicious smile I couldn't see beyond the bodies of the charging vampires.

The first enforcer reached us, and in one swift move Nathanial sent him crashing into the next. Two enforcers jumped in the air, flying toward the high ceiling. Then they twisted, diving at us.

Crap.

Nathanial glanced at them, his full lips drawing thin. His eyes darted from me to Bobby. "Guard her," he commanded. Then he was in the air.

I don't need guarding. We needed a way out.

Bobby met the next attacker head on, and they both went down, rolling in a blur of claws and fists. Samantha rushed forward, barreling into the next vampire.

A howl ripped through the air behind me. A low, angry snarl followed. I cringed, my spine stiffening. *Oh crap.*

I whirled around as Steven charged. He'd shifted to an advanced mid-form, more wolf than human, and his blue eyes were wide, mad.

Wolf. A rogue shifter in wolf form. *I'd rather deal with vamps.*

I didn't get a chance.

Taloned feet scraped the ground as Steven leapt for me. I caught his arms, keeping his claws from as much of my flesh as possible, and absorbed his weight. I let his momentum push me to the ground. I rolled with it, tucking my legs and bringing my feet up as my shoulders hit the ground. Steven's stomach landed against my feet, and I shoved with my legs. He flew over my head, flipping in the air and slamming into two oncoming vamps. All three went down. Blood flew as Steven tore into them with the ferocity of insanity-driven rage.

I rolled to my feet, tearing at my stupid tulle skirt as it tangled around me again. The rasp of scales on stone warned me of the snake's approach. I tensed, but let him slither closer. Content to let him think I hadn't noticed. I closed my eyes and blocked out the sounds of fighting raging around me, focused on the soft rasp behind me.

Closer.

Closer.

The sound stopped, and I imagined the snake rearing back,

preparing to strike while I was unaware. I spun and dove in the same movement, letting my ears guide my claws.

I caught the snake in the soft flesh under its jaw. My claws sank deep, and I slashed downward, tearing a gash three feet long down the snake's belly. He hissed, toppling backward. Blood sprayed from the wound. The snake thrashed, contorting. The skin thinned, peeled back, and a man, not a snake, flailed on the floor.

A long gash split his chest, his lungs and other dark organs visible. *But a vamp might heal from those wounds.* I'd healed from nearly as bad.

"Gildamina!" I yelled.

Magic zinged through the air as she popped into the room. Her eyes widened, and I saw her swallow as she took in the fray. I saw the questions forming on her lips.

"Mage turned vampire," I yelled, pointing at the thrashing vamp.

Her gaze snapped to him, a familiar spark of curiosity lighting her features. She rushed forward, and the injured mage tried to twist back, away.

He wasn't fast enough. "What a specimen," she said.

Magic tingled through the air as her hand landed on the vamp. He vanished.

"Take the skin to Biana," I said, pointing at the black, cast-off skin. It was a shredded mess at this point, but at least I could pay one debt.

Gil gathered the skin, nearly tripping over her boots in her haste. "I'll get you out too," she said, stepping forward.

"No." I backpedaled. "We've got this covered." I was *not* letting her throw me into the void. Not now. Not while I might be needed here.

Besides, it was true. As I spoke, Nathanial threw the last aerial attacker to the ground. The vamp didn't get back up. Two bodies lay around Bobby. He was soaked in blood and had a dripping bite wound in his throat, but he was up and running to help Samantha, whose arm hung at an awkward angle as she struggled with Ronco, the last enforcer standing. Neither of the vamps under Steven were moving—and probably hadn't in a while. The rogue continued tearing into them, reveling in his first kill.

I'll have to deal with him. But first we had to find Elizabeth.

Content we had the fight under control, Gil vanished. My gaze flickered around the room, searching.

A small prick pinched my shoulder, the smallest sting. I whirled around and Elizabeth jumped back, an empty syringe in her hand. An empty syringe that reeked of poison.

"You've over-extended your usefulness," she said, letting the syringe hit the ground. She lifted her dagger. A dagger still glistening with the Collector's blood.

I stumbled back. I could feel the poison, cold, a creeping deadness. "Nathanial!"

As if to combat the seeping cold of the poison, heat boiled out of my center. A spreading, growing, skin-tightening heat.

Nathanial landed beside me, wrapped me in his arms. "I have you."

He pulled me tighter to him, but the heat in my body kept expanding. It jittered through my muscles, sparked through my flesh. Pain shot down my back, and the skin over my spine tore open.

My skin was slipping.

Chapter Thirty-Four

"Let go." I shoved at Nathanial, but his arms only tightened around me.

"Kita?" Bobby crept toward me, his eyes wide.

He can feel the energy pouring off me.

I shook my head. "Her, get her."

I pointed where Elizabeth had been. I could barely see anymore. Pain radiated through my body, some the poison, some the change. My gown vanished, my clothes always disappeared when I shifted. *It's really going to happen.* But Nathanial couldn't be touching me as I shifted.

He jerked as his hands touched my suddenly bare skin—skin that was ripping away, trying to reverse itself. When I shoved him again, he let go, and I backpedaled. I stumbled over something and hit the ground with a thud. Whatever I tripped on tangled in my legs. A body. *No, not a body.* It moved. And it was covered in fur.

Steven.

I couldn't move. Couldn't push away. It was too late. My skin slipped off as my muscles rearranged. My joints popped. A yelp tore from my throat. It was matched by a howl—a howl that morphed into a hoarse human scream.

My shift is forcing Steven to shift.

It was the last thought I had. Then I passed into the moment of the shift when I had no hearing, no vision, no thought. Just pain.

Then it was over.

My skin sealed around me, and my dress reappeared. I looked down. I was in human form again. I hadn't changed. *Well, my claws are gone, but . . .* I hadn't become my other form, a calico cat, and I hadn't even reached mid-form. There was no shift.

But there was also no poison in me anymore. I could smell it on the stone, but my non-shift had purged it from my body.

I pushed off the floor, detangling my legs from Steven's as I moved. He was in fully human form as well. My shift had carried his along, pulled his wolf body apart and reconstructed it in seconds, and he was left naked and healed from his encounter with the silver. *Well, his body is healed, at least.*

Once I stood, he hugged his legs to his chest and curled into a ball. His eyes squeezed shut, but tears slipped through them anyway. Chunks of the vamps Steven had shredded surrounded us. Blood soaked into my dress and Steven's hair. Soft, pained sounds escaped him—pain that had nothing to do with his body.

I turned away. I couldn't deal with him yet.

Friend and foe alike stared at me like I'd just sprung a second head—*or rearranged my body.* I focused on Elizabeth.

"You wasted one of my nine lives," I smiled. "My turn. How many lives do *you* have?"

Elizabeth's eyes widened until her pale-blue irises swam in a sea of white. Not that I knew how I'd back up my threat. My claws were gone, and I was shivering. Not just cold-shivering, but *starving* shivering—slipping my skin had taken a lot out of me.

"Aaric, travel to us," Nathanial called, his voice echoing in the room.

The giant's scentless form stepped into the space in front of Nathanial.

"Did you call, Hermit?" he asked before he was completely solid. Then he looked around, his large jaw dropping. "What is this? What happened?" His body went stiff, his gaze freezing. "No. Marina?"

I twisted, following his line of sight straight to the Collector's head. *Marina.*

The Traveler rounded on Nathanial, his large fists clenching. "What happened?"

"Your companion happened." Nathanial nodded to Elizabeth.

She startled and blinked at the Traveler before vigorously shaking her head. "No. No, Aaric. He lies. Look for yourself."

She extended her arm and seemed to realize too late she still clutched the dagger.

"That's the Collector's blood," I said. "On her dress, too."

Elizabeth dropped the dagger, and it clattered to the floor. "No. I . . . I . . . " Her lips pursed. Then she dropped her hands. "It's true. But I did it for you. All for you. You're free of her now. We all are."

The Traveler looked around the room, his eyes pinching as his gaze trailed over the blood, the twisted bodies. He turned back to Elizabeth.

"My companion," he whispered. He held out his arms, and she rushed to him. His hands moved to her face, and his fingers stroked her cheeks. "My lovely, gentle companion."

He kissed her lips, a tender kiss, and I looked away. *Is that it? She's a hero now?* My stomach twisted.

A blur of movement caught in my peripheral vision. My gaze shot up as the sound of bones snapping filled the room. The Traveler still had his hands on either side of Elizabeth's face, and he twisted until her head ripped from her shoulders.

He caught her body before it hit the ground. He lowered her slowly, a tear slipping from the corner of his eye. Pressing a kiss to her forehead, he placed her head above her shoulders, as if her neck were still connected.

She was beautiful in death. A small porcelain doll covered in blood. A broken, deadly doll.

He knelt beside her, staring at her still body. I backed away, my feet moving without thought. My arm brushed Nathanial's, and his hand locked around mine, his fingers gripping mine. But he didn't say anything. None of us said anything.

The Traveler straightened.

"This is an ill-fated place of death and darkness." The Traveler looked away as if he gazed at something the rest of us couldn't see. Then he turned to Nathanial again. "Take no offense, Hermit, but I hope to never see you again." He faded from the room.

"That's it?" I asked, knowing it wasn't. We were surrounded by blood. By bodies. Even if we left now, I'd have new nightmares, and these wouldn't belong to the rogues I'd created.

Speaking of... I turned to Steven. He was still curled in a ball in the gore. Small, mewling sounds fell from his mouth.

"He's gone," Bobby whispered, the words distorted through his half-cat mouth.

Bobby was right. I knew he was, but I still crept closer and knelt beside the curled man.

"Steven?"

He didn't respond. I reached out and laid a tentative hand on his shoulder. He rolled from my touch, and then sprang into motion, lunging forward to tackle me. I hadn't expected the move, and I slammed backward, my shoulders and head hitting the floor.

Steven straddled my chest. His hands locked around my throat, strangling out air I didn't need.

"See what you made me do?" he yelled, squeezing tighter. "See!"

His flat nails dug into my neck. Then they were ripped away, his weight lifting off me. Nathanial held the struggling shifter by his throat.

"Put him down. He can't breathe." My voice was hoarse after the abuse to my throat, but the words came out clear enough.

Nathanial's eyes flickered to me. He lowered Steven, but he didn't release him. The shifter whined, a sob ripping through his chest. His eyes squeezed shut. "Please. Please just make the nightmare stop. Kill me. Don't make me do that again."

"Kita, you heard him," Bobby whispered. "I'm your second. I will do it, if you can't."

I shook my head. I'd tagged Steven, he was my responsibility. Besides, Bobby and I were all the clan Steven had known, and I was his surrogate *Torin*.

What would my father do if a tagged shifter begged for death?

He'd grant it. Especially if the shifter were as unstable as Steven. Hell, my father would never have hesitated. He knew a *Torin's* responsibility to every shifter in his clan. Steven was a danger to himself and everyone around him. My father would have already found a way to quickly and humanely end his suffering.

I pressed my lips together and took a deep breath. Let it out. "I'll do it."

I stepped forward, and then stopped. An idea bubbled at the edge of my mind. An idea I hated, but . . . "Steven, what do you want done with your body?"

The shifter rolled his eyes to look at me. "Bury it, burn it, leave it to rot. The hell would I care? I'll be dead."

I nodded and untied the small pouch on my necklace containing Avin's ring. My hand went numb as soon as I slid the ring on, but I ignored the pain. Nathanial stepped forward, but I shook my head. "Trust me." Then I called, "Avin."

Magic chilled the air, and Avin popped into the room. He looked around, torn eyebrow lifting. "Babe, this better not be a double-cross." The bauble of my blood appeared in his hand.

I pointed at Steven. "Will this body do?"

Avin stepped closer. He nodded. "Yeah, I like the look. Let me cast my circle and prepare."

Avin walked the room, chanting and stepping over scattered bodies. Samantha started to interrupt, but Nathanial stopped her with a raised hand. He was watching me, his eyes measuring.

When Avin indicated it was time, Nathanial released the city-shifter and backed out of the circle, but only as far as Avin made him. He hovered around the edge, ready to burst in if anything went wrong. Bobby appeared to agree.

"Will this hurt?" Steven asked, shuffling his feet.

"No," I whispered. Then I sank my fangs into his throat.

I needed the blood. I didn't realize how very cold I was until the heat of his blood filled me. Then his mind opened and I fell into his memories. I experienced bits of his life as him, knowing all the while he'd never again remember the football tournament we won, the first girl we kissed, or how much we looked up to our older brother, Tyler. Once the blood flow slowed, the memories faded, and I was left holding an empty body.

I lowered Steven to the ground. Then I turned to Avin.

"My blood?" I held out my hand.

He dropped the bauble in my palm. "Nice doing business with you, babe."

The charm broke as soon as the globe touched my skin, turning into just a drop of blood. I wiped it on my dress before turning away.

Walking out of the circle, I reached for Nathanial's hand. My gaze swept over the room, the bodies, the blood. "Still want me to be more like Elizabeth?"

Nathanial froze, and I shook my head. *Just teasing.* It was maybe two hours after dark, and it had already been a long night. I leaned against his body.

"Take me home."

Chapter Thirty-Five

The door to the cabin slammed behind me as I leapt down the porch steps. I landed a foot past the bottom stair, snow crunching under my toes, and I stared at the expanse of snow separating the cabin from the woods. I could cross it in two heartbeats. Easy.

I didn't. I was done with running.

Instead I stood there, drawing in deep breaths and letting them out. That's why I'd come out anyway. To get a little distance. A chance to breathe.

I squeezed my eyes closed. The house had become claustrophobic. There wasn't room for Bobby, Nathanial, me, and all the things we weren't saying. *Or the things we are.*

Bobby and I had been arguing all night. No, not arguing. Just talking *at* each other. At the top of our lungs.

He wanted me to go back to Firth. But I wasn't. I couldn't.

My skin had slipped, but I hadn't shifted, and now all that heat, all that magic of Firth, was gone again. *Locked away in a dead coil.* Maybe I'd reach it again, someday. And maybe then I'd go back to Firth. *Maybe.*

We were both on edge. The gate would open tomorrow night, and we both felt Firth's call. Not that it was unpleasant. The call hummed through my body, soft, cooing. It made me think of lazy summer days spent lounging in the grass, catnapping to the sound of a trickling stream.

I opened my eyes and realized I'd turned the direction of the closest gate. I frowned and forced myself to turn away. The call was the same as it had been before I'd become a vampire. I'd ignored it every full moon for the past five years. I'd ignore it this month, too.

The cabin door clicked open behind me.

What now?

It swished closed, and I waited, not turning around. *Nathanial.* It had to be—Bobby would have spoken by now. I didn't hear him trudge down the steps, but his heat suddenly filled the air behind my back. His hands landed on my shoulders, and then his fingers moved to my hair, gently combing it.

I had the urge to lean into him, to wrap my arms around his waist and breathe in his scent. Frowning, I stepped away from his hands and turned. Danger had drawn us together in Demur, but now we were home. *And we need to talk.*

But my tongue was too thick in my mouth, deadening my words. My feet itched to move. *Maybe a quick walk through the woods . . .*

No.

I'd made the decision to stop running. So here I was, facing things. I swallowed and hugged my arms across my chest. It wasn't that I needed the comfort, well, at least that wasn't all of it, but more than anything, I was afraid I'd reach for Nathanial if I didn't restrain my hands.

"When are we supposed to see Tatius?" I asked, because something had to fill the silence.

"He will allow us a few nights before he demands our presence. We should report to him of our own volition before that time."

But he didn't suggest we go now, or even later tonight. Neither of us were ready to deal with more vampire politics yet. But we'd go. Eventually. We had to. And then we'd find out exactly what Tatius had meant when he said *"our companion."* I wasn't looking forward to the conversation.

But before that happened, there was something else I had to know. And that meant having the other conversation both of us had been avoiding all night.

"So what is the deal, Nathanial? The way I feel about you, is it real? Is it me? You? The stupid, mooncursed vampire bond we share? What is it?"

He let out a breath. "Kitten, my powers control perception. The ability to trick the eye, the ear. My abilities have no sway over emotions." His gaze dropped. "Yours do."

My hands fell to my sides, and I stared at him, but I barely had time to register his words, much less to respond, before magic crawled over my skin—magic that didn't feel like Gil's—and a green light flashed behind me.

I whirled around. The judge stood several feet behind me. He frowned at the snow surrounding his polished shoes. With a wave of his hand, the snow melted in a three-foot radius around him. A heartbeat later it evaporated. Nodding his head in a self-satisfied manner, he straightened his already pristine suit. Then he looked at me. Nathanial slid his hand over mine, and I grasped it.

"Hello, my little endangered abomination," the judge said, his lips curving to show flat white teeth. "I have a job for you."

Coming Next In Kalayna Price's
Haven Series
Book Three: THIRD BLOOD

Going home after five years is difficult. It's harder still if you've changed species in the interim.

Kita Nekai, once the smallest shifter in Firth but now the newest vampire in the city of Haven, has no intention of returning home or informing her father and clan what she's become. Not that she has a choice. When the mage who holds her death certificate in his hands demands Kita return to Firth as his errand runner, she has to comply. Of course, there is no leaving her sire, Nathanial, behind. Which means introducing daddy dearest to the man—well, vampire—she may be falling for and confessing that she's lost the ability to shift. Talk about awkward.

Her homecoming goes from bad to worse when an attempt is made on her life, and Kita finds herself facing an unknown threat in a hostile world she never fit into in the first place. Can she survive long enough to complete the Judge's task, stand trial before the elders for the rogues she created while on the run, and help defend her father's territory from an encroaching band of misfit shifters? Or is this cat down to her last life?

જે • ⟨ૐ

About Kalayna Price

Kalayna Price is a fan of the fictional creatures that go bump in the night, but wouldn't want to meet one in person. She draws ideas from the world around her, her studies into ancient mythologies, and her readings of classic folklore. Her stories contain not only the mystical elements of fantasy, but also a dash of romance, a bit of gritty horror, some humor, and a large serving of mystery. She thinks hoop dance is about the most entertaining form of exercise on the planet, and has been known to hula-hoop with fire. To find out more, please visit her at www.kalayna.com.

❧ • ❦

A Special Note From Kalayna

To encourage new writers, I hosted a writing group on my blog during National Novel Writing Month in 2009. Congratulations to Cher Green, Tyhitia Green, Heather Kenniz, Ginger Lego, and Kaila A. Sage, who all wrote over 50k words during the challenge. I hope to see you in print one day soon.

❧ • ❦

CPSIA information can be obtained at www.ICGtesting.com
Printed in the USA
LVOW050111070313

323095LV00005B/137/P